VAIN & VALOUR

VOLUME 1 – VANITY

JUSTAN AUTOR

Vain & Valour

First Edition 2023

Published by Staten House

Cover illustration by Justan Autor
Cover and interior design by Justan Autor

A CIP catalogue record for this book is available from the British Library

ISBN: 979-8-88940-423-1

Dedication

To all who accompanied me on this journey, whether for the long or short haul.

Thank you to Edita, Karen, Katerina, Tarah, John, and the living memory of Lizzie, which spurs me on.

A special thank you to my wonderful father, without whose support I would not have been able to focus on completing this project; and my mother, who long ago handed over the kernels of a story that sprouted and burgeoned into the narrative as it now stands.

Table of Contents

PREFACE

Good reader,

Wishing to spare you the fright of a narrative so vast it may induce cardiac arrest, I have judiciously segmented this epic tale of circa 500,000 words (or perhaps a tad more) into five manageable courses. Please, therefore, enjoy each volume as if 'twere a satisfying dish in a fine dining experience — an appetizer to whet the palate, followed by lighter fare, building to the hearty main course and so on to a sweet denouement.

That said, while each installment has been laboured over as to possess its own narrative arc, threads of the broader tapestry are interwoven throughout the series. Thus, like Tolkien left dear Frodo and Samwise stranded amid the fires of Mount Doom, and Rowling abandoned Harry to anguish over the fallen Dumbledore, and Martin deserted Tyrion to languish in captivity, I, too, must, on occasion, leave readers dangling at a cliff, longing for resolution.

But take comfort. For the next volume is never far off.

Disclaimer:

Please be assured, none among my acquaintance have inspired the fictional belles, beaus, blackguards, or crones that parade through this prose. Any perceived similarities to persons living or dead are purely coincidental — though do feel free to take a lesson from them, if you will.

No animals were harmed in this production

And now, without further ado, let us begin! The first course awaits.

"In vain doth valour bleed ..." — Milton.

Act 1

20 November 1791

---

02 December 1791

20 NOVEMBER 1791

His eyes flashed open; he gasped for breath, coughing up frigid salt waters. Cold shock — like a lightning strike — tore him from unconsciousness. Hyperventilating, heart thudding, and chest constricting, he thrashed against the icy waters, which, cramping his limbs, dragged him back under.

Engulfed by a silent murkiness, he sank fast among the swaying weeds, pressure pounding in his ears. The paralysing chill clamped around his chest as he grasped futilely upwards, screaming soundlessly for air. Suffocation besieged him. Up flipped with down. Time swirled slow and rapid. Terror crowded his fading mind: scenes from his life playing out...

Just then, a fiery flare darted through the deep, cleaving the blackness. Perceiving his chance, he chased the light and broke through the surface, discharging the bitter waters from his airways.

All about was a violently churning blur of black and rufous. Confused, convulsing, and choking on involuntary swallows amid the struggle to stay afloat, he had to get out of the lake.

With enfeebled strokes, he swam to the nearest bank, onto which, exhausted and breathless, he slumped at the muddy verge of a pine grove.

Each laboured gasp scorched his lungs. His numbed fingers curled; he clawed the sodden ground. A torturous whooshing burst upon his hearing, and he slammed his hands tight against his head.

What is happening?

From the maelstrom of his thoughts, he strove to recall how he came to be in the waters. All he could summon was a vague recollection of having traversed the castle's western wing.

With effort, he raised his dripping, muddied face and looked back.

Good Lord!

A fire blazed so intensely that, even from these forty metres at least farther up the shore, its blistering heat singed his cheek. Struggling upright, and with his hand screening off the glare, he surveyed the raging wall of flames serrating the southern wing of Oberhofen Castle.

A reverberant boom rent the air, its force felling him back to the loamy ground. Rocks and fabric crashed into the lake; tumultuous clouds of molten orange and crimson billowed into the black skies. Upon the atmosphere swelled a crackling and roaring as the stench of charcoal, saltpetre, and sulphur rushed into his nostrils.

Gunpowder? Of course!

He had been in the vault, pursued there by his accuser, only to be then blockaded by the fire which spread throughout it.

Again, forcing himself up and screening his eyes from the blaze, he searched for the window from which he had sought to jump.

Heavens!

It was now a vast hole spewing out an inferno. Doubtless, the first explosion had breached the fabric and ejected him into the watery depths, rendering him unconscious.

And that I am still alive?

Another thunderous rumble reverbed as part of the castle wall collapsed into the waters.

In his still spiralling mind, fragmented images of what led up to this near fatality coalesced: letters exchanged with the French; arrest and imprisonment, awaiting trial on the morrow; the masked liberator facilitating his escape — his eyes stretched wide: *the scroll!*

Panicked, he checked his inner garment. The now saturated parchment was still there; also, the equally sodden bag still girded his waist.

Sudden agony pierced his temples and a vertiginous-like nausea coursed through him. Overwhelmed by these symptoms, he vomited.

"Search the waters!" came a familiar shout from near the castle, followed by the clatter of armoured men. "Find that traitor!"

Teeth gritted against his afflictions, he (whom we may suppose is this accused traitor) hauled himself up against a rock and staggered into the thickening wood, where, beyond the orange glare, deep shadows merged with the evening's darkness.

Each arduous step growing more difficult, intensified every throb and searing pain. Stumbling into an elm, he clung to it for support; then reaching for his stomach, he prodded beneath his tunic; the immediate excruciating fire brought back to his mind his injury: a sword wound, inflicted upon him by that dangerous man, the banneret.

Hand drawn forth, he extended it into a shaft of moonlight which darted through the canopy. *Blood!*

Since his journey had been most severely compromised, he needed to secrete the bag safely away. But where? — *the tree!*

He turned back and at length found his way through the woods to the hollow oak on the shoreline. Beside it, he collapsed and reached inside its cavity, fingers scraping about until they closed around something. This had to be the sack! Pulling it out, he rummaged through it and found a white cravat; this, he applied it to his injury.

Heavy cloud gatherings stole across the crescent-moon. Thunder murmured in the distance. And in the rising winds voices carried from up the shore:

"See anything?"

"Naught here."

"Keep searching the waters. You! Search the banks. You, the lane. You, the woods!"

Hastily, he untied the small bag from around him and shoved it inside the hollow. He would return for it later. The sack now flung over his shoulder, he pulled himself up and retreated into the deepening darkness.

With one arm outstretched, he stumbled on until arriving at a rocky outcropping. One side sloped down to the lake; the other a continuation of the forest.

Out of breath, faint-headed, and believing himself out of immediate danger, he sank against an oak.

Though strength regathered in his heaving breast, an inrush of violent emotions beset him. How he despised whoever intercepted his correspondence and how he abhorred the wretch who had condemned him to his present flight.

That I should be subjected to this appalling plight! Forced to suffer the wrath of—

A shudder stopped these thoughts. Other words spoken to him by his masked deliverer offered not hope but new distress: should he somehow succeed in this mission, only then might he stay the schultheiss' vengeance and find forgiveness; perhaps even favour.

But what of the gunpowder? From where came such vast quantities secreted in the vault? Surely, there was some ominous reason? Doubtless, he would be impugned for this!

Whoever were his enemies, should he get to Zürich and stay the calamity, he would not rest until he had exacted vengeance upon their heads.

The distant vesper bell of Oberhofen Monastery tolled the sixth hour. Its solemn chimes struck his agitated soul and rang through his throbbing skull while his wound swelled with pangs as if pierced anew.

He glanced at the cravat. The steady blood loss had already blackened it. He must treat and dress the wound.

Voices murmured in the whirling winds.

Are they upon me already?

To outpace his pursuers, he desperately needed transport.

While racking his mind for a solution, the inn at Gunten came to the fore. He would find horses there. And it could not be above two kilometres up the shore?

A gust swelled behind him, bending branches and stirring up leaves. Again, voices rushed towards him. He looked back. Torchlight flickered among the trees, wending their way closer. The next rustling wind carried upon it the sharp baying of hounds.

Whipped and snagged, tripped and stumbling, he fought his way through the woods until he burst from the forest termination.

It *was* Gunten!

Wet cowl pulled close, he hastened on for the stables; yet in his hurry, he collided into something solid.

"Watch yourself!" came a stern male voice. "For what cause do you run so wild?"

Barely looking up from beneath his cowl, the traitor remarked a patrician indignantly wiping his habiliments. Anxious to get away from this man, he tried to sidestep him and proceed.

The man, however, obstructed his path. "I insist you explain yourself!"

Irritated by his persistence, the traitor went to curse at him, but his voice produced only an agonised rasp as he doubled-over, coughing. Just then, a gust tore the cowl from his face, exposing him to the assiduous, glaring eye of this man. Alarmed, the traitor turned and fled down a lane.

"Come back here!" shouted the man after him.

The stable doors being left open and unattended gave the traitor pause. Cautiously, he peeked inside, spying no groom present. A small wooden stool sat beside a crate turned on its end, upon which was undoubtedly an unfinished repast, a cup of wine, and an extinguished tallow candle. Wherever the ostler had gone, he would return anon.

Quickness being of the essence, the traitor fixed his mind upon securing the equine beast in the nearest stall. Yet as he entered, it was likely his aggravated state and bloodied scent that startled the several horses and roused a slumbering Bernese coach-dog tied nearby.

Fangs bared and foam gatherings seething about its maw, the animal got up and fixed its menacing stare on him; its reverbing growl agitating the horses, who sensed the impending confrontation.

Suspecting that the dog would let out a thunderous bark, the traitor grabbed the ham off the plate and held it out. "H —" rasped he, his voice failing to utter "here."

With the expected roar, the dog launched forward and with such force as to break free from the rope.

Horrified, the traitor staggered backwards and tumbled over the crate, at which the catapulted ostler's dinner came crashing down about him.

Fortune, however, spared the traitor's leg; the hound rather sank its teeth into the ham. Between its slavering jaws, it swiftly devoured the morsel and then every other scrap. But before long, the ravenous beast recalled its duty and, on the intruder, re-fixed its baleful stare and stalked slowly forward on claws nigh glistening like blades.

Indeed, the traitor gasped.

To be sure, the dog snarled.

The traitor recoiled.

The dog sniffed.

The traitor curled into a ball, at which the dog pounced.

Yet, rather than rip flesh, it lamely licked the traitor's trembling hands before seeming to roll off him.

Eyes uncovered, the traitor beheld the dog lying on its back and whimpering up at him; its slobbered tongue dangling from its mouth; salted ham wafting on its repellent breath.

What sorcery is this?

Its silver collar tag presently flashed in the flickering torchlight. Thus, moved by impulse and finding the animal to allow it, the traitor examined it.

Znüni? He stared harder at the nametag. *Is it really you?*

The dog jumped up and licked him with avid cheer.

It *was* him!

The now ostler — a former groom to the traitor's family and gifted this animal upon completion of his service — had early observed in the dog's puppy nature a perpetual appetite. Thus, to name it after that Swiss German expression depicting a welcome snack taken around the ninth hour in the morning was most apt for this ever-hungry animal.

"Z—" tried the traitor, but his voice still failed him with the rasp of air that scourged his throat.

As happy a reunion as this was, since the ostler could return at any moment and discover the traitor and perchance report of it, his exigency to quit Gunten grew immeasurably.

He grabbed the extinguished candle and, relighting it from a torch, then entered an empty stall. Whilst watching the elongated shadows pass by the stable doors, he stripped his sodden garb to his undergarments — all with torturous motion.

To close his wound, he held the melting candle over it. The first drop hit the laceration; he jolted at the fiery scorch, a strangled gasp escaping through his gritted teeth as the wax bubbled and sizzled within. But it had to be done!

Grimacing, he continued until the wound was sealed.

Just then, hooves heavy upon the ground struck his hearing. Next came the barking of hounds. The former turned in another direction. But the latter still neared, doubtless fixed on the traitor's scent.

Seized by wild agitation, the traitor's thumping heart nigh burst from his chest. *How am I ever to flee from here?*

From near the shore, the church bell pealed the eighth hour, sparking a cunning stratagem: were the traitor to steal a boat from the harbour, cross Lake Thun to Spiez and, from there commandeer a horse, not only would he elude the dogs and riders but make up for the time already lost.

Baying loudened on the air.

Think! Think!

Znüni presently sniffed at the blood-soaked tunic at his feet.

Aha!

Into several shreds he tore the bloodied tunic and, scantily saddling four of the six horses, tied a strip to each. With the whip, he then drove them out of the stables in opposite directions.

Anxiously, he listened, wiping the sweat from his brow; but the pulsating clamour in his ears drowned out all else. Only after the uncertainty had almost strangled him of breath did his hearing clear enough to confirm that the hounds had diverted.

Not another moment was to be lost.

Against the grievous smarting of his injury, he took the incognito peasant clothes from the sack and changed into them. His own wet raiments, he crammed into the sack, and flinging about him a dry cape, he then bid a culpable farewell to the dog and quit the stables.

As he neared the harbour, he spied from the assemblage of torches a prodigious crowd along the jetty. Up the winding lakeshore they gazed, pointing at the fiery glow which diluted the black skies. With so vast a multitude gathered, it would be impossible for the traitor to steal a boat unobserved.

Meanwhile, on the atmosphere swelled a heavy sulphurous taste, moistening the bitter dryness of his mouth. The growing blasts blew bleak and cold, chilling him to the bone. He took shelter behind a rock and looked on impatiently, hoping that the approaching storm would drive those irksome spectators homeward.

With the turning in the winds that swept around him, of a sudden, several distant yelps stole among them. Doubting not these yowls' origin, the traitor's heart struck him with self-reproach. These were the squeals of the guilty receiving the whip for devouring his master's repast and allowing the horses to escape.

He glanced back, noticing several riders at the top of the lane. Then, with the next agitated thump of his heart, there returned the roaring of the hounds. To his left, at a distance along a street, several torch-bearing figures were being dragged in his direction.

He turned back to the jetty.

Curse these blasted peasants!

Somewhere along this shore there had to be a boat concealed by the night? Eyes shielded from the swirling grit and dust, he surveyed the waterside. On the margin nearby appeared a vague feature. But his vision being stung by the begrimed gales and obfuscated by the blackness made it impossible to make it out.

A break in the clouds, however, allowed the moonlight to momentarily diffuse across the waters which undulated in the winds, revealing an object driven up and down.

A boat?

The riders' heavy thudding neared. The barking hounds were loudening.

What if it is not a boat?

Nevertheless, it was now or never. With swift and unsteady steps, he reached the shore. It was indeed a small vessel. Without checking for any oars, he pushed it out.

Soon waist deep in the frigid waters, he clambered inside the boat and, lying flat, prayed for the current to carry him away and the night to conceal him from those seeking his doom.

Wind and water swelled about the creaky vessel. The traitor's heart pounded. Taking courage, he peeked just over the bow. Indeed, the shadowy outlines of riders and men lingered at the very spot he had embarked from. Some waved their torches along the shoreline, others to the ground, where the hounds yet sniffed about.

A minute more, they finally dispersed.

A tremulous sigh exhaled, the traitor sank onto his back. The darkness and the distance drifted were both thankfully enough.

For the oars, he now searched, discovering but one aboard the wretched tub. *Marvellous!*

As if matters were not already stacked against him, storm clouds, having blotted out all moon and starlight, betokened in the air a tempest of monstrous fury. In that instant, a thunderbolt burst over his head, attended by a violent rumbling. Intense flashes lit up one horizon, rolling thunderclaps answered from the opposite, as if Wodan himself were about to unleash his destructive force.

With but that sole oar, the traitor exerted his all towards the distant light of Spiez Castle.

As the storm grew ever more violent, icy, glass-like shards of rain lashed down upon him. Blinded by the squall slicing across his face, he, with increasing difficulty, struck harder at the turbulent waters, only to be driven a frenzy; no sooner did he climb one swelling wave, he was pushed back by another towards the shore he was battling to escape.

Ravaged by these exertions, his vigour fast diminished. And the searing spasms that erupted from his wound only compounded his miserable plight.

Already forced against his will on this desperate mission, anguish wrenched his heart, for each instant lost to obstruction served only to obliterate, word by word, the contents of the scroll. Failure to deliver it to Zürich on the morrow would not only effectuate a militant upheaval, but ignite war with the French. Absolute pandemonium would be occasioned across the confederacy, and the annihilation of his own soul would surely follow.

Still, the thunder roared overhead while the vessel beneath creaked and groaned as if about to break apart. Capillaries of lightning tore through the surrounding blackness, revealing waves of monstrous height, rising and rising, posed to smash his fragile skiff with their mighty explosions of foaming sprays.

Overborne with desperation, he raised his stinging eyes heavenward. *Are you also bent against me?*

As if in response, the tempest only redoubled its fury: the waves towered only the taller, the lashing rains fell only the heavier as to overcome the boat with more water, threatening to swallow him into the watery abyss.

Now consumed as much by ire as despair, he raised a clenched fist to the skies. *Come at me then! I will not be undone!*

In the next instant, a most vivid flash lit up the black, bright as day. The listing boat, already near to capsizing, was now borne by the whipping blasts straight towards the rocky shores.

I shall be dashed to pieces!

In vain, he struggled to steer. The storm-blasts were unyielding and the waves, still destructively increasing, threw the boat against the rocks.

On coming back into himself, he found the storm had abated. Upon the yet agitated lake, the returning moonlight revealed what remained of the vessel: a few planks, floating here and there.

How long he had lain insensate, he knew not, nor his exact location, on the shoreline. With a searching gaze, he scanned the banks in both directions. At last, in the distance to his right, the hazy outline of Spiez Castle mingled with the changing skies.

Over the several hundred metres of jagged rocks, he now clambered towards the castle — its bell tolling the eleventh hour.

Could it be so late already?

Upon the towering stone quay, torchlight swayed, limning a phalanx of Swiss Guard, who pointed towards the tumult at Oberhofen, visible across the water. Indeed, the flames still rose tall.

As he quickened along the foot of the southeast rampart, his cloak snagged on an overhanging bough of an oak. As he struggled to free himself, hollow footfalls echoed on the still air, reverberating through the fabric of the rampart and pausing above.

No sooner had the traitor glanced up than his blood ran cold.

Through a wide opening in the foliage, he observed a silhouette — a sentinel! *If he should look down now and see me!*

Fortune, it seems, had shone her ray upon him, for the sentinel merely cleared his throat, crooked his neck and spat; his footsteps then resumed and faded, thankfully, into oblivion.

Not without tearing his cape did he wrest free himself from the tenacious, snagging oak, and hasten his steps beneath the looming white walls and brown turrets.

On reaching the end of the walls, he climbed a steep grassy slope which opened onto the garden lawns. From here, he stalked across the green, weaving among the shrubberies, lest his shadows should be observed by any soldiers on the walls.

With guarded tread, he approached the streak of faint light outlining the stable doors. A padlock secured them shut. Grabbing a nearby heavy stone, he exerted its blunt force against the obstinate barrier, springing the lock open.

Hay crunching underfoot, he entered the dim interior.

From the soft glow of a torch, he spied a pitcher of water on a table. Much relieved, he availed himself of several deep swigs before setting to the task of saddling a sturdy-looking mare, shuddering at the worsening pain caused by the motion.

He was just fastening a buckle when something caught his ear, stilling his movement. Scarce daring to breathe, he listened. Only the groaning, returning whistling gusts whipped through the stable, rattling chains and stirring the straw across the floor.

Banishing such anxious imaginings, he resumed readying the mare.

Barely had he brought it out of its stall when voices echoed among the winds. Hurriedly, he led the horse outside and mounted it, about to bolt off, when:

"You there! Dismount at once!"

Against the fiery agony which darted through every limb, he pulled hard on the reins and turned the horse, only to confront a guard — bayonet aimed at him.

The horse, rearing in fright, knocked the man to the ground.

Frantic, the traitor spun the mare in the opposite direction, at which the same occurred: the horse reared, knocking a second armed guard to the ground.

Beyond fraught and nearly unhorsed by the mare's wild motions, the traitor clung on and again, turning the horse, took off.

Several frenzied heartbeats later, a pistol-shot clattered through the air; a musket ball pierced his right shoulder in an explosion of pain.

Still, he rode on, arm dangling uselessly at his side, each pounding gallop sending shockwaves coursing through his tortured frame. Already assailed by a violent thumping dizziness, nausea twisted his stomach and an enervating weakness invaded his trembling limbs.

Soon in a state of swirling disorientation, he knew not where his steed carried him. But on reaching the Hamlet of Reichenbach im Kandertal and remarking the church spire, he realised his err; he had gone south into the valleys as opposed to east, along the lake.

He would have corrected his course, but there came from behind a distant rumble of horses.

Farther thus into the landscape he rode, vision blurring and surges of unendurable agony at each jolt in the saddle.

After some distance, he entered the blurred and blackened confines of stupendous, rolling wooded massifs — mere hills, however, for yonder, vanishing into the black concave studded with blurry stars, climbed the tremendous, jagged granite masses of Gehrihorn, Dreispitz, Ärmighorn, and Zahm Andrist.

With the use of only one good arm, he pulled back hard and reined in the horse, slowing their headlong rush.

It must have been over a decade since he traversed this remote region; its terrain was now so strange and unfamiliar to his recollection. That he had deviated so far off his path and knew not which way to go nor how to recuperate the precious time lost, disheartened, he sank back into the saddle.

But as he strained his eyes to search the land for any familiar feature, a star shone forth from the innumerable milky blur. Drawn by its sudden luminosity, he looked up. Like a beacon lit by the ancient bear-god Artio to guide lost wanderers, the path he needed to take flashed in his mind: though circuitous — a journey of around fifteen hours through mountains and valleys — it was probably the safer route. The horse would be tired. The traitor would barely make it in time. But 'twas his only option.

After some leagues of winding forested slopes and folding glades hemmed in by rocky masses, he came upon a divergence in his route. Veering left, he entered another valley, which abruptly narrowed and steepened into a gorge.

Forced to dismount, he led the mare over the broken ground strewn with jagged stones and large boulders.

How he hoped, prayed, doubted this was the correct way.

Loud, rushing waters dashed against the rocks and echoed between the limestone walls, piercing his aching skull most grievously. Night-birds hooted and wolves howled close by, alarming the skittish horse as much as himself. It was the distant ursine baying, however, that drove the blade of dread deep within; that haunting memory of his mother's gruesome fate.

Shuddering at this recollection, he dragged the horse with haste.

Breathless and trembling all over, he reached the head of the gorge. Before him lay a darkened, forested declivity; this, he descended and reached its termination. The aspect opened onto a broad trough vale. Just silvered by the returning moon, the tall woods and the deep shadows of the cliffs rising on either side at last formed an appearance of familiarity.

This was the way.

Clouds though swallowed the waning moon and enveloped the land in impenetrable blackness.

How am I to proceed?

The trickling of a rivulet crept upon his hearing; recalling its path, he followed its rocky margin.

Soon the exponential burning in his abdomen spread to his limbs, and he stumbled to the point of almost falling. Desperate to abate these symptoms, he sat a while atop a fallen tree and willed himself to quell the subsequent sickness that twisted through him.

Just then, from somewhere behind, a disturbance broke on the air. As he vainly peered into the darkness, an icy gust swept over the peaks; the surrounding boughs creaked as they bent to its force. Accrediting the disturbance to the wind, he stayed his racing heart. However, there charged upon his recollection the famed bandits of Du Pont — the malefactor liberator — who might still roam this isolated area, searching for their leader.

Fresh alarm constricting his breast, he strained anew to pierce the shadows. *Is that shifting forms near the gorge?*

Mingled in the next gust, he believed there came the voices of such mercenaries, echoing with ominous intent.

Was it indeed they, and should they seize upon him, they would leave him for dead!

Hazarding not his safety to any doubt of imagination, he pulled himself up and, barely mounting the horse, heeled it forward.

Yet, before long, a fierce spinning reclaimed his mind. Hot and cold, he flushed. His hands grew numb and, losing their grip, the reins slipped from them. Off the saddle he slid and flung his weakening arms around the mare's neck, only to tumble earthward nonetheless, crashing with shock-waves of searing agony.

Injured, frozen, trembling with pain, and now fighting so heavy a drowsiness, he could ride no farther this night. Shelter must be found. With heaving breaths, he grabbed the stirrup and hauled himself up, lodging his good arm beneath the saddle to stay upright.

Led by the mare, he staggered on through the gloom.

At length, a faint flicker emerged from the night's pervading veil.

Drawn as if by providence, he stumbled towards the lone light. A bleary, swirling form of a window briefly solidified. It was shelter and it would provide sanctuary for the night.

First, he must secrete the horse somewhere capable of concealing so large an animal.

As he glanced about, his eyes momentarily found strength enough to descry in the returning moonlight the appearance of a ruin on an elevation on the far side of the vale. Hence, with immense difficulty, he led the equally exhausted beast up the steep.

The door to the stone structure sagged off its hinges. This adding to his nauseous enervation, he dragged it open with but use of that one arm. Near-blinded by the gloom, he guided the horse inside, fumbling his way around the blackness until he found a wooden protrusion, upon which he looped the mare's reins.

Forgive me for leaving you in so wretched a place. With his trembling hand, he caressed her mane. *But it will shelter you from the elements. And we shall be away on the morrow.*

Back into the night, he stumbled and, using up the strength left in him, pushed the door to.

It was with a near impossibility that he descended the rocky slope and alternately staggered and crawled across the basin towards the faint, dimming glow of a window.

By the time he reached the casement, it was in vain he knocked, for his rap was so faint that the inhabitants could not have heard him. And that his voice still produced only a muted grunt, stopped by the knife-like fire that pierced his vocal cords — doubtless a result of the explosion — he could only rap at the glass, however feebly, a second, third, and fourth time.

Please. Hear me.

Exhaustion having now gained the ascendancy of his will, he collapsed and his body thudded against the exterior...

21 – 29 NOVEMBER 1791

A pervading blackness met his opening eyes. The air was arid, heavy with lavender essence and edelweiss. His mouth, dry and athirst, he endeavoured to moisten with saliva. *Water. I need water!*

Wincing at the pain in his shoulder, he turned his head to the right. Again, only blackness. He turned the other way. Several slanted shafts of tremulous light — upon which dust motes danced — darted through closed shutters.

It is daytime then. But where am I?

— a creaking sound struck his hearing.

What was that?

No sooner did he permit himself to again breathe than the same sound reoccurred.

This time, lifting his head and regretting it instantly as a violent throbbing beset his brain, he noted a vermilion glow of embers on a small hearth on the opposite wall.

Perhaps what he heard was merely that of a log snapping as it collapsed?

However, a chesty cough now broke upon the baked air.

From the feeble glow, he descried the outline of a chair near the hearth. It presently moved, and a shadowy form rose from it and advanced towards him.

Alarmed, he struggled to rise, only to discover his right arm was bound tight across his chest. *What devilry is this?*

Not until after an, albeit croaking, female voice insisted he lie still and a soft hand pressed gently upon his shoulder did his wild apprehension abate and his racing heart slow. Even so, knowing not who she was, he went to demand this; but a burning, agonising rasp ripped away his voice anew. *I still cannot speak?*

The woman's obscure form traversed the blackness to the shutters, and as she swung them wide, the sunlight did rush in most violently, stabbing through the traitor's squinting eyes.

Gradually, her outline separated from the glare: she was of a slight and diminutive stature, scarcely four feet and notably hunched at the shoulders. As her features took on clarity, her stooped head, crowned with white, wiry hair wrapped atop, held certain resemblance to the bedraggled nest of some avian creature. And her nose, or rather beak, did protrude remarkably far from between two wiry bushes posing as eyebrows; its marvel was of such astonishing length that even her own eyeballs were perpetually inclined inwards, as if also fixated by so ghastly a snout.

But notwithstanding her otherwise unthreatening bearing, which might permit one of a sound mind to believe her of the friendly species, she did then unfurl her lips into a grin. From one elephantine ear unto the other, her crinkled mouth spread most alarmingly wide, exposing two rows of crooked, uneven, yellowed teeth.

Truly, she mirrored more closely a goblin than any daughter of Eve.

Though ignorant of the superstitious horror her visage provoked, the woman was not insensible to the staring of her guest. "You'd better close that orifice," said she, "lest you desire to sup on flies for morning repast?"

With a cheery morning greeting that rather tolled like cannon-fire in our hero's appalled brain, she now approached, causing him to recoil from her as if she were the Devil himself.

"Calm yourself." She outstretched two leathery gnarled tree branches. "I don't know what happened to you erenow, but no harm'll befall you here."

Such words little comforted our hero; he only shrank the further from her misshapen proximity, wanting to douse the monstrous peasant with holy water.

Finally, she pulled away, eyeing him as if he were the repugnant spectacle and not she. "Well..." She twirled her curly stubble about her knobbly finger. "You'd have me believe you'd met with a mountain troll — No! The *Erlking*! But I guess you be confused. Not surprising with so many injuries. No matter. Guess all'll be well once we get some victuals in you."

Consequently, with that same frightful smile overspreading the grotesque folds of her frightening phiz, off hobbled the merry-ugly-lady-goblin to prepare a "fine breakfast".

Breakfast? He had not the time for that for he had to get to Zürich!

Battle he now did to get up. But each attempt to rise saw the chamber spin, and he sank back onto the wretched hay mattress. Thus, waiting for the spinning to stop, he tried once more; yet his wounds tore with the motion, his legs gave way, and he collapsed to the floor.

Writhing with pain, perspiring heavily and trembling from the exertion, he clambered back into the crunchy bed, only to suffer the additional onset of a violent headache.

These afflictions, granted no reprieve, were heightened by the indelibly conspicuous view of a chamber which not even the sun's dally rays could add cheer to. Naught but dull, rough-hewn timbers, lending a dreary air above, about, and — his now stinging, grazed knees informed him — below. Alone, furnishing the small space, a dismal dark-wood chair, which he feared may sprout claws and fangs, faced a crooked mantel, which sighed on the wall with equal misery.

As for the bed! He pressed his hand into its lumpy surface. The crunch of hay made his skin crawl. *That I should recline on anything other than a cotton or feather-stuffed mattress!*

At this moment, a clip-clop of wooden clogs announced the return of the cheery peasant goblin-woman bearing the promised bowl of fare and a clay pitcher of water.

With startling strength belied by her size, she levered her patient upright and forcefully fluffed his pillow.

Onto this, he sank back, abhorred, shuddering, and curling his lip at her, lest her ugly aspect should somehow, like the plague, transfer to him through touch.

The wretch now tunelessly hummed as she poured a cup of water. That she dared went to administer it to his parched lips, he snatched it from her — despite the pain it caused him.

Indeed, she gawked at him as he gulped the water down without gratitude or manners, only to then hold out the cup like a boorish lord demanding his fill. Anyhow, the cup refilled thrice more, she finally handed to him the promised zmorge.

Our hero did eye the ugly wooden bowl as one might a venomous snake. The wicked wretch had only passed upon him a sentence of water-gruel!

Oblivious to his mouth turned down in disrelish, the crone pulled up a chair and, taking the indigent wooden spoon, scooped up a serving. "You won't find a better oatmeal in the *whole* valley," spiritedly declared she as if it were a golden spoon bearing ambrosia.

I very much doubt that! He shoved it and her away.

Natch, she was not less determined to force the cheerless morsel into his mouth than he was to fight it off. "Now, open wide!" Weapon in one hand and his chin in the other, she squeezed hard enough to dislocate his noble jaw. "Such heavenly sustenance will put you to rights."

Mouth sealed tight, our hero did dodge the barbarous instrument until his cunning aggressor plugged his nose, causing him to gasp like a landed fish, and got the first dollop past his lips. "My husband says I make the best gruel in the *whole* canton," said she with a chuckle.

The oatmeal — an unpardonable far cry from his usual fare of veal pie and entrée of cutlets in fricandeau — only punished his epicurean palate as the thick, salty graininess slithered down his retching gullet; as did the next dollop, and the next...

Mercifully, she paused the offensives to stoke the fire. "You be welcome to stay here until — Oh! You look pale?" After several struggles, her hand at last assessed his temperature. "You be coming down with a fever."

In point, his wounds had yielded to the earliest signs of infection, and, almost at once, he sank into a deep, feverish sleep with the ill-cleped "heavenly sustenance" churning his insides.

***

As the next day progressed, the traitor's disorder assumed a serious aspect. His fever soared to infernal heights. His skin flushed as if kissed by old Lucifer. Mild shivers grew to violent shakes that rattled his very bones. He perspired heavily, he became clammy, his body knowing not whether to freeze or boil. His quivering lips and spluttering chokes revealed the derangement of his mind. And his irregular, skipping pulse evidenced his poise on a precipitous brink.

"Heavens!" would cry the woman as she flew back and forth with rags and cold water to mop his brow; overwrought, she ordered her husband to fetch tisanes of mixed herbs for the fever and compresses of wild garlic, edelweiss, and arnica, to redress the wounds. "He's at death's door."

"We'll need to bury him out back with our poor boy," bemoaned the man.

Notwithstanding the prayers and solicitudes of his two nurses, by the third and fourth day, his fever became so high as to bring raging delirium. His eyes rolled back. His body gave way to fits. Hallucinations most horrific seized him: the scroll set aflame; bloodied blades gathered at his throat; guards' faces — spectral and elongated — laughed at and taunted him among billows of hellish smoke. Overcome by these conspiring symptoms, he plunged into oblivion.

***

On the sixth day of early morn, his fever finally broke.

While our enervated hero was still lying in his itchy cot, several circumstances, though imprecise, fast claimed his consideration: the woman's lamentations, auguries, invocations uttered aloud with sobs and pleas to the deity; and the man's threat of near interment.

Easily, our hero perceived he had scarcely cheated death.

But to think that I — I of all people — might have drawn my last breath in so isolated, so insignificant, so ... The scratchy crunch of hay re-issued beneath him as if to mock his fallen state ... *vulgar a dwelling!*

Scarce above a week ago, friends, family, and fortune surrounded him. The finest attire, suavest society, choicest equipages, foremost abodes and sumptuous feasts had been his daily staples. But now, divested of all, he was surely ostracised, destitute, ruined. And having failed to reach Zürich, he was deprived of hope.

A sourness filled his mouth. If only he could get his hands on the very rogue who had reduced him to this gross state. The muscles in his arms quivered. Woe to them if he should somehow re-emerge from the shadows. Like Tell's arrow, he would find his mark.

Yet who would dare to raise a heel against him? Had this strike perhaps come from one of his own people? Who else could have intercepted his communications to such a ruinous effect?

Meantime, what of the events that must have already overtaken the world? Images of cantons in chaos and leagues in tatters flashed through his mind. Riddled with such menacing thoughts, he again grew anxious to leave. But where was he to go? And however bereft of allies, he could not simply languish as one paused between life and death. He had to do something!

His stomach interrupted this strategic musing with an ungentlemanly growl, and encountering a sudden light-headedness, he determined to explore the dwelling for any sustenance other than gruel.

Though the throbbing tenderness of his injuries had much abated, still he laboured to rise while the chamber span about him anew and his head thumped afresh.

After the shape of the gloomy chamber had re-coalesced, he cloaked himself against the morning chill and ventured forth.

A shadowy space, separated by a column of light entering a half-opened shutter, met his eye. To his left, beyond a ladder to a loft, emerged a log table upon which appeared a fruit bowl?

Drawn thus across the creaky floorboards, he snatched up the bowl and extended it into the light. Only withered apples and a few clusters of shrivelled berries. *How naïve to have desired anything better!* All the same, he collected two apples for the horse.

"Tick-Tock," caught his ears.

"Tick-Tock," stole his eyes as he searched for the source.

"Tick-Tock," subsequently lured his cold, bare feet across the rough planks to a thick oak mantelpiece, where, as he read the hour, he perceived the outline of a French ormolu. So powerful was our hero's disbelief that he did rub his eyes to ensure the treasure was no illusion.

How did such an elegant item find itself here — wait, what is this?

Squinting closer, he distinguished a honeybee finial. *Can it be?* The steady ticking throbbed beneath his fingertips as he traced the emblem.

Where before had he seen this clock?

"Tick-Tock. Tick-Tock."

His mind hurtled back several months earlier to the revelries of a ball he attended solely for the opportunity of observing his half-brother's political activities. Was not this the very clock gifted to his sibling by that visiting French emissary? Before they withdrew to the library to exchange pleasantries... or was it something more sinister?

"Tick-Tock. Tick-Tock."

Its steady ticking grew louder, invoking that feeling as when time is running out.

But how is this here?

"Tick-Tock. Tick-Tock."

Much like the movement of gears and cogs concealed behind its dial, how he wished to penetrate his half-brother's facade and to unravel the machinery behind his betrayal alike.

Just then, there issued a creak of the floorboards and he turned, only to be met by such a startling sight as made him stumble back, dropping the apples.

Pitchfork poised in hand, the husband was about to smash his skull like a ripe melon. "'Tis *you*!" said he. "We heard the floorboards; and, seeing your cloak, I was certain you be a robber!"

The woman descended the ladder, swung wide the shutters, and joined her husband.

By the golden light of morn, our hero did stare open-mouthed at the pair: from beneath both cottier nightcaps protruded ears of such prodigious size they could double as sails; long white hairs jutting out every which way while veritable hedges of scruff did perch on each chin. Quite likely to make even the pluckiest rodent out a-foraging for morsels turn tail, ten twisted brownish talons extended from each horrific foot. But 'twas the man's nose that held the attention most steadfastly; not less hooked, crooked, and overgrown than his wife's — drawing even his own eyeballs haplessly to its mass — it bulged between two white forests as to put one in mind of a mighty Alp. And with the four rows of yellowed and eroded gravestones that rather formed a grimace than a grin, their likeness was irrefutable:

Heavens. With his elegant hand, our hero crossed himself. Never had he beheld creatures more fantastic outside of the pages of a chapbook of fey folklore. *They are both the very image of an ambling troll!*

Inattentive to the hero's critical a gaze, the ogress picked up the apples, and, after lighting the cooking hearth, she bade him sit and took her own place opposite at the table next to her husband. With apparent curiosity, they eyed their guest; their hideous heads tilted sidewards like inquisitive vultures; their droopy eyes a-blinking.

"Feeling *better*?" said the woman.

Still so astounded at their folkloric looks, the traitor scarce managed a nod.

"'Tis good to hear." She watched his wide eyes twitching back and forth between her and her husband. "I see the tea I brewed has restored you wonderfully."

In truth, her tea, much like her gruel, had tasted naught but like lukewarm ditchwater.

The man took an apple and bit into it. "What's your name?" garbled he.

The woman snatched the apple off him and took the next bite. "Where you be from?"

And without waiting for any reply, they stormed their guest with question after question, all the while chomping on and spewing apple shrapnel. Thus, repulsed, irked, and dodging the fleshy missiles, the traitor looked only this way and that, uncertain through which door to escape.

"You be a quiet one!" The woman's brow ruffled. "Don't ya care to talk?"

Indeed, he did not and cared even less for their nosiness. Howbeit, to quell their chatter, he tried to utter something — anything! But naught emerged save an incoherent grunt.

Looking blank, the woman crooked her neck and, with her finger plugged into her ear, wiggled it about. "Begging ya pardon dear; say what?"

Further effort at speech did produce only slack-jawed bewilderment. She turned to her husband. "Have I gone deaf?"

"Nay, your hearing's as fine as the day we wed," declared the oaf, finger raised. "'Tis plain as the wart on me nose." With his hairy knuckle, he struck the table. "He's a mute."

A new expression stole over the woman's unlovely visage. "*Oh*! He's *dumb*?"

They now turned their pity-filled eyes on the traitor, who, skin a-prickling and shaking his head most vehemently, bid to correct them. But drowning in their ignorance of his supposed tongueless affliction, they set about guessing his name, firing at him: Jakob, Jean, Jeton, Joachim, Josef, Josiah, Jean — again — Johan, Jörg, Jodocus, Joder, Josiah — again; and many others.

Finally, face a-twitching, head a-pounding, and stomach a-churning with frustration, our hero leapt up. He would somehow offer them a name, though a fake one.

Over to the cooking hearth, he marched. The charcoals burned his fingers.

He stomped back across the room to a rough pine dresser and rifled through its draws and shelves. Nothing! Defeated, he flung his eyes about the space. *There has to be something with which I can* — he spotted the wooden spoon — *Aha!*

Over to a cracked washbasin in the kitchen area, he now stalked and snatched the spoon up.

Scarce had he simulated the custom of writing, when the woman, eyes fixed on the hand wiggling the upended spoon in it, cried out: "He's desperate for gruel!"

Incessant prattling was all that seasoned so already bleak a dish. Well over four tedious hours did drag at a slug's pace as the oaf and half-wit prattled on about their dull histories; the series of dull coincidences leading to their betrothal; their parents' dull origins and dull coincidences in matrimony; asserting with bucolic conviction the divine providence guiding every mile-marked event that did abound in their dull legacies. But at long last, they concluded the wearisome chronicle, lamenting the life of their dearest and only son, who sadly met an untimely end.

Death by hellish tedium, I imagine!

Anyway, still puzzling over their guest's strange arrival to their flower-bed, they now fell to quarrelling heatedly over the probable cause but at last agreed it must surely be the work of notorious brigands known to haunt the surrounding valleys.

"Fear not," said the woman, noting our hero's dismay at the mention of such rapscallions — for he now recalled having spied shadowy figures lurking near on the night of his arrival. "They'd have no interest in our tiny vale, as we've naught worth plundering."

"Naught worth plundering?" echoed the oaf. "But what of the chickens? And the pigs?"

"What of them? There be chickens and pigs aplenty all over the canton! Besides, my good friend in the village claims she saw a pig, fat enough, near Spiez, that would feed a whole bandit army. Our little pen — scrawny as rats — wouldn't half-fill even two or three."

Pacified by her argument, the man agreed the raiders would prefer to steal a fatter pig.

Of all wretched places to have sought convalescence, by ill fate I chanced upon a sanctuary for hideous gruel, famished livestock, and simple-minded lunatics!

Doubtless, they now noticed their guest's escalating annoyance, for they cleared their throats and, however, continuing the tales of their barnyard, took a more macabre path.

Beginning the narration, the man related how their son had spoken of some devilish invention called Mr. Guillotine's beheading machine, and its employment on a certain notorious highwayman named Nicolas, or Jean? The woman interrupted to insist the rogue's name was most certainly the latter. The man protested it was most certainly the former. Consequently, did they violently dispute over this weighty point of nomenclature.

Nicholas Jean Pelletier! With his fingers, the traitor could not help drum his ennui onto the table. *Must I endure another day here?*

While the man heaved a weighty sigh at his stubborn helpmate, she, paying him no mind, only commandeered the narrative for herself. This wicked French fellow "Jean!" losing his head, had put an ingenious idea into their own. Distracting his wife with a fly that dared to land on her withered fruit — at which she passionately chased it to the window — the man stole back the story. In a spirit of vengeful invocation, they named their poultry after the abhorred wohledelgeboren's (Swiss nobility); for example, von Bern, von Affry, von this and von that; not forsaking the Schultheiss von Villeroy. Having ejected the winged intruder, the woman returned triumphant and, stopping up her husband's mouth, reclaimed the telling. Thus, for the ill-fated fowl, the ritual of decapitation was a sure omen of bringing the same fate upon the heads of all they that lorded it over them.

Howl they did with laughter, rolling around in their seats, clunking their teeth and clutching their bellies as our hero rather involuntarily grabbed at his own gullet in horror.

The woman, however, remarking this, halted her crackling. "You look unwell again?"

Her fortuitous observation, quashing her husband's merriment, thus put an end to their paltry political rant. That said, the tirade did bring forth the fullest recollection of how desperate the traitor's situation was; a despondent gust raced from his sinking chest. Even was he to perpetuate his life in hiding, without friends or connections, his fate hung on the penurious philanthropy of galling, garrulous, peasants. How was he ever to endure this?

Even without his valet, it was too great an incon — *Of course! Ludwig!*

Before fleeing Oberhofen, our hero was instructed that should he have failed to reach Zürich the next day to hide until the next full moon and meet Ludwig in Lucerne. The scroll would then be conveyed to the garrison there. Though delayed, this measure should, pray, still obviate the looming political chaos and mitigate, to some extent, the ramifications the traitor would undergo.

His spirits revived at this remembrance, new resolve flowed through his veins. *Then I must get to Lucerne.*

Struck as if by a thunderbolt, he only now remembered the poor mare left to starve. Under watchful eyes, he grabbed two apples and, communicating with two fingers — which he walked across the table top — a wish to stretch his legs, sallied forth for the ruin.

The vexed-looking beast, presently chewing on a miserable-looking tuft of grass, did light up at the sight of the apples and did instantly spit out the grass.

Beast thus fed and door shut fast, our hero exhaled his relief; come daylight, he would be on his way to Lucerne.

He had taken but a few steps down the slope when, alas, his foot twisted and he tumbled down, slamming right shoulder-first into a jutting rock, sending an almost blinding wave of agony through him. As he sat up, he saw his shoulder hanging at an odd, misaligned angle.

With smarting difficulty, he got back to the cabin, where the man, rightly guessing the injury, seized him and, rather too heavy-handedly, shoved the joint back into place — unleashing fresh waves of nauseous, fiery chills all over him.

Kinder with her hands, the woman applied them to preparing a tea of dried willow and meadowsweet. That said, she nonetheless ushered him back to the table, where, together with the oaf, she then pelted him with much tedious and bothersome talk.

At any rate, the sun finally fled the sky. Their tongues at last ran dry. And off they toddled to their roost, releasing their prisoner to his straw-stuffed mattress, where he yielded to the tea's sedative powers and escaped in sleep every odious circumstance that surrounded him.

***

By morning, his shoulder was, as we might expect, so inflamed that he could barely move it, rendering departure impossible. Neither could he leave the next day. To be sure, this interim did inflict a most repetitive torture; each morn, interrogations about his daily disappearing off with fruit; each afternoon, unending sessions of ear stabbing palaver, inept platitudes, erroneous wisdom, and the repeated (accidental, claimed they) calling him by their late son's name, Jonas.

Furthermore, they even bequeathed upon our hero the dead boy's rags!

If only they knew upon whom they practice such inapposite charity and rhetoric.

Anyhow, the hours did daily crawl by at a cripple's pace until moon chased sun and dawn freed night; when would this tedium ever end?

Come early third morn, our ailing hero felt much recovered, suffering more from a dull ache and stiffness in his shoulder. Tomorrow he would most definitely decamp.

Anxious to elude his obtrusive hosts so to sneak off the ruin, he resolved on tiptoeing to the meagrely restocked fruit bowl. Thus, assessing the route less prone to betray him with creaks and groans, he stepped out of the bedchamber, one toe so gingerly forward.

As soundless as a prowling tom, he was... at first... for several treasonous creaks did then soon erupt on the air.

Next, footsteps sounded in the loft.

Blast!

Tendrils of fire coursed through every fibre of his being, down through his clenched fists to the tips of his twitching fingers. He would a-swift snatch and dash. Thus, eyes on the prize:

Creak! — C... r... e... a... k! Creak! It truly was a symphony of creaks! — Creak-creak-creak-creak-creak!

"Ho there!" came the unwelcome hail. "Up before the rooster, are we?"

Confound it! Irk repressed, the traitor faced him. "And good mor —" The stolen fruit indeed fell from his clutch as his hand caught his gasp.

"Well, kiss my foot!" said the man. "You *talk*?"

"I *do*?" His voice was, however, faint and rougher than its natural state.

The man verily scratched his balding head in bewilderment and would have summoned his wife were she not already at his side fixing the mess on top of her own. "God be good!" She tugged his sleeve. "My prayers was answered! I spent a *whole* five minutes before bed, begging the Lord that when blessing those in need, he grants a voice to the oppressed. But never would I have dreamed of so miraculous a result."

Consequently, heated water soon announced three things: herbal tea, the sentence of celebratory water-gruel, and plenty of prattle.

Ironically, now our hero could respond to their torrent of questions, it was all for naught. He squeezed in only that his name was Pippin — which it was not, and that he had come from Uri Canton — which he had not. As his hosts were rather still bent on talking than listening, neither could he probe the origins of the clock. And since such a *miracle* had occurred, they fell to whispering before hurrying off with their rickety hand-drawn cart to the village in the next valley to collect provisions to celebrate, promising a speedy return.

Once they had shrunk from view, the traitor snatched two more apples and, along with the sacred slops he fooled the woman into letting him keep for later, hastened for the ruin.

While the animal merrily munched away, several alarming thoughts crossed the traitor's mind as he pondered the implications of his restored speech. *What if the villagers should speak of Oberhofen or Spiez? And what if the oaf and his wife should suspect who I am?*

But over a week had passed since his escape. Such talk must have died down by now? Besides, if his hosts' trip was brief, they would have little opportunity to talk to many people...

It was, though, some hours before the travellers returned; they had enthralled the villagers with the stranger's bizarre arrival, the healing magic of gruel, the powers of saintly ministrations, and his restored speech; tales told with such pride that they quite lost track of time.

A foreboding chill slithered up the traitor's spine. "What did they have to say about this?"

The villagers had all agreed how very miraculous it all was.

Surely, had she heard something of import, she would mention it? Yet perchance she dissembled? Her countenance and her eyes, however, evinced only sincerity.

A feast later sprawled across the table: vegetables, fruits, legumes, sourdough bread, Älplermagronen, Rösti, and their fattest fowl, von Castella de Berlens — beheaded, plucked, and roasted with all the violence intended on the person of that name!

Having too long suffered naught but vile, gritty gruel, our hero devoured every morsel heaped into his oft-replenished bowl.

It was only that the light outside dimmed the traitor turned to the mantel to read the hour. "Ah! You have moved the clock?"

His hosts exchanged awkward glances.

The traitor cast his eyes around the room. "Where has it gone?"

Confusion did plainly claim their features.

Witnessing this and sensing opportunity in their confusion, the traitor believed he could at last, and discreetly so, occasion the particulars he desired. "It is a remarkable piece," said he. "From where did you come by it?"

A shade of grief seemed to steal over their expressions.

"I believe it is of French origin," continued our hero. "Was it a gift?"

Grief it was; tears swelled in the woman's eyes as she explained it was a gift from their child. She turned to her husband. "He must have been in France?"

"Fret not." The man tugged her watery cheek. "We'll get it back. Somehow..."

Get it back? Briefly relinquishing his own interests on the subject, the traitor looked hard at them. "What has become of this clock?"

Likely made uneasy by our hero's gaze, the woman looked away while the husband reluctantly explained that, in wanting to speed up his recovery, they had pawned the item in Spiez.

The traitor leapt up. "You pawned it in order to buy this feast for me?"

Their stunned faces and nods conceded as much. The woman, now growing tearful again, forced onto her unlovely face, her unlovely smile, which, in this moment, revealed to her critical and vain guest an unexpected, wholly unobserved erenow, inner beauty.

Even to so reproachful a heart as we have observed in our hero, he could not help encounter a spasm of admiration mingled with self-reproach injecting its venom into that organ of his breast. He slumped back into the chair. Unable to account for such generosity and selflessness in so indigent a dwelling, it rendered him for some moments silent.

Possibly wanting to dispel the mood, the woman claimed she recalled something important from the village she forgot to relay. "We heard a queer report from the butcher's wife," began she, "who had it from the ironmonger's wife, who was told by the shoemaker's wife..." Here, she paused to verify the accuracy of this chain with her husband, who avowed her a most trustworthy reporter of gossip. "There be some incident." Her eyes darted left to right as though searching for eavesdroppers. "At Spiez! Guards, just yesterday, were asking about an outlaw — and a horse!"

Here, she again turned to her husband. "What colour was it?" The man looked at a loss but said it was brown. "Yes, a brown horse," repeated she (though it was, in fact, black), "and there be a healthy reward to whoever should find this villain and the horse."

Our hero's heart did hammer violently within as instantaneous conviction struck him. *Since they have trumpeted my presence to the entire village, doubtless, when pawning the clock in Spiez, they blabbered the same tale there! Anyone possessed of half a grain of wit will easily guess at who I am and summon the authorities forthwith!*

"And what about Gisela?" appealed the woman to her husband, who raised his eyebrows. "Gisela, my friend from the village," explained she to the traitor, "asked if I thought you might be the outlaw they's all hunting for...?" Though chuckling, she appeared to watch him as if to read his reaction. "Stuff and nonsense, I'd say."

"Indeed," hastily concurred the traitor, striving to stay his clamorous emotions.

Notwithstanding their peasant foibles and ignorance, the possibility of their making a connection between the reports and the traitor's presence was a certainty in waiting.

He had to leave and without them knowing it.

30 NOVEMBER 1791

After nervously awaiting evenfall — each dragging hour fraught with every dread and apprehension imaginable of a sudden ambush and capture — the overly prolonged past midnight retreat of his hosts to their creaking loft at last arrived.

Stood in the doorway to the bedchamber, scarce daring to breathe, our hero listened. Mingled with the growing breezes which swelled about the cabin, creaking its wooden exterior, there gradually floated the rumbling sounds of snoring from above.

The moment had arrived.

To provision himself and the mare for so long and tiring a journey, he stealthily packed into his sack ample victuals from the leftover remnants of the feast. Full of unease as he was, his ears were pricked by every creak he imagined his hosts must have heard — and now the loud creak he himself caught.

Heart shuddering, he froze and turned his ears in the direction of the loft. 'Twas only the wind outside still buffeting the trembling wooden walls.

Last viands gathered, he slung the bulging sack over his shoulder and, casting his ill-contented eyes about the hovel which had, all the same, saved his life, sighed his relief to finally quit so alien a sphere; to quit such irritating hosts and the endless days of insufferable, irksome, unrelenting, prolix yakking that did set our hero's head to pounding.

Several tip-toeing steps later, he was just about to sneak off, when lo, a peculiar sensation did cling to his breast and stay his feet at the door. Unable to shake off this feeling, he glanced back; his eyes drifted about the dark space to the now empty mantel — a lonesome, forlorn-looking shelf, touched by the dwindling glow of several crumbling logs on the hearth.

To think they gave up so precious a gift from their son for my benefit.

Eager to discharge the unwelcome feelings this consideration occasioned, he crept over to the table and dropped a small bag of batzens on it. One last glance about the wretched hovel, he made his way to the ruin.

First, he fed the shivering mare several apples and other comestibles, and not before long, she was soon re-energised and ready to leave the ruin and be led gently down the slope.

Scarce had he reached the valley basin when echoes of hoofbeats and the flashing of torchlight emitted from the wooded gorge at the valley's far end.

Good lord! Could it be they are come already?

Heart lurching, he bundled the provisions over the saddle and, vaulting astride the horse, drove it in a breakneck gallop towards the far side of the shadowy vale, flying past the peasant couple's hut and into the forested slopes.

Anon, the densely wooded acclivity steepened sharply. Low-hanging boughs and branches making more arduous the path, impended over the narrowing rugged trail, tearing at our hero's face, snagging at his garb — near unseating him in the uphill struggle as he grasped at the horse's mane.

But pushing through, they persevered along the rugged path.

As the mangled view ahead only darkened the more, and the buckled foliage and low branches only enclosed the more on them, a stream cut across their ascent. At his right, an opening appeared, framing a small moonlit glade in the distance.

With sudden intense discomfort in his shoulder, he wrenched the labouring creature sideways and galloped through the stream. Soon they entered a grassy opening and then another wood, pursuing for some time its rude, gloomy winding ascent.

Gradually, the oppressive trees thinned out and unveiled a saddle-shaped clearing against the chilled night sky. To his left rose the granite slopes of Urschelgrat, and beyond, the tremendous snow-capped Drättehorn, towering at more terrific heights. To his right, the uneven range of Zahm Andrist, Hundshorn, and Schilthorn crowded the environs like a huge black rampart.

His direction lay beyond these intimidating massifs.

A few moments of rest taken, he urged the mount onwards.

Now and then, he strove to steal a glimpse of any movement in the vale, but all was lost amidst the next mass of rustling pines which blocked the view.

Some way farther up the stony steep threaded between the brooding cliffs, he glanced back over the tops of the pines and descried a momentary flicker.

Pulling the heaving creature to a halt, he turned in his saddle and stared hard; there in the dark vale far below, next to where must have been the peasant's cabin, tiny pinpricks of what resembled torchlight appeared.

To think I was almost seized upon!

Meanwhile, the mutterings of a storm rumbled amongst the distant peaks. Bright flashes snaked amidst the rolling cloud masses, heading inexorably closer. Such ominous scenes corresponding with our hero's already aggravated spirit and gathering disquiet, he spurred the nervous mare into a headlong gallop, seeking to outrun the approaching storm's wrath.

Deeper into the menacing range they pressed as granite walls rose in threatening majesty to blackened heights on all sides. Yet as fast as they rode, all too soon, the pursuing storm gained upon them.

Biting gusts rushed over the ridges all around; bending the pines far below and converging in the rocky heights above, they formed furious blasts, discharging their head-force upon him.

No longer safe to ride, he dismounted and cautiously led the mare along the jagged ridge onto the scarcely trodden passes where the last vestiges of vegetation yielded but to rock, stone, dread, and awe, and piles of eternal snow.

They had but gained the already terrifyingly vertiginous icy peak of Schilthorn, when a thunderbolt tore apart the turbulent black firmament. Dreading the deafening peals above might provoke an avalanche below, he hastened down the narrow ridge towards Birg, shuddering at the possibility of stepping across a snow-filled crevasse and plunging to his death.

Here, at this freezing altitude, an inundation of thundersnow, mingled with sleet pellets and spears of intimidating lightning, fell from the furious heights. Frostnip seared his skin. His eyes stung against the icy snow blasts as he dragged, with aching, heart pounding difficulty, the equally petrified mare.

In time, spying a hollow in the mountainside, he took shelter with the horse, looping her reins over a rocky protrusion.

Scarce had he set about kindling a fire and brought forth the flames, when, as the gales howled louder, roared fiercer, and groaned more ferociously, a thunderclap, so loud as if to split the mountain, startled the skittish mare. Letting out a fearful snort, she reared tall, pulling loose her reins and galloped hard into the blast.

"No!"

Into the blizzard, our hero tore after the creature. But the blinding squall, near knocking him off his feet, drove him back to the rock.

"Curse that horse! This mountain! This storm! This —" *Oh no!* "The scroll!"

Overwhelmed by sudden exponential torment, he stomped around and kicked at the fire, and, at length, collapsed to the rocky ground. He could not let the horse get away. Yet, all the while he waited for the storm to abate, alternately tortured by the existing urgency of his plight and fired with agonising vehemence for this added burden, he could only curse with bitterness every detail of this wretched misadventure.

Since the storm raged relentlessly on, trapping him within the rock, the damp, cold, tiredness, and dejection at length overcame him. Drenched cloak flung off, he sank next to the fire, and, staring into its flames, his eyes gradually grew heavy, shut out its glow, and his mind resigned itself to sleep.

***

Dawn's early light entering the cavity pulled our poor hero from a lingering nightmare, awakening him only to fierce hunger and a recollection his mount had fled with their provisions. The embers, too, having long relinquished their last embrace, found the morning chill drive him out from the rock onto a rude winding trail towards the hamlet of Mürren; how he hoped to happen on the horse along the way!

As daybreak continued to spread over the land, the horizon blushed with pink and orange, and the sky melted in hues of cerulean and lapis, promising a clear and unclouded day.

In the solitude of this region, it was almost possible to believe the world was free from all difficulty and distress; that he was not hunted; not in danger; not desperate.

Departing the tremendous rocky walls and glacial rivers of compacted stones of ice, he continued his descent for about an hour, after which the terrain took on a less oppressive aspect. To the brisk morning breeze, a grassy landscape swayed, sending a stream of damp autumnal balm into the air; upon which the waking birds diffused their melodies and the blue turaco, gliding overhead, called out its ko-kok trill. Amongst the mossy boulders and soaring cedar copses, scattered herds of curious chamois watched his despondent trudging.

No stray horse was, however, to be seen anywhere.

About another hour later, there came into sight the pines and rustic dwellings of Mürren's green slopes, perched atop the Lauterbrunnen precipices; a minute foreground frowned upon by the immense rocky Schwarzmönch, Jungrau, Gletscherhorn, and Äbeni Flue faces soaring yonder — their bellies hung with black forests that disappeared into a belt of mists, from where their jagged gray, blue tinged faces rose still higher to their summits of snow and reflected light.

Disappointingly, no wandering mare had apparently been seen to have passed through the hamlet. Thus, in need of another and still possessing his money bag, our hero enquired from where one might be procured. He was advised to go to the valley below, where he could hire passage to Gsteigwiler and obtain a colt at a fair price.

Though this prospect lifted his mood, it drove fresh agitation into his breast, for the Matten bei Interlaken garrison was but a short distance from Gsteigwiler.

Be that as it may, it was his only recourse.

Though unlikely it was that any search for him could have yet reached these remote hills, still our hero would have departed straight away. But with hunger pinching sharply and the villagers importuning their famished guest to break fast first, he put aside his aversion for such vulgar company and fell ravenously upon the hearty victuals provided.

It must be an inborn quality of the peasant mind — this compulsion to prattle needlessly while others try to eat in peace. With such annoying fervour did they bend his ear, plying him between mouthfuls with their tiresome questions:

"Whence do you hail, lad?" — "What brings you to these parts?" — "Whither travels you next?"

And this was merely the start:

"Have you no family to go home to?" piped up one uncomely dame as she plonked herself on the bench so uncivilly close to him as to near shove him off its edge. Disregarding his scowls, she did then set about pouring him more milk, only for it to spill over onto the table in her distraction, blessing him with her batting lashes, wonky smile, and the crimson rosiness of her pudgy cheeks which did challenge the scarlet threads of her embroidered neckerchief and her flushed, ample, heaving bosom.

"No sweetheart waiting for you in some distant vale?" bombarded another bulbous nosed busybody, refusing our hero a moment's respite from such impertinent interrogations as she too shoved herself uncivilly next to him on his other side with such force as to drive the other dame off the opposite edge of the bench.

"Why not settle here with a comely young lass?" proposed a toothless greybeard opposite. His eye roved suggestively about the pine-panelled room at the several uncomely dames, who — fluffing up their floral skirts, puffing up their puffed sleeves, smoothing out their homespun bodices, dropping curtsies, and stepping on each other's toes in their quest to claim the most eminent position in the line — did smile uninvited smiles in eager, albeit deluded expectation.

"What occupation has thee, young master?" sang out a ruddy matron from the back of the queue, determined to have her turn.

Our put-upon hero did turn from this spectacle to glare into his slowly dwindling plate; he cursed under his breath the babbling rustics who delayed his flight and his every mouthful with their vexing twaddle.

Not done with simply interrogating him, several others now set about bemoaning their impoverished lives and plaguing his ears with the talk of taxes and levies.

A man — evidently chief to this mob of uncouth and incorrigible denizens — built like a rain barrel, slapped the table with hands the size and texture of cured hams and loudly declaimed that the spirit of the famous peasant uprising of 1653 was again inflaming the hearts of the canton. His helpmate, a skeletal wretch bedecked in naught but depressive-looking black garb and deep orbs about her eyes, scrunched her crooked conk and railed against the schultheiss for despatching his dastardly bailiffs to their insignificant hills to steal their little hard-earned coin. With a grievous sigh, she avowed if the world were fairer and didn't force off sons as cannon fodder to fight rich men's wars, their young nephew would still be at home with them. With a grunt, her husband bemoaned being but a mere settler here, unable to have baptised the boy in the city or set up a tombstone over his unmarked grave outback.

From the fireside now crackled the voice of another man who — prodigiously long pipe in one hand and wreathed in pungent coils of white smoke — looked as if he had been carved from the very beams which propped up the low ceiling. Cramming a finger up his cavernous nostril and excavating vigorously, he swore the land needed only another Leuenberger, Schybi, or Henzi to lead them in overthrowing the oligarch thieving tyrants who bled the land dry.

At this, a salt and peppered browed matron with grey locks spilling out beneath her linen cap rushed over and clamped her hand over his mouth. "Best watch your tongue, lest the bailiff hear and clap you in irons!"

Clearing their throats with enough force to power a stiff mountain breeze, though the mob indeed changed the topic, still on and on they droned, till the traitor thought his ears might bleed. Load the air they did now with wearisome trifles and mundane facts as they traced — for the pleasure, claimed they, of their guest — their lacklustre family trees and branches back nigh unto Adam.

Indeed, our hero only fancied he spied the image of a glistening pair of sharp pruning shears flit across his bored mind. To escape these rambling hayseeds could not come quick enough!

Farewelled at last by a chorus of the villagers' cheerful if more tedious prattling, the traitor took his eager leave of his ill-mannered persecutors, fairly fleeing along the winding track as pointed out to him.

What an ordeal to have been the unwelcome cynosure of almost an entire hamlet's collective rustic curiosity, pelted with impertinent interrogatories like one sat in the stockades. Still, he had, albeit with much interruption, gained a full belly — even if at the near cost of his sanity!

Smothering a derisive snort, he hastened on.

Certainly, in order to confound any pursuers who might yet happen upon this hamlet and learn of our hero's passing through, it was prudent henceforth to adopt at each further stop a different alias and feign as much in his words as his rags the dialect of a paysan or paisano.

Our hero's mind did momentarily wander back to the simple-minded peasant man and his wife in their rude timber hut. Though he owed them naught — for had they knowledge of his true identity, they would have grasped the full extent of obligation they were under — still, the fact they had relinquished their only worldly treasure to serve our ailing hero's needs, it continued to trouble him, like a pebble lodged in his boot.

What curious power had that timepiece? He had never met the dead lad, nor forged any meaningful bond with the parents beyond the happenstance crossing of paths. Perhaps it was the brief glimpse of authentic paternal grief that pricked his soul? One that he would likely never know again! Or was his ill-ease to be found in recognising the depth of sacrifice in their small gift while they expected nothing in return? Few, if indeed any, of his own gilded circles would ever surrender their finery to aid a vagrant, regardless of any imagined gentle breeding.

Uncomfortable with this consideration, he shook it off.

Over the crisp air, the climbing sun spread its golden warmth. Upon the morning silence, broke only the crunch of our hero's tread, a distant church bell, the shrieks of the bearded vulture echoing in the mountain hollows and the dull roar of the nearby cascades. Lulled by such circumstances and revived from breakfasting, this permitted his thoughts to roam beyond his inward disquiet and out onto the vastness of the environing exterior.

Across the wide arch of a perfect blue, birds flew and circled in playful pursuits. Along a distant slope, a shepherd boy and his dog led their woolly flock. Among the tumbling grassy steeps bestrewn with tall pines and autumnal woodlands, babbled a glistening brook. Now and then, a humble log cabin appeared, precariously perched atop a crag, where a herdsman and wife reposed upon a balcony and gazed out at the gigantic, seemingly concave rock masses that made the world appear cupped in a giant's palm.

Such idyllic scenes, a last barrier to the dangers that lay beyond, could not help but draw from the traitor a wistful sigh and inspire an Arcadian-like idealisation:

Should he just live out his own days in this remoteness? Covet an abandoned cabin and make it his home? Perhaps he could, in time, accustom himself to the pastoral life? *Perhaps even the comfort of schlosses and the allure of wealth might, in the end, give up their powers to a life of simplicity and indigence?*

Such illusory hopes, however, quickly imploded; he was grown too habituated to the life into which he was born. Moreover, even were he to sequester in such seclusion, the long arm of imperilment would in time ascend these slopes and grasp ahold of him.

Within about a half-hour, he reached Grimmelwald, where, high above a steep crag gushing white foam and spray, he crossed a crude alpine bridge. From here, the village of Stechelberg was visible on the distant valley floor, enveloped in the mountain shadows.

After about another hour's walk, he arrived at the recommended hire's dwelling.

Out from a chalet of stacked timber beams and shingled eaves, emerged a young man of Italian lineage; dark curls framing his swarthy countenance. "What brings you here?"

Assuming a paisano character, complete with gesticulation and accent, the traitor stated his needs.

"Very well," replied the man, "there'll be several stops along the way, mind you, and I go only as far as Gündlischwand; from there your feet will need carry you."

"That will do just fine."

Thus, obtaining his passage under the name Pagolo, our hero wrapped his cowl about his face and mounted the provincial conveyance; a wagon of bleating animals and a splintery wooden bench that offered little comfort.

Barely had the rickety wagon begun rolling over the coarse ground, when he was obliged to suffer the following interrogation:

"So, where d'you come from?"

"Turin," lied the traitor while staring at the road ahead.

"Quite the distance, that. I'm from Bergamo."

As if the traitor cared.

"And how d'you come this far?"

The traitor turned his now impatient stare on his interrogator. "By horse."

"And where's the horse now?" persisted the driver, undaunted.

Irritated at this question, the traitor looked away and distracted himself with the scenes passing by. From the encircling heights, the foaming torrents of Staldenbachfälle, Mattenbachfälle, Mürrenbachfall, and Trümmelbachfälle flashed and thundered as they crashed into the still-shadowed vale, churning up thick white sprays. Mists floating between the sheer limestone precipices diffused the slanted golden rays of the sun just now appearing above the stupendous peaks, which towered at intimidating snowy altitudes.

"I say, what became of your horse?" repeated the driver. "Did you lose it...? Sell it?"

Exhaling sharply, the traitor glowered at him. "I sold it!" And before more questions could spew forth, he whipped his head away.

To his left, in the shaded meadows, shepherds were driving their noisy flocks to the barns. Following them, children laughed and played together.

Such scenes could not but conjure bittersweet memories of his own carefree youth, when his mother allowed him to play openly with other children, dress like other children; join with them at the joyous Alp Aufzug procession of cattle driven to upland summer pastures to the sounds of peasant herdsmen singing, dogs barking, and cowbells ringing. That last spring. That final untainted remembrance of her before her cruel death; before she had...

Shaking off so melancholy a reverie, he re-diverted his thoughts to the present. Again, he strove to piece together the slivers of events that might, somehow, unmask the architect of his labefaction. If truly undone by his own circle, who amongst them could the viperous scoundrel be? No face or name came to mind. Had something crucial escaped his observations? Nothing tangible could he trace back to in the wretched preceding events. But then, from among his beclouded musings, there emerged a recollection of the clock and his second younger half-brother.

Could he have been behind my undoing? Might he be the viper? Was this a retaliatory strike for having foiled his grasping after power and defending the elder half-brother's claim instead? Or had the serpent perchance caught wind of the quiet investigations into his activities and pre-emptively struck to protect his interests?

Again, that clock: *how did such a timepiece ever find its way into the peasant hands of that deceased lad?* 'Twas impossible that it could be the very same clock his half-brother had been earlier gifted. It had to be another of its kind, if not a copy? Yet, again, how could such an item come into the possession of persons of such inferior consequence? *Could there have been some connection between the dead lad and that French emissary? No, that could not be — could it?*

Indeed, the more our bemused hero sought to disentangle this accursed mystery, the more the clock itself conveyed only an ill-air, conjuring images of obscure intrigues which unfold behind elegant closed doors, and where corrupt diplomats and nobles exchange clandestine secrets over glasses of fine cognac by the flicker of ornate candle fixtures. What was his brother up to? And who was this French man? *What dangerous alliances might they have brokered? Alliances that must surely endanger far more than family harmony and —*

"Why d'you sell it?" resumed the driver, breaking the silence of several minutes.

That blasted horse! Hot with anger, the traitor rounded on him. "Mind your own affairs!"

Discombobulated of countenance, the driver averted his face and hummed what was doubtless a Swiss mountain peasant song.

Satisfied in having quashed the bothersome chatter, the traitor stared steadily ahead.

Now bathed in the high forenoon sun, the valley floor unfolded the meandering pastures he recollected on happier occasions. Suffusing the November air came the scent of late lavender — his mother's favourite flower. On either side, skirting the enclosing limestone walls, the chestnut, oak, larch, ash, and maple forests, gave up the last yellows, oranges, reds, purples, and browns of their foliage to the approaching winter — his mother's favourite season.

After bombilating the annoying melody a dozen times, the driver said, in a sort of suggestive tone, a riderless horse had been spotted about the valley earlier that morning.

"Indeed?" hastily replied the traitor. But checking himself, he proposed it had likely escaped a local stable. Eyeing him dubiously, the man insisted the steed belonged to none known in the vicinity. Hence, affecting a casual interest, the traitor probed, "did anyone capture it?"

It had bolted up the valley, explained the driver. In which direction, asked the traitor. The driver pointed ahead.

As much as this reinvigorated our hero's spirits, it depressed him to the same extent. For as his eyes searched his surroundings, he knew that though the horse could be so near and he could retrieve the scroll, it might also have already outpaced reach by now.

Above the distant treetops, the brown spire of Kirche Lauterbrunnen village tolled the eleventh hour. As they rattled past it and beneath the tall boughs, the road narrowed with the encroaching valley walls closing the canopy above them.

Now enveloped by thick gloom, this evoked in the traitor's mind his frantic flight from Oberhofen that fateful eve: *To think that I am, every minute, in danger of arrest and annihilation.* Only three days remained ere the full moon. Reaching Lucerne was imperative. *Should I survive through this, my enemies will pay!*

By around one in the afternoon, they reached Gündlischwand.

The traitor alighted from the wagon and hastened for Gsteigwiler.

When the village bridge came into view, he spied a blockade in place. Swiss Guard presently inspected a wagon trying to cross it.

Blast!

He required another route over the river. This he found by returning to Gündlischwand and crossing a bridge there. Though fatigued from the circuitous trek, he evaded the checkpoint and, with his cape drawn close about his face, slipped into Gsteigwiler.

First enquiring of the farrier, who directed him to a groom, who in turn led him to a yardman, the traitor was sent to an inn. There, he was assured, he would find the French-born liveryman likely swilling ale and gorging himself on Swiss cheese fondue.

There, indeed, in the bay window of the gloomy dark wood and peeling paint guest-house common room, sat the rotund fellow, glutting himself on the very dish. Certainly, his beady eyes, it could be perceived from the outline of the person, proved to be far smaller than his belly.

Grieved that he had to resort to such a negotiation, our hero now assumed the descent and dialect of a paysan and grudgingly introduced himself to this grave-countenanced man.

"Looking for a colt, you say?" spewed the liveryman through a mouthful of dripping bread. "And how d'you come by name?"

The poorly kept interior was as unsavoury as the grease which presently pooled indelicately over the sides of the man's dish onto the crusted table.

"In Mürren," replied the traitor, averting his eyes in disgust.

With a grunt, the man eased his trousers at his bursting waistline with his greasy thumb. "Mürren, you say?" Then, asking for the name of who told him where to come, he continued to gorge himself whilst scrutinising our hero's face with an odd look of enquiry that made him shift uneasily.

"I don't know his name." The food traces dangling from the ill-bred man's beard were an abomination against every etiquette. "But methinks his hut was next to the inn, there."

Something flashed in the liveryman's eyes. He paid a significant glance at his unsavoury companions — one, a stout, bald brute, scars to boot; the other, rail-thin, rotting teeth, nervous tick in his sunken eye; the both of them, staring at our hero alike, then traded the same meaningful glance with the liveryman.

Notwithstanding the dreadful mien of this dubious trio, whatever their glances implied, such looks were far too familiar to those whom are often well-versed in the surreptitious arts.

"Where d'you say you came from?" said the liveryman; food bits dropping onto the dish.

Bile swallowed down, the traitor looked away. "I didn't." Now he began to suspect the man was more a horse peddler than a liveryman. The sooner this business was concluded, the better. "Can't you hurry?"

A thought evidently passed across the man's mind. "Those in haste oft pays more."

Impertinent and underhand! Nevertheless, wishing to be gone, our hero did jingle his coin purse temptingly.

What might have taken a half-hour to eat and drink vanished in several mouthfuls, several swigs, succeeded by several putrid burps directed at him.

"Come along, you two," ordered the liveryman as he rose from his seat. "We've work to do." And addressing the traitor with so obsequious a bow, he bade he would follow them.

The muddy, dung-strewn streets were churned by the passage of wagons, horses, and feet. A sizeable crowd gathered about a notice board; they studied some posted announcement of apparent importance and commented on a reward.

Though our hero could not make it out, there was something inauspicious about the whole; danger clogged the fetid air.

Again, he drew close his cowl and hung his head low as they proceeded.

In time, they came to the village outskirts, where a dilapidated, abandoned-looking stable adjoined a run-down cabin confined by a broken fence.

The traitor turned from this horrid hovel. "The horses are kept here?"

Answering him with only a nod, the liveryman rather instructed his men to wait at the gate before beckoning the traitor after him.

No sooner had our hero entered the decrepit structure when he saw the stalls were all empty. "What trickery is this? *Where* are the horses?"

He spun to confront the liveryman, but the man was gone.

The stable door slammed shut — the drawbar scraping the outside, announcing it locked upon him.

"What the devil is going on?"

30 NOVEMBER – 01 DECEMBER 1791

No matter how fiercely our hero beat upon the stable door, splintering his knuckles. No matter how violently he vented the outrage simmering like molten lava in his pounding breast. No matter how repeatedly he hurled a wooden stool against the boarded-up casement, no response came from his dastardly captors.

Only after his spirit had relented to over-exertion and the ill-boding silence of captivity stole over him did he cease his screaming demands and slump to the floor.

Indeed, he bitterly reproached himself for having so confidently — nay, foolishly — flaunted his money-bag before the eyes of three suspicious characters. The blame for his present confinement lay squarely on his own shoulders!

Yet, if robbery was their aim, for what purpose had they trapped him? *Would not they have already committed the act?* Had their cunning perhaps speculated a crime of greater value and they meant to prosecute such villainy under the cover of night? *Or have they, perchance, recognised me and mean to ransom me off to my family?* No. This could not be it. For it was hardly credible that such coarse souls had ever even glimpsed his face before.

The floor, damp and uncomfortable, forced him to his feet. "I must get out of here."

As his eyes scoured the gloomy, damp interior, they landed on a dark stain on the slabs at the far side. Drawn by uncertainty, his weary footfalls crunched on the hay-strewn slabs and, kneeling down, he examined the stain more closely.

"Blood?"

Upon the eerie air, a distant, solemn church bell struck the third hour.

With his foot, he separated the straw clumps and uncovered a sanguine trail. Though every instinct screamed for him to desist, he followed the meandering smear across the slabs to a mound of hay inside the farthest stall, from where a muffled buzzing stole upon his hearing.

"Surely not...?"

Compelled by a macabre curiosity and noticing a pitchfork nearby, he grabbed it and began sifting through the pile until the metal prongs plunged into something solid.

Like one dealt a phantom blow, he shuddered from his twitching fingers to his splaying toes. "Impossible!"

But determined to corroborate the worst, he wrenched the implement free, at which a vile stench of decay spread about him ensued by swarming flies.

Fork dropped, he reeled backwards, burying his face in his sleeve.

What dire fate befell whoever is buried thus?

So repugnant was the fetor and the horrific tableau his imagination conjured, he had to turn away.

What similar fate do they intend for me?

No such destiny would he surrender himself to. He would extricate himself at once.

Each casement was, alas, boarded tightly over. In checking fastidiously the wide-planked walls, there was not any loose board to be found. Eyeing the skylight above and the thick beams beneath it, he then grabbed the now broken stool. Balancing atop the unsteady piece, he ventured to climb up, only to find the rafters were still beyond his reach.

Presently, voices outside caught his hearing.

"I've got a bad feeling," spoke a male.

Another hissed at him to be silent.

In low tones, they continued conferring.

To better hear, the traitor jumped down and hastened to the doors, ears pressed against the gap.

"If master finds out," continued the first, "he'll kill us both."

"Silence! Else I'll do the same to you and bury you next to it!"

Our hero glanced back at the haystack.

Who are these savages?

"And if we're wrong? If it ain't him? They'll do to us the same as the criminal they's all searching for."

Criminal?

"Master ain't wrong. The man's face matches the posters. Think of the reward!"

Horror did cleave our hero's every vital organ. It was now impossible to doubt the purpose of his confinement: *they mean to hand me over to the authorities!*

Such a fate he could not hazard to chance. He must escape through the skylight.

Frantically, he re-investigated the stable, finding a coil of old rope inside another stall.

Rope in hand, he re-mounted the shaky stool and, flinging the rope over the beam, strove to pull himself up. But the height of the timber, the swaying rope, and his injuries all conspired against him and he crashed to the ground.

"This is insufferable!"

Foot slammed into the stool, he sent it hurtling across the stone slabs.

If arrested, he was as good as dead.

Beset by a renewed pounding of his brain, he fell against a stall.

This was too much. He could see no way of getting out. Gripped by exponential anxiety and scarce able to breathe the wretched air which clogged his lungs, he held onto the walls and staggered to the doors, desperate to gasp at the draft seeping through.

With difficulty mastering himself, he refocused and sought any detail he may have overlooked. As he re-searched the interior, his eyes frequented the rope still dangling from the beam. Surely, it was better to hang himself than be captured!

However drastic such a notion may seem to our expectant reader, our hero, so swayed by the consideration, was almost ready to go through with it. Yet the thought of placing a noose about his own neck and being strangled to death just as quickly drove the plan from his mind; as much as his heart burned to deny his enemies of such a conquest, still it equally blazed to survive.

Perhaps it was a maddening desperation, perhaps Fortune wishing to assist her plaything, but it was at this moment that another idea came fast to his mind: *the pistol!*

We now learn that among the items retrieved from the hollow of the tree was also a gun. Since it was still in his possession and that it was impossible to break out from his confinement, his only chance of escape was to occasion his captors opening the doors to him.

Yet to pull the trigger alone would unlikely suffice. To entirely dupe his captors, to draw them in, a more drastic spectacle — more grotesquely convincing — was called for. And the necessary effects were to be found rotting beneath the hay.

Again, grabbing the pitchfork, he set to plunging it repeatedly into what he, to his disgust, discovered to be the festering carcass of a poor canine.

What beasts would contrive to kill such an animal?

There was no time for such moralistic grievances.

With stomach twisting, nauseating aghast, he plunged his hand deep into the gory lacerations and scooped out blood, innards, and rotting flesh. With further gut-wrenching repulsion, he slapped the putrid flesh against the side of his temple, simulating the aftermath of a gunshot wound.

The foul, putrescent reek near choked him to the point of vomiting. But determined to gain freedom, he re-covered the carcass with hay, shoved the pitchfork back into a stall, and then splayed himself across the slabs.

Deep breath taken, he took aim and fired the pistol into a stall.

Several agitated heartbeats later, the stable doors flung open. Still holding fast his breath, he listened for movement. For some seconds, there was none. But when the first distress, which had doubtless overawed his captors, yielded to the next, they rushed over.

"They wanted him alive!" shrieked the one. "The Guard'll lynch us!"

Sprawled as our hero was, the men cursed the fate which now hung about their necks and, without substantiating his condition, fell to heated recriminations.

With both captors doubly distracted, now was the time to act. Our hero leapt up, quite stunning the ruffians. Launching his foot into them, he sent them crashing into the stalls.

On his heel, the traitor turned and bolted outside. Not without first slamming shut the doors and barring them did he hasten into the nearby woods.

Through the perpetual twilight of the cold, damp, mossy, dense forest, and along the pine needle strewn trails, he hurried back towards Zweilütschinen.

Soon, he reached a broad track bisecting the woods, connecting a steep elevation on the left to a lane on the right that ran to the village. Pausing to look around, he saw no threat and was about to proceed when lively music and song swelled on a stiff breeze that rushed between the trees. Knowing not from which direction the sound came, he hid in the dense growth.

The melodies faded as the breeze died down, only to swell again on the next gust, bringing the rattle of wheels, the jingling of harness bells, and the clopping of hooves. From the elevation at his left, emerged a procession of horse and mule drawn gaily painted wagons, their sides decorated with scrolling patterns and floral motifs. Sturdy horses drew gilded carriages with red velvet curtained windows following behind. Interspersed throughout were ambling mules hitched to simpler coaches piled high with trunks and props.

As the caravan drew nearer, the drivers and their companions came into view. From their flowing skirts, embroidered bodices, ears glinting with jewellery, striped trousers, short coats of velvet and brocade, and wide-brimmed hats adorned with feathers; from their laughter, innuendos, bawdy jokes, and farcical revelries, operatic strains, and music of the zither and hackbrett; from their liberal swigging from bottles of pungent emerald absinthe and filling the air with clouds of tobacco, it was apparent they were a Wanderbühne itinerant troupe.

More wagons rolled past, followed by six Haflingers, tied to a coach in front, pulling the last of the wagons; driverless; likely used for storage.

Rather than continue along the lane which led to the village, the train turned onto a trail that ran parallel to the forest. Seizing his chance, the traitor hurried after them and, catching up with the rearmost wagon, hauled himself onto its step.

An unlocked padlock hung from the travel latch; removing it and lifting the latch, he pulled on the handle and found the door open to him.

Harlequins, hanswursts, marionettes, pulcinellas, and mascheras rattled and swayed side to side, their sinister painted wooden faces smiling upon him. Various costumes, accoutrements, and appurtenances common to the commedia dell'arte, swung on the rails as the caravan traversed the rough ground.

Wedged amidst the clutter, the stowaway could easily remain hidden until safe to disembark. His spirits rising at this brighter futurity, he now sat on a wooden chest next to the small, round window, and watched the forest drift leisurely by.

Our hero had but permitted himself to relax when a cascade of papers avalanched from a shelf above as the wagon tilted sharply. Against the round pane, he pressed his face; the trees were diverging from the wagon's route. "Why are we —?"

Among the documents scattered over the floor were several flyers advertising the Wanderbühne's upcoming performances across the Interlaken district. His eyes grew wide with dawning horror. The travellers were likely bound for Gsteigwiler, having perhaps only taken a wrong turn before re-routing back towards the village!

This was a tragedy worthy of any sentimental Wanderoper stage itself. To have contrived his escape, only to be conveyed back to the village and then discovered by the troupe. To be then flung out, head-first, into the mud before the jeering villagers and then seized upon by the Guard. To have been the Prinzipal, the choreographer, and tragedian Pickelhäring of his own public demise was beyond even hellish invention.

"I must acquit this accursed wagon at once!"

In trying the door, he found it had locked itself from the outside. "What?" Throwing his weight against it was to no avail. "Of course!" He struck his forehead. "The latch!"

Desperately, he sought for something to pry open the door. But each tool he used was in vain. The door was as impregnable as any fortress. Even after he smashed the small porthole's glass and straining to reach through it, the exterior latch remained maddeningly beyond his grasp.

"Blast!"

A sudden halt of the wagon sent him stumbling; again, he pressed his face against the window. A curve in the lane showed the caravans bending towards the Gsteigwiler bridge. They had turned from the village. Evidently no performance was scheduled there after all.

But the blockade?

While the inebriated and obstreperous itinerants disembarked their wagons and gathered at the bridge, cursing at the guards for prejudicing and harassing innocent travellers, two patrols separated from the main detachment to inspect the caravans.

"Good lord!" Even were our hero to break free, it would be straight into their hands. And a thorough search must inevitably reveal him, even secreted amidst the costumes.

Circa five minutes later, the patrol reached the rear wagon. Engaged in scornful talk, the guards laughed at and ridiculed the travellers who still harangued their comrades at the bridge. Then a betraying clatter issued from the wagon and it rocked momentarily.

"There is somebody inside!" said one of them.

Blades unsheathed, they surrounded the wagon. Two guards moved to the door: one rifle aimed, and the other, lifting the latch, threw the door open.

Their expressions will, I dare say, be so far removed from that which our dear readers' imaginations may have depicted. Stare, these guards did in astonishment, in appall, in exquisite confusion at the man whom they could only presume to be one of the travellers.

Face, neck, and stubble powdered spectre white. Rounded cheeks and pouting lips rouged vulgar red. Shadows of smudged royal blue encircled the eyes most dramatically. Crowning this visage, a white perruque, pomaded to preposterous height, festooned with flowers, ribbons, and a toy frigate, teetered beneath its own weight. But what farcical spectacle would be complete without an equally preposterous, as wide as the wagon panniered gold silk chemise a la reine! — all in an irreverent ode to that certain French queen.

"*Bon après-midi, mes chéris*," drawled the queen, in no less an exquisitely frolicsome French accent. Empty bottle in one hand, ostrich fan in the other, he swayed left to right, as if drunk. And natch, he just had to eruct theatrically. "Have you come to save this poor queen from that wicked guillotine?"

The two men, incontrovertibly bamboozled, did draw their comrades to their sides. Equally stunned, they could not but help join their men-in-arms a-blinking as their jaws dropped speedily aslant as we might imagine of the aforementioned glistening blade of terror.

"Why do you gawk at me so?" implored Madame la Reine from behind the fan, now fluttering his hastily glued on lashes. "Where are my *Cent-Suisses*?" Once more, affecting a drunken belch, he held out the empty bottle. "And my champagne?"

These farcical speeches compounding utter confusion, the guards let out a gasp — which stifled a half-laugh — which stifled unintelligible diction — which stifled —

"Let us rid ourselves of this vagrant!" rasped the gun-bearing man, slamming the door. "The quicker they quit our vicinity, the better!"

As the fourth hour pealed on the distant air, the wagon lurched forward, and our triumphant thespian collapsed onto a thick rug, feeling for his heartbeat. "That was *too* close!"

All relief was short-lived. He jerked back upright. "The door!"

Evenfall had begun its descent on the world outside, casting it in that same sort of gloom common to the souls of the afflicted. The purpling shadows whispered of his captivity as he watched the Zweilütschinen bridge pass by — the very direction he needed to go!

Who knew where and when the travellers would next stop?

Oppressed by increasing exasperation, he again sank on to the rug and stared up at the puppets swaying overhead in the shadowy ceiling. So lost he became to his maelstrom of misery, he noticed not at first that something underneath the carpet dug into his shoulder. But shifting his weight, revealed a section of the floor now depress. "Could it be?"

Sitting up, he flung back the rug. "A hatchway!"

Promptly deposing himself first of his royal raiments, he lifted the hatch and held onto the edge as he dropped to the ground; at which the wagon carried on over his head and the capricious sky appeared.

The dark was coming on fast when he got back to the bridge at Zweilütschinen. Keen to wash off his gaudy visage, he faltered down the steep bank to the river and was just kneeling when he slipped and was thrown headlong into the waist-high, frigid current.

"Blast!" screamed he, slamming hard the waters with his fists.

No time to tarry, he scrubbed away the red, white, and blue and then clambered up the far bank and hastened on to the village of Gündlischwand.

Clothes clung to his skin most unpleasantly and chilled further by the late November air, our hero sought the help of a lone stranger, silhouetted in the doorway of a small log cabin.

"I am in need of a fire," said he through chattering teeth as he neared the gate. "I shall reward you accordingly. And I will detain you not any longer than necessary."

An elderly woman tottered forth, clutching her humble linen shawl most fervently around her shoulders. "Fire, is it?"

She raised her night light — whose flickering flame did cast her craggy, weathered countenance in the ghastliest shadows beneath her crumpled linen cap — and eyed him with a most unpleasant proximity.

His answers appeasing her subsequent questions and perhaps that he shivered so violently — nay, deafeningly — she granted him access to the fire of her humble hearth.

"Pass me your cloak," bade she, with a smile. "Lord! It's wet through." She prodded his chest with her stubbed finger. "As is the *rest* of you, I'll say?"

"An unfortunate slip into the river."

Craning her withered neck, she thrust her face into his, nostrils aflare and sniffing most rudely. "No spirits about you, I see?"

He stepped back from her. "That is because I am *entirely* sober!"

Not without closing the gap and sniffing about his face again in a most unwelcome fashion did she finally withdraw. And not without watching him keenly whilst several thoughts visibly scurried behind her eyes like the rodents, he imagined resided here with her, did she push back her puffed sleeves, smooth down her black felt bodice and plunk her hands into the recesses of her hips, from which flowed a faded skirt; its original hue, difficult to discern.

"You'll catch your death of cold," pronounced she at last.

Over to an old-looking pine cupboard she clip-clopped in her cracked clogs and, rummaging through it, brought out a pile of garb. "He wasn't as tall as you, but they'll do."

She clip-clopped back over — the faded wool of her skirt swishing — and, plunking the pile into her guest's hands, pointed out an adjoining room. "Go change in there."

From the bedchamber, our hero soon emerged in the dry yet most ill-fitting and absurd ensemble imaginable. The homespun wool tunic, darned to excess by its previous inhabitant, did hang on his frame like a tent. The breeches were no better; befitting a man twice his girth, they would verily have tumbled straight to his ankles had not he a belt to tediously hoist them up.

Damp clothes taken off him, she draped them with meticulous care about the fire. "Won't take long to dry out," sang she, motioning to a rocking chair next to the hearth — no more than a few bricks stacked together, above which dangled a blackened pot bubbling over the fire. "And you go warm yourself."

About her waist, she tied a threadbare linen apron; from a solitary oak dresser that furnished her kitchen area, she grabbed a pot and, chopping several vegetables, adding them to the pot, busied herself at a stove.

With attentions almost gracious that contradicted her coarse manner, the old woman sat her guest at a small wooden table, its surface worn yet scrubbed clean, and served the modest meal of vegetable stew in an old pewter bowl — tarnished, dented but polished to shine — along with her best, or perhaps only, dry bread, and wine in a chipped earthenware cup.

As our hero set about eating, the woman, deeming it just to entertain him, entered on some light conversation, at length, warning him to pay attention to the road. "Guards were up and down the valley all day hunting an outlaw," said she. "They put a poster on the local board and bade us to report to the village headman any sight of him."

The stale bread did scrape our hero's throat. "Did you," said he, reaching for the wine with a cough, "perchance... see the poster?"

She nodded. "Thrust right in my face."

Assuming she must have recognised him and had sent him to change in order to alert a neighbour, a sudden dread gripped him. He sprang up, toppling the wine in his fright.

The woman entreated he would sit back down and, fetching a cloth to wipe up the spillage, apologised for alarming him. "The criminal will surely be long gone by now."

"What did the poster claim of this... villain?"

"Perhaps you can tell me?" returned she.

A sickening dread pulled at the corners of his mouth. "Whatever do you mean?"

Explaining she had a poster, she searched her living space for several minutes, vexing herself for forgetting where it was. But finding it stuffed into a drawer of the kitchen dresser, she handed it to him. "You keep it. My eyes are grown so clouded these days, the fiend could walk right up to me and I wouldn't know him from the butcher."

Unsure whether to trust her, he scrutinised her narrowed orbs; even in this light, they appeared clouded. She spoke truthfully.

Satisfied, he rolled out the crumpled poster. *Heavens!* His hand flew to his mouth. Sensing that even the partly blind woman must have read his reaction, his eyes slowly gravitated to her.

She was already busying herself, rearranging the clothes around the fire.

He studied the poster. The likeness was unmistakable. He passed his hand across his jaw. *No razor shall touch my face again!* Reading the text, he saw no reference to his name; only that he was a dangerous outlaw... an enemy to the confederacy... "A reward of how much?"

With the cabin being so warm, his clothes were soon dry enough to be packed. Handing thus to the woman the promised payment — a batzen — for which she furnished him with a wrapping of grapes, stale cheese, and the stale bread remnants, he took his leave.

From behind the rolling clouds, the waxing crescent moon glanced now and then, throwing a faint glow on the sleeping habitats of Grindelwald. The tremendous limestone faces of Eiger, Mättenberg, and Wetterhorn brooded above the vale like mountain trolls watching to crush him. Made uneasy at this sight, he averted his eye to the snow-ladened Klein Welhorn, which scowled with equal menace above the distant eminence; the direction his path led.

After about an hour's steep ascent, he gained the brow. Here, he took a few moments to regather his breath and to pay a final look back at the blurry mass of civilisation nestled in the shadowy basin below. From this point forth, dwellings would be few.

Continuing on, he followed a rude, winding declivity which entered a rocky terrain of grassy hillocks and shadowy pine groves. Save for the occasional sighing breeze, which rustled the tall blades of grass, the silence and solemn stillness impressed upon his captive heart a sense of freedom. But the illusion passed as quickly as the faint gleam of silvery moonlight which touched the earth, leaving only the blackness of resentment.

And those accursed posters! How eagerly the world will clamber to collect the bounty, desperate to serve those they claim to loathe! This is a despicable fate.

As he walked on, the gigantic Wetterhorn and Welhorn mountains, which had earlier glowered from afar, rose in intimidating forms at his right. Across their jagged faces, shadows leapt about, conjuring the mythical forms of Berchtold and his spectral huntsmen in pursuit of hapless quarry. Able not to look away from these flitting shadows, he found even the large black recesses took on the forms of Hotap's wide-open mouth, hungry to devour him. A stiff gust whipped past, and, as it turned towards the mountains, roaring in the tops of the pines, a distant wolf howled — its cry echoed on the opposite side of the vale.

Over his shoulder blades, a shiver crawled. He doubled his pace.

Soon, a dense wall of forest halted his progress. With the land cast in an impenetrable veil, he could see not several feet ahead. The babbling of a stream, though, crept upon his hearing; he followed the edge of the forest to its source and discovered it cut through the woods.

While he pursued its banks, attentive to the sounds which carried on the whispering winds, he detected a rustling somewhere to his left in the trees. He halted, holding his breath. Only his heart thumped in his ears and the stream rippled in murmuring echoes.

But then it came again. Someone or something drew steadily nearer.

"Who goes there?" challenged he the darkness.

The crunching of fallen leaves, the snapping of branches alone answered.

Fearful of being set upon by bandits, a lynx, a wolf, or worse, a bear, he drew his pistol and, availing himself of courage, pointed it into the blackness. "Stay back, or I shall fire!"

Barely had two minatory eyes flashed forth from the gloom when the mystery creature charged forth.

With the next thunderous beat of his pounding heart, he pulled the trigger.

But, of course, the pistol was spent; its shot used back in the stable.

Panicked, he turned to flee, only to slip on the damp grass, twisting his ankle as he tumbled into the frigid stream, cracking his head against a rock and losing the pistol to the depths.

"Confound it all!"

Vision stinging and blurred by the water, he looked back.

A large, Alpine Ibex brandished its horns and reared tall, snorting menacingly.

"Heavens forbid!" Believing the animal was poised to attack, he scrambled through the water to escape.

Fortunately, the beast only struck hard on the ground with its hooves, turned, and vanished into the blackness.

Utterly stunned, panting uncontrollably, our hero clenched at his rapidly heaving, hammering chest. Why was it that even nature seemed to conspire against him?

Heavy drops of rain now fell from above. This, conjoined with the icy winds which penetrated his soaked garb, drove him shivering and limping downstream in pursuit of fire and shelter.

After some distance, a break in the forest presented a bridge crossing in front. Communicating with it, a path to his left led towards a structure. The measured dashing of paddles gave to his understand that it was a mill.

A thick chain and large padlock bound the doors fast. But spying a nearby axe, he seized it and delivered several blows until the lock gave way and he could enter.

Musty air and sawdust indicated the various obscure objects were those of a small sawmill. It will be easy to imagine his joy when, from the moonbeams entering a window, he discovered a log burner at the mill's centre with a pile of chopped wood beside it.

After the interior had warmed up, he stripped off the damp and intolerably itchy garments, cleansed and bandaged his bleeding forehead, and reclined next to the burner to repast on the provisions.

Soon lulled by the crackling logs, the rattling of rain against the window, and feeling the heaviness of sleep dampening the dull throb in his head and swollen ankle, these symptoms stole him away to the oblivion of sleep.

***

Awakened by the early sun darting its rays through the window, our hero lingered awhile, soothed by the purling leat and cheered by the gleeful birds heralding the new day. However, as the light shafts moved across the interior, so too did the probable dangers of overstaying here pass over his thoughts. He must be off at once.

The baked air of the mill finding his throat parched, he reached for his costrel. But it was empty. Consequently, half-dressing himself, he then stepped outside to refill it.

As he breathed in the crisp air, a pensive wakefulness infused his mind. His gaze roaming his environs, fixed on the forest steeps of Klein Welhorn, opposite. Its bold grey summit, warmed by a lone sunbeam was, much like his brain, for the most enveloped by impenetrable cloud. It was hard to believe that as a boy he had roamed these very regions with his family with zeal and gladness. Occasions so diametrically the opposite to what he presently encountered. Now, he beheld these scenes with only indifference. Independent of his present turmoil, too much had changed since then.

A chill lifted the hairs on his clenched fists; he shifted his focus onto the skies. That fiery brilliance, common to dusk, while painting the drifting clouds in brilliant hues, touched the valley more with a portentous solemnity. Danger, like a cold gust, swept within.

Eager to drive away such feelings as though dwelling on them might bring about the ominous, he forced his thoughts on the possibility of soon reaching Lucerne. Only one more day he would need to suffer this treacherous ordeal. Tomorrow he would meet with Ludwig.

Kneeling down next to the leat, he remarked in his reflection the blood-stained bandage about his brow. "What cruel disfigurement awaits me beneath these rags?"

From under his habiliments exuded the pungence of stale sweat. Noting also the grime under his nails and the filth streaking his hands, he would have washed had not the following cry rent the air:

"Get away from there!" boomed a man's voice.

At some distance, a figure bore what resembled a dog-lock musket.

"Get away from my mill!" The man quickened his pace. "I'll shoot!"

Inside, the traitor flung. Gathering up his garb and grabbing his sack, he quit the structure, narrowly avoiding the lead ball with which the shooter, apt with his rifle, splintered the doorpost.

Fraught with terror, our hero rushed along the side of the mill and faltered up the ascent of the stream; trailed by the miller's nearing shouts.

Since the slope steepened and the aspect opened out, the traitor retreated into the woods at his left and hid behind a thick trunk, gasping for air and rubbing his smarting ankle.

Can I pass not one day without danger, or —

Nearby, the ground crunched beneath stealthy footsteps.

Fearing even to breathe, our hero covered his mouth.

The miller's heavy footfall drew steadily nearer. "I know you're here!"

Crouched as the traitor was on his injured ankle, it buckled under his weight; fiery pains bolted up his cramping legs and his foot slipped out from under him.

"I hear you!" The miller must have been just on the other side of the tree. "I'll have you for breaking into my —" Abruptly, he fell silent. "What's that then?"

The man seemed to turn on the ground and retreat down the slope.

A tremendous, pent-up, quaking breath burst from the traitor's lungs. But wary of the peril he might encounter in moving, he waited for some minutes before cautiously peering out: no sign remained of his stalker.

Swiftly putting on the rest of his clothes, he then ventured a few paces out from the wood to survey the declivity. The miller was certainly gone.

Trusting it now safe to do so, he limped along the open acclivity, teeth gritted against the fiery pain; his ankle twisting, his toe dragging with each stunted step.

A few minutes later, there came a recognisable thudding and a dreaded cry:

"There he is!"

Whether his heart or his legs first failed him would be difficult to say; but as he glanced back, the traitor saw three mounted cuirassiers in red coats rapidly gaining ground.

"You there," cried another. "Stand fast!"

"After him!" yelled the third.

Trapped, he stared at the steep slope ahead — his only hope of escape.

Too soon, however, as he struggled up the ever-steepening hillside, his foot dislodged a loose rock and he crashed facedown. Gasping for breath, he glanced behind; his pursuers were nearly upon him, their shouts ringing in his ears.

Dragging himself upward, he scrambled desperately on, clutching at the tall blades of grass, which, concealing clumps of spiny thistle, drove mini daggers into his palms.

Assailed by the agony roaring from his punctured, bleeding hands, he lost his balance and toppled backwards.

This time, having tumbled so far down the slope, when he attempted to regain the lost ground, it was too late. One guardsman had dismounted and advanced forward with such swiftness that he was instantly upon our hero, throwing over him a weighted rope net.

01 – 02 DECEMBER 1791

However dire our hero's present state, it called not for despair but fortitude. To attempt escape would engender only further trial and misery. Thus, resigning himself, he was bound with rope and led back to the mill.

***

Now, the circumstances leading to this capture went as follows:

As we earlier saw, the miller had pursued his prey into the woods and was about to storm his concealment, but a disturbance near the mill stole his attention. Distinguishing a general blur of the Swiss Guard — ten cuirassiers, a phalanx of footmen and a prison cart — his curiosity impelled him back down the slope.

From the many guards, several of whom drank from his leat, the miller estimated who was the most senior of rank. To him, he bowed. "What brings you here?"

Dismounting his white steed, a colonel, emblazoned in bright colours, a morion, plumes, and so polished a cuirass as to blind the miller, approached with an air of haughty superiority.

"We are here on matters of the schultheiss," said he, eyes fixed imperiously upon the miller, who lowered his own. "It is our understanding that bandits are in this region."

"Bandits?" The miller dared lift his gaze.

Raising a harsh brow, the colonel nodded.

Again, lowering his eyes, the miller said he knew of no bandits, only a criminal he'd chased from his mill.

The colonel's brow did invert in curiosity. "A criminal?"

Now meeting the colonel's harsh gaze, the miller, in his simple-mindedness, explained how the fiend broke into his mill, used his stove, and his firewood too! But did scurry off no braver than a hare when threatened. Probably observing the colonel's impatience, he added, "for sure, he was a criminal. Everything about him screamed he didn't want to be seen. I'll wager he might be that outlaw who —"

"What did he look like?" interrupted the colonel, drawing forth his dazzling sword from his bejewelled scabbard.

Startled nigh witless at the sudden sight of the naked blade, the miller could only stutter incoherently while the colonel ordered one of his comrades to bring over a poster forthwith.

"Was *this* the knave?" The colonel shoved the poster up to the miller's whitening face.

Transfixed rather by the glistening sword, he barely glanced at it. "I can't say for s —."

"You *cannot* say?" The colonel did swing most mercilessly the sword up to the miller's quaking neck. "Dare you to trifle with the Guard? Surely you saw the blackguard's face?"

The miller's stuttering only grew in perfect proportion to the colonel's menaces. "I swear," insisted he, teeth a-chattering and limbs a-trembling, "I saw him only from afar."

A growl hissed between the colonel's bared teeth. "Which way did he go?"

The miller hastily pointed out the direction. Sword resheathed, the colonel despatched his footmen and cuirassiers in several directions, directing three up the stream. Hence, those three riders it was that captured, bound, and led the traitor as human spoil back to the mill.

***

Meantime, pacing the ground with fiery impatience, the colonel regarded the captive at a distance, at which his steps halted. Astonishment mingled with uncertainty did overspread his phiz. But when closer observation afforded itself, his expression wore the undeniable satisfaction of vengeful triumph.

"Here we were," said he, "despatched after mere rats disrupting the peace of our patricians and the just rule of our régime. Yet, we find you. Another malignancy in need of excision from the world!"

This colonel, a most dedicated partisan of his second younger half-brother, would too easily relish at the slightest symptom of desperation in his captive. Thus, making no comment but with looks of resolution, our hero concealed the hopeless sentiments that internally plagued him.

A volatile twitch played about the colonel's meticulously curled moustache. "You foolish traitor!" He struck him across the face. "Did you believe you could avert the inevitable?" But meeting with only a disdainful look for his reply, the colonel stared back, astounded. "Have you nothing to say?"

Suppressing the violence that raged within his soul, the traitor remained silent; he would neither amuse this man's corrupt disposition nor satisfy his lust for brutality.

With undisguised detestation, the colonel shifted his tyrannical leer onto the men holding the captive bound. "Confine him to the wagon!"

The colonel then addressed the still-trembling miller. "You have performed an invaluable service to the Confederacy this day. Since a bounty is on this man's head, you must attend Burgdorf Castle to collect it."

No doubt marvelling at the mention of a reward, the miller soon forgot his stutterings and tremblings and insisted that the colonel enjoy some of the finest hospitality in the Swiss mountains at a popular sternen.

This invitation, the colonel declined outright, whereupon the miller, counting the guards, did immediately importune him with the very likely disappointment of his nine daughters — the bar keepers, who, he extolled, were reputed the fairest in the Alps. Hearing this, the colonel's men likewise importuned their leader to accept.

***

What a cruel contrast there was between the lively inebriated temper of the guards, and the traitor fettered in the wagon. The former did revel without restraint in Swiss song and dance around a roaring bonfire, boots stomping, crushing the grass. The latter, with not even a drop of water to lessen his thirst, could only look upon these scenes with sickened disdain.

Captured as our hero was, bound to the manacle of dreadful uncertainty, their freedom he both scorned and envied as they flirted with and faux duelled for the prettiest maidens. For him, a branded traitor, there remained only to be brought before the malice of the schultheiss, whose forgiveness knew neither mercy nor impartiality, and whose retribution knew only unstinting vengeance.

At intervals, the soused guards, goaded by their ill-humour and increasing intoxication, would break away from their debauched pursuits — hussies dressed in white ruffled necked blouses, dainty white stockings, blue knee-length dresses and white frilly aprons — to parade round the wagon. With exaggerated yodelling, skipping steps, twirls, and bows, and brandishing their rapiers, they did denounce their prisoner with insidious oaths and acerbic taunts; while the Jezebels, for that is how they verily behaved, bedecked the occasion with their own trilling laughs, hisses, and mocking curtsies, delighting in his tribulation.

Such a stream of crapulous invectives failed not to press the object of their ridicule deeper into the chasm of bitter despair. Yet as his spirits caved beneath the weight of oppression, his crumbling thoughts were punctuated by the following:

"Though every dictate of justice proscribes such an indulgence to one so treasonous," slurred the colonel, breathing malodorously through the bars, "in deference to your family, I proffer you a drink."

With a cold stare, he held up to the bars a cup of beer.

Was such a known beast truly capable of such a symptom of humanity? Too thirsty to ponder this, the traitor reached for the cup. But the colonel instantly yanked it away, and swigging prodigiously the contents, he then spewed them into his face.

A raucous outburst reverbed on the wretched air. Insults, invectives, and injurious mockery rang all around as the colonel raised the empty cup in mocking triumph.

Stung by such principles of cunning and contempt, our hero sank back into the corner of the cold, tenebrous wagon to repent of the gullibility of his own.

The profuse amounts of intoxicants guzzled down by the rowdy militia having finally affected its secondary powers upon their brains, they each grew oscitant and fell one by one under the decisive alchemy of drunken slumber.

Though spared from further taunts, the passage of hours would abandon our hero only to a sleepless dejection. Born of an exalted rank, bred in state, and conditioned to the most slavish attention, how he yearned for the dissipated life he once enjoyed. But again, for one branded as treasonous as himself, there awaited only the foulest dungeon into which he would be flung. Not merely to rot away from existence, no! This would be but an added menace before an ignominious trial and sentencing; a mere prelude to the sword, the axe, decapitation, or the scaffold. Even would he somehow escape his present confinement and somehow live out his days in hiding, the very notion of poverty he despised more than death.

These considerations so eclipsed his fortitude, he sank into the abstractions of the blackest affliction.

***

Morning, grim morning did come creeping over the mountain peaks, the stench of urine and stale beer marring the once fresh alpine air. Though not a cloud wafted across the brightening sky, our hero's mind was obnubilated by a storm, which neither chance, ingenuity, nor enchanted brush could paint away.

The guards soon awoke, groaning, cursing, each claiming, according to their recollection, the most joyous of nights, however tarnished by the harshest of hangovers. Eager to restore the men's vitality, the bar maids — more so the eligible ones — served a light collation of bread and cheese while playfully stealing away with the bachelors' handkerchiefs in exchange for their own embroidered ones.

Finally, with amorous goodbye kisses and inappropriate, grasping squeezes, the detachment led the creaking wagon along the acclivity, waved away with rosy-cheeked smiles, and a few downcast farewells.

Beyond the wagon bars, the inn gradually shrank into the background, soon lost behind the woods which enclosed it from sight.

Though, as we earlier saw, the traitor had no share in the prior eve's pleasures, this merry inn would be the last such establishment he would look upon; a dissonant memory etched as with the point of a blade into his mind until — No! He would not dwell on this now.

Desperate to distract himself, he turned his attention to the guards' talk; their coarse voices echoed on the thinning air; some engaged in boastful badinage, each exaggerating their exploits and conquests with the prettiest wench at the inn; others conversed the universal astonishment their cargo would soon produce.

Impossible as it was to disprove the evidence to our hero's disadvantage, there had to be some way of averting his present fate? But without the scroll, such a possibility was unattainable.

Perhaps he should throw himself at the schultheiss' feet? Beg for the lowest servitude in exchange for his liberty and life? Perchance that imperious man would yield to his desperate entreaties? Be altogether unmoved? Or become only the more resolute to execute his wrath...

As the rattling wagon left behind the gloomy green forests, a barren and oppressive aspect met the prisoner's view. Rock upon rock rose intimidatingly all about, crowding close on all sides, giving way to sheer precipices, which endlessly plunged. Neither tree, shrub, nor living creature appeared here; only a sombre mist hung low, crawling over the coarse ground before rolling over the cliffs; swallowed as if by dispiriting, spine-chilling abysses.

... But whatever the schultheiss' ruling inclination may be, the traitor would try. He must!

While his thoughts did continue to swing back and forth between vain design and black despair, there obtruded on his hearing the colonel's loud exaltations. Proclaiming himself the hero for having rendered so sacred a service to the canton, he grew impatient to receive his distinction sooner. Consequently, abandoning entirely his commission to apprehend the bandits, he commanded the detachment to avow there being none in these regions. The order was given to cut across the mountain to Lake Brienz and to hasten their return to Burgdorf.

The guards, sore of head and already suffering from the fatigues of their hangovers and the rugged acclivitous tracks, needed no great persuasion and rerouted accordingly.

The tall recesses of projecting rock through which they now passed concealed them entirely from the face of the sun. This cold and shadowy seclusion was of such a sinister potency that even the mountain's stern faces seemed to scorn the traitor's temporary presence in their realm. And the farther the creaking wagon progressed into the gloom of the rocky steeps looming overhead, the more isolated and ill-boding the journey felt.

Truly, only the most desperate and villainous of souls would be welcomed here.

As the cold mountain air crept through the bars, a growing apprehension chilled our hero's bones. If bandits did, indeed, lurk in this region, this location, being so far removed from civilization's grasp, would most likely have been their haunt.

Seemingly oblivious to any possible dangers, the guards only rejoiced at the Schwarzhorn and Wildgärst ridges, which loomed in the distance, where, yonder, they would again tread a declivity.

Barely a moment later, the wagon ground to an abrupt halt. A confused murmuring rose from the vanguard. The colonel's smug aspect shifted to marked consternation, and he spurred his mount ahead. Next, an indistinct sound carried on a sharp breeze. Several guards surrounded the wagon with their fusils held at the ready. Then, almost immediately after, a commotion erupted from the rear guard.

"Bandits!" yelled the colonel. "Defend the wagon at all costs!"

The slick sounds of unsheathed schiavonas, rapiers, and Walloon swords swelled on the air, followed by the noise of these steels clashing furiously, fore and aft.

Gripped by mounting agitation, our hero clung to the bars, straining to see. The bandits outnumbered the guards twofold. "As if my wretched fate was not already deplorable enough!"

Back into the far corner of the wagon, he shrank, panting and perspiring. "I cannot simply sit here!" Exerting his all, he tried to tear his fetter chains from their bolts in the interior wall. "Blast these infernal chains!"

Chaos and clamour continued to reign outside. Vehement expletives mingled with heavy groans of mortal pain. Artillery bursts thundered among the rocks — the deafening sounds rebounding, startling the wagon horses, and they bolted forward.

Tossed about violently as the wagon bounded the treacherous ground, the traitor cried out to the driver, "rein them in, man!"

But the relentless breakneck pounding continued unchecked; the dreadful noise of which reverberating through the wagon. "What are you doing, man? Halt this deadly contraption!"

Rather than any reply, there came only an agonising groan, ensued by what sounded like the thud of the driver's body falling to the ground and the jolt of the wagon going over it.

"Surely not?"

Again, the wagon jolted and lurched madly, hurling our battered hero into the wall.

Struggling to steady himself, he grabbed onto the bars, at which point the wagon, once more jolting, tilted almost to the point of overturning and flung him against the opposite bars.

Unbridled terror it was that vanquished his last shred of courage. Down, so appalling a drop, he gazed as the wagon careered so terrifyingly near to its edge. "That I should die so cruel a death!"

"Ya! Ya!" burst on his hearing, cutting through the menacing din.

A dark shape rapidly gained on the careening wagon from behind.

"Ya! Ya!" again came the shout, nearer now.

Wrapped in a black cloak and sat atop a stallion as black as midnight, a hooded figure galloped past the bars.

"Ya! Ya!"

Scarce had this unknown rider overtook the wagon, when the maddened horses let out a fearful snort and the wagon was somehow brought to an abrupt, teetering stop, mere inches from eternal oblivion.

Trembling uncontrollably, our hero did collapse to the wagon floor.

After a few words of reassurance being spoken to the horses by this unexpected saviour, the wagon was turned on a broader section of the ridge and proceeded back towards the earlier scenes of violence and bloodshed.

Barely had our hero come back into himself when he realised in which way the wagon went. Impossible, it is, to inscribe the extent of agitation which envenomed his palpitating heart. Knowing not which of his two foes Fortune had spared, his mind leapt from one shocking image of his own fate to the next.

He was not, however, long abandoned to such uncertain visionary terrors. For soon an enthusiastic noise of a crowd loudened on the air; a general hum of coarse celebratory speech referenced plundering the Guard.

The bandits had prevailed.

Uncertain how many of the vanquished camp yet lived, our hero could only hope that his captors, as soon as they would discover him, might join him to them.

"Are they dead?" shouted the unknown rider of the wagon.

"All of them!" answered a ruffian.

What? All dead? The traitor's eyes did gravitate to the scenes outside the bars; but he instantly restrained them. What if these men happened to be the very bandits of Du Pont himself? *Had only the wagon plunged over the precipice!*

"Excellent," replied the rider. "We have done a noble work this day."

Another miscreant approached. "I extracted from one of them their purpose here," said he. "Do you wish to hear it?" The rider answered in the positive. "The schultheiss despatched this very detachment to apprehend us all."

At this, the rider laughed. "And to affect his glorious cause of wiping us 'degenerates' off the earth, he thought to commission such poorly trained soldiers and only one wagon should he have imagined he would succeed?"

The mob now did jeer in wicked amusement.

"Naturally, I thanked him for so invaluable intelligence," resumed the ruffian. "And to show my profound gratitude, I ran him straight through on my blade."

Overwhelmed by the concert of sinister laughter, the traitor sank further into the corner. From the sickening dread which cleaved his innards, it was as if that same afore alluded to bloody blade had pierced his own heart through.

Fortune had truly worked her most striking blow yet. For to be seized by the Swiss Guard under his present condemnation, and to be handed over to the schultheiss, was an outcome already most dreadful. But to be carried off by such persons whose infamy lent itself to unprincipled and unscrupulous creeds, and whose comrades perceived and obeyed no laws but their own, was something else!

And should they, indeed, be Du Pont's men, and discover who our hero was, it would be for certain that they would content themselves not until they had flayed, sundered, and incinerated his individual members.

"What of the spoils?" said the rider, at which an inventory was called out. The rider again laughed. "We have once more put the taxes to better use. Down with the corrupt régime!"

"DOWN WITH THE REGIME!" repeated the murderous mob.

"Curse the patriciate oligarchies!" cried another ruffian.

"DEATH TO THEM!" roared the others.

"*Vive le futur Empereur!*" shouted the driver.

"*VIVE LE FUTUR EMPEREUR!*" shouted all.

Future Emperor? Hearing such a bizarre sentiment had potency enough to momentarily pull the traitor from the blackness of his own ordeals. *Is there a new power rising somewhere?*

Footsteps neared; another brigand pronounced they had one difficulty. Asked of it, the bandit gravely referred to the prisoner.

Prisoner? Thunderstruck, our hero did certainly gasp.

This brigand continued, saying that the prisoner was wounded during the cross-fire.

Wounded? Confused, the traitor felt his body for injury.

The rider demanded if the prisoner still lived. He was told yes, though likely mortally injured.

Another ruffian rasped why it even mattered. Collateral, came the reply; though the rider intended to keep the prisoner alive only until necessary. Thus, despatching a comrade to fetch a certain surgeon from the village of Meiringen in the valley below, the rider then ordered his men to bring the prisoner to the wagon.

Hearing this, our hero did involuntarily jerk, rattling the fetters which detained him.

"Hush!" said the rider. "Do you hear that?"

Though the men denied it, he insisted, "inside the wagon."

Was it now that Fortune would execute her final menace?

Demanding the keys be brought in haste, the rider jumped down and peered through the bars, at which the traitor, fearing he might be recognised, lowered his head.

Keys soon jangled outside, the lock turned, and the door swung open to several staring faces.

"Who are you?" bellowed the rider.

Mute with dread and wishing for the gloom to swallow him, our hero kept his head turned away, eyes riveted to the filthy wagon floor.

"I said, who are you?" repeated the man, his voice louder and searing.

That one ruffian interceded he was perhaps a foreigner and was unable to reply, the traitor now dared to meet the eyes of his masked persecutor.

"There is one way to find out," said the rider. And pulling out a pistol, he aimed it squarely at our hero's head. "I'll ask once more. Who are you?"

Staring thus directly into the black, loaded barrel, it was impossible not to finally answer. "Merely a fugitive with a death sentence already hanging over his head."

Some surprise and curiosity seemed to dampen the man's ire. "A fugitive, you say?"

But the bloodthirsty mob, filled less with curiosity than corruption, murmured amongst themselves and demanded he be shot, lest he escape and reports them.

"Fools!" snapped the rider. "Considering that he is fettered, and we possess the keys to his freedom, how do you suppose he should escape?"

From the instantaneous silence commanded by this man, it was clear he was the leader of this vicious mob.

"Besides," resumed this leader in a calculating tone, "when he deigns to fully talk, who knows if we might find that he proves of use to us? Bring the other prisoner."

At length, this young man — red coat, dark blue lapels, cuffs edged in white embroidery — bound with ropes, was confined to the wagon's far side.

From his corner vantage, the traitor studied his person. Was he of the same detachment having put him in his present captivity? *No; they were declared all dead.* The guard's wheezing presaged the likely culmination of his injury. He appeared barely conscious, slumped against the slats. A dark stain discoloured his coat breast. The white shoulder belt dangled, torn and askew from his left shoulder.

Why had these monsters taken him prisoner? Against whom did he serve as collateral?

The man's head slumped to one side; longevity favoured not his stricken countenance.

Momentarily withdrawn from his own difficulties, our hero leaned forward and scrutinised the young man's features. Was he perhaps known to him? *Perchance he had served the schultheiss, if not this canton?* But the soldier's face was so contorted by the agonies of his injury; and that his head now slumped the other way, recognition proved impossible.

"You there," whispered the traitor, "who are you?"

The prisoner only groaned incoherently. Thus, the traitor leaned closer, extending his hands as far as his chains would permit. "I cannot make out what you are saying?"

Slowly, the young man turned his head to him. His phiz grown more cadaverous, glistened with droplets of fevered sweat; his eyes half-opened, he again groaned through bloodless lips. Surely, it was the affliction of misery, not ammunition, that haunted those eyes. Some profound grief avowed a spirit shattered beyond all remedy.

Had circumstances been different, curiosity and perhaps humanity may have compelled our hero to attempt understanding the man's grief. Compassion might even have impelled him to succour and strengthen him. But circumstances being as they were, it was better the soldier should die. Was not he, after all, a Swiss Guard? And if he was aware of the search for a traitor and were to recognise our hero, he might too easily endeavour to preserve his own endangered soul for one of greater value and importance.

Suddenly the man violently convulsed, twisting against his bonds. He stared wildly into the traitor's eyes. There was a character that bespoke a fear of approaching death or the relinquishing of something other not less material than his soul.

The fetid air thickened with tension. And while the man struggled to speak, spluttering words, which, utterly unintelligible, seemed to convey the request of delivering a dying wish, he let out a protracted groan, and his glassy eyes, rolling back into this head, fell shut.

Good lord! Has he perished?

"Throw the dead off the precipice," came the leader's cruel voice.

What? Could they not at least leave them to be found and receive a respectable burial?

"Tonight, we shall pass at base, but tomorrow we must relocate elsewhere. It will not be long before the next swarm of these rats comes searching for their comrades."

Raw fury did crackle beneath our hero's skin as he peered through the bars at the bandits. *It ought to be they, and not the schultheiss' men, thrown to the bearded vultures!* More beastly was the sinister joy carved in the brigands' faces. In pairs, they carelessly pitched the slain over the cliffs — the macabre hollow thud of their bodies, at intervals, reverbing among the rocks; a sound forever scarred on the traitor's memory; a scene forever sullying these environs.

***

The skies were handing over to the thickening evenfall as the prison wagon straggled along the margins of boggy lakes and ponds towards Chaltenbrunnen Moorlandschaft.

Having stared overlong at the lifeless prisoner, the traitor sought distraction from his surroundings. Only sinister crimson and ochres punctuated the spreading shadows as the sun sank behind the mountain summits. Wisps of pale fog crept across the desolate moorland like ghostly tendrils. Ponds, like spectral mirrors, slithered past, offering upended catches of those distant peaks now vanishing into the advancing darkness — these confused reflections corresponding with the overturned state of our hero's mind.

The wagon slowed to a gradual stop within the marshy wasteland. Doubtless chosen for its difficult to penetrate wetland and peat-land, this high moor was the bandit settlement.

A strained groan burst from the prisoner. He was alive! But from the stench of blood and the worsening tones of this man's muttered agonies, his waning condition was unmistakable. Upon the eerie atmosphere, there now broke the sound of horses approaching. Gruff voices then directed the new arrivals towards the wagon. Soon, the door swung open and in peered a man, his torchlight illuminating a searching look of concern.

"Which one here is the patient?" said this man.

The scar-faced bandit next to him indicated the wounded guard.

"We must act swiftly," continued the other, evidently the surgeon. "Assist me."

Together, the surgeon and ruffian laid the soldier across the one side of the wagon; no sooner had the surgeon employed his dexterous hands, than he commented on the patient's precarious state.

"It is rather fortunate that I have benefited from the surgical arts of

France," said he whilst probing without sentiment the torn, burnt flesh surrounding the nearly blackened gunshot wound. The prisoner writhed and groaned in new agony against these necessary torments. "Bring that torch closer." The surgeon scrutinised the injury. "The French truly have developed the most remarkable techniques for regulating such bleeding."

A thin jet of the soldier's blood abruptly shot forth, splattering the surgeon's face. "Military combat has become quite a speciality these days," said he, unfazed as he wiped away the red with a handkerchief. "Especially when dealing with explosive, or in this case, gunshot wounds. *Merci* to Jean Louis Petit. Now where are you? — aha!"

He held up the lead ball as though it were a personal trophy.

At this very moment, there resounded from just beyond the wagon door a heavy thud, as of a collapsing body. Ironically, a bandit had fainted dead away at the sight.

Next, scalpel in hand, the surgeon performed what he termed the *"debridement,"* to ward off infection. From his portable leather dispensary, he took a bottle of benzoin and liberally disinfected the wound. Lastly, with an air of efficiency, he applied thin adhesive strips around the wound's edges before packing it with clean lint and neatly bandaging the patient.

"There!" said he in a self-congratulatory tone. "That should see you aright."

Casually, he now seemed to recall that a second prisoner did languish too, confined to the wagon. Extending his flickering torch, he examined our hero. After which, he simply quit the wagon without comment and the door was again slammed shut.

Ere long fires were lit, their smoke clouds mingling with the cold, black, starless firmament. All around the camp, there soon erupted riotous merriment and raucous strains of drunken balladry.

Anon, the fatty, rich aroma of roasted hog meat, wafted enticingly into the dank wagon confines. Despite his dejection, our hero's mouth could not but otherwise well with saliva most profusely. "You there!" called he to a nearby knave. "Bring some victuals, will you?"

With a murderous, stony stare, the man scowled at him.

"Bring me something!" again tried the traitor.

The ruffian only ignored him and strode away.

In turn, soliciting another rogue proved equally fruitless; our hero's demands went unheeded. Thus, while every environing rapscallion filled himself most greedily, the traitor had not even a scrap of meat to subsist on. His evening only crawled along most awfully as his gut did rumble most fiercely.

Of a sudden, from among the general raucous cacophony of brigands loudly claiming their plunder to be the superior, there arose the noise of a heated disagreement from nearer the wagon.

"I say we ought not to keep either prisoner alive."

"That is not for you, or us, to decide."

"And who are you to tell me —"

"Best to slit their throats now," interrupted another. "What if that prisoner of the Guard is some notable scoundrel? 'Twould be best we offload such a liability now than hazard drawing the canton's minions after us."

At this bluntly practical notion, several drunken voices chorused in agreement. More ruffians now joined themselves to this topic; soon, a vociferous debate did engulf the rogues as they argued most violently over the captives' fate.

"I say we do away with them."

"Aye!" slurred the unruly and uncivil mob. "Kill them *both*!"

Angst and fury did vie within the traitor's pounding breast.

"'Tis for the leader to decide," rejoined several other rogues.

Bitter invectives and expletives, most unfit to pen down here, did the two factions now trade as they fell into feisty hostilities. Why, they were just getting to brawling when:

"Friends!" cried a new voice above the fray. "I've a capital notion!"

At this, the mob desisted their scrapping and, quietening down, asked to be told of it.

"Let's drag him out and discover what great crime he has committed —"

"Fiddle faddle!" interrupted the many. "Let's just *kill* them —"

"Hear me out!" interrupted the other in his own turn. "If his villainy merits no special consideration, once the leader is done with him, we shall amicably wager which one of us shall have the luck of putting a lead through his skull!"

"Aye!" roared the mob. "Bring him out! Bring him out!"

02 DECEMBER 1791

Whatever the terrors of the night were to be, our hero was about to endure them. And if they were Du Pont's men, those terrors would most likely culminate in his execution. The creaking wagon door swung open, presenting the inebriated countenance of the very ruffian who had orchestrated this cruel enterprise. Rusty iron keys dangling from one hand and wagging a finger with the other, he ordered him to come forward.

"I have no wish to come out," answered the traitor. "I am not your sport."

This bold remark did clearly astonish the ruffian. For several long moments, he stood rather slack-jawed. But finally turning to his comrades, he loudly cried, "he says he's got 'no wish to come outside'!"

Sneering and laughter rang all around.

"Perhaps," jeered another, "he'd prefer to join the slaughtered?"

Though wholeheartedly averse to indulging such rogues, our hero did perceive the wisdom in acquiescing. Thus, with as much dignity as he could muster, he shuffled forward. The smug brigand unfettered his feet, and the traitor stepped out into the chill of the air, passing with uncomfortable proximity the face of his persecutor, who, leering at him, saluted him with a pompous, exaggerated bow accompanied by an elaborate roll of the hand.

All around, bonfires crackled, throwing their hellish flames against the blackness, casting the marshy world in an infernal tinge. Ominous figures swigged from bottles and jugs as they moved and danced about the blazes to folk music and song. Though roasting hogs still turned on spits and their aroma still permeated the air, dread despoiled our hero's body of hunger; of a sudden, the enticing smell seemed more like burning human flesh.

Forcing so grisly a portent from his uneasy mind, he averted his eyes to the blackness beyond the reach of the fiery glow. His hearing discovered to him the presence of yet more brigands concealed in the gloom. Their hulking forms lurked among the twisted trees, where, though obscured by the darkness, they appeared mingled with countless tents; the muted outlines catching the occasional pale cold moon-beam.

They are practically an army.

Our hero's feet inclined him back towards the wagon, but the brigand pushed him forward.

"Bring him here!" shouted countless voices from around a nearby fire.

The traitor turned his wary eyes their way, uncertain what fate might await him here. Their countenances, as shown by the red glare, evinced souls scorched by years of corruption. Their cruel dark eyes, fixed keenly on him, evidenced their mischievous bent.

As he entered among the group, they ordered him to sit on a log.

Whether they were Du Pont's men, the air was no less thick with evil intention. Bandits, they were all the same. Our hero's time among them had already taught him this.

"What was your crime?" spoke several ruffians opposite to him.

So, they were not Du Pont's men?

Fortunate it is that despite every circumstance which mounted against our hero, he was possessed still of presence of mind to conjure a means of making himself seem, if not useful to his captors, at the very least equally villainous.

"Murder," answered he.

"MURDER!" echoed they, unfittingly taken aback.

He nodded, leering as he smiled.

"Who did you kill?" demanded they.

Answering them not directly, he first availed himself of as savage an air as he could muster. Then, with a wicked sneer, he lent forward and fixed on them his best menacing gaze. "A much better question would be, how many..."

"HOW MANY?"

The astonishment on their faces, corroborated by their voices, drew several more rogues into the conversation. "How many d'you kill, then?" said they.

With a precision and art that would fool the wisest philosopher and the basest brigand alike, he claimed to have assassinated hundreds — not less than three-score — as a hired killer for the illustriously powerful and notably corrupt nobles; all of whom paid him a salary worthy of such atrocities.

This narrative naturally produced a general wonderment. "And how'd you get caught?"

"A treacherous, unworthy friend."

His audience, which grew with every gloriously atrocious sounding syllable he uttered, fell into discussing amongst themselves the marvel and injustices of this account. Verily, that afore-alluded to friend was deemed the worst of scoundrels, deserving of a death most vicious.

Cognisant of the successes of his tale, our hero did relax a little; as his eyes drifted to a roasting hog, he found his hunger race upon him with exacting vengeance. *I will, somehow, get my fill.*

Anyhow, those men who had before plotted the traitor's demise now did agree not to destroy him, but rather to restore his corrupt spirit. Thusly, a plate of hog and grains was thrust with eagerness and compliments into our hero's hands.

Meat was never so succulent and savoury; he could not swallow fast enough. Seeing his hunger, the ruffians refilled his plate again and again.

As our hero feasted most heartily, he failed not to take advantage of studying his distracted captors. Of the most, their garb was that of the lowliest proletariat and meanest peasant echelons: homespun linens, wool, and worn leather. Of others, theirs was a sartorial elegance: fine French coats, Austrian vests, German embroidery, and Italian silks; these luxurious raiments being undoubtedly the acquisitions of robbery and plunder. Yet, as he gave greater ear to their varied manner of speech and scrutinised their general carriage and deportment, he marked that they bore the incontrovertible stamps of aristo. There must be some truth in what he had heard: the disillusioned nobility *had* joined hands with these savages.

Those same rogues who had before questioned him were now staring at him over the flames. They appeared to be locked in some sort of disagreement. Unsure how to interpret their looks but feeling an ominous whisper creep over his skin, the traitor turned away to disguise his ill-ease and continued to feed the strips of succulent flesh into his mouth.

"We know who you are," loudly declared one.

Starting at these unexpected words, our hero nearly choked on his mouthful of meat. A brigand just now sitting beside him passed over some spirits, which he gratefully gulped down. "What do you mean?"

"Aren't you Du Pont?" came the astonishing — nay, *confusing* reply.

At the mere mention of this name, more miscreants rushed over, clamouring to know who spoke of it. One of the accusatory men stood up, nearly toppling backwards drunk over his seat, and pointed a wavering finger at the pretender assassin. Loudly, he proclaimed how, having once glimpsed and overheard Du Pont speak, he was convinced our hero was the very notorious Machiavellian villain himself.

All glinting eyes did now fix upon our startled hero, which, none of them bespeaking of a decent soul, did force him to lower his own.

"Are you really Du Pont?" cried the rogues most insistently.

Acquainted as our hero was with every deed of this infamous malefactor and au courant of his recent imprisonment — a covert operation known only to our hero and those involved in his prosecution — once all alarm and confusion subsided, a cunning scheme took shape in his mind. Since some similarity of age, build, and resemblance did exist between them and, moreover, the striking similarity between their voices (this, he now realised), perhaps he could assume the mask of this most elusive villain?

"You have found me out," avowed he in as devious and sombre a tone he could affect. "I am Du Pont."

"DU PONT IS HERE!" shouted the brigands, at which the fireside crammed with countenances innumerable and conceivable only of the most wretched and wicked.

There was one person, however, who shared neither the enthusiasms nor the encomiums of the credulous majority: their leader.

Stationed atop a large rock overlooking his rapt comrades, this ominous figure looked down intently at our hero. His eyes, reflecting the blaze, betrayed an inscrutable yet terrible purpose, flashing with severity and suspicion as the firelight glanced across his stern features. There was in his air something terrible; something resolute and vengeful. And wrapped still in his black cloak, all under apparels black with various weaponry hanging from his holster, it was as if he lived to meld with the night itself.

The more our hero stole glances at him, the more he felt some vague familiarity as if they had crossed paths before. And if this were so, was it not also then recognition, mingled with contempt, that flashed in those eyes which stared back at him?

Again, our hero lowered his own.

Of a sudden, a loud groan burst from the wagon. It was soon discovered that the injured prisoner had breathed his last. Despite the surgeon's efforts, blood poisoning had taken its early hold. Cursing this ill-turn, the leader ordered his men to strip the corpse of its uniform. To the bandits' no little bewilderment, he forbade tossing the body into a bog and rather demanded it be bound with cloth and kept safely in the wagon.

Though macabre was this intermission of distraction, it at least offered an escape from the leader's piercing, nigh, intimidating gaze. That said, all attention soon re-engaged with the regaling tales of Du Pont, and the leader returned to the fire-side, reclining on the log opposite.

Though that man listened to all that the pretending notorious agitator avowed in narrative, he seemed more to examine him only with that same suspicion; he leaned into the shadows, watching him from the mistrustful slits of his eyes.

***

Morning broke upon the land. The Du Pont pretender, having, in the credulity and veneration of the mob, gained a full release from the fetters, was given the privilege of a warm blanket and a tent, in which he passed several hours in a sound slumber.

Half-awake and beguiled by a lingering dream, he spoke out loud: "Ludwig!" He pulled the blanket over his head. "Draw the blasted curtains."

"Who is Ludwig?" came a gruff voice.

These words and the voice that spoke them wrenched our hero back to reality. *Did I truly call out my valet's name?* Half-reluctant, he turned to the bandit. "I must have been dreaming."

The ruffian, with whom he had shared the tent, stared down at him, half-yawning, half-laughing. "Dreaming? You're a fine dandy. Draw the —"

"Are you always so overbearing in the morning?" interrupted Du Pont, and, throwing off the blanket and cutting the man with a contemptuous glare, he exited the tent.

Outside, all was still and quiet. Not a soul was to be seen. Even the icy breeze crept silently, stirring not the tall grass. Pitched for some considerable distance across the curling mist marshland, the tents, he now perceived, were beyond counting: round, rectangular, large and small, made of white linen canvass or coloured cloth.

As he glanced around for a horse to steal, a lone female emerged from one of the larger tents and made her way to a fire, where the previous night's pot still hung. Dressed in men's garb — leather jerkin, wool breeches — she moved with a masculine gait.

Perhaps feeling his gaze, she looked at our hero and, smiling, beckoned him over. There was something familiar about her. Drawn by curiosity, he thus approached her.

Again, she smiled; a smile which the more he studied, the more it seemed he knew it.

"Hungry, I'll warrant," said she. "Since you're first up, try this, if you please."

Before he could espy what filled the pot, a spoon was shoved in his mouth.

"Argh!" He spat it back out. "Gruel!"

The woman's smile did instantly vanish. Had not footsteps drawn near with rough good-mornings, she would certainly have brained our hero with that same spoon. "A fine one, ere!" snapped she at a ruffian who, half-dressed, presently shoved his head into the pot. "He has the audacity to insult the coveted rank of taster."

After plucking his reddened face from the pot, the rogue warned, "insult the maiden's cooking at your own peril."

Caring no more for the masculine maiden than for her gruel, Du Pont answered them both with the same glare. The woman's cheeks did rush quite a-crimson with that sort of violent heat common to a female bandit's temper. She slammed her ladle into the pot with a look verily suggesting she was rather about to launch than serve the next slop.

Staying her wrathful arm, the ruffian apprised her that he who'd spat out her culinary delights was only the finest fiend and example of criminality the confederacy had ever contended with and would aid their own cause in half the time. "*This* is Du Pont," said he.

This pronouncement did cool the woman's warm complexion. Now eyeing our hero with an expression that evinced a warmth of a different species, she, with a coy smile, insisted on knowing his preferred fare. But no sooner had she heard it, she laughed like bells in a stiff wind. "Signor Do Pont!" she probably mispronounced the rebel's name on purpose, "even could you bring down the heavens, you'll not be finding such noble fare ere! I care not for which tables you've plundered, so unless you wish to starve, you'll eat what I serve."

At that, she rationed a rude tin bowl brimming with the odious grub and forcefully shoved it into his hands. That our hero did look at it with increasing disgust, the wench snatched it back and threatened him to remove himself at once, lest she toss him into the boiling pot.

"How dare you address me —" he let burst before catching himself. "Give it to me!" Forcibly grabbing back the despised bowl, he then stomped off to a log, which he slumped down on and glared at the miserable grey lumpy gruel, torn between ready hunger and stubborn revulsion.

"That's the leader's sister," explained the ruffian, joining him. "And unless you're bent for the courageous and treacherous scruples not to terrorise the female species, I'd advise you not to get on her wrong side for she'd scruple not in poisoning you."

"Poison me?" Our feigning Du Pont did let out a derisive laugh. Yet as soon as he looked back at the woman, though she presently stirred the pot, her eyes stayed fixed on him. Indeed, her face told she was about to invoke thunderbolts from the heavens if not already plotting how she might in fact poison him.

No! 'Twas quite impossible. Our hero could never have known such a wretched woman.

About an hour later, the leader emerged from his tent. Though his air was not less terrible and avenging in this morning light, there was something of sorrow that stole over his stern features; as though circumstance and not temper had led him to his present mode of life.

He fixed upon the Du Pont pretender his inquisitive eyes and, after speaking in low tones with a comrade, mounted a horse and rode off as though he were about to execute an urgent assignment.

Though unable to account for the man's purpose, instinct whispered to our hero that the departure related somehow to himself. And recalling the leader's dubious scrutiny the night before, an ill-boding did claw at his breast. Truly, he needed to escape this camp anon.

Presently, a rather slender brigand, silhouetted in a forest-green frayed coat and matching waistcoat, shouted out that a meeting was about to begin. Like pigeons descending upon scattered seed, the unworthy masses flew from their tents and flocked about a small stage, upon which the man now began to feed them his words.

With the camp now quite distracted, Fortune, it seemed, did extend her fickle charity. Several suitable paths emerged among the now unoccupied areas of the camp. Easily, our hero could slide between the tents and vanish beyond. He glanced about to check he was not observed, yet the subject of the meeting piqued his interest, rooting his feet to the spot.

"We have lingered long enough under the gilded boot heels of the Bernese," proclaimed the ostensibly learned former noble. "They, those self-appointed rulers — self-professed Gnädige Herren — increase their monopolies! Gorge on the blood and tears of workingman! Stealing forests and lands to construct their palatial manors while the world plea for crumbs!"

Our hero crooked his ear more in that direction as the audience growled its disapprobation and pumped their angry fists.

"And the so-called reformation! Served only to line further their pockets and to consolidate the strength of those silk-stockinged parasites. Drunk on power, they tax and extort the rural folk to starvation and debtors' prisons. Just this past July, they violently crushed the cotton spinners protesting their wages!"

For revenge, the gathering screamed while gnashing their teeth. To rend the patriciate tyrants, limb from wretched limb, they shouted.

"But friends," the speaker endeavoured to calm the mob, "remember, though past revolts increased the general suffering and instability, they were still the first chinks in the oligarchs' authority. Again, the common man will brave to rise against their tyranny. Soon, we will entirely shatter them as earthenware and remove even that cursed schultheiss from his seat!"

While believing himself touched by a moment of madness, our hero could not help turn full about and make his way back to the gathering. To be privy to such rebel intelligence was a unique opportunity which would never occur again.

"And the once proud pacts of the cantons?" continued the noble. "Those sacred bonds that brought low the Austrians centuries ago? Utterly betrayed! The rotten tyrants have hacked at liberty's roots, enriching themselves as the common man toils in chains!"

Death, called down on all patricians, echoed from one vile mouth to the next.

"Not only do they close off economic opportunities and sell citizenship for colossal sums, they take on the roles of the heirs of William Tell! No! It is we who share the spirt of that one. We will have freedom whatever the cost! We must destroy them first!"

Down with the régime, was again chanted; as was "*Vive le futur Empereur.*" Several ruffians grabbed drums and instruments and, joining their noise to the voracious speeches, produced strains of music such as perhaps not even Hell itself could ever conceive.

Such a fulmination could not but otherwise arouse political passions in the traitor's own breast. Certainly, there ran a deficient vein throughout the world — this he now knew from personal injury. But to suppose that this future emperor and these marauders and their egalitarian puerilism could barely attenuate, let alone eradicate the reputed inequity they clambered to obviate, was madness in its most garish colours.

Stifling a scornful laugh, he turned face away. To think these brigands could yet move so freely about the world whilst he was hunted like a wild animal was a monstrous atrocity and failure of order!

"Have you naught to say?" came a voice from his left.

Though jolted from reflection, our hero ignored the man.

"How can so famed an insurrectionist be so coldly indifferent?" persisted the brigand. "You'd persuade me to believe you're without a care of the oppressed."

Incensed, the traitor rounded on him. "*Oppressed*? You *woefully* misjudge oppression's true nature and source! Is it not the impoverished who perceive their plight simply for rebellion? Justifying it according to their envy of the —" He stopped himself. He had said too much. "I fight only my *own* battles now."

Done with speaking, he cut the man in half with his glare and moved away to another part of the camp to finally slip away from notice; but several rogues, having sought him out, obstructed his path and insisted on more of his terrible tales.

The high noon sun announced the leader's return. He drew a small group of his comrades to one side; whatever words he spoke with them, he repeatedly glanced at the traitor. His briefing swiftly concluded, the men dispersed whilst the leader hastened inside his tent.

Danger prickled beneath our hero's skin. Soon lost in uneasy contemplation, before he was aware of it, he was seized upon by the very brigands whom the leader had spoken with.

Clamped once more in irons, our confused and outraged hero was dragged back to the wagon and flung inside of it next to the foul, decomposing corpse.

"Do you forget who I am?" shouted he. "I am Du Pont!"

The brigands, however, answered him not.

In time, the leader approached. "I did say he might be of use to us," said he to a comrade who argued that Du Pont should surely be better used to help them. "But the monetary recompense is of greater advantage," replied the leader, "and with less the trouble."

Monetary recom — a reward? The stunned traitor did instantly grasp the implication — the posters!

A swell of voices complained about Du Pont's presence at the morning's meeting. But the leader assured his men that whatever Du Pont had heard would be of no threat to their security. "For the authorities would hardly believe such a report from such a beast."

Did the leader still believe our hero to be Du Pont? He must, therefore, have referred to the bounty on that villain rather than his own? Even so, the rising peril amounted to the same.

The leader laughed. "Besides, I'll implicate him in the guard's murder."

What? Like a pistol-shot to the head, horror, grief, dread, and disgust assaulted our hero's brain all at once.

This journey of around an hour was perhaps the most awful yet. For not only was the traitor already hunted for sedition, rebellion, and failed deposition, but he was now being conveyed to his prosecutors with the added infamy of murder. This was a most treacherous arraignment! Forby, as he glanced at the foul cloth-wrapped corpse, this gave to his imagination the cruel prophecy of his own destiny.

The roaring of plunging waters steadily grew louder, and the wagon jerked to a halt. Heavy boots thudded on the ground, and the leader passed the barred casement. Rusty locks clanked, and the wagon door creaked open.

"Out!"

Whether bewilderment or awe were the leading emotions of his heart, without hesitation or word, the traitor complied. Stepping stiffly out, he recognised between the spreading branches, which threw their shade all about, that they were at the head of Reichenbach Falls.

"Why," said he to the man, "have you conveyed me here?"

The leader bent upon him a peculiar brow; his eyes were aflame with something beyond interpretation. "Now, tell me truthfully. Who are you?"

"Who am I?" stammered our hero.

For his holster, the leader reached and, pulling out his flintlock, he pointed it at him. "This will indeed be the last time I ask you. Who the devil are you?"

Unable to withstand the intensity of such a piercing gaze or conjure words to answer him with, our hero remained silent, and his eyes fell to the rocky ground. Clearly, his disguise had failed entirely on the man. But who then did the man believe him to be? He must have seen the posters!

At the height of the falls, the traitor glimpsed. His chief impulse was to hazard jumping from them. But sanity had not entirely left the seat of his reason; he restrained himself and, looking at his persecutor, firmly replied, "I have already told you who I am."

"And yet I know you are not Du Pont." The man picked up a sack and cast it to him.

No sooner had the traitor caught it than he recognised it. "Where did you find —?" spoke he without thinking. He threw it back to the ground. "Why are you giving me this?"

"I suspected as much." The man returned the gun to his holster. His stern expression softened. "Your voice is not how I remember it, however."

"My voice?" *Who is this bandit speaking so familiarly?* "Do you pretend to know me?"

"The only thing I have pretended to is in allowing my men to believe you are Du Pont. And he, you most certainly are not. I know this because it is I who tricked the real Du Pont into the hands of the authorities."

Astonished, confused, and alarmed, our hero did stare in silence at this man.

"Fear not, my friend," said his accuser, "for it is I: Franz."

Recollection did not come fast. But the character of the man's eyes, undoubtedly made harsh by life, and the smile, which now widened his face, brought back to our hero's memory who he was. "Franz? Is it truly you?"

He nodded and, stepping forward, closed the gap to embrace him. "I knew in my heart it *had* to be you!"

It really was Franz. His childhood friend lived! Our hero could not help but hold him tight nor perplex at how he had ended up a bandit — and a leader at that! "You have been gone these three-and-twenty years." He stepped back from him. "I believed you dead?"

"Now is not the time to explain. All I can say is that I am finally at liberty to repay the bravery and compassion your mother showed to my own and, my sister, and me."

"Your sis —? Of course! That feisty cook?"

Franz laughed and with a nod confirmed it was her.

"Heavens!" Our hero did scratch at his temples. To be reacquainted with so cherished a soul and under such extreme and singular circumstances, conjoined with the tender mention of his own late mother, proved altogether too much for him. Encountering a sudden dizziness, he sought to support himself against the wagon.

"Come." Franz grabbed his arm. "You must go now."

"Yes, yes." He put his hand up to him. "But how...?" He glanced at the sack on the ground. "*Where* did you find this?"

With swiftness, Franz explained that when on patrol, he happened upon the wandering mare — which he now indicated was hooked up to the wagon. The sack he had searched and, discovering the scroll bearing the schultheiss' seal, he broke it and perused the communication. His first vengeful impulse was to destroy it. But the message being so extraordinary stayed his hand. Moreover, certain that something not less extraordinary must account for the absence of its courier, and being somehow convinced the envoy would soon appear, he kept secret this matter from his fellow ruffians.

"When were you so sure it was me?" said our hero, still the more amazed.

Concerning this, it was whilst Franz had studied him at the fire-side, knowing him to be an impostor, that a vague remembrance did touch his mind. It was not until morning, though, when he saw his face more clearly, that the vagueness dissolved. Believing he saw in the Du Pont impersonator the image of his old friend, he visited the village of Meiringen to corroborate his suspicion. This investigation, having resulted in the affirmative, he hence determined to do all he could to set him free.

"Such fortuity is near impossible to believe," uttered our hero. "Yet, how do you know my voice is changed?"

"Again, not now," answered Franz as he gave him a second bag which contained the regimentals of the deceased. "Dress in these."

"You want me to don a dead man's regimentals?"

Franz nodded firmly. "And we should dress him in your fineries."

"Are you mad? Drape a corpse in my silks?"

"It's the perfect ruse." Franz now explained this was, in fact, his motive for having stored the dead man. "Considering your enemies seek you and not him, if we garb him in your habiliments, and push the wagon over the precipice bearing the body, both of which will shatter into a thousand pieces, it will be impossible to identify the tattered remains. All will believe you are dead."

Inwardly repulsed as our hero was, he nonetheless conceded. Donning the regimentals, he then helped Franz clothe the stinking corpse in his own fine raiments. As the traitor solemnly went through these grim motions, weighing up the alternative, he could not help but see the scheme's ruthless cunning. Besides, it was a temporary solution. As soon as he would complete his mission, he could dispose of the regimentals and reassume at least some tatters of his own life.

Together with his old friend, he manoeuvred the wagon to the very brink of the precipice.

One final nod exchanged, they executed the stunt and pushed with all their strength.

The wagon teetered, then plunged over the edge.

A mere three heavy heart beats later, it crashed at the foot of the watery basin with all the destruction, disturbance, dust, and debris as to be expected.

"I wish you success," said Franz as he embraced him once more. "With guards all around Lake Lungern, I suggest you take the hidden valleys to Graustock, then onwards to Lucerne by cover of darkness if you can."

One last heartfelt embrace, then they stood back, gazes locked.

All now fell silent as past and present eerily converged. Happy memories of their vanished boyhood commingled with present uncertainty. Bereavement on the one side was balanced by newfound joy at this reunion. On the other, sentiments of something equally profound were written in his face.

A brisk wind swept about them, howling among the rocks and trees.

"Come with me," implored our hero.

"Our ambitions differ," replied he, coolly. "But should fate allow, we shall meet again."

"Very well." With the scroll secured inside an inner pocket of the bag, our hero wrapped this about him and mounted the horse. "Ah! Pray, what is all this excited talk of a future emperor?"

Franz did not answer at first. "As faithful a friend as you were, I can only warn you that a storm approaches and it will ravage all who resist it. If you're wise, you'll know how to weather it."

"A storm? Can not you say anything more? Per se, when this storm will come?"

Franz's eyes and countenance were equally resolute. "I've now repaid all that I owed. I'm under no further obligation to say anything more — even to you. Go now! Stay safe!"

A heavy groan did burst from our hero's breast. "Marvellous!"

With a last farewell nod between two friends, they parted ways.

In a hard gallop, the traitor drove the horse and crossed the Innertkirchen bridge towards the deep forests which rose before him as a thick curtain. Through this he cut and entered a valley, which stretched endlessly ahead, hemmed in by looming forest slopes that, with each thud of the horse's hoof, faded into the approaching dusk.

The chilly evening air which rushed past him was only fresh and reinvigorating. Imbued with a tingling warmth that seemed to strengthen his whole, he clutched the reins with renewed confidence. Despite his reclaiming the scroll and being so close to reaching Lucerne, it was that his friend lived, which was perhaps the most galvanising news yet. A smile burst from his heart, stretching wide across his mouth. If futurity would be so good as to reunite them, perhaps they could make up for the years lost, and he could also then extract the intelligence pertaining to this threat of a storm...

***

It was just before midnight when he reached the municipality of Oberdorf. From the slopes of the Büren hamlet, he could just distinguish, by the growing moonlight, the distant town of Stansstad. Beyond, the faint glow of Lucerne flickered across the lake.

He patted the mare. "Almost there, girl."

As he crossed Stansstad bridge, there emerged from behind a steep lakeside cliff the ominous glow of torches. From the gleam revealing a group of shadowy figures, the marked colours of the Swiss Guard alarmed him.

Thrown into momentary confusion, he veered the horse left. But again, in the distance, another patrol appeared, headed in his direction.

Heart a-thumping, he looked this way and that; yanking the reins, he turned the mare onto a steep forested acclivity.

Barely had he entered the woods, stooping beneath low-hanging branches and jumping over fallen boughs, when something startled the horse. Into a frenzy, the mare broke, snorting and rearing tall.

Flung off while he endeavoured to restrain the panicking creature, our hero hit the hard ground with force and, tumbling down the slope, smashed headfirst into a tree.

As he struggled to get up, the whirling world scattered from before his eyes, vanishing into an impenetrable blackness which overspreading his mind...

02 December 1791

Act 2

03 December 1791

—

17 March 1792

03 DECEMBER 1791

"*Was einmal war, das kommt wider,*" so says the old Swiss proverb which, when translated into our mother tongue — or that which the gentle reader does comprehend — imparts that "what once was, will come again." But speaking in simpler terms, as is the narrator's wont, the venerable adage implies that ofttimes in this mortal coil, history has a habit of repeating itself.

A hum of indistinguishable sounds crept into our hero's ears. As he pried open his blurry eyes to the rude sunlight's invasion, a nebulous human form swirled before him.

"What hap — *Ohgh*!" exclaimed he, clasping at his throbbing noggin.

"You are awake?" spoke a woman, whose voice, warm and benign, glided through the church bell tolling discordantly in his head. "Please, do not disturb yourself."

Her soft hand settled his own beside him before she slipped away, soon returning to dab his temple with a damp cloth.

Blinking back the fog in his befuddled, pounding brain, he focused on her. There was in her countenance a charming warmth. Her eyes, clear as a summer sky, spoke a sincerity mingled with compassion worthy of an angel. And her spreading smile was as graceful as it was soothing. A lace kerchief, tucked into the neckline of her simple muslin gown, fluttered as she leaned forward. But alas, recognising her not, he turned his eyes on the bedchamber.

Rustic whitewashed walls bedecked with a small crucifix, and several inferior-looking fripperies met his study. About a modest little window, a humble lace furnishing draped; several ribbons and dried flowers, evidently employed to prettify it, dangled each side. Beside it, however, a commode of an elegant, bombé shape — marble topped, parquetry rosewood draws, gilt bronze ormolu mounts, large handles, and escutcheons — caught his fascination.

Again, he scanned the chamber. There certainly was not its complement to be found in any other fixture. Why this incongruity piqued his curiosity, he could not decide. Still, recognising not the room either, he turned back to the woman. "Where am I?"

"You are in Bubendorf." She slid her warm hand under his head and raised it just enough for a trickle of water to touch his lips. "Drink this."

The water was as refreshing as if she had drawn it from the springs of St Moritz — wherever that was? "Bubendorf?"

"Of the Canton of Basel." First lowering his head back onto the pillow, she plunged the cloth into a small bowl, wrung it out, and with it, repeated the office of dabs to his forehead.

The stink of an extinguished tallow candle on a bed-side table assaulted our hero's nostrils with its repugnant, animal-fatty inconvenience. "Basel?"

Since he could drink and appeared refreshed by it, the woman insisted he should eat. Thus, taking a bowl and spoon in hand, she served what she promised would speed his recovery. But scarce had the sustenance entered his mouth when, most unceremoniously, he spat it back out. "*Ohgh*! Gruel!"

This shock further punishing his pounding head like a brigade of drummers, he again reached for it with a pitiable groan. "What happened to me?"

After hurrying the offending bowl of fare back to a tray, the woman returned to the bedside. "I cannot say," replied she, again laying his hand gently down. With a pensive air, she glanced at the commode, upon which were his sack and liveries. "Perchance your injuries result from your employment?"

"My employment...?" His sore, blood-dried brow gathered heavily above his eyes as he rifled through the empty chambers of his brain for this.

"From where have you come?" She wiped the crusts from his perplexed brows. "Which canton or country did you serve ere these injuries befell you?"

Striving for recollection only redoubled the pounding of his brain. Hither and thither his eyes did search as though the answer lay hidden in some dusty corner of their sockets. "I... I cannot ... recall?"

In her own expression, she evinced perplexity. Her serene forehead formed a frown. "Do you... recall nothing of it?" That our hero only stared vacantly at her, she rested her hand on his and intoned, "tell me your... name."

At this, he gulped hard. For above all, this he ought to know. "My name is... that is to say... My name... My name...?"

The woman's eyes widened. "Surely, sir, you know your *own* name?"

Hot irritation burned like reflux. "What a *ridiculous* question!" He ventured to rise, but his splitting head forced him back to the pillows. "My name..."

His chest tightened. "I am called..." He struggled to breathe. *Good lord!* His entire frame fell a-trembling, and in desperation, he turned his own widening eyes to her. "I can recall not my own name — what is wrong with me?"

"Tranquillise your spirits, please!" She restrained his trembling hands.

In the grips of terror, he seized her wrists. "Why can I not remember?"

"I know not, sir." She wrested herself from his grasp. "But you are Peter."

"*Peter*?" Such were his agonies that, scarce speaking the name, he screamed out a string of unintelligible utterances and, succumbing to a wild paroxysm of groans, sank into a stupor.

"What's all this ruckus?" said an elderly man, rushing in; his clogs reverbing; his weathered tricorn hat askew atop his head.

"Did he awaken?" shrilled an elderly woman, rushing in behind him; clogs also reverbing in discordant echoes; petticoat clutched in her sturdy looking hands.

The young woman did tremble. "Indeed, he stirred, but..."

With a deep sigh, the man looked at the stranger. But the woman rather let out a great harrumph as she cast her narrowed eyes at him and shrilled, "he can't stay here!" She turned her glare to the older man, the ribbons on her linen cap quivering. "You and your Protestant stupidity! Where shall we put him?"

Paying the older woman's outburst no mind, he fixed his hat and addressed the younger: "He did wake, you say?"

Before she could answer, the older woman interrupted. "Who *is* he?" She knotted her woollen shawl about her shoulders. "Whence came he?"

Rather reddening than replying, the younger woman fell quiet. But prevailed upon to speak, she gave the older woman the name Peter. Then, while biting at her lip, she explained he *seemed* to know neither that nor from where he came. "I fear some misfortune has robbed him of his memory."

As stupefying as this was to her auditors, who verily glanced several looks of amazement at each other, the older woman, gifted with one of those certain rapidity's of tongue, rejoined, "can a person lose such a thing?" Over her bemused face stole an alarming expression. "What if the Devil is in him?" She grabbed the man's sleeve. "What if he's possessed by Beelzebub?"

The man went to rebuke her, but:

“I’ll put him out!” continued she with sour shrills. “A bit of hardship’ll soon remind him who he is and whence he came!”

“Mother!” The young woman’s cheeks glowed. “How uncharitable.”

The man, who we shall suppose is the husband and, consequently, the young woman’s father, verily accorded with this stricture, annexing to it his own, which may have produced heated words had not the young woman added, “as it happens, I know very well who he is.”

At this, the parents goggled at her as if she had two heads. “You *do*?”

From them she turned and regarded the stranger lying on the cot, dazed and confused. The corner of her bottom lip drew in as several thoughts seemed to pass over her mind.

“Well, spit it out!” snapped the mother. “Or would you have us wait till spring?”

Flushed of countenance, and tremulous, she replied, “this is Pet —”

“Yes, yes!” interrupted the mother. “You’ve *already* told us this much!”

Begged to be quiet and listen, the mother stopped her shrills, crossed her arms and only scowled like a gargoyle. Thus, permitted to now do so, the daughter took a bracing breath and explained, “this is *the* Peter.” Her meaning, however, they discerned not and rather stared at her as blank as cows. Hence, again after a deep breath, she elucidated, “the handsome volunteer to the Guard I have mentioned before; with whom I have an understanding...”

First to recover from the general astonishment, the mother replied, “*well*!” Her eyes verily now twinkled where before they had only glowered. “I’ll be damned!” Her countenance brightened. A smile erased all vexation from her mouth as she gazed more favourably upon the inamorato, laying still dazed in the cot. “Even with all those bruises, he’s the *handsomest* there ever was.”

For certain, had it not been for a rapping at the front door, she would have lingered, fascinating, smiling and doting over the handsome lover. “Oh, *curse it*! That’ll be the farmer. Whatever shall I tell him?”

Since our hero was entirely insensible of his surroundings to pass any remark on, we shall depart for a moment to observe what was about to go forward at the front door.

“Hans, my good man.” With syrupy sickliness, the mother smiled.

Tidying her cap and apron, she then curtsied. "How very good to see you again."

The man's eyes were fixed on a pocket watch dangling from his hand. "Edmunda." With a snap, he closed the timepiece and bowed. "I confess I'm early to call, but as you know, I'm not one for tardiness. Look what an effort he made." Hans, whose ticking eyes beamed with pride, joy, and expectation, indicated his son stood behind him, dressed in his best brown woollen jacket and breeches. "He's counted the very hours till this blessed day."

"That you mention it," replied Edmunda, paying no regard to the son still bowing, "this puts me in mind that I perhaps ought to tell something of a small matter." Ergo, asked to know what it was, she explained, "we've been in confusion all morning! But would you believe it, the mystery lover — and he's mighty handsome too — has appeared out of thin air. Ernest found him lying half-dead in a ditch somewhere near Lucerne."

In turn, having asked to know whose lover this mystery half-dead ditch-dweller might be, and being told of it, Hans' astonishment and indignation were more than apparent. "What?"

"Yes," avowed Edmunda, brightly. "Until this day, we didn't believe her for a batzen —"

"*Indeed*?" interrupted Hans, whose agitation increased with each breath she drew and every thoughtless syllable she let slip. "This is shocking to hear!"

"Indeed, it is," continued the oblivious woman, downright insensitive to his feelings. "And I'm sure none were so shocked as me. But it might be an ill-fated romance, for he doesn't even know his own name; where he's from; nothing! But she knows him, so, wedding —"

"Enough!" again interrupted Hans as he assumed the colour of his prized beets, which had won him only second place at the village fête. "What wench would have us the sport of —"

"*Wench*?" interrupted Edmunda, irritated in her own turn, grasping not the merit of his righteous indignation. "You'd better sew up that tongue; else the Devil will make good —"

"*Devil*? I'll give you the — what about the baker? He's already baked the cake. And Father Francis? He's already reserved the date to give his blessing. And what'll we tell the village? My son and your daughter need to still get engaged! *I* need help on the farm!"

At this, Edmunda threw her head back and laughed so hard that her eyeballs rolled around in their sockets. "A fine prophet you make, sir! Preparing for sunshine when rain may fall. Do you sow wheat and expect to reap barley? Flog your eggs even before they've been laid? And your little lambs, do you name'em ere they've popped their little fuzzy heads out from the dam's hindquarters?"

Much like two overripe peas would burst out of a pod, Hans' eyes looked ready to explode out of his head. "Was it your aim to make sport of me? You and your wanton daughter —"

"Wanton?" Edmunda's own colour assumed that of her best radish, which had won her first place at that same aforementioned village fête. "I'll rip out the wily tongue of yours —"

"*Wily* —?" The farmer did choke on his splutterings.

"What's happening here?" intervened Edmunda's husband, drawn by the rising voices. And remarking his wife's eyes dart at her broomstick, he hastily stepped between the two, divining the use she had doubtless conjured for it.

Meanwhile, the son, stood mute as a statue amidst the squabbling, sullenly working his jaw as though chewing the cud, glimpsed something move in the nearby window. Sacrificing his father to the fight, he slunk away and pressed his face to the glass. Within he gazed, spying the very man abed, who, easy it was to deduce, so happened to be the mystery lover, presently enjoying the solicitous attentions of his no-longer intended.

Subsequently, the youth's countenance, which was not unattractively framed, metamorphosed, resembling rather strikingly his father's prized pig, which had also come in second at that twice-earlier-cited village fête. At the unwelcome usurper, he snorted — nay, exhibited a want of decorum we might have expected in that same pig had it been obliged to share of its carobs. Whether he was conscious of it, with his right foot, he pawed the ground.

Just then, Hans grabbed him by the ear and pried him from the window ledge as one might pull a reluctant pig from its trough. "Come away, boy!"

With a face still burning with vexation, Edmunda flung back into the bedchamber. "To think I was bent on you wedding that barbarian's son!" While unruffling her face and skirt, warmth of a different nature overspread her cheeks. "But it all turned out for the best. What a fine creature he is; even when sleeping." She nudged the daughter. "You'll be the envy of the church, the village — nay, the canton! And such handsome children you'll make together."

"Mother!" The cloth fell from her fingers. "How can you talk so?"

"Very easily! You'll not make us wait another decade for that too, I hope! Don't you dare dally overlong in the marriage bed!"

Indeed, the daughter's gasps choked up her remonstrations.

Of a more dubious stance about this romantic tale, the father demanded proof of it, at which the daughter, increasingly crimson cheeked, insisted her words were precisely that.

As the two sparred in a tournament of disaccord, the mother grew infuriatingly confused. To know who to credit with her hopes, she begged and demanded. Then, noticing the lover-in-question stir and open his eyes, she flew forward. "Hark!" shrilled she. "What's your name?"

That she (despite being enjoined otherwise) begged, bothered, and badgered with such zeal: "Your name? Your name?" Our hero did allow to drop off his tongue the fate-sealing designation: "Peter...?"

"Praise the Lord! The Pope! Father Francis!" Edmunda clapped and, snatching the cloth up off the floor, with it fanned herself ecstatically.

Natch thunderstruck, the father gawped in astonishment, arms dangling limply at his side, blinking at the purported lover as if the man had sprouted horns and a tail.

Peter, therefore, which appellation we shall substitute for all those prior, now found himself the unfortunate object of the overly effusive Edmunda's rhapsody.

"How you've restored joy to a heart as dead as stone from all the disappointment! You must have handsome parents?" She awaited his reply. But getting none, she added, "what about siblings? Do you have any?" Again, she waited. "Don't remember that either, do you?"

That she had elicited not any reply, she diverted her attack and pelted her now shrinking daughter, who stammered out that yes, Peter had claimed his parents to be handsome, and, no, he had no siblings; this statement she furnished with a sharp clearing of her throat.

Satisfied, Edmunda turned to her husband. "Ernest, be so good as to fetch me a chair."

Ernest — we now discover his name — brought in the chair and, after gazing still incredulously at Peter, commended the daughter for her conduct, determination, and devotion to a man who nobody believed existed. Frowning at him, Edmunda might have said shush, but mid-flow in his next praises, Ernest stalked to the casement. "That heedless farmer! He's only gone and left the gate open. The pigs'll get out again!"

And off hurried he to avert the swine catastrophe.

"The misery you've subjected us to, child," said Edmunda, rounding on the daughter. "You ought've produced him sooner. We were convinced you'd perish an old maid."

"Better an old maid than wed to that dolt of a —"

"Hold your tongue!" Edmunda flung the cloth at her. "Speaking such folly! You're bent on sending us to an early grave. I blame it on those books you're always reading; those — those *novels* putting such foolish notions into your head."

A certain abashment crept over the daughter's countenance. But 'twas most likely a cognisance of her mother's ignorance than any conscious shame of deserving such a rebuke. "If anything," rejoined she, "novels rather encourage than curb romantic attachments."

While Edmunda either listened not to this correction, or affected having not heard it, Peter, not yet discerning who this narration pertained to, paid it some curious attention.

"Still, I blame you," resumed Edmunda, "for entering an understanding with one man while leading another down our garden path, only to break his poor little heart."

The daughter gasped and asseverated that not once had she *ever* encouraged the suitor. Edmunda, however, maintained her prosecution, referencing all the poems she knew he sent to her, and those she had secretly sent back to him.

At first, understanding not this averment silenced the daughter. But likely revolving in her mind the allegation and finally deciphering it, she responded, "I returned to him only what he sent to me."

Edmunda now gasped. "Whatever for?" The daughter sat up stiffly and explained how she had merely corrected the young man's many scribal mistakes. This extenuation by no means appeased the mother. "How could you be so cruel as to send back his poems? I now wonder at the boy's courage for showing himself here today."

"'Cruel' is not the word, Mother. 'Tis not a wife he should yet be seeking. To express himself through the pen, he ought to first apply himself to spelling."

Having huffed and tutted, Edmunda rebuked her for her want of sense and marvelled at her failure to see that rather than driving him away with her corrections, she'd only gone and filled him with hopes.

Indeed, the daughter had not foreseen that. Able not to coin a shrewd reply, she bowed her reddened face and fiddled with the trimming of her apron.

Ernest returned, declaring he had prevented the pigs from getting out.

"He'll have to stay where he is, for now," said Edmunda, smiling upon Peter. She turned to the daughter. "You'll have to sleep with us in the attic. But we must keep this to ourselves; at least until we've removed him to a room of his own. We don't want a village scandal."

"And somebody'll have to go visit Hans," said Ernest; at which utterance Edmunda urged him thither directly.

Curious about Peter's character and skills, Edmunda asked the daughter about them. Hearing he was always honest, kind-hearted, *and* diligent — this virtue especially pleasing — she turned to Peter and placed her hand on his. "You'll make half the village sick with heartache, and the other half with envy."

He jerked his hand away, glaring sharply. *What nonsense is this?*

That rejected hand retracted to her breast, Edmunda's eyes flashed with exquisite satisfaction. "You'll make the handsomest husband there ever was."

Though recollecting not who he was, from where he came, or anything else, he scrupled not to dispel the woman's delusion. "What insolent talk is this? Husband? *Whose* husband?"

Taking them both by surprise, Edmunda took hold of the daughter's hand and his and united them. "*You*, silly." She flicked her eyes in the young lass' direction. "Husband to *my* girl."

While choking on his own gasp, he snatched his hand back. "*Me*?" (The daughter too withdrew her trembling hand) "While I confess there are many circumstances I cannot recall, I positively swear I have *never* seen this..." he ventured to raise himself as he motioned away the daughter as though she was a pesty fly, "... this *creature*!"

Indeed, the daughter scowled at this affront.

Circa three seconds later, Edmunda burst into a fit of laughter. Sharply, she repudiated his confidence, declaring he was incontestably the hero destined for the damsel, who, in this instance, was her daughter, and, who, in the same instance, he'd dragged both from the doom of spinsterhood and the brattish farmer's son. And not yet done terrorising him, she did promise him also in this instance too, that should he venture to ungallantly abandon her, he would meet with the Stollenwurm, if not her broomstick.

***

After somewhat soothing Peter's sufferings, the daughter begged leave to take the pony into the village to buy, said she, medicinal herbs to ease his anxiety. But her errand was not solely as she claimed. First, she visited the neighbouring Protestant and Catholic churches and scoured their records — just in case Peter was a local. However obliging the minsters and the Fathers, and however every baptism and census was stored alphabetically, neither provided a sufficient match for the Peter in her bedchamber. Next, she visited the Liestal garrison but found no such absent soldier registered with them. The garrison would, in the meantime, send out word to the other cantonal garrisons — Lizzie being instructed to return in the next weeks to obtain an update.

So, not without that purchase from the village dispensary, she returned home, where she found the mother in the kitchen, complaining and calling down evil on the convalescent.

"What took you so long? Handsome he may be, but, oh, what a temper! And if he persists in it, I'll verily put an end to his life myself!"

The daughter placed her basket on the table and asked what she meant.

"Though that knave forgets who he is, how he forgets his manners, I don't understand. I took him gruel, at which he waved his arms in such a temper and sent the bowl flying!"

Exhaling a gale-force sigh, she slumped into her chair. "I'm sorry to say it, but he verily acts like a raccoon."

A mirthful blush escaped over the daughter's cheeks. "I believe you mean buffoon?"

Except for her few favourite Psalms, Edmunda was illiterate. But having espied the smiles and contemplative expressions on the daughter's face whenever reading, her own curiosity had been piqued. Thus, asking what she read and, on one occasion, catching the word 'buffoon', and on another, 'racoon' — for the daughter enjoyed not only novels but compendiums on nature and the continents — she often got the two words mixed up.

"Mind that tongue, missy!" Edmunda darted her best bulging eye at her. "I don't need my daughter correcting me."

***

As it may, by now, be apparent that our mysterious hero is perhaps no more Peter than our heroine is his prospective betrothed, please allow me to elucidate, lest the maiden be accused solely of shameful duplicity.

Let us turn back the clock to the earlier hours of dawn when the daughter returned home from nursing an ailing neighbour all night. At the gate, she found her father exiting it, face furrowed with irritation. The mother stood at the chalet door, brandishing her broom, cursing him for bringing home a complete stranger on the very day the farmer was bringing his son.

"Your mother will explain," said Ernest. "And I hope you'll be kind to the farmer's son."

"Even were I seeking another beau, he wants in so many of the basics."

Ernest's brow did crease only the deeper. "He'll work hard and provide for you." With a reproving shake of his head, he hurried off to the fields.

In the kitchen, Edmunda raged like a bull, vilifying Ernest for bringing back God only knows who he'd found in a ditch; an item of pottery dropped from her grasp. "Hang it!" She scowled at the shards. "I'll toss him out! We've no room for him! We'll all need to sleep in the attic! We'll all eat less for it too!"

Not content with disparaging her husband's charity, she berated the daughter for being away all night. The wrath of heaven she betokened she would verily heap on her head if she should look at all the less pretty for it, or dare refuse the young farmer's romantic advances.

"He's in your room!" Edmunda thrust into her hands a tray bearing gruel, a cup of water, and a bowl and cloth. "Go tend to him!"

So preoccupied with the impending visit, the daughter did not at first regard the patient with any peculiar interest. But after wringing out the cloth and dabbing his head, cautiously expunging the dried blood, she noted the appearance of a handsome face. Closer she leaned, studying the shape of his nose, his strong cheekbones, his long lashes, his delicate mouth, and manly jaw. Then, at the sideboard, she glanced, noting the red coat.

Hence, drawn to inspect it, and having no insight into how our hero had come into possession of these regimentals, she naturally supposed he was of the Swiss Guard.

Curiosity gaining the ascendancy of her mind, she opened the coat, and out fluttered a folded paper. Presuming it fell from a pocket, she picked it up with the motive of reinserting it. But since this entire set of circumstances was so uncommon, curiosity, again, acted as sovereign. Stealing a nervous eye at our hero, she then unfolded the paper and discovered lines — ostensibly authored by a blood-smeared name 'Peter' at the page's bottom — of what, however unsteadily penned, resembled a poem:

Oh! Were I the moon, I would gaze forever upon you;
in the darkness of night, watching over you.

She paused and glanced at the man in her bed. This was all so curious. But resuming:

Fear not would I of the twilight stealing you away;
For the sun does set each day,
Dearest, loveliest Eli —

"Elizabeth of Bubendorf?" Starting at this, she almost dropped the paper. "Does the apparent owner of your heart share not only my name but also that of my village?"

At last, we learn the appellation of our heroine.

Suspended between disbelief and amazement, Elizabeth reread the composition several times. Its verses, their character, she found poetic, yet intelligible; their sentiment, warm yet noble; their sensibility delicate yet manly.

Feeling a peculiar warm sensation in her breast, she turned her incredulous gaze to the supposed author. "An unalloyed, almost ethereal admiration directs his pen." Yet, there was that one stroke which touched as much as it confused her heart. "*Who* is this Elizabeth, inspiring you thus?"

She revolved her recollection of the villagers but recalled none of her name, or of a suitable age for such dedicated enamours. Neither were there any who lived near, or had since gone away.

To the verselet, she returned her attention and lingered at its inscription. Was she somehow acquainted with him? Again, she scrutinised his battered face: no flicker of recognition stirred. Notwithstanding her certitude, doubt sustained a contrary consideration. Perhaps he somehow knew her?

"*Elizabeth*!" A tingling perfused her cheeks. "What *are* you thinking?"

Despite every plausible dubiety, her soul became so deeply interested in this subject that her wish to discover the mysterious Elizabeth of Bubendorf thus rose with every beat. And contemplating the stranger's ostensible mode of expressing himself, and his employment, she supposed him to be a man of principle, honour, *and* courage. Hence, that his character, in this light, appeared already worthy of her approbation, she deemed him deserving of her protection and determined to help him.

She then slipped the paper back into a pocket and refolded the coat, choosing not to mention her prying, and returned to the bed-side. Awakened now to a profound concern for the patient, the more she studied him, the more she could not help believe him the handsomest.

As we have already seen, the traitor opened his eyes and, knowing not where or who he was and, being without recourse to family or friend, was thence cast upon the mercenary mercies of Edmunda. And here it was that Elizabeth, soon to be sacrificed at the connubial altar, thus contrived to avert two equally deplorable fates with the same swoop.

Having, I trust, exonerated our shrewd but benignant heroine, let us resume the narrative. But first, whilst we find ourselves in this calmer intermission, it would behove us to delineate the general disposition of the several dramatis personae thus far introduced.

Firstly, Elizabeth, who was of a good age (nine-and-twenty to be precise) to be yet unmarried, possessed a character and person rather fortunately, so wholly the reverse of her mother. Though not of that trope of paragons we oft find sprawled across the pages of fashionable novels, her manners were sufficiently dignified to term her a heroine. Her comportment, adequately elegant. Her temper, though hardly subdued, endued with becoming timidity. Having benefited from a wealthy patronage — a most charming fellow, whom we shall meet anon — such an edification did naturally bestow a clear, vigorous comprehension, which, when engaged, evinced, as we have heretofore observed, an ardent imagination.

Not to be forgotten, she was an avid reader of the aforesaid novels, whose virtuous heroines did inspire in her an emulous desire to succour the suffering in others and breathe to her very pretty soul a forbearance and sufferance of her own privation.

It was, however, perchance, her graceful and airy steps conspiring against her exterior charms, in that she could enter and quit the bedchamber with little notice of her patient.

But we cannot speak the same of Edmunda.

"Good lord, woman!" would cry Peter. "*Must* you *stomp* in and out like an elephant?!"

So, wholly unlike the daughter, Edmunda boasted neither beauty nor fine proportions. Her complexion was not soft and fair. Neither was her hair radiant red, curling in bewitching profusions about her neck. It was brown and seemed only to obey the wild disorder which nature, not fashions dictates intended for it; speaking plainly, it was as wiry as an old mop.

As we have observed, her manners were unbecoming and uncouth. And her temper, which needs no introductions, quicker to ignite than gunpowder and burn down a cathedral. Though hasty for the broom, it would be unjust to omit that she was quickly appeased and willing to forgive — for she prided herself on her Catholic mercifulness. And despite lacking an education, she was not ignorant of the form of an elephant. For having once seen such a beast in one of her daughter's books, she castigated her defamer and controverted the comparison, stating how verily, from her memory, she could sketch its appearance.

Oh! And since it is rude to speak of a woman's age, let us delicately say that she had seen around fifty-five winters.

By-the-by, Peter, having likened her to that mammal, would have certainly felt the full weight of her trunk — I mean, her hand, or her broom, smacking him about his head, were it not for Ernest's intercession. But I digress.

So, Ernest, a man having endured nigh on fifty-eight long and gruelling harvests was, wholly unlike his wife, not of rotunded proportions, nor was he of a short, treelike stumped stature. He was as slender in frame and height as a willow. Of his swarthy features, rugged and expressive would best describe them; doubtless furrowed by the storms of an opinionated, quarrelsome, and querulous spouse. Though indeed weathered by her every shrill, his mandible was not so worn out as to deny him of a countenance otherwise animated and light.

The greater part of the daylight occupied him as farrier, farmer, fiddler, fixer of looms and spinning wheels. But when spared from such menial mundanities and marital menaces, he proved a most devoted father, a faithful friend to the village, and a hearty welcomer of waifs and strays — as we have ere observed in his rescue of a total stranger in our hero.

Oh! And beneath the humble garb of clogs and lederhosen beat the heart of a nobler conviction: the precepts of Protestantism, which, in constant conflict with his wife's Catholicism, most truly, we shall see, this long-suffering Job did need.

As for the mysterious and broadly supercilious Peter, that we are no more informed of his history or his other parts than he is, it would be unjust to speculate on such and whisper in his ear things he lacks the wit to remember. We must rely solely upon his cogitations, discourses, and general conduct to discern the lineaments of his person, if not the true complexion of his character. For even prior to his misfortune, it seems his innermost secrets were closely guarded within his bosom, protected by a breastplate of staunch reserve.

Therefore, in the absence of certainty, let us proceed as the tools of Providence and observe whether this blank slate be etched by Fortune with the edifying letters of virtue, or the scrawls of vice — that is, in plainer terms: for better or for worse.

And if neither should emerge, we may just take up our sharpest satire and prune away at the fellow ourselves until some semblance of a personality peeks through!

10 DECEMBER 1791 – 13 JANUARY 1792

About a half-month passed since the learned physician had attended to our hero. Post-traumatic dissolution of memory was the diagnosis; likely resulting from the several blows successively applied to his pericranium. His corporeal ailments being much easier to address than his mental confusion, he was prescribed the most suitable ointments and panaceas.

The sun had already risen, though the clouds did steal its light and pelted the windowpanes with heavy rain. Since our hero could again stand without succumbing to dizziness, he tottered towards the casement to investigate what was outside; in so doing, he recalled the commode next to it.

"What an insult to your manufacturer. To be forsaken to so incongruous and irreconcilable a chamber." He ran his sympathetic hand along the fine woodwork. "I wonder that I am possessed of such discernment to distinguish the fine from the vulgar...?"

He did chew on his lip for a moment. Already his soul whispered he belonged elsewhere. The regimentals and the sack stacked in the chamber's corner caught his eye, accompanied by a feeling he should perhaps probe them. But Edmunda presently entered and, supposing his restored perambulation betokened the restoration of his mind, assailed him with a thousand questions. Her shoulders soon slumped as a gust of disappointed air escaped her lungs. However, with a robe thrown over him, she shoved him out of the chamber and along a poky hallway to the kitchen.

The gloomy room was precisely as grim-visaged as Peter's imagination had painted it. The insufferably low, beamed ceiling hosted several pots, baskets, and clutter that seemed only to gravitate towards his elevated pate. Save for one delicate tea-set — a diamond in a dung heap — the few shelves were stacked with only utilitarian objects. The hearth, presently aflame, rather vented itself in smoke; great plumes of which entirely filling the room. Yet the windows, which were open, served only to welcome in the wind and the rain.

"Have I descended into Hades' scullery?" Peter coughed theatrically. "Am I to die of asphyxiation?"

"Sit, sit," cheered Edmunda, steering him to an ugly pine chair as she flew to a cooking pot. "And there'll be no dying from a bit of smoke here!"

Certainly, something *was* wrong. "Why do I feel I belong... *elsewhere*?"

"Speak no more nonsense," chided Edmunda. "You belong with Lizzie, so you belong right here with us!" She beamed uncomely, eyes aglint. "And I'd have you be *nowhere* else."

Though bereft of his memories, Peter's tastes had somehow remained entirely unaffected. As expeditious to remark as he was to reproach, from the general commingling of faded pine forming a dresser, table, and several chairs, two seats whispering of French luxury — one at the table's head and the other at its foot — fixed his eye.

Drawn thus closer, he ran his hand over the smooth, gilded finish of one such chair, finely carved and upholstered in the richest blue brocade. "Perhaps I have a claim here, after all?"

Anyhow, this seat being exactly best-suited to his noble personage, he pulled it out and sat down.

Barely had his backside kissed the fine padding when Edmunda, stirring away at the pot, commending his recovery, declaring he would, henceforth, eat only at the table, glanced his way. "Why you *rapscallion*! That's Ernest's chair!"

Instantly, she drove him off it as one would an opportunist nabbing a vacant landau. "And that's *mine*!" Her quick eye following his, she chased him faster than an avalanche back to the ugly chair. "Here!" She drummed it with her irked finger. "*Beside* Elizabeth!"

Naturally, Peter's toes and fingers did curl in contempt. "Is there not even a cushion?"

Here, Elizabeth now entered, at which Edmunda urged she educated her lover on the order of precedence, lest she herself educate him with the order of the broom. Before Elizabeth could query this menace, Ernest came in with a young man, who greeted them and fell to staring at Peter as if he were a performing hog in a wig and gown.

Certainly, the gawking agrarian youth was not ill favoured in countenance; yet neither had he benefited from the same spring as his sister; he resembled more his mother. His slender proportions were goodly enough, however; clearly the legacy of his father.

The lad was just about to introduce himself when a loud rapping issued from the main portal. With a most prodigious huff, Edmunda advanced upon the offending door. Some meagre moments passed before she returned. It appeared guards from the local garrison had come a-calling, enquiring after any "suspicious characters" lurking within the vicinity in the last weeks. With quite the patriotic fervour, Edmunda had not only assured them they'd be the first to know about it if such rogues dared to darken her doorstep, but she'd personally deliver them, bound and gagged, if necessary, to the garrison's very gates.

"But never mind that!" shrilled she. "Hurry and sit! All of you! Food'll get cold!" And with a tremendous thud that shook the very rafters, down went the cooking pot on top of the table, and a billow of steam erupted from it.

As she served Ernest and then Emil — for this was the youth's name — she explained to the latter's curiosity the strange fellow's presence. With sudden enthusiasm, Emil declared he always wanted a brother. Then, as if checking his zeal, he apologised. Edmunda now stared gloomily into the cooking pot. But, letting out a long, equally gloomy sigh, she resumed serving. "Here you go my dear," sang she with smiles and sighs more of joy as she passed the bowl to Peter.

One look at its contents was all it took. Huffing and puffing, he pushed it away. "I *refuse* to eat any more of these culinary offences." All eyes turned to the disagreeable epicure. "Why do you gawk at me so? It's barely fit for fodder."

"*Fodder*?" Edmunda jousted the serving spoon at him across the table, careful and deft to catch the splashes and hurry them to her mouth. "Think yourself above your station, do you?"

"Whatever my *station*, madam, I —"

"Wasn't you a mere volunteer to the Guard?" interrupted she, pushing the bowl back to him. "Or do you pretend they fed you at the colonel's table?"

Aghast at this treatment, Peter stared at the odious bowl. "Oh! How I crave veal pie! How I yearn for *entrée tourte* and *entrée* of cutlets in fricandeau!"

"Ontray what?" replied Edmunda.

This question proved rather difficult to answer. Our hero could not recall what those viands were or where before he had ostensibly eaten them. He groaned and slumped into his seat.

"He really *does* have *no* memory," said Ernest with a light laugh.

"My memory I cannot vouch for," rejoined Peter, again shoving the bowl away with a scowl. "But my palate *convinces* me that gruel is not less beneath my predilection than *any* table I — OUCH! What *is* this attacking my —? Can there be a *chicken* beneath the table?" He stamped at the feathered foe, hammering its beak most violently into his toes. "Away, thou villainous fowl!"

Edmunda swept up the now squawking bird, whose wings did flap in feathery fury, and whose pea-sized orbs did instantly glare at Peter as though it rather now wished to peck out his eyes. With threats not to terrorise "her Edith" — the eggy chicken — Edmunda thrusted the bowl back to him. "Now eat!"

Alas, with that shove of the bowl, Edith so happened to fall from Edmunda's enclasp. All waffles, hackles, and feathered breast, the hen charged across the table at the enemy, clucking battle cries like warriors of old.

Anxious to elude the orange talons launched at him, Peter tilted so far back in his chair that he toppled over, crashing thunderously to the floor.

Fortunately, Elizabeth apprehended the plucky bird before it disembarked the table for Peter's head. Yet no sooner did our hero sigh his relief when, with a horror equal to the suddenly gasping Edmunda, he spied the head of another beside his own; its glassy eyes fixed unforgivingly on him.

"Good heavens!" He vaulted to his feet and retched uncontrollably.

With threats he should mind more Hell than Heaven, Edmunda, in a profusion of tears, flew around the table to retrieve the beheaded (she called it) benefactress of eggs.

So, this unfortunate fowl (named Enya), a feathered favourite of Edmunda *and* Edith, had, amidst the foregoing fracas, unceremoniously entered the kitchen, clucking innocently by, only to be slain by the weight of Peter's chair.

While our hero stared at the decapitated bird on the bloody floor, an image of a guillotine flashed across his mind and a name rang in his ears: von Castella de Berlens. (Our readers should recall earlier on in our narrative the kindly peasant couple, who invoked the glistening blade upon the necks of all those patricians). "Who is... *von Berlens*?" implored he of all at the table.

"Never mind *that*!" shrieked Edmunda as she scooped up the murdered hen's limp carcass. "Look what you've done to my poor Enya!"

Of course, Peter denied it and protested the disaster was entirely the feisty Edith's fault. Of course, Edmunda would have none of it and reminded him who was sitting in the chair. Suffering not this accusation either, Peter again denounced the gruel. "I will sooner swallow my own vomit than eat any more of —" His traitorous stomach interrupted him, rumbling loudly. "I *refuse* —" Rumble, growl, and rumble. "I simply *cannot* —" More rumbling and groaning.

In conclusion, his obdurate eyes performed obeisance to the bothersome bowl and the ravenous spoon scraped it clean all the while under the astonished watch of his audience.

The exterminated Enya enjoyed a brief wake before Edmunda tossed her feathery corpse into a bucket, declaring she would make that night's sup. Upon hearing this, Edith performed a near about-face, eyeing her askance, and with a very indignant-sounding ba-gawk, she wrested free of Elizabeth's grasp and bolted for the yard as fast as her little drumsticks could convey her.

Talk of gruel was dropped, and Emil's travels were taken up.

It was all storms, lightning, and foolhardy sheltering under trees. There he found a stray dog, as terrified of God as himself, which he had brought back with him. "Oh, and I bumped into Johannes' manservant." The consignment the servant had been sent to collect were the usual expensive and dusty items. "I don't know why Johannes sends him here and there to fetch those fancy things, which he says are worth more than all his servants' lives."

Though Edmunda agreed how frivolous it was to be sent traipsing about for such vain luxuries — perhaps forgetting the chair she presently sat on was a gift from Johannes' son — she was more interested in the dog. It seemed to please her well to lean that upon arriving in Bubendorf it leapt from the wagon and chased a rabbit over a hill, never to return.

"The Swiss Guard were all over Bern," went on Emil, "hunting an outlaw," who, a sotted lower ranking guard had let slip, was likely behind a plot to murder the Bernese schultheiss. Edmunda asked if there was a reward. While glancing somewhat oddly at Peter, Emil said the WANTED posters offered one thousand batzen. "I brought one with me," said he, at which he hastened out of the kitchen, leaving an interlude of suspense in his wake.

He returned, clutching not a crisp proclamation, but a sodden, pulpy mess. The ink, once bold and accusatory, had bled across the page in an indecipherable blur, transforming the outlaw's fearsome visage into a grotesque smudge. The afore-related storm had, it seemed, conspired to grant our hero a temporary reprieve, cloaking his identity in a shroud of watery obfuscation.

Immediately, Edmunda bemoaned the spoilt poster and lamented the blackguard came not to their village so she could haul his carcass off to the garrison to claim her booty. "But why d'you stare so at Peter?" said she to her son.

"His face..." answered Emil with a dubious look. Needless to say, it would have seemed impossible for his sister's lover to have been the very 'wanted fugitive' himself. "No matter. 'Tis naught..."

Deeming whatever had snared Emil's fancy beneath his own interest, Peter, in his amnesiac state, found his mind wander off, fixing on an empty sixth chair at the table and the bowl of gruel before it. "You await another guest?" said he to no one in particular as he signalled the chair and bowl.

While most fell silent and turned grave of face, Elizabeth, evincing in her own aspect a share of disquiet, whispered she would explain another time.

***

Several weeks had passed. No sooner did the physician declare Peter was fit to be removed to a chamber of his own than Edmunda led him outside to one. "I'm sure," said she, all sweetness and courtesy, "you'll find it comfortable enough."

Incidentally, Edith — the testy hen — stood central to the yard, seemingly tapping her middle claw upon the dirt, as though staring down Peter. As if *this* was not odd enough, her feathered comrades gathered about her, clucking minaciously as though they, too, were caballing some sinister scheme.

"And here we are!" Edmunda beamed widely.

However eager for privacy and a respite from Matron Edmunda, incredulity and astonishment chased each other about Peter's brain. For some moments, he could neither look at her nor make a reply. But at length: "What derangement" said he, "could have possessed you to bring me to this — *this...*" Words he could not conjure for the ghastly barn that rose before him.

"*Oh,*" cooed Edmunda. "'Tis not suitable for you?"

Peter looked at her with so disapproving an air not to be mistaken.

"*Oh,*" cooed she again. "Perhaps I have something better. Follow me."

Taking this as a happy omen, he followed. *Mayhap she is not so unhinged after all?*

Alas, how quickly can one's hopes be thoroughly dashed.

"I think," said she, nodding at the pigs, "you'll find the company apt to your temper."

Small wonder that Peter's head wobbled. Again, he had no words to answer the despot with, who, curtsying and stifling her laughter, asked if "Her Lord" preferred the barn to the pigsty. For certain, interpreting his silence as the wretched grief she sought to inspire, and knowing he would choose the barn, she led him back thither and pointed out a ladder that ascended to a loft. "The heat rising from the animals will keep you warm. Now settle yourself in."

Whether stupefaction or antipathy most assailed Peter's brain, I cannot say, but on realising he was in fact not in one of those dreams termed nightmares, he turned to lambast the madwoman, only to find she had already vanished.

Upon gaining the loft, he inverted the occasion, likening the ladder not to that of the Biblical Jacob but to Dante's inferno — a contrast he now wondered how he knew of — for whether he went up or down the rickety rungs, one damnable fate was traded merely for another. The gloomy space, barely lit by a small aperture, presented a creaky wood floor dusted with hay; a rumpty rocking chair; rude stool; rusty washboard; and a mangle, which, in giving it an experimental turn, he caught a finger. Three rusty bedpans protruded from beneath a small bed draped with threadbare blankets, upon which, despondent, he sank.

"This *cannot* be my life." The horrid hay mattress crunched beneath him. "Why do I feel such unease? And Peter? That name just so *ill-befits* me."

Beside him lay the liveries and his sack. Desperate for some crumb of history, he again emptied out the sack: blood-stained silk cravat; black wool breeches; brown fustian waistcoat — this time, an ornate silver pocket watch fell from a pocket. *How did I miss this?* Its lid was dented; its engravings obscured: "Val —?" *Whose is this?* With difficulty, he pried it open: shattered glass covered the dial; a damaged watercolour of some unfamiliar woman claimed the lid's inside. *And who is this?*

Alas, that black vault of his mind yielded nothing to his recollection; neither did he spot the slight bulge within the sack's lining (a bulge, dear reader, caused by the scroll). He was lost in a repellent world. A prisoner to a loathsome existence. And now relegated to a disgusting barn, abandoned and alone and —

"Mooooooo!"

"Buk, buk, buk, ba-gawk!"

Good lord, no!

"Baaaaaaaa!"

"This is Hell itself!"

"Maaaaaaa!" answered the cheeky goat.

"When my memory returns, perhaps I will find I had a better life? Yes! And if not, I shall make it so. But what about now? Am I to linger in this loft?"

No! Tomorrow, after breakfast, he would go in search of his *true* history.

Evening quickly arrived, and exhaustion having overtaken him, he resigned himself to the lumpy mattress and sank into a fitful slumber...

A vast hall pulsed, a blur of lords, ladies, and faces that swam with an unsettling familiarity. As Peter pushed through the throng, clutching a weighty document, a vice-like grip clamped onto his arm. Steel flashed — swords swung at his neck. A harsh voice clawed at his ears: "Arrest this traitor! At once!"

The scene shattered. Iron, cold and absolute, bit into his wrists, chaining him within a lightless, suffocating cell; leering eyes burned through the bars. An explosion — sound and pressure. Then, a figure coalesced from the gloom: "You must finish what you started! Do not forsake your duty!"

Peter jerked awake with a gasp, his heart thrashing, clouds of dust swirling about him in the gloomy loft. *What a strange dream! Arrest? Duty?*

"The only duty I have is to *quit* this *wretched* place!"

***

Far too early the next morn, the accursed cockerel's serenading — nay, screaming — at the sun's return did jolt him from an insufficient sleep. And neither was his day about to improve thenceforth. First, a pounding headache beset his brain. Second, he battled the innumerable cruel emotions poking at his heart. Third, in descending the ladder, ere he reached the bottom, his foot slipped, and he fell — nay, flew — onto the dung heap.

Easy it is to feel his rage as he clambered up, only to slip back down while the turkeys gobbled, Edith clucked, and, in fine, the entire animal mob ganged against him, revelling in vengeful triumph, clucking, gobbling, mooing, maa-ing, ba-gawk-ing, and baa-ing.

In presenting himself thus at the chalet, so great was Edmunda's shock — for her hands caught her gasp — a *whole six seconds* expired before she regained her tongue, and then the broom, which had, in that gasp, fallen from her grasp. Calling him the stupidest there ever was, she chased him off, threatening dire punishment should he dare sully her threshold again.

Aghast and choking at the chilly air, Peter demanded to know where the water closest was. But Edmunda, darting at him her hell-fire gaze, flung inside, yelling he would not stink out her privy, and returned with a rag, which she flung at him, ordering him to go bathe in the lake.

Wishing not to expose our hero to further ignominy, we shall pass over the undignified ablutions in the frigid lake scene and proceed to the next, where, at the breakfast table, he declares he now knows he *cannot* be Peter.

"When I first emerged from Morpheus' realm into this hell," said he, "she" — he pointed a stinky finger at Elizabeth — "enquired of my name and origins as if I were a total stranger."

With a blush, Elizabeth replied she had but wished to probe his state of mind. With a huff, Peter stood up and, taking several steps away, back kept on his auditors, insisted they speak his name aloud. This they dutifully performed; several times, too, much to their befuddlement.

"You *see*?!" With great triumph, he pivoted on them. "Surely, if I *were* this 'Peter', I should have turned at the very first mention of that name?"

Needless to relate, all at the table exchanged looks rife with satire and reminded him that, in his having no memory, he made no sense at all.

Nettled by their logic, he now pulled out the timepiece and challenged his name on the pretext of its partial engravings — to which a reddening Lizzie swiftly said it was likely a relative's watch. Further nettled by this plausible account, Peter avowed anew his indelible aversion to a proposed union, of which he had no recollection, and his intent on quitting so alien a sphere.

With some nettled looks of her own, Edmunda vowed to hunt him to the ends of the world, should he dare try to flee.

Beyond Peter's sullen return to the table, and his questioning afresh that empty chair and extra bowl — about which Elizabeth whispered into his ear concerned her eldest brother — naught else of note transpired.

Let us then move along to see what came of Peter's great escape.

Come mid-afternoon, we find the ill-starred defector once more retreated to his loft. Thwarted at every turn by the broom-wielding Fury who so effectually guarded all exits, Peter did believe her to be the three-headed Cerberus incarnate. Moreover, this odious woman-hound was bent not only on shackling him to the underworld but had the brass to impose upon him hard labour.

"I will perform no such *vile* thing!" Had Peter the thunderbolt of Zeus, he would gladly have dropped it on Edmunda's head. "Go into the fields? In this *bitter* cold? Do it yourself!"

Fortunate it is that Edmunda had not in her vehement leer the abracadabra of Medusa, else our vainglorious hero would verily have found himself cast into a most unbecoming pose, crashing through the boards under the weight of his own vanity. Nonetheless, with all the vengeance of Nemesis, Edmunda, broom in hand, did charge the ladder, at which our hero, borrowing of Apollo's foresight and divining what would occur should she ascend it, expeditiously drew it up beyond her grasp. Further enraged at the "lazy, good-for-nothing" and "undeserving of her daughter" for "deserting her as a cuckoo would its young", Edmunda vowed she would "spare him the trouble of fleeing" and pitch him over the gate herself.

That Peter refused to come down until she desists her unpardonable tyrannies, Edmunda swore she would, if need be, stay where she was all night and starve the ingrate out.

"What?" Peter stood wide; chest puffed out. "You would not dare!"

"*Wouldn't* I?" Since Peter was as stubborn as she was determined, she spoke shrewdly. "Tis a pity you're bent on dying aloft. I roasted the ham... to celebrate you getting better..."

At this, Peter's hands did form a happy clasp of anticipation. "You *did*?"

"Yes," smiled she. "Though 'tis a pity, too, you're so loath to labour..."

Like the bound-at-noonday Proteus of old — sans knowledge of the past or future — our hero returned to a form his captor could more easily persuade. He lowered the ladder and descended it, stipulating she had won his compliance solely out of consideration for his own health and for the ham going to waste.

To the toolshed she led him and, passing him a hammer and nails, took him to the afore-threatened field. Here, to the many fallen rails and several naked posts she now pointed. Then, eyeing him doubtfully, she left him to it.

"How difficult can this be?" said Peter, knowing not where to begin.

Incidentally, back at the chalet, a visitor called. "Jago." Edmunda curtsied, ogling the hamper presently passed into her grabbing hands. "How very good to see you, my lord."

"The pleasure is ever my own." The benefactor wiped his hessians before following her inside, whereupon she put the hamper on the kitchen table and said she had no tea to offer him. "It would appear that Providence whispered into my ear," answered he, directing her to a replenishment tucked just inside the hamper.

This nobleman, Jago (Johannes' son), the bringer of tea, furniture, and other goods, was a man of around thirty and of an uncommonly handsome appearance. Having descended from an ancient family — von der Mühll; saddler and shoemaker merchants; masters of the trade, grown wealthier in the cotton and silk trade — his carriage, manners, and understanding were those precisely to be expected from one of elevated rank.

Notwithstanding the prohibition of patricians using their titles in this canton, this dissuaded not the von der Mühlls from asserting their pedigree in whatever way they could. And this son, seemingly assiduous to exert his influence for the welfare of the poorer families of the village, thus visited frequently to curry their pleasure.

There being several loose seams in his finest suit, and his preferred tailor being gone abroad, Jago stated he would send his valet round with it later that day for Edmunda's expert attention. Ever eager to be of help *and be paid for it*, she insisted he sit in her chair (that earlier gift from Jago). With ingratiating smiles, she served the brew in her finest porcelain (another largesse from Jago) before seating herself unnecessarily close to apprise him of the latest goings on.

"A lover?" Jago slowly stirred his tea. "And he has *lost* his memory?"

"Yes," tutted she. "But if you only heard his haughty tongue. You'd think his life was *never* in any danger. And I'm certain he believes *us* obliged for *his* staying here."

Jago balanced the spoon on his saucer. "Indeed?"

"He's set on abandoning poor Lizzie — treats her like the plague. I don't know where he thinks he can go; he doesn't remember a soul. Besides, nobody would have him; even if they were bribed!"

Elizabeth presently entered. She blushed and curtsied. "Jago."

"What in the world d'you see in him?" interrupted Edmunda as she rose from the table and stalked to the window. "*Now* what's he doing?!" Trying Peter was, every which way, to fix the rails to the posts, only for the tacks, the hammer, or all, to come repeatedly crashing down and more oft than not on his feet. "I know the Lord said let not our right hand know what the left is doing, but I wonder if he's done a day's graft his whole life?"

She opened the casement and shouted, "Peter! Peter! ... PETER!?"

But no reply came.

Thus, apron wrenched away and flung onto the table, she stormed out, seizing upon our hero from behind. "Why don't you answer when I call?"

"Why?" Peter made a face at her. "Is it not obvious? I still *cannot* get used to *that* name."

With a laugh, she poked him hard. "And *I* still can't get used to *you*!"

Meantime, Jago asked Elizabeth about her lover.

Having suffered too much of his temper and insults, she instantly declared him an ungrateful, conceited, egotistical, insolent, uncivil, and infuriating pig. "I wish I could send him back to his family!"

With a quizzical brow, Jago queried why she therefore still considered him for her future husband. Elizabeth did colour condemningly but insisted Peter had not shown such churlishness ere his mishap. Head titled in thought, forefinger circling his mouth, Jago asked if she had yet received word from his family. Eyes averted and hands folded, she said it had slipped her mind — quick to add that with Peter being bereft of all memory, and though she had tried every manner of question to spark his memory, "'tis impossible to write them."

Jago now enquired of his canton. Though ignorant of it, Lizzie, after another condemning flush of the cheeks, gave the very distant Republic of Geneva.

Edmunda burst in — naturally stealing all attention — huffing, puffing, and pulling at her hair.

Turning from her, Jago offered to write Geneva's Council on Elizabeth's behalf. Lizzie's colour did indeed rise and fall several times. She thanked him, but, with a tremulous voice, insisted she would take care of it herself.

"And be quick about it, too!" squawked Edmunda. "I should verily like to know *who* gave him that temper and *who* his stupidity?"

Perhaps to moderate the palpable, crackling tension and to alleviate Elizabeth's discomfort, Jago turned the talk to his recent jaunt out of the canton. "Here is something for you; November last, while I sojourned on Lake Thun, a great tumult erupted at Oberhofen Castle; tall flames and loud explosions. Gunten was all a frenzy; Swiss Guard everywhere in pursuit of some villain, who, I am certain, collided with me in his escape, almost felling me to the ground."

Though still heartily distracted by her vexations with Peter, Edmunda, all huffs, puffs, and frequent tutting, eagerly avowed the fiend, when found, should be clapped in irons and carted off to a land far away.

"On another note," continued Jago, "Bern and Zürich seem to have since fallen on very bad terms — with France in the mix, too! Something to do with a devilish fugitive. The fanatic won't be able to hide forever! It will be all over the press soon. My father tells me the animosity has already escalated to —"

A red-faced Peter now burst in, blood dripping from one finger and a splinter sticking out of another. "What *torture* must I endure for a strip of ham?!" He flared his nostrils at Edmunda and turned to implore Elizabeth but now remarked the man so ill-suited to so indigent a habitation, fashioned after the baroque-style in blue, gold, and vermilion, finery. "Pray, and who are you, sir?"

Jago rose to speak, but Peter put his injured hand up to him. "You are come to rescue me from this *bocardo*?" His chest filled out with every atom of melancholy kitchen air. "To reinstate me to the life that I am *certain* awaits me?"

Jago's brow did slowly form a perfect arch of bemusement. "Pardon?"

Peter moved towards him. "You are a relative, perhaps?" Stepping back, Jago said he was not. "Friend?" tried our hero. Again, no. "Saviour?" persisted Peter. Jago shook his head. "Liberator, at the very least? For why else would a man of irrefutable elegance choose to call upon so impecunious a family?"

"I am sorry," said Jago, coolly, "but I *do not* know you."

Peter did fling himself most dramatically into a chair. "Oh! *Treacherous* folly!" He clawed at his temples. "Oh! *Poisonous* poniard!" He gestured emphatically. "What god has cursed me with this plight!" He clenched his fists. "Is not this Hell itself? And that woman there..." gritting his teeth, he pointed his bloodied finger at Edmunda, "... the very Devil herself! And you, sir," — he now flung himself at Jago's feet — "are not you an angel? If not an angel, then a saint? If not a saint, then a ... I *beseech* you! Release me from this purgatory!"

However poetic this overripe diatribe, inspiring in Jago's countenance intrigue and bewilderment, Edmunda's bulging eyes did dart at her broom. Observing this, Elizabeth gathered Peter up and urged him away to her chamber, where she would attend to him and bind up his finger.

"And be sure to bind up that unmannerly tongue of his, too!" shrilled Edmunda. "Why he refuses to bow to his betters and speaks like a noble, yet acts the very rascal, I can't fathom!"

At this remark, Peter's feet did stop abruptly at the door. "A noble, you say?" He spun around. "Of course! I *must* be a patrician!" His heart and cheeks burned with conviction. "But, from which illustrious family do I descend?"

Seeing the fiery magma diffuse its warning across her mother's ballooning cheeks, Elizabeth flew to the door and shoved Peter into the hallway. "*Go*!"

Soon after, with boiled water, vinegar, a cloth, and a dressing, Elizabeth followed and found Peter slouched on her bed, silent and lugubrious.

She sat beside him and asked for his hand. So distrait was he, however, she had to reapply for it. But again, receiving still not his hand, she took it.

As she cleaned and bound the wounded finger, she appeared to note how soft and uncalloused his hands were. Visibly surprised, she took hold of his other, discovering the same absent signature of toil and industry.

By gradatim, our hero lost in a maelstrom of misery, did now recover the use of his senses. Seeing his hands held by hers in so toweringly inappropriate a way, he yanked them away. "What *insolence* is this?" He sprang off the bed. "How *dare* you touch me so, so — you *adventurer*! You *siren*!"

Edmunda and Jago came rushing in. "What's the matter now?" demanded the former.

"*Your* daughter!" Peter stabbed his freshly bound, however accusatory, finger at our heroine. "An *audacious* seductress! Fondling my hands as though — though they were... *kittens*!" He glared at a trembling, uneasy white Elizabeth. "I have already forbidden you from laying even a finger on me until my memory returns!"

13 – 21 JANUARY 1792

In such circumstances as these, it is to be expected that misunderstandings can arise. Believing a parental obligation upon them, Ernest and Edmunda congregated in the tool shed to confer on what was to be done.

An oddity had overcome Elizabeth's temper since Peter's arrival, agreed they. She seemed more awkward than joyous. Was she hiding something?

Given the lovers' long separation, 'twas likely they had entered — pray, not clandestine — assignations. Then again, that Peter was so clearly possessed of antipathy towards flirtation, they believed whatever his temper, vanity, and other deficiencies, he must be of some merit. That said, since he lacked his memories, who knew what principles he had forgotten?

Edmunda next perplexed over Elizabeth reading novels of virtuous heroines, yet being so remiss to hazard her own respectability. Ernest pondered her education, particularly of the Holy writings, praying no defiant spirit had entered her heart. Finally, moving onto Peter's gift for brattish grandiloquence, they worried he had possibly filled Elizabeth's ears with persuasive poetry that might inflame certain passions. Thus, our two pastoral philosophers could not help take this as a portent they should have sooner perceived.

In turn, desirous of hazarding no further impropriety which might stain their own reputations, they fixed on tackling the lovers that evening.

***

Only after much importuning did Peter and Elizabeth agree to being in the same room, and dinner was finally served, the ham speedily relished, the plates cleared away, and the rebels accordingly dealt with.

While Edmunda, broom in hand, shooed Lizzie to her bedchamber, Ernest bade Peter to remain at the table. Kitchen door closed, he hesitantly began his avuncular homily, approving the promise of morality which had, all the same, occasioned their present interview.

"And this wholesome advice," said he, "I hope will prompt a swift soberness, lest the omen lose its force." Citing the Divine texts on chastity and prudence, he claimed had his wife admonished him, "she would advocate the harsh doctrines of Catholic tradition." He, however, being Protestant, would apostle only the discipline of the Christ. Next, he illuminated the Divine's provisions for they who intentionally or not take a step to the right or to the left: "Best not to err. But if tempted to mortal sin, always confess directly to God."

Concurrently, Edmunda upbraided Elizabeth with every Catholic condemnation, insisting had her father (in this instance, Ernest) spoken to her, she'd not have the advantage of the full weight of her guilt. "If you ask me, *and* the Pope, these Protestants forgive too indulgently." Likewise, she addressed confessions: "Always unbosom to me, then your Father," (in this instance, Father Francis) "but never directly to God, lest you offend his ears and he strikes you down with his fiery bolts! And remember, like Mary, mother knows best; not your father," (in this instance, Ernest) "so, you'd better listen!"

"This isn't what my wife, or any Catholic, would have you believe," continued Ernest, "but only Jesus mediates. Ask nicely, and he'll pass your prayers to the Almighty, who forgives generously; as He did wicked King Manasseh."

Neither was Edmunda done. Professing a wish to inspire penitence and to show God's impartiality, she told the woeful tales of Uzza, a presumptuous stubborn king dethroned for his irreverence, and the misbegotten wench at the local inn, rendered loathsome by her canoodlings. "The both of them, driven out from the camp of the righteous; the one with leprosy and the other infamy!"

And she was quick to add: "You ought to take this as a warning from Heaven!" And: "You ought to get down on your knees begging forgiveness of your Father," (in this instance, Father Francis) "before dreaming of your lover getting down on his!" And: "You ought to thank Providence your reputation, not your neck, was nearly fractured!" And, averring such a fate was reserved for her for some future occasion, she added with stinging emphasis: "Had you been in the wilderness with Moses, you'd already be six-feet under a pile of stones!"

Returning to Ernest: at long length did he arrive at his peroration and reprimand all who pursue carnal pleasures, Protestant or Catholic, stating all debauched paths led to the same fiery hell of impenitents. Back to Edmunda: in this tenet she agreed with her husband: should the daughter not better behave, she'd verily end up in the same red-hot cauldron as Peter.

***

Sleep did bring Peter again to the boisterous bird bursting upon his hearing. He sat up rigidly — the prior evening's admonishments still raging in his recollection. "It is insupportable that such indigents dare hold so ill an opinion of me." More fixed than ever that his origins must be as far from this hellhole as Heaven, he resolved to remove this stain against his character before leaving.

Scarcely had the last scraping of gruel entered Ernest's mouth when Peter began authoritatively: "The reproof which, last night, you felt so pertinent to impose upon me, behoves me to counterstrike in my defence!" Natch, every eye fixed on him. "I know not what the general code of conduct is for such an establishment as *this*, but I assure you, I possess no proclivity for such exploits which warrant the censure of my conduct."

Ernest finally swallowed his gruel and might have answered, but Peter put a hand up to him. "And I am not less certain that my parents, could I but remember them, have *rigorously* instructed and fashioned me in the elegances contrary to debauchery."

Brow crooked, he slid his eye towards Elizabeth, who gasped as all stared her way.

"Such fine speeches, indeed," now said Edmunda, while admitting she understood not the half of his lofty phrases. "Whoever birthed you, did *poorly* to let you prate so fancy or blame others for your own bad conduct. But if you're set on clearing your good name, you can start so with the cow."

Our hero did demand his business with the bovine. Edmunda did explain should he wish to drink any more milk, then he has a business with the bucket. Rising in a huff, Peter readily confessed he would soon drink his milk elsewhere. At this, Edmunda too stood, and a clash erupted. Elizabeth soon rose in her mother's defence and urged her father and brother to take up family arms. Seeing the knave outnumbered, Edmunda cried victory and demanded his surrender.

But pride forbade defeat. "While I appreciate that your reason is not less desolate than this table wasteland which separates us," boldly declared our hero, "let me be clear; superiority, madam, should never bow to its inferiors!"

Consequently, the designated inferior now sought recourse to artillery. Barely had Edmunda swung her broom on its first revolution when Peter cursed the Trojan horse in his treasonous lover, remarked that he lacked spear, helmet, or shield, and chose flight over defying the Achaean and meeting his death — like Hector, Deiphobus, and Paris. Thus, pride abandoned to the foe, he flung out of the cabin, trailed by the cannonry milk bucket, which, discharged with such prowess as to strike not his heel but his head, sent forth a church bell-like knell as it felled him, face-first, to the mud.

So, yet another setback to Peter's taking to his heels. As the day wore on, swellings and sharp pangs plagued his battered skull. But by gradatim, overcome by extreme mental lassitude, he fell under the spell of slumber and, transported to that enchanted realm, where reality and fancy intertwine, now enjoyed an interlude, albeit an odd one, perfectly disparate to his present state:

A yawn, a stretch; our hero opened his eyes to a lavish bedchamber and a valet attending. "Ludwig! Oh! Happy Ludwig! Such a ghastly dream I had!"

Soon dressed in the finest of finery and hailed "Lord" by the happy Ludwig did feel oh! So restorative...

Two lofty golden doors swung wide; he stood atop a rivulet staircase, down which he skipped — nay, splashed — to a luxuriant red carpet, leading to an elegant equipage of extravagant equines and exquisitely attired footmen.

Inside, he sprang, finding a most elaborate hall of a most magnificently appointed assembly, all bowing and curtsying. Oh! Such harmony...

Coruscating crystal ware drew him to a table laden with wondrous feasts. There, before his hungry eyes, did sparkle slices of veal, braised in white wine and cream with mushrooms — entrée of cutlets in fricandeau!

Salivating, he scooped a serving; yet barely had it touched his lips when, oh cruel trickery! It became naught but gruel! Which he flung away in dismay!

He reached for a tantalising thigh of roasted fowl. Alas! The rascal sprang to its legs and, ba-gawking, flapped featherless wings and flew away!

Next, a scintillating bowl of ground veal, fluffed up in a flaky pastry crust — entrée tourte! He tried for this, too, but beer jugs raised with applause, and bottled champagne shook, shooting off corks, torrents rained down upon him. A mass of Swiss Guard and pretty barmaids saluted a glistening guillotine, through which fowls, bedecked in frippery and donning tiaras and crowns, leapt to a lively Ländler as the blade went up and down, up and down ...

"Tick-Tock. Tick-Tock," swung the huge pendulum of a golden clock.

"Valentin?" came a voice from behind.

Hearing his name — his true name — he turned, excited, to a Versailles-clad maidservant, who, in a blink, became a foul pitchfork-wielding goblin; who, in the next, a manservant — "your carriage, sir"— who became Ludwig, handing over a weighty document — "Godspeed, be careful, Viktor will be enraged" — who became a masked ruffian; who became the wicked Edmunda, flinging our hero into a prison wagon, which became a bridal chamber bedecked with gown and trousseau, crashing off a precipice —

Gasping and sweating tremendously, Peter jolted awake.

"What a frightfully *grotesque* dream...!"

That a storm presently raged above, he discerned the applause was but the rain pelting the roof and the champagne but the downpour penetrating its cracks and sprinkling his face.

***

The night being now fully passed, the cockerel screamed, and Peter awoke, taxed with hate, resentment, hostility, revenge, and what was most distracting, a still very much throbbing head. Knowing not what further injuries might befall him, he resolved to march forthwith to the garrison and bring his violent afflicter to justice ere fleeing this blackest hell on earth.

By-the-by, the milk-bucket colliding with his head resounded so like the church bell, it beguiled the pigs into believing their owners had gone off to worship. Out of the sty came they a-charging, as was their wont each Sunday, eager to dig up and gobble down Edmunda's crops and plantings. But espying Peter a-fallen and she in the doorway, they turned full about with all the speed their conniving little hooves could carry them — but again, I digress.

As Peter hastily stowed his regimentals, warily watching the barn entrance for his persecutor, his fingers caught on a slit in the sack's lining. Probing it, he discovered a pocket and pulled out a crumpled parchment bearing a fragmented emblem. "G.V.V.?"

Rightly connecting this to his lost past, hope did rekindle in his soul; his pulse roared as he unfurled the creased scroll with trembling impatience.

> *My faithful friend. Trust every word of this grave despatch, and believe still in the consonance of its inscriber and our alliance being neither diminished nor tainted according to the mendacity which will soon reach you. Do not —*

The next sentences were, because of watermarks, wholly illegible; as were in part the last:

> *— — — we are for preserv — the regime and not ab — doning —.*
> *Therefore, I beseech —, send urgently your — to defend and not destroy us. I fear for my l—, — if anything should happen to me, know that my last request is to the raven: release the dove.*
> *Your faithful, unwavering ally Gu — — —*

"Finally!" Peter's heart pounded. "Something of my past." Utterly confounded, his every thought of fleeing did vanish. "I *must* show Lizzie."

No sooner had he exited the barn than he collided with her, barely catching her up in his arms before she struck the dirt. For a very brief moment, they were rather charmingly framed, faces a few inches apart, staring askance. Yet as quickly aware they both were of so romantic a posture, Peter, first to redress it, did let go and she fell to her backside to the earth.

Visibly more concerned for her pride than her soiled garments, Elizabeth clambered to her feet. "I was come to ask after your injury?"

"Never mind that, see here!" He waved the scroll before her. "It was secreted inside my sack. What think you of its message?"

She took and read it; her eyes stretched with astonishment. "Heavens!"

She gave him an incredulous look. "What a message!" And re-reading: "Frustrating; the signature is blotted out."

"Look." Peter showed her the seal. "G.V.V. — the emblem, is it not?"

Scrutinising it, she concurred. "Does this stir any memories?"

"Regrettably not." An impatient sigh escaped him. "Oh, the cruelty! To possess such a clue and be yet still bereft of all recollection. What ought I do?"

"Come. We must take it to the Liestal garrison. I shall ready the cart."

***

At some small distance from the chalet, the red roofs and brown gables of Bubendorf village sprawled in a disorderly way across a meandering basin confined by turfed slopes and forested hills heavy with orchards and vine crops.

None of it, though, stirred in our hero even a flicker of recognition.

At the Liestal garrison, despite every plea, neither the korporal sat at his desk nor the man-at-arm at his side could make any more of the cryptic scroll than Peter himself. They agreed only on its apparent urgency and to send word to the main garrisons of each canton.

"But the seal!" Peter jabbed a finger at it. "Do you not recognise it?"

Since countless gentlefolk might share those initials, it was deemed impossible to trace this unknown author. Thus, dejected at this dead-end, knowing nothing of the unknown author, nor any more of his own history, Peter turned to take his leave with Elizabeth.

At that moment, several guards rushed in yelling for aid: a schloss was attacked in the night; its patrician family fled; now rioters mobbed another nobleman trapped inside his coach in Liestal's square.

"Let us away quickly," whispered Elizabeth, taking Peter's arm.

"You there!" came the korporal's voice. "A volunteer guard, you say?"

Peter turned in surprise. "Me? Yes. But why?"

***

"Down with the aristocratic tyranny!" chanted the fist-waving, crude-implement wielding mob — aprons askew and breeches dust-stained — as they pressed upon a detachment guarding with difficulty the aforementioned patrician inside his stranded carriage; the horses were nowhere to be seen.

The korporal ordered the reinforcements and a trembling, bayonet-holding Peter to force their way through the mob. That the masses refused them passage, the korporal fired his musket skyward, scattering the rabble momentarily for the unit to hustle through as ordered.

Upon reaching the carriage, Peter rather hid behind the guards; but the korporal shoved him forward. "Hold the line, men!" bellowed he as the mob, now chanting a protest song against tithes and taxes, charged again.

Faced by a phalanx of bitter, frothing faces, Peter pointed his bayonet at which rough hands seized it, nearly wrenching it away. A face streaked with dirt and desperation begged for an end to the toil which enriched only the nobles.

"You overstep yourself!" rasped Peter before realising it. "Get back! Consider how generously the elite have provided you work and land."

These words, somehow heard over the screams, only stoked the crowd's fury. A hammer crashed against a soldier's morion. Swords and scythes clashed. Rocks and debris filled the air.

Amid the swelling tumult, an equally chaotic vision seized Peter's mind: darkness; claustrophobic confinement; a violent clatter of steels; soldiers in familiar red and white battling bandits beyond the bars; chained to a wall, he could not escape. *What is this?*

Overwhelmed by terror and confusion, his limbs failed him; as his mind spun, a stone glanced off his temple, and he crashed to the earth...

***

Back at the kitchen table, a silent Peter, gloomily stirring his cold gruel, nursed his pounding brain and bemused over so frightful a remembrance. In his stead, Lizzie related their fruitless errand, the scroll's mysterious contents, and the events at the town square. Her tale quite begat astonishment in the listeners towards Peter. The scroll implied great trust in him. The call to arms painted him as heroic. These circumstances did naturally conspire against their better judgement of his character and capabilities; of which a still sceptical Edmunda hoped to soon see better displayed in whatever tasks she would henceforth assign him.

Furthermore, the very same korporal who sent Peter to his near death had further appropriated his present idleness and want of employment. Orders had arrived from Bern for a small contingent to meet a Bernese detachment at the cantonal borders. A convoy of ammunitions were being sent to Basel city, along with a stash of certain WANTED posters for distribution across the canton; the assigned contingent was to escort the convoy the rest of the way from the border.

This commission was set for the very next day.

Easily, we may deduce the perils attendant upon such a journey.

And so, speeding the narrative along, the light of dawn had barely brushed the horizon when our hero, garbed once more in martial regalia — his bayonet gleaming faintly in the cold morning air — marched resolutely towards the Solothurn border that marked the gateway to Bern canton.

A crisp air clung to his skin, heavy with a strange portent. The previous day with its ordeals had possibly unlocked some fragment of his past. But again, what? Why was he chained as if a common criminal or captive? Was that even him or someone else? Certainly, where before the scroll had served to illuminate the tenebrosity of his past, a darker shadow now stole over it, filling him with dread. He bore with him a nameless apprehension, a shadowy whisper skimming the edges of his thoughts.

Across the ground, a pallid mist curled like ghostly fingers about the gnarled roots of the trees lining the forest path. The birds were silent; even the rustling of the wind seemed subdued, as if the very earth itself held its breath.

Glancing up at the korporal, who rode alongside, Peter noted in his stern features how his eyes scanned the horizon with the vigilance of a hawk. Riding beside the korporal, an attendant spoke in low tones, fractures of which caught our hero's hearing: "... the fugitive... wanted... posters..." A more distinct tone uttered oaths and vows of bringing the wanted fugitive to justice at all costs — even if delivering the scoundrel onto the edge of his sword.

Stirred strangely by these words, and encountering a visceral, almost magnetic pull, Peter asked of the attendant what was known about said fugitive. Not without first reiterating his determination to find and deliver the dastardly villain to the authorities, did the man aver that he was, according to reliable intelligence, not only the very cause of the disharmony between Bern and Zürich

— even going so far as to have attempted to blow up the Bernese schultheiss — but had colluded with French revolutionaries in an attempted coup.

To be sure, an inexplicable anxiety and unease instantly seized upon our hero's breast. The sensation was of such potency that, while attributing it to an innate sense of injustice, even he could not help but second the attendant's oaths and vowed to personally hunt down the miscreant himself!

At length, the party reached the borderlands, where the forests gave way to rolling hills and the faint outlines of a Bernese watchpost appeared through the fog. Here, the detachment and contingent were to rendezvous.

But what greeted them was a scene not of martial expectation but ghastly desolation. The watchpost lay in ruins — smouldering embers hissed where once sturdy timber had stood. Remnants of a fierce struggle lay strewn: shattered muskets, broken halberds, and the twisted wreckage of a once-proud wagon.

Mingled with the breeze, a thick acrid stench of smoke and blood pressed in upon the arriving contingent. A silence, profound and unnatural, hung over the devastation.

The sight was of such hideousness that Peter halted, unable to move. Some moments it took before he regained the use of his limbs and motioned to the korporal, whose face was turned ashen beneath his Basel-patterned helmet, adorned with the canton's insignia.

"What..." tried our hero, "what happened here? Where are the men?"

The korporal's gaze swept the scene. "Gone... all *gone*! Slaughtered!" His eyes fell upon the form of two legs which protruded from behind a shattered palisade. "Ambushed by bandits, no doubt — likely Du Pont's ruffians!" His widened, anger-filled eyes darted wildly about. "And the convoy... *Taken*!"

A cold dread seeped into Peter's bones. Notwithstanding the barbaric slaughter, the knowledge that the WANTED posters, the very means to hunt the fugitive, were lost to this raid struck with a peculiar, almost personal blow.

Just then, upon a sudden gust, a fragmented sheet of scorched paper, as if tossed by some mischievous sprite, tumbled along the ground in our hero's direction. Spotting it, he snatched it up.

'Twas but a burnt remnant, a mere teasing sliver of what was evidently the very top part of a poster. Blood-stained, but in bold letters: WANTED rested above a delineated broad brow and a partial eye — a mocking visage that seemed to leer at our hero with cruel amusement.

Still and all, 'twas a fleeting thread of truth. Peter stuffed the remnant inside his jacket, his fingers curling tightly about it.

***

Two-and-a-half days did suffice to diminish our hero's wretched headache and shrink the monstrous swellings to mere bumps. Deeming him no longer a fright to the Catholic-half of the village, and possibly wishing to show him off, Edmunda insisted he attend Sunday service. Incidentally, having found and kept secret his money purse for reimbursement of his stay, she presented the Sunday clothes she had *graciously* bought for him.

Though not disinclined to hearing the Divine despatches, Peter rather hoped his attendance might bring back to his mind what effort could not — his memories. So, he accorded. Oh! But when inspecting the aforementioned garb later that morn, he found the fabric far too coarse; wove of fustian. The style, far too agrarian. And the colour, mud-brown! This *would not* do!

Off hastened he to the chalet to declare his disgust.

Edmunda was absent from the kitchen.

Perhaps the workroom?

He tried the handle; the door creaked open to two spinning wheels, two chairs, a large table, and cotton-sacks stacked on a tall shelf in the one corner. Still no Edmunda. As he turned to leave, something on the table snared his eye.

Thus enticed, he investigated what was a garment bag woven of a heavy satin damask. Verily, his eyes did suddenly widen. A splendid silk suit, all in the French mode, gleamed within as if graced by celestial light, winking as if to say: "Choose me, *choose me*, and at long last be dressed as the gentleman you know yourself to be!" The double-breasted green-blue frock coat appeared precisely his fit; as did the striped waistcoat and breeches of deepest blue. Compared to the homespun rags that befitted only destruction, there could be but one choice...

Some quarter hour later, our vainglorious hero paraded about the kitchen, quite satisfied with his new finery, when Edmunda entered bearing buckets of potatoes. Espying his brazen theft, she dropped her load, and the spuds scattered every which way. "What are you —?"

"Run along and fetch silk stockings and fine leather shoes," interrupted he, putting a hand up to her. "Only *then* will my ensemble be perfect for church."

Instantly, the virago charged forth. But slipping on the bouncing tubers, and being not of a comely frame, she crashed down with the weight and noise of a cathedral — pans a-swaying, shelves a-rattling, potatoes a-ricocheting underfoot.

Amidst the chaos, our nimble hero likewise lost his footing and he, too, slipped. But with some struggles, they each gained their feet and a merry, albeit unsteady table-circling chase ensued, tossing spuds: Peter, fleet as a hare; Edmunda, lumbering ominously as a bear.

Ere her claws could snag even a strand of the finely woven silks, our hero flung outside into the yard, provoking a pursuance, which generally went:

"Take them off!" — "Not on your life!" — "I'll tear them from your back, you thieving knave!" — "You will need to catch me first!"

This spectacle would have continued had not Peter blundered into a freshly turned vegetable patch and, again losing his footing, upended the order of nature, lending height rather to his heels than his head, and crashed on his back in the mud.

"Quack! Quack! Quack!" went the mocking duck, waddling by.

'Twas soon realised that the filched garb was soiled beyond even Edmunda's formidable powers of remedy. Subsequently, estimating the damages, she castigated the culprit and, seizing him by the ear, dragged him to her workroom, where, under the glaring watch of Elizabeth stoking the hearth, she stipulated he must labour hours on end in penance, spinning wool like the lowliest wretch!

"I shall perform no such *dismal drudgery*!" Peter made for the door.

Edmunda blocked his path. "You've a *ruined suit* to pay for!"

"But had you not *chased me* like a wild boar!"

This retort did choke Edmunda's fury higher! She locked the door, vowing he would not leave the room until he'd spun ten sacks of cotton, and, grabbing a fire poker, swore she would brand him should he again dare refuse.

Consequently, our cornered hero leapt atop the table, once more contending she must catch him first. And so, the circus recommenced; the one brandishing the hot iron and mounting the fortification; the other forced to abandon it.

Across the air, our hero vaulted like a mountain goat onto the shelving and scaled it, crying victory, only for catastrophe to follow. The groaning wood collapsed beneath his weight, sending him a-flying and the cotton sacks cascading downward and across the floor into the:

"Fire!" shrieked the horror-stricken Edmunda and Lizzie.

***

The following morn dawned as gloomy as the smoking embers of Edmunda's workroom. The flames had spread so fast that not only did those ten cotton sacks go up in smoke, but five more.

"How shall we ever repay this loss?" Edmunda's shoulders a-slumped amidst the ruins. The peddler expected two-dozen skeins by month's end — seventeen days away. Failure to deliver would occasion bailiffs and prosecution.

So bitterly disconsolate, she brooded for many a-hour until her ire overcame her gloom. With curses, most unchristian to pen down here, she did scold Elizabeth for entangling herself with the stupidest of men: "Honest? Kind? *Hard-working*?! That's what you told me. I doubt even the Schmutzli could abduct him and bring him back reformed! No! I want him gone immediately!"

Scarce had Elizabeth gone gladly out than Edmunda shouted with great violence for her return, countermanding the rogue to present himself to answer for the damages. Out went Lizzie a second time, though with less gladness in her step, when Edmunda accused herself of want of resolution. She re-summoned her, determined to turn the wicked Peter out. Barely had Lizzie crossed the threshold a third time when the wily spirit Verwirrgeist did whisper doubts into Edmunda's ear; thus, resolve warring with mercy, she called Lizzie once more, demanding to see Peter. But again, Lizzie had not travelled posthaste before Chlungeri (the impish spirit of distraction and confusion) did taunt poor Edmunda without mercy — certainty to uncertainty to rage and back, leaving the woman quite overwrought. Hence, she called Elizabeth back, yet again.

"No! I'll go see Hans," decreed she with fresh vigour. "I'll sooner wed you to that dullard of a farmer's son than this demon from Hell!"

Here, Lizzie did protest, begging she restrain her waverings. "I shall hire him out. Even if he has to work day and night, he will earn back the losses before the close of the month."

Meantime, in the barn, Emil heartily advised Peter to practice kneeling and begging Lizzie for mercy or face sleeping amidst the swine. Natch did prideful Peter refuse, doubting Elizabeth could be so barbaric, whereupon she appeared at the entrance, pitchfork in hand and vehemence on her face. Though indeed unsettled by this sight, an unrepentant Peter still lacked the needed genuflection. But with swift intervention, Emil lodged his foot nicely at the back of Peter's legs, and so went our hero down to his knees on the floor...

***

Though spared the sty, the next days brought new tribulations unto Peter and, by extension, Elizabeth, and Edmunda, too. For wheresoever hired out, our hero returned not with honest wages but only further debts and dues: for neglecting his charge over the cows and refusing to retrieve the truant beasts; for leaving the faucet a-flowing and flooding the fishmonger's store; for locking the blacksmith from his forge and losing the key; for laxity with the baker's stove and burning his bread as black as pitch; and sundry other failures besides.

"He'll ruin us all," shrilled Edmunda after receiving a procession of bitterly angry tradespeople at her door, demanding recompense. "He has that — that — that 'Miners touch'. But all he touches turns only to chaos!"

Had not she herself so despaired at the wastrel who stirred up only mischief and financial catastrophe, Elizabeth would have corrected her mother, for 'twas Midas, not Miners, whose touch turned all to gold. Anyhow, determined to free not the prodigal from his yoke, Lizzie vowed that by fair means or foul, Peter would reimburse each soul he had robbed of peace and prosperity.

At that, out went Lizzie in search of him, finding a somewhat despondent hero slumped on the yard bench, with pocket watch in hand, but his eyes rather staring into a void. No need had she to castigate him, for he had already pondered his litany of failings. Vainly had he rubbed bright the remnant etchings of the timepiece, hoping to summon thence some genie of memory. But no spirit stirring within, he relinquished all recollection as lost and begged she acquaint him with whatever trade he could claim prowess at.

Lizzie did not at first answer him. But having clearly given some thought to his question, she replied, "you once spoke of the pleasure you derived in ploughing, seeding, weeding, chopping wood..." Doubtless, she wished as much to punish him as to unearth any talents he might possess. After studying the yard some more, she resumed listing tasks suited to his penance: "Drawing water, feeding fowl, collecting eggs, milking cows, mucking sties... Yes, things of this nature — Oh! And you claimed to finish a day's work by noon."

"Ah." Mouth-agape, Peter blinked. "But I do not feel I was ever... *good* at these?"

"Mere rust from disuse. Now come... your body will recall soon enough."

Not ten minutes later, a commotion drew Edmunda to the kitchen window: "What's he doing?" muttered she.

Hens harried our mud-spattered hero as he flailed with the seed pail. Ernest suggested he was likely trying to feed their feathered friends.

About another quarter hour passed. "Now *what's* he doing?" shrilled Edmunda. Eggs dropped everywhere; the poultry, in battle formation — rooster vanguard — set upon the luckless fellow anew. Even Elizabeth hurried after him, looking fit to tear out her pretty red locks. "And what's *she* doing?"

Soon after, angry mooing drove Edmunda to the kitchen door. "What *is* he doing *now*?"

The hapless, near to tearful labourer presently fled the cowshed, doused in milk amidst the bovine's displeasure. Noting Peter's swollen pate, Ernest delicately proposed it had acquainted itself with the cow's hoof.

Later still, squeals and snorts announced a swines displeasure at an intruder in their domain. "That *blundering* oaf!" Edmunda raced outside to behold the porcine chaos unleashed upon her yard; Peter lay quite trampled under the disgruntled cloven feet, becoming, in Ernest's gentle phrase, quite plastered in natural bounty.

In drawing water, Peter tumbled into the well. In ploughing the field, he broke the plough. In splitting logs, an errant axe head flew off, beheading poor Erika — Edmunda's third favourite bird and Edith's second-best bosom fowl. Indeed, Edmunda could endure no more folly. "Why d'you encourage his bumbling?" shouted she at Lizzie. "We've proof enough of his uselessness!"

Edmunda lamented this second slain bird (as she had the first). Then snatching up its feathery carcass (again, like the first), she flung it into a bucket, proclaiming it their dinner.

***

"I have to own," said Peter as he rode in the cart with Elizabeth to take the plough to be mended, "axes are *devilishly dangerous* things. I am most definitely cut out for gentler pursuits. Every man has his string to his bow. Though I am astonished that you so *woefully* misapprehended my gifts."

A heavy sigh exuded from Lizzie's nostrils; but no words followed.

"Your silence I find *extremely* vexing," continued Peter.

Now, she replied. "*Everything* about you *I* find *extremely* vexing! What is worse, you persist in your arrogant airs and noble talk. If only a noble you were, your failures would not matter. But we have a debt to pay off — which you caused! How do you intend to recoup such an expense when you are so utterly useless at every task assigned to you?"

Her words cut our hero to the quick. "Do you not think how difficult this is for me? Remembering nothing of my past, my talents, or who I am?" He turned away to hide his hurt. "You ought to soften your strictures."

"*Soften* them? Would to heaven that I could find out whatever you did in the past to have possessed so critical a despatch!"

At this reference, Peter convulsed within.

"Had only my father not plucked you from that ditch!" continued Lizzie. "And had I *not* taken pity on you! You would be somebody else's —" here, she stopped herself.

Peter turned back to her. "Whatever do you mean by that?"

22 JANUARY – 17 FEBRUARY 1792

Sabbath morn being now arrived, and we find our hero, sat on his cot, early in ill-humour looking at the rustic attire he was to suffer at church. But then, spying a small parcel deposited at the top of the ladder, he discovered therein a tolerable double-breasted woollen suit in sage green.

Though not as fine as those silks he had ventured to pilfer, 'twas a marked improvement upon the mud-hued fustian alternative. Beneath, lay respectable white stockings and heeled black leather shoes. Quite amazed at this boon, he could not help but ascribe to Edmunda the motive of an olive branch.

"Does she finally sympathise with my piteous plight?" Again, he eyed the suit. "I shall accept her conciliatory gift."

Arrayed thus in the suit of Edmunda's atonement, he waited outside the chalet to express his approval of her conduct while admiring his reflection in the window. Ernest, Emil, and Lizzie now came out in their Sunday best, smiling. No sooner did Edmunda join the party than her face turned as sour as curdled milk and Peter realised the err of his former reasoning.

"Where did you —?" begun she, but stopping, she turned her nettled looks on Ernest. "This is *your* doing, I'll warrant!"

Certainly, Ernest's reddened face did confess his crime. "'Whoever lends to the poor is lending to the Lord'," tried he quoting scripture but immediately quailed beneath her fury.

More certainly, had it not been the Sabbath, her broom might well have had many a stripe to give. "Let the Devil tend to his own!"

Ignoring her, Peter enquired about the absent wagon; with instant disamusement, he learned it had dislodged a wheel and, consequently, his feet alone would convey him to church. "You expect *me* to *walk*?!" demanded he.

"As does the Lord!" Lizzie further admonished him with narrowed eyes.

He cast his own orbs heavenward and repudiated the Lord could ever be such a tyrant as to allow him to trek like a mule and ruin his new shoes. This response stole away quite a few breaths, less the termagant Edmunda, that is:

"D'you think if the Lord spared not his own gentlefolk forty years' traipsing about a mountain, he'll spare you a few muddy miles? Besides, if I didn't fear your mischief, I'd forbid you coming for the shame you've brought on us!"

***

Beneath a gigantic clock counting down the minutes till that day of fiery damnation, Peter, suppressing a shiver, entered St Blasius Ziefen's lofty portal.

Indeed, the dreary half-lit interior accorded well with that depressive cheer he envisioned common of Edmunda's denomination. Yet 'twas not for sermons of salvation he came, but for the Holy Ghost to restore to his brain what the Devil had clearly taken. For despite whatever torment he may invoke upon himself, he had to uncover something — anything! — that may negate some of, if not all, the dread which daily clawed at his breast and darkened his thoughts.

Ushered along the draughty nave to the only pew still vacant — the foremost (one of three benches few braved to sit in) — Peter had barely obliged Edmunda by seating himself beside Lizzie when he noted the vaulted ceiling was no nearer Heaven than the parishioners' piety. Their prying glances he could not help catch, nor their whispers that floated to his ears:

"Who's he?" — "Family?" — "Friend?" — "Lover?" — "Didn't you *hear*?" — "No?" — "Tsk-tsk-tsk!"

More whispers, more tutting preceded references to the farmer's son, the fishmonger, the baker, and such, leaving Peter quite stranded at the sea of scandal he had evidently waded into.

Up the squeaky staircase, Father Francis presently ascended to his pulpit. Plunking his large Bible atop the lectern, he surveyed his flock with the piety and stern appropriate for one of his trade. When his eyes landed on Peter, his shaggy brows bounced several times — perhaps the effect of having spotted this new addition to his cloistered domain? His eyes then darted left and right, landing on Elizabeth; his brow descended like storm-clouds, colliding with his pointed snout. Next, his orbs bolted to the aisle, where possibly the farmer and his son sat; his brow turned disapprovingly asymmetrical.

Purpose perceivably recalled, he opened his great Bible, removed a leather bookmark with a scourge-like snap, which jolted the congregation, and thunderously pontificated two of the seven enemies of the soul: lust and sloth.

That he frequented his gaze on Peter and Elizabeth, they, stung by such accusatory attention, both looked away: the latter, at the next bench full of young men, wiggling their grubby fingers; the former, at a troop of females on another bench, all smiles, fluttering lashes, hushed giggles, and delicate fingers adorned in lace gloves no less off-white than their want of holiness.

For above an hour, the Father ran on with sacramental pearls, hurling his holy axioms and aphorisms at the libertine, incorrigible, and customarily sleepy swine, who, now wide awake, did ogle the handsomest fellow and maiden. Though try he did to conceal it, envy — that offspring of Satan — verily played about the holy man's face. For a fact, by the time he reached his peroration, he looked much tempted to hurl his weighty book at the decadent rebels!

But let us draw the curtain of charity over Father Francis' struggles against the enemies of his own soul.

No sooner had the lovers risen from their pew, so too did the lusty belles and beaus hungering to espy their idols. Observing more of this than the frowns of those past such blooms or the scowls of the tradesmen, Edmunda urged Lizzie and Peter stay exactly as. Her proud chin then lifted as she cast her proud eyes over the bewitched idolaters, catching sight of Harris and Hans — their faces still full of that bitterness common to the rejected, jettisoned, and discarded.

Father Francis now descended upon them. Bending one eyebrow at Ernest, glancing at Edmunda, glaring at Elizabeth, and ignoring Emil, he scrutinised Peter with a condemnatory eye. "They *must* marry!" decreed he to Ernest. "It is a *sin* for the man while yet unbound to be living under the *same* roof of his future bride. I will brook no scandal stirring up *my* flock!"

The fiery Father now darted his hell-fire gaze at the nosey sheep! Oh! How they either ducked behind pews, hid behind fans, buried noses in hymnals, cleared airways, checked watches, fiddled with ribbons on bonnets, or affected straightening lace gloves.

Visibly satisfied in putting godly fear in his flock and seeing that neither Ernest nor Edmunda dared oppose his thunderous words, the Father added, "I shall visit you mid-week. Lest you wish to face Heaven's wrath, *dare not* to displease me, as you did Hans *and* the baker."

At this, a trembling Elizabeth slumped to the pew. Though she had evaded the boorish farmer's son, now a worse ensnarement awaited. Even was Peter the last of men; wed one so arrogant, so condescending — so stupid? Impossible! Yet were she to confess the truth, while she may evade the misalliance, she would be forever stained with disrepute; or worse, the farmer's son might still wish to secure her, even as his infamous, tarnished wife.

Trembling more from zealous indignation, our reluctant Romeo went to object at the bridal noose; but the holy zealot had already vanished.

As our hero made for the exit, he became trapped in the crowded aisle. Incidentally, from a darkened alcove slid a stealthy shadow and hissed in his ear, "think you can *hide here*? I've *seen* the bills. When they take you, I'll reclaim what is *mine*! Your sins will find you out..."

"Who *is* this?" Peter fought against the masses to whirl around but saw only painted puckered lips blowing kisses his way. "Where did he *go*?"

***

Notwithstanding the perturbation beget in Peter's breast by the alarming speech of that lurking knave and the additional affronts of the holy Father, yet did his preoccupations tend chiefly to the scroll.

Heretofore, he held it to sun and candle, steamed it over bubbling pots, rubbed it with coins, doused it in oils and vinegars, even dusted it with charcoal, all to raise the faded scrawls — enough to drive him near to madness! What is more, with each glance at the scroll came phantom feelings of danger, of disgrace, of damnation, like muscle memory, inflaming his anxiety. And as if such torment were not enough (perhaps owing to the sundry knocks applied to his pate of late), condemnatory visions, released like lightning strikes, would snake across his mind, unlocking to him catches of unsavoury activities.

"Can it be the scroll contains only damaging secrets? Perhaps even implicating *me*?" Maybe 'twas better to destroy it? To leave the past buried forever in oblivion's vault? Yet where even the lowliest of knaves oft believes himself the most upright, there came a refusal to believe himself capable of any crime other than refusing to milk the cow. "These hell-sent visions must pertain to another life entirely? They *have* to!"

Again, taking up the scorched poster fragment, he passed his scrutiny over it. Whoever was the missing face belonging to that one eye staring back at him, he — as an indecipherable urge swelled within, as an unconscious feeling constantly found his heart racing, or sudden shivers cloistered about his breast — grew the more determined to discover the mysterious fugitive's identity.

***

With his waking thoughts, the sundry inconveniences of his own, still obliterated past and identity crowded fast to his mind; there came a powerful urge to do something about it. If his present world would reveal nothing to him, then he would have to reach out beyond it.

Of course, wholly unaware of the dangers he courted, he straightaway begged Edmunda to fund a notice in a Basel paper, appealing for any soul acquainted with him or the scroll's history to come forth. Alas, still aggrieved at his debts, the virago promptly refused his requests. Her meanness did stoke our hero's temper to new heights. He despised her the more for it and accused her of the coldest of hearts that not even the hottest violence of her own temper could ever melt. Thus thwarted — for now — Peter grew downcast and irascible.

"What delusion ever led me to this threshold?" mused he while pacing his prisonous loft later that afternoon. "Could I truly have bowed at destitution's altar, all for a pretty face? Of which I have no remembrance? Bound myself in a betrothal against my heart's desire?"

Here, he stopped. Experiencing his brightest illumination since waking in Bubendorf, he assayed his heart more assiduously. Adjudging by his feelings, his sentiments, he sketched up several methods to test his suspicions. Fixing on the aptest plan, he set off for the chalet.

With no little surprise did Edmunda receive our wild abandon hero at the chalet door as beneath her arm he swooped, nearly knocking her off her feet.

Rushing to Elizabeth's door, he rapped on it in a frenzy.

Startled, she opened it.

Full of zeal, Peter stepped forward, causing Lizzie to stumble backwards, losing her balance. She would have fallen had not he caught her up in his arms.

Ernest and Emil now appeared and joined Edmunda in the passageway, forming a small audience, quickly beguiled by the promising impromptu dramaturgy. Poised as the pair was — the heroine immobilised by his daring; the gallant assured of his cunning — they presented a very fine tableau brought to life. But let us not neglect the purpose of this performance:

His veiny neck overstretched, our hero did press his lips to hers with much irreverent ardour. The saucy smack rang through the chamber and passageway alike. For some moments, Lizzie remained stunned in his embrace, eyes gaping wide, slightly crossed at Peter, whose own squinted shut amid the kiss.

"Blessed be Pope Pius VI!" Edmunda clasped her hands. "Blessed be Father Francis!" She tugged Ernest's sleeve. "He remembers his darling."

Fain, she would have flown to wrap them in her wings were it not for what came next.

Gentles breezes, so often unsuspected by the inexperienced cultivator, tend rather to presage a perfect hailstorm. "Unhand me this instant!" cried Elizabeth; freeing herself from Peter's unwelcome enclasp, she dealt his cheek the disdain appropriate in a stinging slap that rang out like a pistol shot!

Their gasping audience, experiencing viscerally this enactment, could not help but grab their own smarting cheeks.

This was, of course, a most bitterly disappointing denouement. Edmunda threw up her hands, writhing through every feature. "Do they seek to *destroy* my patience?! When *she'll* have him, *he* won't have *her*; and when *he'll* have her, *she* won't *him*!"

But as vexing as love already seemed, Edmunda's choler would only rise higher still when she demanded an éclaircissement.

"Though remembrance still evades me," explained Peter, nonchalant, "my feelings I trust are a sufficient cicerone during my present sojourn in this wilderness." This sophistry was clearly lost on Edmunda, so he repeated it in plainer terms: "Though one may forget one's memories, I do not believe this is the case for one's feelings."

This amendment, more easily grasped, Edmunda dismissed his words as bovine, accused him of losing his mind and not just his memories, adding that even her cow, would it be separated from its young for decades, would have the good sense to remember it.

Ernest, at first, silent, perhaps giving greater latitude to his mind, upheld how sensibly Peter spoke. But meeting his wife's glare, he quickly added: "Still best to wait until your memories return. 'Tis a fact even us non-amnesiacs find their feelings come and go as they please."

We shall omit the naïve Emil's adolescent notions and attend to the indignant Lizzie's response: "You accost me with neither my consent," cried she, "nor my desire, and then —"

"Words are unnecessary," interrupted Peter, loftily staying her with his hand. "This kiss was but a mode of divining truth. Your recoiling heart, mirroring my own, obliterates any doubt I had until now suffered." Back and forth he now toured with the swagger of a Caesar. "I suppose I have only *myself* to blame for having countenanced the whim of so *dilettante* a rhapsody to so *infelicitous* an object of so *depreciated* a consequence."

His words did render Elizabeth gasping and speechless. Not less rendered mute were Ernest, Edmunda, and Emil; though their silence doubtless hinged on their failure to comprehend such superciliously chosen words. Thus, the next prosecutions bursting forth between the combatants, duelled with equally eloquent and elaborate wording, very likely went something like this:

"Blablabla! And blablabla!" retaliated the heroine, all hues of mortification at this slight.

"Something-something-something! And something-something-something!" pursued the anti-hero; all fire and zest in his voice.

"This-this-this-and-that, that-and-this, and-this-and-that!" rejoined she, voice a-trembling, cheeks a-flame with indignation.

"Such-and-such, and such-and-such!" retorted he, colour rising faster than mercury till the wronged woman choked, face turning of a sudden ashen.

As this was a conversation, or rather conflagration, not to be missed, here is its verbatim:

"You, sir," had cried Elizabeth, stung to the quick, "I repine, are not less *insolent* in person than *impudent* in practices!"

"And you, Miss!" had said Peter, priding his opinion. "I avow are not less *indigent* in prospects, than clearly *impecunious* in understanding!"

The looks she then gave him might have shown any man not blinded by his own vanity how much she was offended. "*Understanding*?!" Here her voice had trembled. "Pray, what ennobled reason directs the tongue in so cruelly *ignorant* and *defamatory* a manner?"

Imagining her ill-humour proceeded only from the want of benison and introspect he had kindly pointed out to her, he continued with taunting exultation: "Truth, pray, is neither cruel, ignorant, *nor* defamatory when represented in its barest, most *faithful* form."

"*Faithful*?! You know *nothing* about me! We have barely known each other a *few* —" Here she stopped, very likely apprehending her err. Not that it went noticed, anyway. Peter was far too worked-up. Their audience were still lost several dialogues back.

"Since there is *no shred* of evidence of affection between us," resumed our hero, "I shall suffer no more here — and *none* shall again thwart me!"

And, at that, off he stormed.

As our indignant hero packed his sack, there so happened to fall from the jacket a certain folded paper. Perusing the unfamiliar lines, he discovered, to his stupefaction, the possible missing proof of endearment. There was the "Dearest, loveliest, Elizabeth of Bubendorf". There, too, his own blood-stained "Peter" below. No longer could he deny what evidence plainly corroborated.

'Twas only now he did investigate the coat for further clues, and indeed, further wonders awaited! In an inner pocket lurked a golden band bejewelled with emerald's brilliant hue.

'Tis beyond my humble power to capture the emotions which raged within his stunned breast. But as the paper did slip from his grasp, and his legs did give way, and that he sank to the floor as if exhaling his last breath, the depths of his dismay, I believe, were plain to see.

"So, this *is* my life." He slumped back, banging his head against the boards. "This *wretched* world I have *no* recollection of." His heart and pride sank to the cowshed below. "Perhaps, before losing my memory, I lost my mind?" Heaving a heavy, dusty, coughing sigh, there he did lie amidst his despair.

Several hours of deepening gloom passed.

Several tears of hope's demise fell from his eyes.

Even Edmunda came by to spy him out without his notice; Ernest, too, snuck out of the chalet with a pilfered repast, ascended the ladder with it, placing it on the floor, and retired — all without Peter knowing of it.

At length, our hero, finally forcing himself up, approached the small aperture. But so abstracted was he that he initially remarked not Elizabeth at her own casement, opposite, gazing heavenward.

It likely owed to the discovery of the poem, but an inexplicable nature cleared his mind of all but the sight of her moonlit face. Her countenance held an elegance and innocent delight, blended with deep musings and serenity; all framed by something of beauty.

Shaking off this observation, he followed her gaze. Yet, finding not the moon's fascination, he returned his attention to her.

Just then, she looked his way, and their eyes locked. Over her face, there crawled something like mortification; perceivably gasping, she withdrew.

"Does she think me grown secretly... *besotted*?" He would have instantly undeceived her, but for the poem and ring. Maybe it was judicious to finally search his heart rather than continually resist what must lie therein? Still, pride, as much as shame, would not yet suffer him to make known to her the ring.

***

Fortune did smile upon our scene, for Father Francis did not visit mid-week as menaced. He was called away to some ailing kin, where soon he would perform the last rites and confessions. Though palliated in this reprieve, still our lovers faced Ernest and Edmunda's nuptial ultimatums, all of which our hero and heroine steadfastly refused under the pretext of memory's lack.

In any case, 'twas now mid-morning. Peter had vainly re-arraigned Edmunda about an advert in the paper. But imagine his joy when the kind-hearted Ernest betook him to the toolshed and was just sneaking him the needed coins — that is until mischance orchestrated Edmunda catching them in the exploit.

"But 'blessed are the merciful'," tried Ernest as she confiscated the coins.

"An 'eye for an eye'!" rasped she, shoving them both outside.

Thwarted again, Peter's fury grew so high as to choke out his words. How Edmunda could be so merciless and how Ernest could have chosen her for his wife, beggared belief!

Later that day, Ernest, after having snuck off on some purported business, found our hero slumped on his bed, communing with this heart on what course to pursue. Ernest handed to him a newspaper and proposed a familiarity with the world outside may stir some memories. Amazed that this notion had not entered his own head, Peter eagerly thanked him and praised his heed but vexed himself that Elizabeth had not earlier submitted so sensible an idea.

After finding naught to rekindle even a glimpse of his past, he would have discarded the paper, but the front-page fixed his idle curiosity: "Bern accused of revolutionary ideals. The Bernese Schultheiss reviling the imputations. French ambassadors arraigned for conspiring a coup. Zürich calling for an emergency Federal Diet. The *Assemblée législative* of the Kingdom of France scorning allegations of dishonouring the XII Orte. And the malefactor, whose failed arrest spurred this upheaval, still unfound."

Here, a peculiar disquiet again thrilled his nerves. Yet, why, he knew — nay — remembered not. A new line caught his eye: "Three suspected collaborators executed in Bern. No mercy for traitors to the Confederation."

A few hours later, as Peter entered the kitchen, a thunder of fists pounded on the front door, startling Edmunda nigh witless from her knitting! Two redcoats entered on the heels of her invitation, stepping aside to admit their captain:

"I am here to review your roster of able-bodied men," announced he.

With tremblings, she complied, shoving Peter forward; only after threats of prosecution for holding back any other men did she reluctantly produce Emil.

"Under orders of the Federal Diet, all cantons must supply additional troops." The captain thrust official notices into Peter and Emil's hands, each document bearing an official state seal. "While the French nibble at our borders, war may soon break out between our cantons. Report for duty at the garrison!"

With a curt nod, he spun about and marched off with his men-at-arms, leaving behind a stunned Edmunda, Emil, and Peter perusing the now unfurled documents, which summarised the brewing national and international threats.

***

January's end came, and as Edmunda had feared, the peddler came-a-calling. Spying with horror, the charred ruins of the workroom and the blackened vestiges of the cotton sacks, his temper quickly flared hot as brimstone, while Edmunda turned ashen as a spectre. Knowing not how to mollify his screams, she offered him tea. Yet, alas! Calico yarn alone, he desired.

"You'll pay for this!" said he, face purpling. "And with *interest*!"

"*Interest*?" Edmunda fell against the sooty wall. "But how'm I even —"

"Aye, interest! And if I see not a coin, I'll send for the bailiffs!"

Here, Elizabeth entered and begged for the peddler's forbearance. After professing he would receive no such lenience from his supplier, he reluctantly conceded an extension of a month to pay in full with interest. Then, storming off, he quit the chalet, kicking the chickens out of his way en route to the gate.

Unused to such comminations, Edmunda slumped into her chair. "Oh, Lizzie. What *are we* to do? That demon *has* to go! Yet I'll be *damned* if I let him leave before he's repaid me!"

"He has to be good at *something*. And whatever it is, even if he tears the flesh off his knuckles, I will have him slaving every hour to recompense you."

As if affairs were not already inauspicious enough, the sound of feet hasty upon the ground preceded a thunderous banging at the front door.

Opening it, to Edmunda's no little dread, there appeared the baker, the blacksmith, the fish-monger, the drover, all with their respective bailiffs in tow, angrily demanding their dues. Though Edmunda prostrated herself before them, weeping and beseeching most piteously, they would brook no more delay and would rather take her livestock in lieu of payment!

Now, it would perhaps be a little unjust to paint only that one face of Fortune, for it so happened that while Edmunda still sobbed, and the mob still shouted, lo, a fine chaise and four clattered through the gate, drawing every eye.

Out stepped a fine bohemian fellow, who strode towards them with an air of confident determination, asking if a Peter lodged here.

Natch, gulping back her tears, Edmunda quavered what losses he came to recoup? Yet to her surprise, 'twas not compensation he sought; but rather he came with an offer of employment. Needless it is to say, the mob did sneer and, with a very vivacious parlance, caution him against this folly. But determined nonetheless, this bohemian fellow, an artist of some renown from Liestal, explained that in having heard of Peter's fine features, he wished solely to engage him as his model for an oil bound for exhibition in the summer.

As Peter would need only to stand in a certain attitude, attired in ornate apparels, the sneers subsided, replaced by the ready acknowledgement that, for such a sinecure task, there could be no foreseeable danger employing a person so self-admiring and otiose as Peter.

Shrewd even when suffering, and sensing opportunity through her tears, Edmunda did shed a few more — but secretly of joy. She jumped to her feet and, verifying the amounts owed to the tradesmen, quickly offered up the scoundrel at the handsome price.

Perhaps sympathetic to her tribulation; perhaps more influenced by the mob and their many sets of impatient orbs burning into him, the artist accepted. Still itching of palm and sensing more profit, Edmunda tried her luck upping the price to include the peddler's debt. But as for this, without the extra pair of eyes glaring at him, the canny fellow promptly declined.

***

Since not even Peter could find grounds to object to the proposed scheme of employment, come the arrival of the very next morrow, he was trimmed, tidied, primed, and despatched to the studio, where, fashioned as he was according to his partiality, he exceeded every expectation.

That even his carriage and air were of such urbanity, the artist could not help marvelling at his versatility, vaunting his beguile, and probing his lineage, which verily seemed to defy the rustic garb and dwelling he found him in.

Indeed, Peter's ears were so wonderfully played to by the harmony of these mellifluous words that he could not but drink up such praise without brimming and spilling over at least a drop or two. Excluding his compliments to the fellow's forte with the brush — for there were ample paintings (though being of that subject which might arouse a few blushes, we shall not delineate to the reader) displayed about the studio — he returned an approbation of this artist's prudence, percipience, and savoir faire. Verily, in the realm of judging and not merely sketching a character, our hero determined this man to be a master.

Consequently, canvassing the very same subject, Peter doubted not that somehow he had lost his way, ostensibly his reason, and very likely his family and inheritance, too; all for the charms of a pretty, however *verarmt* woman.

As it is indeed in vogue among such artsy sorts to indulge and glorify certain amorous affairs, the fellow naturally believed he had grasped his model's predicament; he appended to it an account of his own liaisons that had already cost him a small fortune — this he said with a conspiratorial wink.

Incidentally, the case of the elusive fugitive came to the docket. As Peter mentioned the partial poster in his possession and the circumstances of it, the artist recalled he had obtained one such poster on a recent trip out of the canton.

"You *do*?!" Our hero nearly fell from the platform with excitement.

"Indeed." At that, the artist got to rummaging through several draws.

Had Fortune, in her whimsical wiles, smiled upon our hero?

Alas, at length, and with a cursory "Aha!" the artist rather retrieved from a bin what was a rolled-up, but equally scorched poster fragment. "You will have to forgive me." He handed over what was merely the very bottom part, revealing but a chin and a partial mouth. "A few too many glasses last night; and in this poster I found recourse to the lighting of several candles."

To be sure, a monstrous sigh nigh took all the air out of Peter. How could the artist have been so careless as to use so important a document to light mere candles?! Even so, this was something. A second piece to the puzzle, so to speak.

***

At any rate, the painting was a masterpiece. The artist exceedingly delighted. The tradesmen's debts settled. The livestock saved from confiscation — now, Edmunda had only to contrive means to pay back the peddler. And Peter, having apprised the artist of his predicament and won his sympathy and help, finally got to place that advert in the column. These were its lines:

> To whom it may concern, & whom may know of it. I, that certain refined person of (yet unconfirmed) consequence &, I dare say, family, am still in possession of a certain communication which, G.V.V. if you yet live, will be so good as to reply to instruct &, perchance, restore me to my happiness &, I hope, fortune.

Satisfied with having placed the advert, Peter quit the printery onto the bustling Basel city street's cobblestones slick with recent rain. Immediately, he noted a knot of men loitering near a fruit stall; their eyes fixed on him with an unsettling intensity that sent a prickle of unease down his spine.

Quickening his pace, hand instinctively moving to his small purse, he glanced back. They *were* following him.

Just ahead, two more dastardly looking men blocked his path.

Confused, Peter turned sharply down an alleyway, hoping to lose them.

But alas, the telltale pounding of boots thundered behind him.

"After him!" bellowed a gruff voice.

Driven by sudden danger, our hero broke into a frantic run — only to find as the alley's exit drew nearer, three more burly figures obstructed his escape.

"We've got you now!" snarled one. "That reward's *ours*!"

"Reward?" echoed Peter, stumbling back, glancing behind at the gaggle of approaching ruffians. "What *nonsense* are you speaking of?"

Knowing this confrontation boded ill, Peter scanned the alley littered with a meager assortment of potential weapons: a broken crate, a length of chain, a discarded broom handle. 'Twas a far cry from the gentlemanly art of fencing, but necessity, as they say, is the mother of invention.

The mob, explaining nothing, lunged at him.

Peter snatched up a crate and swung hard. With a sickening thud, it connected against a brigand's shoulder, sending him sprawling to the ground.

Seemingly stunned, the miscreant's comrades hesitated.

Seizing the moment, Peter drove the wood's edge into another's midsection — the already weakened wood snapped in half with the force.

Two more of the motley crew rushed forward, fists clenched.

Grabbing the broom handle, Peter parried one directly to his chest, taking the wind out of him, then swept another's legs from beneath him.

The remaining assailants charged forth.

But our hero met them with swift thrusts and jabs, wielding his humble weapon with surprising dexterity, sending them reeling and scrambling back up the alleyway, clutching bruised limbs.

Eyes fixed on a last, reluctant brute, who presently stumbled to his feet, Peter shoved him against a wall. "What reward?" demanded he, pressing the brigand's shoulders against the bricks. "Why are you attacking me?!"

The thug, eyes wide, only stammered incoherently; then, with a shove, he broke free and fled.

Left alone in the now-quiet passage, Peter tossed the broom handle aside. A rush of confusion beset him. What had just happened? Who, in the world, had these ruffians mistook him for? Despite his indignation, there stirred beneath a creeping unease. This attack, as much against his pride as his person, he could not so easily dismiss as happenstance — this encounter seemed more than mere chance; it felt like a dark echo of a past he still could not yet recall.

***

Mid-February being arrived, Jack Frost's icy embrace had tightened its grip, blowing his frigid breath and snow across the land. Incommoded by winter's wrath obtruding on his draughty lodgings, our hero did shiver and chatter as though his bones were a set of castanets.

Hence, off to the chalet went he to apply to Edmunda.

"I refuse to sleep any longer in that barn," said he. "It is so devilishly cold that I fear my blood may freeze in my veins ere spring arrives to thaw them out."

Sat in front of the warm hearth, Edmunda paid him no heed. Thus rebuffed, our hero rallied every effort at civility and asked that she answer him. Edmunda now looked at him. "What would you have me do? You know I've nowhere else to put you. But as I was need to go to the village for sugar, if you go in my stead, I'll give you an extra blanket."

Peter cast his eyes towards the window; thick snowflakes tumbled like a torrent. "I will be swallowed whole by such a blizzard!"

Edmunda only chuckled and repeated her offer, adding she would have no trouble chipping the icicles off his frozen corpse.

Though tempering the fury which shot to his brain, he could hardly look at her without wishing for the fire to spill over and burn her to the same charcoals of her workroom.

Ernest, having entered, volunteered to go; to which Peter said he would; to which Lizzie said he would only get lost in the woods and they would need to go search for him; to which Peter, all the more irked, flung his cloak on, saying if he should die on this mission, they have only the mother to blame.

At that, out went he into the blizzard, trailed by Edmunda's shouting echoes to stick to the lanes and not take any shortcuts.

White skies, slopes, and blanketed forests, all in want of apricity, soon blurred around him. Moreover, several snow blasts then tossed him into a snowdrift. That it was naught but white above, about, and below, he knew not in which direction he screamed.

Certainly, Edmunda was the most maleficent crone he had ever known!

While he struggled to get up, voices mingled among the whistling gusts.

Looking around with stinging difficulty, he perceived two hazy figures in the distance. Fractured words caught his hearing; the words unpleasant and directed at he knew not who.

Imagining they perhaps argued among themselves, Peter trudged on.

So distracted he became in cursing Edmunda, and so intense grew the blizzard, it took only several wrong turns for him to lose his way.

Stood at the margin of a large snowpacked field confined by black forests and, believing it to be the right direction, he went to cross it.

But then, recalling Edmunda's injunctions to stick to the lanes — which wound too vast a distance about the field for such an intolerable blizzard — he again cursed her for only adding to the pains of his journey.

Hence, simply to defy her, he crossed the piles of snow.

About a minute later, an unsettling thunderclap-like noise brought him to a halt. It reverbed exactly like a gunshot.

Behind him, at the edge of the field, two figures waved their arms; one of them bearing a rifle.

"Surely, they fired not at me?"

He pushed on until a second booming echo tore through the biting gusts.

But it was not rifle fire; the snow tremored beneath his feet.

In the next instant, several more thunderclap-like rumbles reverbed all about. He lost his footing as the ground sank aslant, and a fissured ice sheet stood at an angle.

Plunged into a body of icy water, black and bleak, he struggled against the assault until overpowered, senses blackening...

17 – 29 FEBRUARY 1792

"*Alle schönen Dinge sind drei,*" so cry the Swiss. "All beautiful things come in threes," echo our English sages in kind. But ironically, too oft in life, the inverse is true for misfortunes. So it seems for our hero. For 'twas curses, not blessings, that rained down on him in triplets terrible as sport for Fortune's twisted pleasure; repeatedly, she rendered him insensate only to awaken in bewildering and alien environments...

"Peter?" grumbled a man's voice. "*Peter*? Can you hear me?"

Indeed, hearing his name uttered a second time, Peter forced open his eyes to behold the sour physiognomy of a fellow so utterly unfamiliar. "Who the devil are *you*?" He forced himself up. "And where the devil am I *now*?"

"At the farm," replied the young man with a huff. "And I am —"

"*Farm*? Which farm?"

To Peter's right, a broad stone fireplace commanded a long wall; a red deer's head furnished the oak wood-panelled overmantel. On the mantel itself, several taxidermy domes exhibited twigs, dried flowers, and nuthatches — of the greyish-blue plumed species, with peach underbellies still vibrant in death. To his left stood a large oak wardrobe abutting a door. And in front of a window, opposite, several glistening glass trinkets ornamented a prettyish dresser, bespeaking feminine influence.

Peter turned to the young man. "How long have I been here?"

"Three days, but —"

"*Three days*?"

They were interrupted by the door opening, whereupon an older fellow appeared. Seeing Peter in a conscious state, he stood as one petrified.

Of a sudden, a shaggy Bernese brute came bounding between the man's legs and, in a trice, leapt onto the bed.

"Down dog," tried the young man, half-laughing as he tugged at the ebullient creature, who, disregarding all commands, pulled the young man atop Peter.

"Get off, you *imbecile*!" With one hand, Peter strove to thrust off the man while, with the other, he fended off the dog's slobbery affections. But the latter was endued with such vigour and vim, and the former such carelessness and clumsiness, that soon all was a tangle of arms, legs, laughs, bedsheets, vexatious grunts, happy licks, and a wagging tail.

Eventually, the older man rushed over and disentangled the chaos, dragging the dog by its collar out of the room. "*Bad* Znüni!"

Peter glared at both men. "What riotous, maladroit heedlessness is this you permit?" He straightened out the bedsheets. "And that Znü —" Something touched his mind. "*Znüni*...?"

The older man removed the key from the door's outside and, closing the door, locked it from the inside. He now explained he found the dog, a hungry one, too, sniffing around their stables about two months ago. Nobody knew from where it came. And since Peter had been here, the stubborn whining creature had refused to budge from the door's other side.

"Indeed?" Strange as this was, Peter rather pondered the key which had before clearly locked the door from its outside. "Who are you both, anyway?"

"I'm Harris," grumbled the younger man. "And that's my father, Hans."

These names rang with familiarity. "The farmer and his son?"

With head hung low, Hans plodded to the bedside; whatever he muttered, Peter failed to hear. Thus, Hans repeated himself. "Begging your forgiveness."

"*Forgiveness*?" replied Peter, in his customary air of disdain.

Hans fell to his knees, hands clenched. "About what... happened."

Already, the presence of these men filled Peter with irritation. "This is a most elliptical conversation. What *are* you talking about?"

Hans raised his head, looking increasingly mortified. "I was meaning us chasing you into that..." he wiped his wiry brow, "... field with the frozen pond."

Cognition slowly dawned on Peter's brain. "Oh! That was *you*, was it?"

Though ignorant of whatever had provoked their pursuit, Peter knew it was his own vexation with Edmunda that impelled him into that hazardous field. Feeling more fatigued than generous towards the farmer's unease, he apprised him accordingly.

Hans' furrowed phiz did overspread with veins like bindweed. Up he jumped. "*What*?! You mean you *only* went into that field to *spite* Edmunda?"

A sudden headache lodged in Peter's brain. "I believe I spoke plainly enough. But as you wish to rival my judgement, then *yes*, that is *precisely* it."

Hans gnawed at his bony white knuckles; he motioned a flick of his head to his son. They both flung out of the chamber, leaving the door gaping wide, at which the dog came bounding in again with canine conviviality.

"Down Znüni!" tried our hero. But the oddly affectionate brute would not be deterred from his happy pursuit. "Znüni... Where have I heard that name?"

Observing the bedstead's reasonable draperies of blue velvet, though dusty from disuse, and the well-kept but equally dusty furniture, our hero wondered whose chamber this once was.

For Hans, all prior sympathy for Peter had blown quicker than gunpowder set to torch. "Didn't I say we ought to let him drown?" said he to his son upon reaching the kitchen. "We ought to have let him freeze to death! Nobody would've known! Then you could've married Elizabeth!"

Harris agreed how troublesome their plans had turned out since Peter arrived.

"And now the thief profits from our hospitality!" Hans hurled a cup of barley into a pot, which would become a hearty meal for his inconvenient guest. "We ought to let him starve!" Grabbing a handful of cured meats, he cast them in. Face twisted with uncertainty, and despite his venomous words, he added another. Still unsure, he added a third. He then bade Harris slice some bread. "No, no, *thicker* slices! He looks half-famished."

Huffing and reddening, Harris complied.

"That wench, Edmunda," continued Hans, "stingy as she is sharp-tongued. And your sister, she's to blame for this, too. Had she only married a local lad, she'd've lightened our burden!"

"Fear not," said Harris with a sneer. "Peter'll soon be gone for good."

Hans gave his son a look which spoke he fervently wished it so.

***

Now, let us forget not that curious incident at church. It may come as a surprise to some to learn that the whisperer at Peter's ear was none other than Harris. Whilst passing through Lucerne, he espied, to his astonishment, a notice board displaying a WANTED poster — the outlaw's face unmistakable.

This occurred on the Saturday morn. And, as envy oft inspires all things invidious, he schemed to remove the obstacle to his own happiness by informing the Liestal garrison the following Monday. Thus, the appointed day came round.

"Have you not the poster to prove your claim?" said one guard.

Harris had not. "But it's him! His annoying face I'd know *anywhere*!"

Alas for him, without proof and with the fresh stash of posters delayed from Bern, the guards were powerless. Harris vowed to fetch one himself from Lucerne. But then, a senior officer approached, declaring his own plans to travel there shortly. If the fugitive remained at large, he would obtain a poster and contact Harris to verify the likeness before taking the necessary action.

Protest Harris did, demanding immediate arrest. But the senior officer threatened him with the jailhouse should he not remove himself from the garrison at once. Disappointed, Harris returned home. Not a word escaped him about the poster, nor did he divulge his plot to overthrow his rival.

***

Having been fed to satisfaction, our hero slipped into an unencumbered repose, whence a host of visions burst forth in wild, fantastical array. One such phantasm of that wondrous realm being of certain import, let us now unfold:

A gilded clock, its face a swarming dance of honey-hued bees, did tick-and-tock like the roar of a cannon blast.

From the dial's depths, a familiar countenance swirled into view, tracing with gloved fingers the lines of malevolent hue; his lips moved in silent, secret council, that settled like poisoned dew.

The form of a corporal, visage half-shrouded by trembling light, drew near, bestowing a weighty writ — "Be careful; be careful!"

Anon, a flash — a roaring blaze. A castle swallowed by flames. A lone figure, face cloaked in midnight's shadow, fled from justice's stern pursuit. A boat upon a storm-tossed lake — hooves striking spray into tempestuous wake. A perilous mountain pass. Swiss Guard in grim pursuit — muskets, halberds, and bayonets flashing 'neath the lightning's ruthless wrath.

Darkness descended. A swaying prison wagon, wherein iron shackles dug deep. White and crimson, mud and blood, the fugitive's face stared back — a mirror darkly cast of none other than Peter's own.

"Ghhhhhh —!" He jolted up, tumbling from the dream's grasp. Breath ragged, lungs seizing as if pulled from drowning's cold embrace, he clung to the blankets, haunted by so grim a vision — a whisper of sins half-remembered, a past yet veiled in shadow.

As for Peter's hosts, sleep proved no less a stranger to their eyes than the three nights prior; though the nature of their agitations, which kept them awake, now sprang solely from resentment.

Hans, like a boar roasting on a spit, did turn on his cot all night, revolving in his mind the capricious injustices of arranging marriages. Likewise, Harris, impatient to avenge his rival, revolved a thousand images of him soon being carted away, and Lizzie, as easily caught in his net as a partridge, showering him with gratitude and blossoming love! Desperate to witness Peter's downfall first-hand, he racked his brains for some scheme to prevail over his father's intent to doubtless eject him come morn.

By early light, every cunning seed had ample duration to germinate. No sooner did Harris broach the subject with his father than he found him equally fixed upon a scheme to amass the best yield from so bothersome a harvest.

"We ought to keep him here as long as we can and continue *exactly* as we've done," said Hans while he swung his pocket watch about a finger. "Already we've won Edmunda and Ernest with our charity to that rat. We need only now win over Elizabeth to our favour."

Not solely would this earn them further encomium, but it would widen the chasm between the "doomed lovers", as Edmunda called them. They could — would — *should* separate the two and re-present Harris as the alternative and superior match for Elizabeth's future.

I need not explain how easily persuaded was Harris at this proposal.

The clock had just chimed the eighth hour forenoon. Ensconced by the fireside, pondering anew the taunting poster fragments, his missing past, and so disturbing a dream while watching a raven in a tree beyond the window, Peter was expecting to have already been brought in his breakfast. But instead, a small crowd bustled into the chamber, gathering about him — ladies with wide skirts, gentlemen, musty overcoats, muddy boots, and generally too much racket.

This impromptu audience comprised the surgeon, the physician, the apothecary, Hans, Harris, Ernest, Edmunda, Elizabeth, and Emil — Oh! And, of course, Znüni. Since the dog recognised Emil, and Emil the dog, a very happy reunion of hugs, barks, pats, and licks ensued before questions pertaining to how Emil knew the animal; whence it came; how it reached Bubendorf; when it disappeared; when it reappeared at the farm; culminating in Edmunda's general avowal of how much better suited it was to living and eating at a farm than from her modest pantry.

A rapping at the front door prevented further comment. Hans attended upon whoever else visited so early and returned with six fair maidens, all of whom (from that earlier scene at the church) claimed friendship with Elizabeth and a tender concern for the invalid.

Since it would be unkind to overlook Harris, as did these doe-eyed damsels fawning over his rival, we shall spare a thought of consolation for him as his eyes filled with such exterior charms. Like the alluring Undines rising from crystal waters — albeit bedecked in their best embroidered dresses, scarfs, red stockings, coats, and bonnets; and not wavy golden tresses wreathed in pond lilies and wet loins clothed in white mist — they gathered about Peter. Intoxicating the air with lusty sighs and longing looks — the rosy colour of which spilled onto their bare necks, drenching their fair skins as far as their heaving bosoms — they pelted him with knitted scarves, gloves, and socks; cakes, breads, and a general cacophony forming their names, and squeaks, giggles, and cooes forming their conversation:

"You're so cruel, Lizzie," said one. "Aren't we friends?" said another. "To have hidden him from us for so long," added a third. "Look at that face," added a fourth as she reached out to touch it, at which a glaring Peter grabbed her audacious hand and thrust it away.

Naturally, Lizzie was the luckiest; Peter, the handsomest; she, the most envied; he, the most coveted. Yet their praise held thorns:

"'Tis a shame he's the useless dolt who ruined the baker's bread," declared one. "The good-for-nothing idiot who locked the blacksmith out and refused to climb through the window on his roof," said another. "The pompous block-head, who lost the farmer six of his cows," added a third. "The dullard who almost drowned the fish-monger's cat," continued a fourth.

Had not Peter been struck paralysed by appal, he would have thrown the entire party out of the room. As for Harris and Hans, erstwhile green with envy, they now snickered between themselves, pink with all humour and satisfaction.

Jago presently arrived as well and brought with him the promise of a most prodigious feast at his father's country seat as soon as Peter was recovered.

Edmunda flew to him and dropped several curtsies. She said how good he was, but not to forget Lent begins in two days. Just bending her knees again, she stopped and turned to Peter. "*Well*? Must I thank him for you?"

Peter was just rising from his chair, but Jago bade him stay seated.

"You have my profound gratitude," said Peter in his politest tone yet.

That Peter thanked anybody, Elizabeth and Edmunda turned to each other; by their looks, they clearly doubted their eyes, ears, and even their senses.

Hans now claimed to be feeling "equally generous himself" to celebrate Peter's health. Since his daughter and his son-in-law were planned to arrive at the end of the month from the Basel Carnival, he decreed he would execute the hog, which he was fattening up for such a special occasion.

"D'you hear *that*, Peter?" said Edmunda, in a tone clearly connoting he should again grovel in gratitude while with her eyes she motioned he ought to retry where he had been refused by Jago.

Anyhow, that our hero wished not to invoke a remission, verily he listened to the learned men's injunctions and promised them his compliance. Satisfied thus with the patient, all quit the chamber; save Lizzie and Edmunda.

With gasps and gulps, Peter now learned he nearly died of hypothermia whilst unconscious for three days. Elizabeth nursed him each day; Edmunda, each night, in tears, blaming herself for sending him to his near death — just before Ash Wednesday, too! Since his own anger with Edmunda had caused his present state, he paid an uncommon heed to her prescriptions for his reform, nodding without objection. Thusly pleased with his apparently newfound obedience, she, with smiles and tugs at his cheeks and injunctions he gets better before returning to the garrison, quit the chamber to join the others in the kitchen, her nose telling her Hans prepared a hearty breakfast.

Our lovers being now thus alone, a silence entered between them. To dispel the awkwardness, our hero offered our heroine his chair. She refused; but he insisted, taking a stool for himself. Possibly, in searching for words, Lizzie asked if any memories about the scroll had yet resurfaced. Peter shook his head; since his advert had yielded no reply, he would write the Geneva garrison. With some quickness, Elizabeth offered to write for him and, with an awkward smile, turned the talk to his health.

"Why put your life in such danger?" She took his hand and caressed it as if with regret mingled with anxiety. "Mother bade you stick to the lanes."

Aware of her recent nighttime solicitudes, our hero felt something he could not decipher; but supposing this mere gratitude or esteem, he readily dismissed it. And as for his hand, held by hers, he felt unwilling or unable to remove — though which he knew not. All the same, contemplating the dictates of duty thrust upon him — she had served his health twice now — he meant to thank her; he longed to thank her. Yet irresolute on what to say, impotent still to command his pride, words fled from his tongue, and he only gazed at her.

Insensible of the perplexing regard she had inspired in Peter's breast, the moment her eyes met with his, she blushed and lowered her own as if conscious of some peculiar effect. "Yet you are safe." She patted his hand before withdrawing her own. "I trust you will draw from this encounter the necessary lesson. Hans insists on your convalescence here until spring — should you... *prefer* it?"

The savoury aromas wafting in made Peter's nose twitch. Also, the warmth of the crackling fire played about his cheeks. And the bed surpassed that of the loft; he again pressed his hands into it: no horrendous hay. The alternative was bitter gruel, a cold barn, and the bitter stink of animals defecating below his bed. And if he *was* to be called away to war — he shuddered at this thought — comforts would be few. "If it inconveniences not Hans, I see no objection."

This answer seemed to please her well; she smiled. Likely, with such an arrangement, she believed herself extricated from Father Francis' menaces.

"Also," resumed our hero, "after suffering from the strangest of dreams last night, I begin to believe part of my past has finally... crept through..."

"*It has*?" answered Lizzie in a tone evincing some apprehension.

"Yes. And I begin to wonder whether... in the recent months still lost to the abyss, I was... perhaps... involved in the pursuit of this... fugitive... And considering, antecedent to this, the inescapable feeling of... the oddest... *whisperings*... I have encountered — I do not know why, or perhaps I do? — I grow, with each passing hour, firmer in the opinion that I have, most certainly, at the very least, crossed paths with this outlaw."

Indeed, unlike before, this last dream had engraved itself most unforgivingly upon his recollection.

***

The 29th February was arrived. After several most gruelling days of martial training at the garrison, wherein Peter interrogated in vain the officers and captains for any scrap of intelligence about the dastardly fugitive — whose villainy had brought about so bothersome a conscription — we find him back at the farm. Having breakfasted some hours ago, impatiently he waited for Hans to finish with the newspaper, which he then snatched away to the bedchamber. There, sitting himself beside the fire, he dashed through the pages to the adverts. Easy it is to draw the sudden amazement upon his face when he read the following:

> To he who will be glad to know he is, indeed, of consequence, family, & fortune. By way of response to your advert, I must, however, caution you: do not, for now, seek that which will reward you rather with greater distress. Until I write again. Your loyal, yet anonymous, adviser & protector.

It is not to be wondered at that his perplexity at so transporting, yet so perturbing a tiding brought on a sudden and most violent headache. He was not long left in this storm, however, for Elizabeth rushed in, gasping for air.

"Come!" cried she. "Mother has been detained. She is to be indicted within hours! Hans will drive us, and we will meet my father there."

Of course! 'Twas the end of the month. The duration of forbearance, the peddler extended, had reached its culmination. Despite Edmunda's efforts and those also of Ernest, she had failed to raise even a tenth of the debt.

***

In a half hour, they arrived at the venerable Liestal's Rathaus. As they rushed up its weathered steps, Peter noticed along the street a trio of men. There was something in their bearing and attire that arrested his attention and stayed his feet. The men were stopping passersby and showing them what resembled a poster? Lizzie's pleas for Peter to hasten with her, however, stole over his distraction, and he followed her inside to the hall of justice.

Within the timbered walls, a disorderly throng ensconced amidst the coils of pungent tobacco fumes that induced fits of coughing in all but the most hardened lungs.

"Lizzie!" cried Edmunda, escorted by two officers of the court to one of the two tables at the hall's centre, at which the principal players in our drama would soon contend.

"Mother!" Lizzie peered through the fog. The plaintiff peddler sat at the other table, drumming his fingers in anticipation of the impending victory he doubtless felt assured of. At the far-side of the foggy hall, Emil consorted with the baker, the blacksmith, the fish-monger, the cattle owner, and those fair nymphs. Letting out a sigh, Lizzie turned to Peter. "Remember what I told you on the way here, lest you bring ruin on us all!"

Over this theatre of petty disputes, presided Liestal's esteemed stadtschultheiss, bedecked in full magisterial splendour, embellished with an embroidered sash and an imposing white powdered periwig that threatened to overbalance his tricorn hat. Flanking him were the village magistrates clad in robes of office.

The stadtschultheiss rose from the bench at the room's head and, with an authoritative rap of his ceremonial sword, called the "rabble" to order.

This being affected, a hush fell over the hall. The stadtschultheiss sat back down and, adopting his most magisterial pose, commenced the trial: that pitiable exhibition of justice that would determine Edmunda's fate.

Called forth to present his case, the peddler approached the bench with obsequious bows and spun his yarn of woes, apprising every ear willing to drink in his terrible tale of the combusted cotton sacks and the negligent defendant who had put him at great financial odds with his merchant. With an unctuous tongue, he failed not to wax long his own magnanimity, or the ingratitude displayed in return.

This account, at first eliciting murmurs of assent from fellow tradesmen, drew prodigious gasps, which, so deep, sucked in several tobacco clouds, clearing several pockets of air, through which Edmunda's shame was easily espied.

The stadtschultheiss bade the peddler to stand down and motioned for the quailing defendant to rise and answer to these accusations. Haltingly she stood and, with unsteady curtsies and convulsive sobs, confirmed the substance of the claims, placing the justice of her cause entirely in Heaven's hands.

Into close consultation, the stadtschultheiss and his magistrates withdrew and whispered amongst themselves. Verily while they deliberated thus, a deathly silence of anticipation smothered all present. Trembling and gnawing at her nails, Edmunda frequented fearful glances at Elizabeth and Ernest.

At long last, the verdict came down in favour of the plaintiff! The court decreed a full recompense to the peddler, including all amassed interest, by direct payment or confiscation of possessions ere month's end. Failure to abide by this ruling would result in an eviction forthwith from the chalet.

Upon this crushing sentence, Edmunda let out a tortured shriek as though she sustained a mortal stab to the heart. She crashed violently to the floor, Elizabeth and kin flying to her aid. The peddler and his cohorts exchanged exultant glances amidst the protests of injustice and shouts of mercy which filled the hall.

So stunned at this ruling and Edmunda's collapse, Peter could utter not a word or move a limb. 'Twas all *his* own doing, yet 'twas *she* ladened with restitution. Abhor her as he might, he must act! But what to do, he knew not.

"Order!" The stadtschultheiss' gavel slammed like a cannon blast, reverberating off the walls and silencing the rowdy assembly. "Though it grieves me to afflict the defendant, justice *must* prevail." After regarding Edmunda with evident pity, he despatched a clerk for the physician and rose from his seat. "As there is nothing more to mediate —"

"Your Honour," said Elizabeth, curtsying hastily. "If I may speak?"

After scrutinising her for a moment with a piqued brow, he nodded and sat back down. Lizzie thanked him and, again curtsying, summoned Peter forth into the curious gaze of all.

"The fault," said she, "indwells not with my mother but with *this* man." Promising extenuating circumstances that would exonerate them both — which, though dubious as it sounded, the magistrates wished still to hear it — she then began: "You will recall several years ago the trial of a certain villager who burnt down her master's property, but being proved insane, she was acquitted?"

The stadtschultheiss and his fellow councillors exchanged furrowed looks. Again, they engaged in hushed talk. And, at length: "Are you implying that *this* man" — the stadtschultheiss pointed his gavel at Peter — "was, at the time of the offence, labouring under a defect of reason?"

"Yes, Your Honour. He is as *insane* as they come."

The peddler jumped up and vehemently objected. But the stadtschultheiss commanded he stand down and bid Elizabeth continue.

"If you will grant me further forbearance," said she, "I can prove this."

Duly granted such, she called upon the testimony of the baker, the blacksmith, the fish-monger, the cattle owner; Ernest, and her brother. Ergo, they averred that the inept, blundering Peter is the most, "doltish" and "imbecilic" — "A loaf short of the baker's dozen" — "A clown fish" — "A slag heap for brains" — "An egg without its yoke" — "Who," interjected Elizabeth, "suffering from amnesia, was rendered further wooden-headedness," and — "Who," now interjected the fair nymphs, "is renowned town-wide for his lunacy."

The magistrates were all stunned to silence. Not so the rabble, who tutted, sneered, and mocked Peter, who, horrified at so scourging a portrait, went to cry out against the vilification, at which Elizabeth, sagely watching him, quickly stopped up his mouth with her hand.

Whether from natural mercy, or more from his wife's persuasive glares to aid her friend Edmunda, the stadtschultheiss, after several more minutes conferring with his fellow adjudicators, overturned his prior verdict. The wretched woman deserved only a full acquittal, herself a victim of the village idiot.

Amidst the peddler's subsequent uproar, demanding a retrial — his merchant comrades chorusing the disaccord — Elizabeth let fall her hand from Peter's mouth; to her instant regret.

"How can such *incompetents* occupy such seats of civil weightiness?" cried Peter. "You administer *not* law and harmony but *mobocracy* and disorder!"

The rabble did choke on their gasps while those "incompetents" sputtered words, condemning him for not merely speaking so offensively to them but failing even to bow.

Of course, our hero did protest he had *never* bowed to *anyone*.

Fearing for his safety, Elizabeth curtsied several times to the magistrates, begging pardon for Peter's stupidity before turning to him and insisting he bow at once. That he refused still, she pointed at his shoes, referencing "horse dung". Natch, a horrified Peter did instantly investigate — head and bow arching forward. "See," said Lizzie to the magistrates. "He is *quite* capable of bowing."

Glaring at her for such a falsehood, our hero might have protested had not other matters needed redress. "While I admit amnesia," addressed he the bench with an air of haughty displeasure, "I am *not* devoid of lucidity *or* culpable of *any* inanity deserving the traduces of these *impertinent* attestants. I am a man of consequence, family, *and* fortune. It is *they*" — he swung a condemnatory, sabre-like finger back and forth — "who are *non-compos mentis!* And it is *you*" — he dared point a bold finger — "who are *clearly* inane to believe them!"

Never has red been found so violent in the countenance of so many. The atmosphere in the hall was ready to burst. Elizabeth again tried to stop up his mouth; but he would be heard.

"And what is more, rather than *squandering* public resources upon so *trivial* a trial, you would much better acquit yourselves in providing me a personal detachment to hunt this cursed fugitive, whom, ere my affliction, I had, I am convinced, almost delivered unto justice!"

Such an audacious claim could not but engender a demand for its foundation — more so, given the fact that the WANTED posters were yet to arrive and all present were desperate to learn what they could of so already infamous an outlaw. But oh, when our hero could furnish naught but the substance of a dream to support his conviction, a peal of derisive laughter swept about the hall.

Made only indignant at this ridicule, Peter, wishing to silence his mockers, launched into sundry laws and legislations — indeed, confounding all present. As if possessed by a sprite from some city archives, bills flashed across his mind, and he proclaimed the proper measures to be met out in a Stadtgericht, rebutted any acquittal founded on such erroneous grounds of "defamation", vowing to repay the debt in full and vanquish every aspersion against his wits.

All that could now be heard was the ticking of the clock hung on the wainscot above the top bench. For our hero's speeches, having indeed silenced the hall, we can safely deduce none present could discern whether it evidenced his firm principles and knowledge of such laws or his consummate folly. But:

"Tick-Tock. Tick-Tock. Tick, tick, TICK...!"

"You really *are* out of your mind!" rejoined the stadtschultheiss. "But as you are so determined, I shall duly grant you your petition!"

Hence, he not only revoked the acquittal, placing the full debt on Peter to repay in a month or suffer a fate of forced labour, but had him carted off for the night to the town's lock-up for his insolent, irreverent, insubordinate talk.

***

Later that evening, after having been handcuffed, hissed and heckled at; hauled from the hall, heaved onto an open wagon and paraded before all to scorn; hurried to the gaol and hurled into a hovel of a cell, with a great clanging of iron, Peter's misadventure had, in truth, scarcely begun.

Obliged to share the incommodious, fetid, stone-walled weeping moisture lock-up with several most unsavoury-looking rascals, he soon became the object of their knavish curiosity.

How he repented for having seated himself beneath a flickering torch. While its friendly glow banished the gloom of night, it also revealed to his gaze those sorts of grizzly countenances which generally tend only to fright.

Away he looked; his glance fell upon another equally unwelcoming countenance. Startled at this sight, he turned his attention to the narrow slit of bars, purposed to separate the good citizens from the bad. A bold shaft of moonlight presently darted through and struck the far wall, where two faces, a trifle less irksome than the rest, peered at him.

"Don't we know you?" said one, an unwashed lout; he leaned forward.

"I think *not*!" replied Peter, recoiling from him.

"But your face," said the other, equally filthy. "We've *definitely* seen you before. Why are you in here?"

Affronted by such persistent insinuations, and determined to dethrone the fiends' faulty bias, Peter did apprise them of his former rank, employment, stating also that his present arrest was but the result of a strict observance to pride and principle. "So, unless I have had the misfortune of apprehending you for crimes committed in other cantons, I can assure you, your eyes must entirely deceive you."

Possibly intimidated by this speech and its haughty delivery, the men withdrew and fell to muttering between themselves — the most of their words lost to the environing groans, until: "... he's *definitely* that traitor they're searching for..."

Our hero's ears pricked up. *Traitor?*

Such utterances could not but have caught the attention of all ears present. In the unsteady torchlight, madness soon glinted in countless eyes, which did now fix upon our hero with unwelcome portent.

Peter instantly shrank from so many malevolent gazes. Yet, anxious to understand the pair's meaning, he leaned forward to better listen; from their next mumblings, he caught only that they hoped to be rescued by their gang, though they doubted they would; that had they acted with better discretion, they would not have been caught snooping about a schloss and ended up detained among such wretches that swarmed in such present regions, putting themselves at the hazard of forced labour, if not conscription.

Thus deeming himself spared from further insults or claims to any malformed acquaintance, our hero sank back against the cold, damp stone walls, soon lost to musing on his confinement. *I shall endure this with dignity.* Besides, it was but for one night. *No shackle or cell shall tarnish me with the shame of upholding my honour. No. And that fugitive, I shall —*

"You're *definitely* that criminal the world is looking for," resumed the two men as they again leaned forward; their dark, flashing orbs fixed determinedly on him. "'Tis your face that is plastered all over Bern."

"*My* face?" Peter jolted up. "What *nonsense* is this?"

"The WANTED posters, you fool," explained they. "Have you not seen them?"

01 – 17 MARCH 1792

Released from durance at the appointed hour of ten, the next morning, our hero was met at the gate to the gaol by Elizabeth, the pony and sleigh, and a thick blanket. With relief, he mounted the conveyance and wrapped himself against the cold. Together, side-by-side, they set off for the farm — neither brave enough to turn a glance upon the other.

As they embarked on their silent journey, Peter's thoughts dwelled entirely upon the alarming asseverations which closed off the preceding chapter. Though averse to entertaining any notion so abhorrent to his ego, he found he could not so easily banish such a shocking accusation from his mind; uttered with such conviction, it had imprinted itself thereon with some disagreeable persistence. And with what happened in Basel, those ruffians and their strange talk of a "reward", this found him staggered with sickening disbelief.

How strange that two men should possess such similar countenances? Yet it must be so, for the only other prospect, that Peter himself was indeed the very alleged outlaw, was too awful to be borne! *There could not have, before now, run through my veins such notorious blood, could there? Impossible! A man of fortune and family would hardly condescend to such degeneracy?*

Eager to banish such considerations, he forced his mind elsewhere. Despite a night's freezing squalor, rather than repent of his daring courage at the trial, he was only the more resolute for having rescued his character from every impudent pig who had sought to hurl it over a precipice. "I can scarce believe you so readily disposed of my character to such degradation, derision, and disesteem," said he, breaking the silence. "And all for the ambition of evading a trifling debt! You are as mercenary, madam, as your mother!"

Natch, with some glares glistening in her eyes, Elizabeth sharply reproached his defective chain of reasoning, explicating with knife-sharp emphasis that the cost of so assiduously preserving his character — which she had sagely counterbalanced barely a breath before his detrimental outburst — might yet be at his future freedom.

Our crestfallen hero could not repudiate her argument and was forced to concede to her point. "I, perhaps, did not *quite* think that detail through enough."

"*Perhaps*? *Quite*?" A long stream of air billowed from Lizzie's gasp. "Nay, you gave it not a moment's thought at all! And how do you propose to repay this debt? I imagine you have *perhaps* not *quite* thought about that either? Unless you intend on hunting down that fugitive and claiming the reward? — if you can even recall what he looks like!"

Indeed, at these words, our hero shuddered. Moreover, able neither to defend himself nor counter her arraignment on this head either, he did turn face away and fall into a deeper, more brooding silence, watching the snowpacked scenes pass by with promises of an inescapable portent.

***

For Hans, that his daughter failed to arrive on the expected day, he suspected some misadventure had befallen her. That another dawn arrived without her appearance, far worse imaginings took hold. But about noon, a slam of the front door announced her at last.

"Lack-a-day!" She threw her luggage at Harris. "Bear these to my room, Brother; my arms are about to fall off!"

Astonished by her dishevelled aspect, Harris neglected to mention that a slumbering Peter presently occupied her chamber — watched over by Elizabeth.

Not less bemused by her looks and tardy arrival, Hans glanced about the yard for her husband. "Where's Heinrich?"

"Don't speak that odious name again!" Cheeks flushed, she pushed past them and to the kitchen glided. From the table she dragged her late mother's chair across the stone floor to the hearth, demanding the fire be lit.

Where Hans, obeying her command, had not the courage to probe her temper or her husband's whereabouts, Harris, having rather left her luggage at the front door, did. "Let me guess; another stupid argument?"

Only after darting her fiercest glare at her brother did she give way to tears. Hans pulled a chair near and begged she explain herself. Damning the deluge, she confessed the awful truth: "He's gone off with another woman!"

At this, Hans nearly tumbled off his chair. "Another woman?"

The waters again broke through, choking out whatever else she said.

Drawn by the weepings and recognising the anguished, wet countenanced daughter, Elizabeth hastened to her side and took her hand. Words of consolation spoken to her, she then offered tea, which the daughter, so distracted as to perceive who was her comforter, accepted; after silently sipping on the beverage for some minutes, she began her pitiable account:

The fateful event owed to a certain strumpet who took a fancy to her husband as they supped at their local inn. "He says he wasn't, but I say he was most inappropriate with the wench! His hand, grasped by hers, clasped the wrong cup for far too long before he heeded my protests."

Harris dragged a second chair from the table for Elizabeth.

"That odious beast," went on the daughter, "blamed his slowness on the beer. I gave him a whack with my umbrella. Talk grew rather heated. The manager bade us leave; but Heinrich and he exchanged words, which led to a few blows. Before I knew it, the manager flung him out of the door, and they got to brawling in the street like two bears for all to see! 'Twas positively humiliating!"

With more awkwardness than grief, she related how she had naturally fallen aswoon but was brought back to herself by a gentleman, who, seeing she was in great pain, went to great pains to console her, providing restoratives to soothe her spirits.

At these intimations, Elizabeth perceived an unfavourable omen. Hand now retracted and folded in her lap, she listened to what came next.

Heinrich was not to be found anywhere. The gentleman comforter claimed her husband's rage had led to his arrest. But what was her confusion when she realised her beverage steamed with alcohol! Here, she reddened; though 'twas not likely the effect of being at the fireside. "I could barely stand."

Pausing, she implored her auditors to swear not to judge her. Hans swore on his prized pig. Harris, his best fishing reel. Elizabeth answered it was wrong to swear on anything, but promised not to allow the account to prejudice her unfavourably against its narrator.

"Well, what a turn of my head when the gentleman carried me into his personal chariot and offered to convey me wherever my heart wished. Yet, no sooner had we set off, he gave very little ear to my objections — he was in the most violent passion! He called me an angel! A goddess! The handsomest there ever was! And in the next breath, he kissed — he clasped me! I tried to scream, but his lips were so tightly cemented to mine, I almost fainted!"

There were, indeed, several strokes in this speech which offended Elizabeth's virtue. But keeping her promise to listen without judgement, she forbore to announce her disapprobation even in her countenance.

"Then what happened?" said Harris; wide eyes, slack-jawed.

The rake of a man, who was anything *but* the gentleman, only ceased exerting his superior strength when a pistol-shot rang out and the carriage stopped. The daughter thought her last moment had come at the hands of a highwayman. Yet, to her vast surprise, the door swung open and in leapt her husband. Natch, she had thought herself saved, but Heinrich, seeing the rake and her — dress in quite the dishabille; hair, and make-up, too, smudged over both faces — vehemently cursed her for the strumpet he secretly believed her to be (and several other vulgarities she dared not repeat) and abandoned her to the rake.

"*What*?" spluttered Hans, rising from his seat. "I'll teach that —"

"There is more," interrupted the daughter. Hans sat back down.

She had run up the lane after her husband, but thanks to the rake and his intoxicating beverages, she lost her balance and toppled into a ditch — headfirst, with her undergarments on show to the entire world.

Harris stifled a small laugh; for which Hans grabbed a small log and flung at his head. "*Ouch*!"

At any rate, with the world whirling about, she, spitting dirt and screaming for aid — which never arrived — eventually found which way was up and stumbled home to explain herself. But Heinrich was not there; nor for the next four days. On the fifth, she received his clerk (for her husband was a lawyer), who handed her the ill-fated envelope — its contents declaring her Mrs Heinrich Hofer no more.

"My heart is shattered! No man shall *ever again* possess a single fragment of it!" With that, she dissolved into the next deluge of tears and flung out of the kitchen for her bedchamber.

What a shock for the slumbering Peter when she burst in and threw herself onto the bed to give full vent to her grief.

"What in *heavens* is *this*?" He shoved her away. "How *dare* you charge in here like a wild animal and ruin my sleep! Who *are* you?"

Znüni, previously dozing by the fire, sprang onto the bed and barked at the intruder before jumping to the floor and sniffing suspiciously at her feet.

As when the Alpine rivulet yields its last drop to the relentless summer drought; as when the shrinking glacier trickles its last refreshment to the vale below; as when the vast lake becomes a desert, likewise, did the well of sorrow run dry. "Which god hath carved thee and dropped thee, divine gift, into this very bedchamber?" said she as she unruffled her skirt, curtsied, smiled, blushed, and fluttered her long, though still damp lashes.

"Pardon?" stuttered Peter, recoiling from her. "What are you —?"

"Hephaestus, perhaps?" interrupted she as she took a step closer.

"*Hephaestus*?" echoed Peter, shrinking farther from her.

"The god of smiths, metalworking, carpenters, artisans, and sculptors," explained she, taking yet another daring step forward.

Znüni, made only the merrier by this intrigue, panting heavily and thrashing his tail, leapt back onto the bed, while Peter, recoiling still the more, fell backwards off it.

He was not long splayed athwart the stone slabs, for his quick eye descried the fire iron next to the hearth. Seizing the improvisatory weapon, he then sprang to his feet, thrusting it at his bedeviller, advance-lunge and esquiver. "Come not a step closer!"

This heroic display menaced not the approaching Peitho. She sprang to the mantel and grabbed a tall brass candelabra, thrusting it in mirthful retaliation.

Znüni, of course, barked only the more merrily as she now duelled Peter with no less deft than one would imagine of the warrioress Zenobia, or perhaps how she had earlier wielded that umbrella over her faithless husband's head.

Drawn by the barking, the furore, and hysterics, Elizabeth arrived, putting an end to the monomachy. His makeshift blade dropped, Peter flew to Lizzie's side. Observing his escape, the daughter likewise discarded her weapon and collapsed onto the bed in a gale of laughter, joined by Znüni, who, now an ally, licked her with avid cheer.

Hans now entered with Harris. "I see you've met my daughter."

"*Encountered* her!" returned Peter as he surveyed the irreverent, indecorous, insouciant family, knowing not who to despise the most.

'Twas was most likely Hans' voice that stirred the daughter to sit up and straighten out her gown. "Father," cooed she, "when were you going to tell me you'd installed such a handsome beast in my bedchamber?"

Hans only laughed heartily. Harris ribbed his side and joined in the laughter, while the daughter, all giggles and blushes, pretended to swoon dead away.

At this spectacle, a glow crept over Elizabeth's cheeks. In her breast, she encountered a peculiar sting. To compose herself and to abate her flush, she moved to the cooler air of the window, where, had she discriminated more impartially her feelings, she might have discerned the impregnation of jealousy.

So, Helene — a variant appellation of that certain daughter whose abduction sparked the Trojan War — was the name of this rather forward girl. Though not the sensiblest of her species, nature's bounty, indiscriminate to rich and poor alike, had somewhat compensated for the want of elegance; she was handsome. That said, her understanding was not without some cultivation, for she had, since her marriage, developed a bent for the Greek classics.

"Lizzie!" Helene now recognised her. "What a simpleton I am." She laughed immoderately, joining her at the casement. "How have you been?" Oblivious to the other's reserve, she prattled on, "I can see very well. You've turned out very pretty. Such radiant locks." She took a ringlet between her fingers. "And your complexion!" She touched Lizzie's cheek. "But what brings you —?" Here, she glanced about the room until her eyes landed on her brother. "Of course! Father wrote me about your betrothal." Arm linked through Lizzie's, she dragged her from the window. "How I have *always* longed for a sister. We shall make the *happiest* sisters ever, don't you agree? And we shall —"

"They're *not* engaged," interrupted Hans with some sharpness.

"They're *not*?" Helene looked back and forth bewilderedly. "But *why*?"

Though our hero underestimated the claws of jealousy raking at his own breast, in his wish to ward off the incorrigible coquette, he stepped forward and snatched Elizabeth from her. "Because she is to be affianced to *me*!"

***

About mid-morn the following day, after returning from the farmer's market, Edmunda was just putting the water to boil and bidding Elizabeth to ready the table, when: "Oh! I nearly forgot." She flew to the hallway and retrieved a letter.

"This came for you two days past, before I was dragged off to the... Never mind."

Its superscription was written in a hand altogether unknown to Elizabeth. Breaking the seal, she found its contents were a letter, written in these terms:

> *To Miss Elizabeth,*
> *You will, I pray, forgive my means of conveying so stern a warning. But circumstances will speak in my defence. Do not, I beseech you, sacrifice your dignity or heart to so contemptible a wretch named Peter.*

Saying it was a note from an old friend, Elizabeth retreated to her bedchamber and resumed perusing this most perplexing correspondence:

> *Though not acquainted with the means by which he has imposed himself on you, I am certain they will be the least of his crimes since leaving me despised, abandoned, and humiliated at the altar. Whatever tale he has fabricated, trust it only to the Devil! Your own virtue, I am sure, will perceive not malice nor vituperation in these lines.*
> *Your most humble, sincere servant.*

Lizzie's eyes fell from the lines. "Who *is* this man that I have hazarded into my life?" Detecting a lingering trace of perfume on the paper only deepened the mystery of this correspondence from an unknown woman, who, having somehow learned of her name and direction, could apprise her of Peter's history.

Considerable indeed was our heroine's predicament, though of a nature quite contrary to that which the epistoler had doubtless sought to inspire. As we know, Elizabeth had not the slightest intention of ever marrying Peter. Therefore, she needed no added dissuasion on that score. Rather, her perplexity stemmed from uncertainty whether to show him this letter.

Verily, we may wonder *why* she would *ever* vacillate. That she had neither a genuine claim to him nor any sincere affection to bridge her aversion, this would have been the ideal moment to be rid of him once and for all.

Oh! How was she to rid herself of this wretch without compromising her own virtue? Perhaps, without revealing the letter, she could simply end their faux amour on the grounds of incompatibility? Surely, none would censure her thus!

But wait! Would not she then be vilified for abandoning a man who, however stupid, was robbed of his memories, with nowhere to go and no family or friends to turn to? Would not aspersions be heaped upon her by the townsfolk? She needed to ponder no such obloquies, for her own conscience forbade this.

"Lizzie!" came Edmunda's shrills from the kitchen. "*Here*!"

Seated at the table, Edmunda was plagued by whatever storm rended her mind and contorted her face. "I *can't* have you wed that *buffoon*!" She paused, likely pondering whether she had chosen the right word. "Yet what to do about Father Francis? *He* won't let you *not* wed him — else face eternal hellfire!"

In this mode, she continued for some minutes, torn between Father Francis' menaces, reprobating Peter's character, and reproaching herself for considering evicting a man who, despite his added stupidity at court, had spared her from destitution. "Mayhap we can foist him off on someone?" Her face rippled violently. "That won't do it! Nobody'll have him!" Her head slumped into her hand. "I have it!" She sat upright, eyes alight. "I'll take a hammer to his brain, and we can convey the senseless oaf back to the ditch where he was found!"

Her expression quickly altered; she let out a great harrumph. "Blast it all! Perhaps the war shall do my work and relieve us of the idiot? With any luck, the fool'll catch a cannon ball squarely to his dense skull, knocking what meagre wit still rattles inside it, prompting him to forget all about us and wander afield, never to trouble us again!"

She again huffed, tutted, and puffed, a new notion taking hold. "But nay! Knowing my luck, Old Nick shall guard his way through shot and shell only to bring him back to our door to plague me anew — return *addled as ever* he will, heaven-bent on tormenting us unto the grave!"

Judging by the rising colour of her countenance and the haste of her twitching fingers, she approached the delivery of her sentence. Yet, it seemed that something, perhaps sentiment, raced in as Peter's advocate. Likewise, possibly pity tried its hand at vindicating his stupidity. Lastly, mercy, who does oft play tricks on all humankind, certainly rose up to mitigate his punishment.

"If only he didn't have amnesia, I wouldn't care a fig."

Ernest and Peter so happened to enter the kitchen from the yard. "Who knew we had such a talented future son-in-law?" said Ernest, wrapping his arm about our hero's shoulder while referencing the remaining section of fence which he had volunteered to mend. "I hear even the garrison sings his praises!"

For once, Edmunda was struck speechless. Lizzie, too.

Such scenes of kinship and camaraderie were, however, shattered by a thunderous hammering on the main portal. Ernest opened it to reveal the familiar, unwelcome sight of a captain and two redcoats.

"Peter and Emil," the captain dispensed with all pleasantries, "are to report to the garrison within the hour. We march for Porrentruy this evening."

"*Porrentruy*?" Edmunda shoved Ernest aside. "Why drag my darling child off there? *Here*, take Peter alone!"

She practically thrust him into the captain's arms, who fixed her with a bone-chilling glare. "Because, *madam*, the Comité de la Commune again attempts to overthrow the bishop's authority and open the gates to the revolutionaries! The French advance faster than expected. And *all* able-bodied men are to report for duty!"

At this rebuttal, Edmunda let out a great harrumph, planting her fists on her hips. "Those dastardly frogs! Why can't they just stay in their own pond?!"

At any rate, resigned to their fate, Peter *and* Emil readied for the garrison.

And so, with tearful farewells and hurried provisions, Edmunda thus waved *Emil* off with all the fanfaronade to be expected of maternal distress.

***

The march to Porrentruy, ladened with an artillery convoy, proved a trial. Not only did Peter endure several petty officers' incessant prods and barks, but he had to succour a whimpering Emil and Harris, who swiftly irritated their fellow soldiers, earning the three of them accusations of cowardice and worse! To be sure, Peter's glares and eloquent, if incomprehensible, rebukes only rendered his tormentors bewildered, gawping back at him as though he was a madman.

Amidst this misery, a snippet of talk caught our hero's attention. Two captains, some rows ahead, discussed the fugitive. The captains cursed the traitor for emboldening the French, exposing Basel to further threat, and vowed to hang, string, and quarter the scoundrel if they had the opportunity to identify him — which, said one, will become quite the competition with the expected arrival of posters in the morrow.

Naturally, Peter could not help but ask the men to repeat what they had said. Indeed, hearing for the second time of the anticipated delivery, a peculiar buzzing clawed at the edges of his thoughts. Verily, with each subsequent marching stride, there pressed upon his chest a stranger and more disquieting tightness. Though he strove to shake it off, imagining such uneasiness stemmed from the present tensions, it only grew in proportion to his efforts to efface it.

As Peter glanced at Harris, he noted his eyes were fixed upon him; found in their expression was a strange, almost distrustful, character which he could not fathom. Made only the more uneasy by such a gaze, he averted his own.

'Twas after midnight when the detachment reached Porrentruy.

Wearied from the long march, Peter scanned the scene; the normally slumbering town buzzed with an unnatural activity: flickering torches darting here and there; barricades hastily erected in the main square; anxious townsfolk peering from behind shuttered windows; armour clanged, and officers shouted commands at companies of soldiers — swelled by the new arrivals — muskets at the ready. The air crackled with uneasy anticipation, the prelude to a storm.

The captain's briefing was grim. "French sympathisers multiply daily. Trust no one completely — even among our own ranks, treachery may lurk."

At these words, Harris' eyes shot towards our hero.

Suddenly, there tore through the night: "The French!" shouted a nearby voice. "They're attacking!"

Chaos erupted. The ordered ranks dissolved into a blur of movement. Muskets roared to life, spitting fire and lead into the darkness.

Emil and Harris, paralysed by fear, stood frozen. A lead ball whizzed past the former's head, singing his hair. He cried out, clinging to our hero.

"Get down!" Peter shoved them both to the ground while shielding Emil with his own body.

With terrifying ferocity, the battle raged on around them.

Outnumbered but determined, the Swiss fought fiercely.

It being now or never, our hero scrambled to his feet, pulling Emil and Harris up. “Stay behind me! Stay low!”

Instincts, as if honed by years of military experience, surged through Peter’s every fibre as he guided them through the tumult, dodging musket fire and falling debris.

Of a sudden, out from the swirling vortex of smoke and shadows, a group of French soldiers emerged. Their bayonets glinting in the torchlight, they charged towards them.

Peter shoved Emil and Harris behind a nearby stack of barrels. “Stay!”

Wielding his own bayonet, our hero met the attackers head-on. The blade, a blur of swift motion in his hands, seemed possessed of a life of its own. He parried a thrust, disarmed another with a swift kick, and, with a shudder of revulsion, drove the pike into the shoulder of a third.

Gunpowder smoke coiling around, the acrid stench rushing into his nostrils set his head spinning... the present chaos seemed to still... every sound stretching thin... and distant... until an eerie silence descended... The world shimmered into something else entirely: a vaulted chamber; barrels of powder stacked like coffins; a sword-wielding figure whose face swam familiar yet unknowable through the haze. Tall flames rose all about; shadows danced and writhed like living things, and then — an explosion that tore through his skull like thunder.

Dazed, head throbbing, heart thrashing, breath seized in his throat, he staggered... the phantom heat still scorched his cheeks when the world snapped back with sudden, violent clarity.

In the next blink, a Frech officer, sabre flashing, lunged at Emil. Peter spun around, intercepting the blow — the impact sent him staggering back.

And so, throughout the night, amidst the swirling chaos of smoke and gunpowder, fought Peter, protector and shield to a terrified Emil and Harris.

As dawn broke over the ravaged town, the fight at last waned with the French retreating, leaving behind a scene of devastation and the stench of blood.

Peter, Emil, and Harris, exhausted and bloodied but alive, surveyed the aftermath, grateful to have survived but grieved to behold the fallen.

***

Around two weeks were gone by. Elizabeth and Edmunda were just arriving at the farmhouse, only to find villagers clutching papers and lined up at the stable.

In no little perplexity did our heroine and her mother catch the complimentary words that flitted on the chilly air. Peter was deemed a "divine arbitrator" — "no longer an idiot" but a "clever fellow" — "and a brave one, at that!"

Out from the stable, a recently widowed townswoman hobbled over, smiling ear to ear. "How charming is your Peter," croaked she, tearing up. "He's no useless dolt. He's an angel of God." A kiss bestowed on Lizzie's cheek, she then hobbled onwards out of the yard.

"Have I died and woken up in some strange afterlife?" said Edmunda.

Helene came out of the farmhouse and seeing their confusion alleviated them of it. "As happy as this is for the townsfolk — and many have come and gone from here today, I assure you — the high-ups and merchants will be most displeased. He's only bringing a monstrous heap of trouble on his own head."

This curious state of affairs owed itself entirely to his theatrics at the recent trial, which, while it infuriated the magistrates and earned him a night in jail, caught the optimistic ears of certain exploited townsfolk. The above-mentioned widow had consulted our hero regarding her late husband's will and was thereby saved from eviction; Peter's expertise had revealed the Swiss guardsman had wisely secured his pension for his wife's benefit should any ill befall him.

Doubting she heard right, Elizabeth hastened inside the stable. There, to her additional wonder, she found a most contented-looking Peter seated at a make-shift desk (two overturned tea crates). Proud as much with himself as for his happy defendants, who had left him as payment, eggs, some wildflowers, a jar of preserves and other humble offerings, he beamed with smiles.

"Ah, Lizzie." He rose from his bench (an upturned bucket).

"What *exactly* did you do in the Guard?" said she.

"If I could answer that, I would *not* be an amnesiac, *would* I?"

Presently, an indistinct sound caught their ears, preceded by the measured tread of soldiers and the clank of martial appurtenances. A commanding voice bade all clear the way — the scuffling of many feet signalled their obedience — before asking after Harris.

Ah, dear reader, you have likely guessed it.

Harris, all sinister triumph written in his face, soon ushered a colonel inside, followed by Edmunda, Helene, Znüni, and several redcoats.

The colonel levelled a finger at Peter. "Is *that* the outlaw?"

"Aye! 'Tis *he*," replied Harris, too excited to draw another breath.

"*Outlaw*?" choked Peter while pointing at his own breast in dread. He staggered backwards, nearly tripping over the upturned bucket as every horror imaginable besieged his mind — the damning jailhouse conversation ringing in his ears as a seeming prophecy.

Poster unfurled, the colonel held it up and contrasted the increasingly pale and unnerved man before him to the likeness depicted. "You say *this* is he?"

Harris nodded eagerly, but no sooner did he cast his own eyes upon the poster than he turned as ashen as Peter. "But?" stuttered he, snatching the poster. "It's him — I mean, it *was* him!"

The colonel wrenched the poster back and flung it with disdain to the ground. "Should I have your useless eyes gorged out and fed to the ravens?" thundered he, drawing his sword. "Do not ever again aspire so incompetently to a reward unless you wish to be fastened to the pillory and flogged. I'll not be so lenient a second time!"

With that, in the same measured tread, the colonel quit the stables, followed by his marching men-at-arms.

Like one struck through the heart by a thunderbolt, Harris was too aghast to answer the interrogations, which hence came his way like rocks and stones. He snatched up the poster and regarded it and Peter. Finally, emitting a wailing whimper, he tossed it back down, quit the stables, and fled to the farmhouse. The slam of the door gave to all left behind little doubt of his disappointment.

Indeed, sage reader, this peculiar turn of events may have raised some quizzical eyebrows! For though we were led to expect a rather dismal outcome for our hero, instead, even in my office as narrator and omnipotent engineer of our tale, methinks some roguish god upsets my plot. But lo, I must not reveal overmuch, lest I forestall my own devices. Suffice it to say for now, that the abhorred poster which should have wrought ruin on our hero's head proved but a counterfeit! Yet produced by whom, you ask? Why, none other than that same colonel whom the greedy Harris had hitherto pinned his grasping hopes upon!

Most confounded was Peter, who, only now coming back to himself, lunged forth and seized the poster. For some moments, his mind grasped not what met his eyes. And as for Harris' accusation, though ostensibly false, it struck him in a way he could not yet comprehend. Who else watched? Who else suspected?

Lizzie and Edmunda rushed forward to inspect the poster for themselves.

"Thanks heavens," said Peter with a deep exhale. Quivering of voice, he began to recount the offensive conversation that had passed at the jailhouse.

But let us set aside all subsequent talk pertaining to Harris and his motives for hoping to betray Peter, for Znüni raced out of the stables barking, and a fresh disturbance stole away all attention to a situation of more dangerous merit.

"Help! *Help*!" A man possessed of wild confusion burst into the yard.

Prevailed upon by Helene to calm himself, the man disclosed with fits and starts, the cause of his terror. "'Tis Johannes, I believe, miss! The horses — they've gone *wild*, dragging the carriage down the lane!"

Peter enquired after the coachman, to which the man turned to Elizabeth in bewilderment. "The coachman, Miss, he's — and *your* father!"

Elizabeth started back in anxious confusion. "My father?"

The man noticed Edmunda and addressed her. "By all appearances, the both of them, *dead*!"

Each letting out screams, Edmunda and Elizabeth collapsed to the dirt.

"Which way did they go?" demanded Peter. The shaking man pointed out the direction. "Helene, assist Elizabeth to the bench over there. And you, sir, please aid her mother."

After hastening into the stable, Peter returned astride a horse; with a determined gallop, he raced off, stirring up a cloud of dirt and debris, pursued some distance by Znüni.

Drawn from his garrison of shame by the commotion, Harris joined his sister as consoler. Together, mouths wide, they watched Peter crest a hill and vanish heroically from view.

"He positively rides like a Spartan," cooed Helene. And overcome perhaps by the flutterings of her heart, she fell into a swoon.

For several tense minutes, nothing could be seen or heard of from the runaway carriage. But upon a stretch of half-wintery wood, intermingled with a blur of scattered chalets and huts which flew by on either side, fresh ruts of carriage wheels appeared in the dirt.

Infused with hope, Peter drove his mount ever faster.

"Ya!"

Within a short distance, the forest terminated and opened onto a broad, frosty turfed aspect bounded by rows of partly whitened pines. The dirt track bent to the left at the base of the wooded hills, but the grooves of the wheels broke from it, entering the grassland and vanishing.

From a break in the distant tree-line, a circling flock of agitated gulls ascended the pallid skies. It had to be the carriage!

Upon reaching the gap, he spied tracks which entered and exited a shallow stream. Eyes lifted, he beheld Bubendorf's village outskirts. Confused peasants milled about, pointing out to each other what was likely the carriage's path.

After a distance, the tracks reappeared, penetrating a wooded eminence.

"Ya!"

On his reaching the summit, the chaise came into his view.

"Ya!"

Quickly he drew abreast of the careening vehicle. The three passengers were being tossed violently about its open-topped interior. One, seeing him, screamed for aid. With a wave to signal his intent, our hero edged the swift beast forward until they galloped shoulder-to-shoulder with the crazed horses.

Ernest was collapsed on the seat, next to the coachman; each were soaked in blood — unconscious, if not dead.

Grabbing hold of one frenzied horse, Peter swung himself across.

Barely had he seized the reins and hauled back with all his might, when a termination of ground opening onto a precipice fast approached!

Thankfully, his yanking on the reins brought the near-calamity to its jarring cessation. Disaster averted, he rushed to Ernest and checked for a pulse. Though it was alarmingly faint, life yet stirred. The blood spurting wound was that of ammunition having penetrated his shoulder.

Ernest's neck scarf removed, Peter pressed it to the wound to slow the bleeding. Then, tearing his own outer garment in two, with one half, he secured the neck scarf about Ernest's wound, and with the other fashioned a sling.

The coachman had most certainly perished. A bullet wound to the chest.

One of the two gentlemen passengers now struggled to alight from the chaise, but his enfeebled limbs already trembling and one wheel collapsing, he lost his footing and fell.

Peter leapt down to offer aid, but the man waved him off.

The second gentleman called for medical help for his wife; she was still too affrighted to be yet removed from the vehicle.

Many villagers riding aback of mules arrived and, eager to be of aid, obliged Peter's request to find a surgeon and a replacement carriage.

More peasants soon climbed the steep slopes and joined themselves to the growing crowd. All commented on the near catastrophe and cheered the miraculous intervention and heroism of the rider Peter.

At length, the requested surgeon appeared with a physician in a wagon, followed by an empty coach. Ernest, deemed safe for removal, was carried to the former. Johannes' wife, only after repeated entreaties, calmed herself enough to be removed from the collapsed vehicle. The other gentleman, anxious to thank the hero, searched the crowds for him.

Directed as he was to Peter, no sooner did he fix his distressed but grateful eyes on him than incredulity and confusion seemed to banish all relief from his face.

Rooted to the spot as if he beheld a phantom, he spoke in a voice betraying the potent confusion of his soul. "Have not... I... met you... before?"

Act 3

29 March 1792

—

01 May 1792

29 MARCH – 03 APRIL 1792

Almost two weeks had trotted by since the misadventure, which concluded the second act. Bubendorf was thrown into a delirium of talk, hatching wild theories about the mystery marksman and his wicked motives. Indeed, did all lament the changing of the times, for while a neighbouring schloss was lately despoiled of its treasures, those two rogues from the jailhouse scene — arrested for plotting another such raid — had been freed by armed men, who waylaid the wagon en route to the gallows.

With the changing also of the seasons, as winter retreated before spring, as the bare branches sprouted their infant foliage, as the melting snows vanished from the valleys, so too did the infamy of the pompous Peter thaw into a more agreeable distinction.

For having already protected Emil in the battle and now also having saved Ernest from certain demise, every prejudice Edmunda held against our hero — frozen like icicles by the Frost Giants — now melted away as if by fairy magic; for their Fairy Queen, who does oft battle those aforementioned icy brutes, had possibly poured her warmth and flowers upon Edmunda's heart. And with the warmer waters which hence gushed forth from that otherwise berating organ, Edmunda found she could hardly refuse Peter anything, be it great or small, lavish or frugal, reasonable or ridiculous.

Likewise, by Peter's bravery and daring, Elizabeth — spared both the deaths of her father and her patron Pier, coupled with her brother's safety — her affections and sensibilities were so profoundly touched that even the accusatory correspondence and its concomitant concerns had quite vacated the forefront of her mind. Thus, with smiles so meek, so fond, so confiding, she confessed, though wordlessly, the dissolving disinclinations of her mind and the emerging emotions of her heart, which could not help but escape into her occasional blush.

As for Peter, his shoulder again injured in his heroics, he was granted temporary leave from the garrison and again prescribed a convalescence in the comfort of Miss Helene's bedchamber.

'Twas during this interlude that Hans, still hungering to separate the lovers, saw several advantages to his daughter's failed marriage. Besides having her to help on the farm, he believed her prettiness, if ploughed into Peter's notice, might bring about certain fruits. And if so, not only could he marry off his son to the one, but his daughter to the other, profiting him three extra pairs of helpful hands. Yet, how to induce in the aloof and unromantic breast of Peter that amorous inclination towards his daughter certainly required Hans to summon his utmost artifice, for Peter was so unforthcoming respecting his heart as to leave him only a-fuming and a-guessing. And Helene, though of a rather forward nature, since she learned Peter was to be affianced to Lizzie, she sank back into the gloomy nostalgia of her divorce, hence necessitating her father's utmost wits.

At length, Hans' contriving heart hit on two principles — if we may call them so. The first, which tends not only to bring forth the hidden rogueries from even the staunchest of wholesome men, but transforms them into the most monstrous of debauchees. The second, which tends both to prevail over the scruples of a vulnerable female and rears them to a full-grown infatuation.

Accordingly, with the claim to expedite Peter's health, Hans prescribed a powerful potation under the guise of a pleasant panacea. For Helene, to buoy her sadness, he proffered a reinvigorating, though equally pungent, cordial. With instructions to oblige, to utilise every opportunity when Elizabeth would be absent, to distract and to entertain Peter's bored mind, Hans then despatched — nay, shoved — her posthaste to the bedchamber.

Howsoever innocently, though not entirely guilelessly, she obeyed these injunctions, once seeing Peter abed, she succumbed to that weakness of which she had already been guilty. The distemper of her divorce was again expelled forthwith from her bosom by the scorpion whose sting beset her with the most violent passion.

But neither her wit, vivacity, compliments, blushes, or smiles made even a meagre dent in Peter's indifference. Her salacious solicitudes, he saw only as vulgar imitations of the sincere, unfeigned, and caring Elizabeth. Her conversation he found tedious and unrestrained. And her quips he perceived were more indiscreet than intelligent. Were it not for the alcohol insinuating its devilish powers upon his brain, he would have remained only increasingly frustrated, imposed upon, and pushed away her advances.

Anyhow, as chance would have it, during this exploit a visitor came a-calling. But Helene, quite feeling the effects of that naughty cordial amidst her merry, intemperate giggles as she fed Peter the strawberry jam Swiss roll she baked that morning, heard not the rapping at the farmhouse door. So, it fell to her brother to answer it.

It will not be difficult to delineate the displeasure, the disgust, the damnation soon written in the visitor's dial. Standing at the bedchamber door, he stared upon the seductress half-sprawled across the bed; fork in one hand, plate in the other, but cake smeared more about the offenders' mouths, cheeks, chins, necks, bodice, and tunic.

"What degenerate wantonness is *this*?" thundered Father Francis, hurling his heavy Bible to the floor as we might imagine Moses had the stone tablets. "Dismount that bed this *instant*!"

Helene turned ashen. The plate fell from her hand and smashed across the flagstones, at which Znüni made exploits and gobbled up the cake fragments.

While crossing himself, the holy man stepped in and snatched up his Bible. Upon the unvirtuous woman, he fixed his fire-and-brimstone glare until she moved not less than several feet away from the bed. Only then did the indignant Father burn his gaze into Peter's soul.

"Hearing of your fame," said he, "I had wished to congratulate you in person and impart the blessing of God. But I see I am deceived by these reports. For I find only a duty to scourge the rotten flesh of your heart and to retrieve you from the shackles of Satan himself."

Znüni growled at the holy man; but frightened into silent submission by an equally damming glare, he crawled with tail between legs under the bed.

Father Francis now launched into the most severe denunciations against men and women, accusing the former of "possessing no attachment but to their selfish and too often libidinous interests" and the latter of being "so equally dependent on vicious inclinations" that "notwithstanding already being married" they can rarely be trusted with the opposite sex!

Helene's colour oscillated red and white. "But I am no longer —"

"I have been away for a little over two months," continued the Father, brooking not her interruption, "and Hell itself has erupted. Why, its fallen angels are running wild, plaguing my parish with the machinations of criminality, profligacy, lust, and avarice!"

Helene's passions were indeed equally tempestuous whichever way they tilted; she threw herself at his feet. "Holy Father! Divine guardian of my fame and peace! I have been a wicked, wicked girl!" Producing a prodigious volume of tears, she bathed the holy man's feet with them. "Please forgive this foolish, foolish girl. For though she has sinned, she recognises that even the best of mankind can never be as divinely good as you."

It will hardly surprise us that a person who lived an entire life to so strict a calling should be so violently shocked at the least deviation from it in another. But surveying the wench in stern silence and perhaps moved by her entreaties — probably more her panegyric — he raised her onto her feet, steadied her with a firm hand to her elbow, and promised to adapt his next sermon to her needs. "Prove yourself contrite, and I will judge you less deserving of Hell."

Assuaged by this pledge of pardon, Helene wiped away the tears and garish streaks of jam, curtsied, and, glancing at Peter a cunning, impenitent smile, departed with an airy stride.

Peter now ventured to vindicate himself, but Father Francis put his sacred hand up to him. "Silence will become you better. Your unworthiness of my compliments remains the same. But there is still another matter upon which I am required to talk with you: your forthcoming betrothment to Miss Elizabeth."

***

The next morn, after breakfasting on a most delicious serving of eggs, toasted bread, and freshly churned butter, Peter returned to bed to ponder once more the scroll. The more he studied the partial text, there gradually crept over his thoughts that he perhaps ought to visit Basel again, to see if people there might know something more. His attention returning to the WANTED poster, which he again compared against the earlier poster fragments obtained, he could not help but observe the several disparities between them.

A rap on the door, however, soon disrupted his musings.

"Yes?" called he.

Elizabeth answered.

Scroll and fragments placed on the bedside table, he bade her enter.

First, determining whether he was well enough for visitors, she then explained two important folks demanded an audience with him.

Once assured they were not Father Francis and the Pope, our hero replied, "that is a relief! For I believe I have never contended with so holy a tyrant! Very well, let them in."

Elizabeth beckoned forth the visitants.

Consequently, a man of some sixty-odd years, followed by a woman of rouge and attempts at concealing her own, entered in so solemn an air that with the silence accompanying it, there was announced an importance to their visit. The former, presently bowing, donned a glistening white cravat and the habit à la française: red and gold silk striped justeaucorps; bejewelled frock-coat with richly embroidered cuffs. The latter, presently curtsying, sported a deep-green heavy sateen and twill damask redingote, white petticoat, gloves, and a sparkling fichu stuffed into her ample décolletage.

After scrutinising them in equal silence, feeling from their pinched countenances as though he were himself under a looking glass, Peter turned his unharmed eyes to Elizabeth. "However pleasantly adorned, who are they?"

She inhaled deeply. "Your parents."

"My *parents*?" He re-fixed on them his now confounded eyes.

"My *child*!" cried the woman, rushing forth. But rather than recline at the bedside, she tripped on the hem of her skirt and disappeared head-first almost entirely under the bed.

The man, looking affrighted, sprang to her aid and dragged her out by her heels, while Peter, far too astonished to move even a limb, simply gaped on.

Thus retrieved, the woman shooed the man off and reorganised her dishevelled state. Remarking a pearl button had popped off her bodice, she dropped to her knees and again vanished under the bed, searching for it.

"*Vous voilà!*" said she in her notably muffled, choking, French accent.

While watching the woman's legs, which did stick out, threshing the flagstones, Elizabeth evinced vast bewilderment; no doubt she perplexed at the mother for esteeming so greatly her missing button as opposed to her son, who was also lost but now found.

The lady soon re-emerged and held up the lustrous item before inserting it in her pocket. Again, she dropped to her knees, this time with an air of elegance, and commandeered Peter's hand, wetting it with her tears. "My dearest child. It *is* you."

As Peter looked at her, he could neither speak nor pull away, doubtful that his heart still worked. For searching within for its beat, he found all was silent; as was his mind obliterated of all order and comprehensibility. Was it truly possible his parents had found him?

"Son." The man's accent was more German. He too dropped to his knees but quickly stood back up, for his joints cracked and snapped louder than the logs ablaze on the hearth. "Our *heroic* son. We have searched the world for you."

"The most tormenting afflictions we have suffered!" The mother glanced at the wall stencilling, the candlesticks on the mantel, and particularly the sparkling trinkets on the dresser. "But at last, we find you. Do you... *remember* us?"

Peter opened his mouth, but words came not to his tongue.

The father perched himself on the edge of the bed and took Peter's other hand. "Elizabeth has apprised us of your condition," said he, with cool affection. "Can you really not recall a single memory of your past?"

Again, Peter opened his mouth; but still so stunned was he that nothing came out of it. The man and his wife exchanged several significant glances and then stared at Elizabeth.

"It is as I explained," said she, shrinking from their stares.

Once more looking at each other, the parents nodded some tacit communication.

"My child!" resumed the mother, producing tears anew of apparent maternal joy and consolation. "We have much to acquaint you with." She gave Elizabeth a certain look, which communicated that she should leave the room.

Consequently, as soon as the door closed: "Who, *exactly, is* that woman?"

Just then, Edmunda burst in. "It's been impossible to discover anything with his memory gone," shrilled she. "Lizzie tried to stop me from coming with nonsense about granting you time to reacquaint. What a fuss about nothing, said I, they've the rest of their lives for that!"

"Elizabeth's mother," explained a most piqued Peter. "Elizabeth," (she was looking verily abashed) "escort my visitors to the parlour. I will join you momentarily."

"And here he comes," said Hans with iron-weighted irony as he aggressively stoked the long-dormant parlour fire. "The hero of the canton."

Edmunda snatched Peter to herself and the mother on an old partially reupholstered green velvet chaise facing the room, which, according to the mother, though spacious and furnished comfortably, was far from her own taste.

As the lady evaluated — all with an air of distinct, though critical refinement — the sofas, the tables distributed atop a large rug, and the several dressers arranged about the space, Peter understood her to be a collector of sorts.

Edmunda now probably aimed to appear somewhat of an expert, too. After casting some envious looks the lady's way, she passed her own remarks on the dark wooden floors, the joisted ceiling, and the half-panelled walls; she stated particularly how, were it not for the light afforded by the many windows, it would be as gloomy as Aladdin's grave.

Peter suppressed his smirks and laughs at her faux pas with a feigned yawn. I am sure my readers divined she meant to say Aladdin's Cave...

Of course, since Edmunda had endured the most insufferable of terms since Peter's arrival, she just had to preside and ask: "Who let him talk so fancy?" And: "Who gave him airs and not manners?" And: "Who gave him books instead of tools?" And: "Who did he get his stupidity from?"

Probably enduring the same rush of violent blood as her husband, the mother, her brow having already contracted little by little each time she listened to the garrulous woman, now frowned with seeming severity.

As much embarrassed as irritated, Peter rejoined, "*cette impertinente va* —" but a gasp prevented his finishing the denunciation. "I speak *French*?"

All eyes turned astonished to him and then to the parents.

"*Oui!*" affirmed the rouged, reddening all the more mother. "You received your education in that *terre glorieuse,* at its finest institute."

All eyes swung back to our hero.

"Schooled in France?" said he. "That would explain it." Pride tingled through him. "I suspected I was possessed of much native genius."

Sighing, laughing, he stood up, sat back down; he could not stay still.

"Ask me anything in French," bade he to Edmunda. He turned to Elizabeth. "Even Italian — Oh! do I speak that *too*?" Immediately, out of his mouth there came: "*Mare, Fuoco, e Moglie. Tre Male Cose!*" (The sea, fire, and wives. Three bad things!) "*Parlo anche italiano*? I *do*!" He turned to the mother. "But *how*?"

For sure, all widening eyes watching him with perceivable awe again turned to the parents, expecting their reply; save Edmunda, that is:

"And *this* is all you remember?" In turn, huffing, puffing, and tutting, she upbraided the parents for having raised him so vain, indulged him in "only pointless things," and not taught him the more important things, like milking the cow, feeding the chickens, and so on.

Too elated at rediscovering such modicums of brilliance to regard Edmunda's complaints, Peter sprang to Elizabeth. "I knew I was no idiot!" He clasped her hands. He was no criminal after all, but only good breading! Surely, there had to be some mix-up in Basel and even more so in the jail? "Can such an auspicious occasion as this be true? How I shall laugh in the faces of they who disparaged me! Thank heavens for these parents who return to me and —" Here, however, a sudden whisper of dubiety struck his mind.

Nonetheless eager to embrace the idea of being the offspring of seemingly noble parents, our hero asked for proof of their claims.

Struck with wonderment was he — nay, *everyone* — when the father presented a birth certificate confirming Peter's name and corresponding so convincingly all manner of circumstances; for example, his probable age and, most stimulating, his so long wished-for noble lineage.

For some moments, all present — including Edmunda — verily lost the power of speech. Likely most affected was Elizabeth, her thoughts distracted by certain terrors gathering fast at her mind: self-reproach for having exchanged her virtue in purporting a complete strange for her faux lover; and the tempest of shame which painted to her imagination the strictures of dishonesty, defiance, and deception she would encounter when making that confession.

As this new reality claimed Peter's mind, dispelling fears of past villainy, he saw he might learn of his history. To the bedchamber, he dashed and returned with the scroll and the newspaper.

"Can you tell me who wrote this?" He shoved the scroll into the father's hands.

The mother loaned her own inquisitive eyes to the investigation. At first, neither was sure how to answer. When Peter directed their attention to the broken seal, G.V.V. almost instantly did this incline the father to believe he found the answer in the Bernese schultheiss — particularly the crumbled cresting.

"The schultheiss?" replied Peter.

"The schultheiss?" repeated Lizzie.

"The schultheiss?" reverberated Edmunda.

The man nodded. "Is not this G.V.V. perchance Gustav von Villeroy?" said he to his wife. "Did not we read, only a few weeks ago, about the rift between Bern and Zürich?"

"That we did!" The woman, lips pouted, looked all intrigue at Peter.

"Von Villeroy?" mused Peter aloud. "This name feels familiar...?" If he served the schultheiss, then he was *most certainly* no criminal! "Is this... *Gustav* still alive?" With a nod, the parents confirmed he was. "That is a relief, at least."

Eager to know his more recent past, Peter now asked where the parents had last seen him. Together answering, the mother said France but the father Germany. They both reddened. Again, together answering, the father now said France but the mother Germany. Once more, they reddened under so many bemused, watchful eyes.

First to clear his throat, the man re-steered the topic. "What is that you are holding?" He pointed at the rolled-up newspaper in Peter's hand.

"Ah, yes." Peter opened it out to the column. "Do you know who may have written this?"

Looking at it, they shook their heads. But referring to the fortune, with a sudden rise in their tone, they asked whether Peter yet recalled where this might be. Peter shook his own head. Looking a little put out, the parents directed the question to all present, who, though doubtless of its existences, were still eager to corroborate it themselves, begged they would help hurry Peter's memory.

'Twas now that the mother addressed Edmunda with biting civility. "That we are all together," said she, "there is another matter needing redress. The prospective betrothal of our children. Since this espousal was ventured upon without our sanction, and since your daughter is..." — she cut Lizzie with an icy glare — "well... it is only right that it be *annulled* at once!"

Instantly did Edmunda jump up, demanding who she was to be telling *her* daughter *who* she can marry. With cruel indifference, the mother replied she commanded only *her* son *who* must marry into a family able to bestow on the alliance all things concomitant to such desirable connections.

"Who are *you* to tell Peter what he can and can't do?" shrilled Edmunda.

As the women were pulled apart but short of a violent culmination, Fortune — that fickle goddess — having other interests in her head, had already conjured the next catastrophe:

Not forgetting Peter's hefty fine, though it was but the penultimate day of March, a loud thumping reverbed at the farmhouse door. As we may guess the visitant, a day early, too, we may envisage the preceding tumult. Finding Peter unable to pay in full, the merchant peddler waved before all the indictment and hauled him into a bailiff's wagon.

***

We shall, however, skip the two days and three nights in the belly of the whale — that is, the cold, wet, and damp gaol — and rather attend the Monday morn. There we find Peter grappling with so early a separation from his parents and about to be sold off at a slave auction for such persons as thieves, brigands, gamblers, misbegotten wenches, and they who set cotton sacks ablaze.

Gathered in the town square to gleefully mock and judge what they deemed the dregs of society, the throngs watching this public spectacle were not shy in denouncing those aforementioned souls lined up, stripped of all worldly goods. Yet, since we are concerned only with our hero, we shall pass over the several imps and urchins, snapped up by the equally villainous slaveholders, and discover, media res, where at a pitiful current price of two paltry batzen, what the mob have to say:

"He ain't worth one batzen," heckled several men.

"He's cursed by the Devil," shouted another; "put him on your ship, and it'll founder."

"He'll burn down your storehouses!" sneered more.

Poor, poor, Peter, stood central stage, delivering perhaps his most tragic audition yet.

There were many other invectives, to be sure, which, though plausible sounding, might make us wonder where were his votaries in his moment of need? Why, they were the very ones in the crowd who hurled these very horrific insults and jibes!

Though Peter had earned some wages from Hans prior to his injury, they were scarce a fraction of the debt. Also, though Ernest had gathered what coin he could, and Edmunda and Elizabeth had prevailed upon another peddler to provide them cotton sacks and spun many yarns and woven many pieces, the remuneration tallied still too little. Edmunda had even re-petitioned the magistrate's wife. But unlike in her first influence, which proved triumphant, in this second, she met with quite the reverse. The stadtschultheiss was so affronted by Peter's insults at that recent trial, he could not be dissuaded from his seat of judgement; not even at the forfeit of his favourite dinner.

Thus, a Catholic-wide effort was concerted to hoodwink all prospective buyers at the auction. And its effect was so remarkable that the crowds received quite a number of threats to be carted off away themselves if they did not shut their traps forthwith!

Anyhow, while the stratagem went according to plan — the buyers disdaining Peter and the auctioneer; the auctioneer disdaining the buyers and the crowds; Peter disdaining the auctioneer, the buyers, the crowds, and his fellow bondsmen, who passed down their own sneers and ridicules to his dishonour — a gaoler approached and whispered something into the auctioneer's greedy ears. This occurrence soon transformed his grunts, fists, and grimaces to hoorays, open hands, and smiles.

All universal wonder as to why our hero was then led away dissipated as the auctioneer declared him no longer available for purchase. A private buyer had already put up the price.

"*What*?" cried Peter as he struggled against the dirty paws of two stocky, malevolent men dragging him off-stage. "Let go! You filthy brutes!"

Certainly, though we tender mortals, safe upon these pages, may venture to partake viscerally of this tragedian's cataclysm, 'tis most unlikely we have ever been plunged into such riotously ill fortune's stew ourselves! But even if you have, stow away your tears and sighs of sympathy, for they shall prove premature. For Fortune, not yet done dallying with him, had other designs lurking up her sleeve.

Still a-struggling and a-screaming, Peter was led to a musty stone courtyard of benches, dejected wretches, usurious middle-men, and mean-looking stewards. With a heart very much pounding, his breath stuck in his throat, and a cold sweat trickling down his back, barely was he unshackled and passed to a pleasant-countenanced steward when along came another of a less-welcoming aspect; a visage rather akin to a bulldog chewing a wasp.

A conversation passed between the two, which, owing to their differing opinions and arrogances, soon turned rather heated, their voices rising to a crescendo of indignation. Were it not for the intervention of the keeper who called on the auctioneer, it might have ended in fisticuffs and nostrils a-streaming.

The acquisitive auctioneer, while counting his coins with the dexterity of a seasoned crook, listened to the red-faced servitors bellow forth their cases; both, with each breath, more bent on securing Peter for their masters.

Indeed, this scene puts one in mind of wise King Solomon's own legendary conundrum with the squabbling harlots, who each bade their claim against the infant. If only our auctioneer possessed such wisdom and had simply drawn forth his sword and threatened to divide poor Peter down the middle, perhaps the disputants would have seen the folly of their ways, and the dispute would have been settled in an instant! But anyway, no metal brandished, he arbitrated in favour of the one who, to the profound shock and dismay of the other, had a prior claim on the booty; the auctioneer decreed Peter be given into the care — dare we call it — of the less-favourably framed steward.

"No!" Peter recoiled from the man, imagining a dreadful life on a miserable, distant, sweaty plantation. "I would much rather go with the other!"

The auctioneer shoved him forward. "You'll go to whom *I* sell you!"

'Twas at this very moment, as our hero resigned himself to his fate, that Fortune showed her hand at last! 'Twas an ace after all up her capricious sleeve, trumping all despair and leaving our poor player quite bedazzled by her whimsy. For rather than suffer the harrowing fate he so bitterly anticipated, Peter found himself suddenly manumitted! Released forthwith, he was granted full liberty to quit this dreadful scene and hurry himself back to the humble farmhouse.

What prestidigitation is this? Confounding, indeed; more so, that two persons, let alone one, should ever squander their coin on a man so infamously worthless. But, in the scenes soon to unfold, perhaps some modicum of enlightenment may bathe these baffling events in sense-making radiance? So come! Let us on then to discover what method of Fortune's madness will illume the page and, perchance, teach a moral, too!

***

The sun had set above an hour. Stood at the window, a still disquieted Peter, rubbing his chafed wrists and sneezing from the chill he caught, spoke with much discomfiture to his father about the awful jailhouse conditions, the equally awful company he kept, and the woeful events at the auction. Receiving much paternal encouragements, the more Peter listened, the more he accepted in the absence of filial recollection, this man to be his father.

A knocking at the farmhouse door produced two familiar men: Johannes and Pier. Edmunda sprang to the former and assailed him with anxious entreaties about Ernest, who still convalesced at his schloss. Johannes only answered her with icy civility, frowns, and gusty sighs, clearly displeased with visiting so modest a property and company.

Seeing this, Peter could hardly believe him to be Jago's father.

Pier, however, gave an impression entirely the reverse. He answered Edmunda with affability and smiles; his brow more favourably framed as to paint the general mood of his mind.

The parents did stare at these additions to the party — particularly Johannes — with something like covetous wonder; this expression was interrupted only by their lingering glares and twitches at Edmunda.

By-the-by, it probably escaped not the reader's notice that our hero's parents were neither to be seen nor heard from during the entirety of the auction events. This ostensibly owed to the father having, directly after Peter's detainment, been taken away ill to his preferred physician, who lived at quite a distance. It was apparently happenstance that they returned just after Peter's release; as it was apparently their own steward who first put up the price for his liberty.

Pier greeted Elizabeth most affectionately and then wound through the gathering towards Peter. With each step, his expression betrayed a most peculiar working of his mind.

***

We return for a moment to that earlier scene where Pier said, "have not I met you before?"

Though an irresolute Peter had answered in the negative, Pier believed he resembled most strikingly someone he once knew. Hence, Pier enquired about his family, which, of course, our hero had no recollection of; neither had they yet arrived at our narrative. While Pier had then mused upon the sorry condition of the amnesiac, curiosity shifted from one brain to the other, and our hero asked who it was he apparently mirrored. Rather than disclose the resemblance, Pier merely dismissed his impression as redundant and bid Peter a swift recovery and reuniting with his memories.

Anyway, the more Pier later reflected on the likeness, the more he endured the most oddly inexplicable whisperings of an aching heart. Impatient to illuminate the confusion of his thoughts, he determined to visit Peter as soon as he was recovered enough to probe further his history.

Our hero, however, having since encountered the several odious circumstances thus chronicled, had thought no more of the occasion.

***

When introducing Pier to his father, Peter noted the former fix upon the latter a most incredulous gaze. This look was then added additional dubiety when the mother made herself known to his presence.

"What is your family name?" said Pier to them.

"Von Graffenried," replied the father.

Pier seemed to ponder the patronymic.

Having escaped Edmunda, Johannes insinuated himself into the conversation. With a crooked brow, he scrutinised the father and then the mother; possibly determining the appearance of sartorial taste, he smiled; his austere air abated and a more temperate zephyr exuded from his person. Most likely wishing to test the quality of these new objects of his study, he engaged the father solely to himself and asked the very same question his companion just had.

With smiles of apparent pleasure, the mother watched the conversation unfold between her husband and the illustrious Johannes, who, though recognising not the family name von Graffenried, was satisfied with the particle 'von'.

Something else of an additional pleasure now flashed in the woman's eyes, and her face exhibited a curious working of her mind. She curtsied to Pier, and rejoining Elizabeth next to Edmunda, commenced an inexhaustible inquisition with a pointed affability so affected that both Elizabeth and Edmunda rather preferred her sincere austerity. The mother asked when Lizzie (yes, she called her that) met Peter, where she met Peter, what she knew of him, whether she might guess at where his fortune might be hidden, and the like.

But mid-flow in Lizzie's awkward replies: "What is that I hear, Peter?" interrupted the mother, somehow maintaining her interrogations while she listened with a free ear to the talk proceeding near the window. "You are offered employment at Schloss Ebenrain?"

This was the chief purpose of Pier and Johannes' visit. Since the latter had need of a new coachman and that Peter had already proved his equestrian worth, it was naturally the best solution to offer him the vacancy. We now also learn the identity of the mystery buyer who had bought back Peter's freedom. The cotton merchant to that unfortunate peddler who lost his sacks to the flames just so happened to be Johannes. Since the account of the combusted cotton sacks had made quite a noise in the region, it had reached Pier's ears. Thus, Pier sallied forth to save our hero and importuned his friend to extend the olive branch. Hence, Johannes reluctantly despatched that servant to the auction to absorb the expense, paying off the auctioneer.

Peter needed not to thank him too profusely for Johannes would deduct the monies from his wages, with a small appended interest.

Again joining them at the window, the mother vouched for Johannes' choice of a new coachman. "Having served His Bernese Schultheiss Gustav," said she, with serenading glee, "I believe is a good enough recommendation."

"The schultheiss?" replied Johannes with some marks of amazement.

"The Schultheiss Gustav?" echoed Pier with some hints of peculiar agitation.

"Yes," answered the woman for her son. "So, you may entrust to him an early approbation worthy of your most prodigious residence, Ebenrain."

Johannes now regarded the mother with evident wonder. "Do you know the property?"

"*Of course*! It would be an insult to the best of men and countries would any person of distinction pass through it without any apprehension of its best houses and gardens."

"I say," replied Johannes, clearly enrapt with this encomium, "you *must* allow me the pleasure of better acquainting you." Immediately, he insisted she and her husband join him at the fire-side.

Easily obtaining their accord, he sat his new acquaintances next to him on the chaise and discussed with incontrovertible pleasure the reports they had heard of his house.

Stood alone now with Pier, Peter remarked the peculiar, uneasy, and watchful countenance of this man. "May I ask *why* you stare at me so?"

Brought back into himself, Pier replied, "forgive me... I..." Then, betraying a character of painful recollection in his eyes, he bowed and hastily departed to join Elizabeth and Edmunda.

Confused by the whole, Peter's own bow was delayed.

As he half-turned and stepped backwards to make his way to the kitchen, he tripped over Znüni — lying unseen behind him — and crashed to the floor.

All joy, tail a-wagging, and happy kisses, the animal leapt onto him.

"Znüni!" Peter laughed. "Down boy."

The dog rolled off him.

Barely had Peter sat up, noting his shirt splattered with the red wine of his toppled cup and the happy dog at his side with its happy tongue still hanging out, when a chilling sensation rushed through his limbs.

His earlier wounds again throbbed and burned as if opened anew. And there flashed before his eyes an image of several horses in a stable and candle-wax being dripped over a laceration, bubbling and sizzling within his flesh.

Confused, he reached for his smarting scars.

The more he pondered these images which grew fast on his mind, an overwhelming sensation left him breathless, as if with panic.

What was this? Memory? Fancy? Or *déjà vu*?

04 – 06 APRIL 1792

The elegant four-in-hand landau coupé, which conveyed Peter to his new abode and employment, turned into the shade of tall rows of pleached lindens, early leafing-out. The trees stretched either side of the promenade into the perspective, providing at its termination a glimpse of the famously handsome edifice: Schloss Ebenrain.

It was a most fine forenoon. The early sun diffused its light all about, dappling the long gravel drive with specks of gold. The air was mild, upon which a fresh breeze stirred the foliage high above and wafted the earthy scent of cut grass as gardeners and under-gardeners scythed the long and expansive lawns at his right and his left.

Into the finely upholstered seating, Peter relaxed, absorbed by his surroundings: the crunch of the carriage wheels turning on the gravel, the clip-clop of hooves, the morning arias of birds; all commingling in a blissful morning symphony. At his side, panted Znüni.

Yet while our hero soaked in such scenes, a creeping unease tempered his contentment. The serenity surrounding him seemed more transient, overshadowed by the warnings of encroaching war. Unease gripped his breast. A darkness grew within, vibrating with premonition at each new decree, calling for citizens to the ready. He shuddered at the thought of again donning a soldier's uniform; not, however, from mere anxiety over battle itself, but from a bone-deep conviction of some prior bloodstained failure that filled him with foreboding. The possibility of war felt oddly personal to him. Yet why, he had still to realise.

As the carriage emerged from the linden promenade and passed beneath an ornate wrought iron archway, Peter recalled his mother's words that one day he could re-establish their name above a pretty wrought-iron gate of his own.

That day could not come quick enough.

The distinctive, luxuriant echo of cobblestones struck his hearing as the carriage rolled into a small courtyard centred on a cherubim fountain — its dashing waters reverbing with that soothing quality. Two footmen clad in velvet overcoats, crisp white stockings, and boots polished enough to be mirrors stood sentry at the entrance, their countenances exhibiting a blank dignity.

With grave solemnity befitting their station, one approached and opened the carriage door. Out leapt Znüni, followed by Peter breathing in an exultant air of pride, delight, and eager anticipation. The perfume of an orangery teased his nostrils and drew his attention to the potted trees in blossom, which bounded the extremities of the courtyard.

"Ah, Schloss Ebenrain, what a refreshing sight for one so long deprived of such pleasing architectural composition."

'Twas most likely due to the stark contrast between his humble garb and elevated speech that induced the footman to look him up and down with disdainful curiosity. Meeting so stern a visage, Peter could not help staring back. Was not this the manservant who Johannes had sent to the auction?

Peter affected a smile, but the footman only glowered the more solemn.

Watching this exchange, Znüni gave the man a warning growl.

The property itself offered a more welcoming aspect, comprising a two-storey main edifice: its walls, white-washed; its shutters, stone quoins, and ornamented masonry arched entrance way, accented blue. Two structures flanking the main building formed the courtyard in which Peter stood.

"Take him and have him dress!" bellowed a male voice from inside the house, ensued by sharp footsteps. "I require the carriage almost immediately."

Johannes appeared beneath the arched entrance, attired in the most ostentatious morning wear, postured in the most ornate hauteur, waving his hands at the footmen. At his heels appeared two proud dalmatians; each austere in attitude, noses upturned, eyes averted, deigning to acknowledge no soul but their lord. Even friendly Znüni's bark went pointedly unheeded.

The footmen's former blank dignity became all unease as they bowed to their imperious lord. While observing this, there flickered across Peter's mind the image of men-servants, more exquisitely attired, bowing as if to him. What was this? A possible recollection of his time serving the schultheiss? Yes, that had to be it. *I must have held a prominent post...*

Without bowing, which quite put the footmen's faces aslant, and dropping also the honorifics, Peter addressed Johannes. "I had hoped I might briefly pay my regards to Ernest."

"I have brought you here under the formality of employment," rejoined he, doubtless scowling at Peter for such informal addresses, "*not* to pay *court* to your future in-laws. And you will need to *remove* that thicket growing over your face! I keep no barbarians in my service."

Stung by so extremely cold and offensive an officiousness and, perceiving his own displeasure discover itself in his countenance, Peter looked away to disguise his face.

Johannes now asked whether he owned such a thing as a blade — which Peter did not. Edmunda would expend on no such luxury nor allow him use of Ernest's; she told him but to wait until sheep shearing when her good friend would be so generous as to clip him for free.

Accordingly, Johannes instructed a footman to fetch a blade for the "ill-kempt junker." Too much occupied by his own importance to penetrate into the feelings or sentiments of another, Johannes paid only another impatient glare at the coachmen, demanding that he change into his liveries rather than sit idling about. "One must keep them in check," continued he, in so privileged yet blameless an air. "Were I not so *forbearing* and *noble-minded*, I would certainly have replaced the entire household a hundred times over before now."

With the sun still low, crawling the eastern sky, as if averse to shedding its lustre upon so acerbic a man, a slanted shadow stole across the courtyard. On the stiff breeze which swept through it, a foreboding shiver ran Peter through.

Johannes' wife appeared at the entranceway. "Peter," said she, "how glad I am that you are come."

Her genteel tone and elegant manners were at such a variance with her husband. Her smiles and gracious enquiries were as warm as her person, her dignified yet fashionable dress mirroring the taste and refinement of her address.

"I need not remind you, I hope," resumed Johannes, "of the obeisance, discretion, *and* silence requisite to serving a family so consequential. And let me dissuade you now from aspiring to any of those indulgences your predecessor most erroneously dared to covet. You will need to prove your worth. And, of course, work off your debt. And you will need to hand over your mutt to the groomsman! The beast can sleep with the horses."

Johannes wheeled about imperiously and stalked so importantly back inside; his proud dalmatians mimicking their master's haughty strut, they followed behind.

After handing over to the stable boy a whimpering Znüni, Peter shaved and, with some pain still in his shoulder, donned the liveries laid out upon his bed; all while the footman stood on the other side of his door, tapping his heel against it with impatient regularity. The few glances Peter stole of the chamber gave to his understanding an unfavourable inkling. Though clean and not immodestly furnished, a cheerless atmosphere whispered of some past or future discomfort. But perhaps these feelings were merely the effect of his soon having to return to the garrison for weekly training once his shoulder had fully healed?

Upon entering the vestibule, Peter observed the property was as grand and spacious as expected of a patrician's residence. A marble staircase rose to the left, and a colonnaded balcony overlooked the foyer, through which Peter followed the footman, whose every regulated stride echoed with unwelcoming dignity.

"The schloss, a recent acquisition, was built by a Basel silk ribbon manufacturer," explained the footman as they proceeded through ornate antechambers and past stone-faced servants. "Fitted up with the modern taste, the family redesigned it entirely after taking up residency," continued he.

Ushered with overbearing pomp to a library, Peter was finally positioned by a tall window and schooled in comportment through a compendium of injunctions against improper glances, unauthorised touches, incorrect stance, and ill-regulated breathing. Though Peter went to protest such formality given his own genteel upbringing, the footman would brook no interruption and admonished him to sooner familiarise himself with the art of bowing.

"I believe," replied Peter, "save for the Bernese schultheiss, I have *never* bowed to anyone throughout the entirety of my life."

"*Never*? Were you in France, you would certainly have lost your head before now."

"But we are *not* in France," retorted Peter.

With some overt looks of disdain, the footman retired, leaving our hero by himself.

Ostentation best characterized this library. Heavy gold drapery. Ornate guild furniture. Gaudy upholstered seating in various shades of hunter, forest, and chartreuse-greens; all clashing against a nod to the Sistine Chapel, frescoed ceiling, complete with cumulonimbus clouds and pudgy cherubs. Though there were books enough, the room aimed more to flaunt the master's vanity than serve his erudition. Around the room's periphery, trotted fancy globes, marble statues, and glass cabinets of terrified-looking taxidermy's, all seeming to fix their glassy eyes upon a high-backed chair at a carved walnut conference desk at the room's centre.

On the desk, a Basel newspaper snared Peter's interest. Since he was quite alone, he stole over to it and flicked to its classifieds. No further communication from his mystery correspondent. Disappointed, he turned back to the front page:

"Tensions between Bern and Zürich reach tipping point" ran the incendiary headline, detailing a recent diet's explosive fallout. Distrust and dissent prevailed towards the schultheiss; the Grand Council's prejudices rooted in notions of dissident ideologies. Several other cantons, now embroiled in disputes over centralised authority, challenged the long-unquestioned supremacy of the Federal Diet. Meanwhile, the Kingdom of France still asseverated their irreproachability, lambasting the confederacy for its duplicity and threatening reprisals for French emissaries assassinated on Swiss soils. Nearer to home, propagandists distributed materials in Basel markets and wealthy Basel merchants fretted over trade disruptions from deteriorating relations. Caught between Zürich and Bern's feud, Basel resisted threats of harsh penalties for refusing to choose sides and continued to conscript more men in anticipation of civil war.

"Good lord! The world is about to blow sky-high!"

At once, his mind turned to the scroll. Whatsoever those obliterated words once were, could they somehow connect to the tumult now engulfing the land? Indeed, the longer the parchment remained with Peter, the more compelled he now felt to restore it to its rightful owner.

I should try again at the Liestal garrison? No, that would not do. *I should take it to Bern.*

His eyes, adrift with his thoughts, landed on the newspaper still spread open on the desk. Sharing its front page, a smaller column declared: "Another schloss plundered in Liestal." The latest in a string of robberies targeting the wealthy.

Fresh unease stirred Peter's thoughts at the proximity of this latest outrage. Liestal being but a short distance from his present location, Ebenrain would make a most tempting target for brigands as any country schloss in the region.

Recollecting himself, he refolded the newspaper and restored it to its former position. From this he turned to the lavish mantel, above which hung a prodigious, self-aggrandising oil depicting Johannes in hunting garb. It was, however, the object on the mantle itself which, despite the footman's earlier injunctions still ringing in his ears, enticed him forwards.

Soon, he stood at such unauthorized proximity, gazing upon a French Ormolu. Rather than arousing admiration for its exquisite workmanship, the apparatus evoked familiarity. The more he studied it, the more his hand was drawn irresistibly forth to touch it.

As his fingertips made contact, his perception of his surroundings metamorphosed; he was no longer in the ostentatious library but a dim, sparsely furnished hovel.

"Liberty!" bellowed Johannes, shattering Peter's reverie. "Liberty!" He rained stinging blows with the rolled newspaper and drove Peter from his transgression back to the window. "What presumption you already aspire to! Pray, avow I have employed no opportunist?"

"*Opportunist*?" Johannes' violent outburst made Peter already half-repent he had accepted this post. With difficulty, he mastered his wounded indignation. "Not at all, it is just —"

"It is *just*?" interrupted Johannes, his very tone avowing distrust. The dalmatians flanking him exhibited similar disapprobation in their haughty stares. "Do I already need to anticipate your premature discharge? Or remind you of your ousted predecessor?"

"If you will but hear me out," replied Peter, "I believe I have seen a clock, much like this one, before." Johannes' brow slid, still unconvinced, to one side. "Indeed, its honeybee motif speaks of its singularity. May I enquire from where you obtained it?"

With each heavy exhale, Johannes' disdainful countenance hardened. "Though I ought to scold you for improperly addressing and questioning me so, I must assume that despite your impenitent irregularity, you are acquainted with some expertise in this realm?"

"Acquainted at least with the knowledge of this clock's rarity."

Gazing at it, our hero felt certain of its familiarity. Yet a sinister foreboding clung to it and whispered of dangers unknown.

Johannes reclined in his seat and fell silent. This conversation seemed to transcend his judgement. "Jago had described you as being of a... *singular* temperament," said he, at length, while idly indulging his pets, scratching behind their ears and stroking their spotted coats. "And perceiving your parents to be of a *dignified* sort, it would be natural to suppose they have adorned you with *some* refinements. That said, were it not for the insistences of my good friend Pier, I would never have countenanced the employment of such *obscure* and, as I am told, generally *incompetent* persons."

Probably imputing to Peter's incredulous countenance adulation, Johannes prolonged his disquisition, incontrovertibly imagining the rightful veneration he inspired with every word. "Those of large and important connections like myself," said he, assuming an air of imperious affability, "can afford not a singular glance the other way." These words he pronounced with a measured emphasis. "There is always some vagabond or vile servant wishing to usurp our rightly deserved positions. And if given half the chance, the most would scruple not in plotting our very downfall. You, I hope, will prove otherwise?"

Indeed, the more Peter studied this man, the more he disliked him.

"And if, indeed, you served the Bernese schultheiss — do you recall anything of this yet?" Peter shook his head. "Pity," coolly replied Johannes.

Since this subject had been approached, Peter said: "There is something I would —"

"Whilst the inferiors of our land may recoil at the thought of war between the cantons," interrupted Johannes, silencing him with a stern gesture, "such a situation, in fact, presents manifold opportunities. Imagine it! Coffers overflowing, trading monopolies guaranteed, and currency speculation and money-lending dancing to my command!" And with so self-congratulatory an air to be despised even by the meanest of men, he chuckled a cold and hollow sound. "Even if aristocratic blood must run in the streets, let it flow along lucrative channels! Let Bern and Zürich rend each other asunder whilst we grow fat off the spoils."

Here he paused as if to receive some compliment or acknowledgement. But Peter, despising to pay him any, merely affirmed his attention with an inclination of the head.

"Should you not displease me in your service," resumed that man, "you will learn that politics is not my only pleasure in life, nor is it my first."

Rising from his throne, he then sauntered to the mantel. "And to answer your question, this masterpiece" — he fiddled with its door — "was, of all places, discovered in an insignificant pawnshop in Spiez."

"Spiez?" Familiarity again crackled in our hero's mind.

"But it no longer seems to work." He slammed its door shut. "I shall send it to Lucerne for repair. Ah! And what were you going to say earlier?"

Some inscrutable force held Peter's tongue. Perchance it was his swelling abhorrence for the tyrant before him? But so deeply etched was this indecipherable instinct, he felt no inclination to re-mention the scroll, let alone divulge his wish of returning it to Bern. As much as something in Peter sensed the need for caution, so too did some quality in Johannes' temper invoke distrust. It was better that Johannes seemed not to recall it.

"I forget," lied he.

***

Later that evening, only after driving the exacting Johannes hither and thither in fruitless pursuit of unattainable pleasures, Peter was at last permitted to attend upon Ernest in a commodious and finely decorated bedchamber.

"Peter," said he with an extended, trembling hand. "How'm I ever to repay you?"

"Your full recovery will be payment enough." Peter gently squeezed his hand before sitting opposite. "Thanks be to Pier and Johannes' wife for insisting on your convalescence here."

So, the unfortunate circumstances which led to Ernest's respite found its genesis in a potential assassination attempt upon Johannes; ostensibly a second such attempt. Anyway, that elegant lord's disposition being what we have so far observed, doubtless leaving him in no want of enemies, had, however, left him in want of a coachman.

Whatever had provoked the predecessor's dismissal, it happened that on the sunny day Johannes collected Pier from the coach inn, a temporary hire had struggled with the already skittish horses. Perhaps Fortune had her hand in the matter, but Ernest just so happened to be there, and it was his kindly interventions that found him placed squarely between the sniper and the intended target, Johannes. The bullet pierced Ernest's shoulder before striking rather the coachman — who inopportunely found himself between Ernest and Johannes; the lead ball plunged into the poor fellow's sternum, rendering him instantly dead.

Tears escaped down Ernest's cheeks. "I hope you'll forgive an old man's wishes before..." He trailed off, eyes haunted by an anxiety natural to one having brushed with mortality. "Hale as I am, this scrape has made me determined to see Elizabeth settled in the world." He paused and seemed to discriminate whether he was understood.

Indeed, Peter understood him. But preventing his discomfiture escaping onto his phiz, he politely nodded that Ernest continue.

"Even had I not my own heart's wishes on this score, I'd still need to speak with you." Ernest shifted uneasily. "Father Francis visited me yesterday. And the short of it is, you and Elizabeth need to formalise your engagement. If not, the Father will expel us from his flock."

A subsequent air of agonising apprehension accompanied Ernest's stare.

Bound rather by duty than directed by the infant affections which had grown unattended to in his heart, our hero gave consideration, albeit tardy, to his proposed engagement, which was indeed, even by standard decorum, long overdue. He could not, without self-accusation, refuse this humble request.

"It will relieve you of your anxieties, I am sure, to learn that I am already in possession of a ring." Ernest's eyes did brighten instantly. "Be assured, tomorrow I shall ask Johannes' leave to visit Father Francis."

***

And so, it was the next day, with permission obtained, Peter paid that visit. Eager to effect at least some air of romance, he entreated the Father to allow him until the Ostern festival to perform the sacred duty. This delay granted, though with admonishments of tardiness to God and want of conformity to good society, our hero was released with promises of blessings from the Divine and, not less, the Father's own good will to follow.

Incidentally, during this requested intermission, whenever Peter would convey Johannes or Jago about the countryside — whether to town, balls, or neighbouring estates — though but a coachman, he was acknowledged and saluted with honours bordering on the noble. His heroic actions with the run-away carriage had fully redeemed his former reputation.

While the distinction naturally confounded Johannes, it seemed to stir in Jago a touch of envy. And if envy it was, though Jago was assiduous in preventing any outward show, it may account for the sudden delay in the fulfilment of his earlier promise of that fine banquet. But Edmunda, not one to neglect her own happiness, would not let the matter lie. She pressed Jago to make good on his word that she might at last celebrate her triumphs over her daughter in proper form. Though doubtless regretting his generous offer, he bowed to her petitions.

And so, the date was fixed for April sixth; Karfreitag.

This did, however, mean that Edmunda would need to abandon Lent a few days early...

***

Karfreitag being now arrived, our party of the surgeon, the physician, the apothecary, Ernest, Edmunda, Elizabeth, Emil, and those fair nymphs, along with the addition of Pier, Helene, and Peter's parents, attended the mid-morning mass with empty stomachs, rumbling with expectant pleasure. Scarce had the church bell pealed before the group burst forth, making posthaste for Ebenrain and its promised feast.

After the alfresco luncheon, Johannes, with dalmatians and wife in tow, led his guests from the wrought-ironed veranda onto the gravelled terrace, overlooking the gardens.

"I flatter myself," said he, "in choosing so perfect a country abode. The formal geometry and ornamental broderies of box hedge offer a touch of the resplendent, while the lawn parterres with carefully chosen fountains, sculpted hedges, and strapwork alleys, you observe there, could rival Versailles itself!"

The party all agreed on how very fine the views were.

Znüni came a-bounding, determined to rouse a playful spirit in his aloof canine brethren. The male Dalmatian completely ignored his convivial overtures while the female did deign to grant the friendly hound a glance. Marking this, Johannes castigated his pet's presumption and ordered Peter to remove his ill-mannered mutt, lest it spoil the occasion.

No doubt eager to claim the rank of first in all things fine, Johannes insisted on a tour of his equally fine house. With an imperious gesture of the hand, he bade his dogs and guests follow him inside.

From room to room, he proceeded with a pomp befitting one so enamoured with castle and self, pointing out to his eager auditors — whose heads did swivel on necks like owls — the chief features of each interior. Here, they observed tall and wide double doors, ample for lavish ladies' gowns; there, they admired stucco ceilings and corner cartouches in the rococo mode. A collection of oils stole fulsome compliments, particularly a large rendering of Venus in the Vulcan's forge. With incontrovertible self-gratulation, Johannes referenced the very cards table which had lost the former owner this house.

While admiring still the striking Venus, Peter's reflections were broken upon by his mother, whispering into his ear how exceedingly well he had done to secure such employment.

"Indeed," replied he; a turning to her, he rather espied Elizabeth stood at a tall window, engaged in tête-à-tête with Jago. Her countenance, smiles, and glistening eyes, illuminated by the light flooding in, radiated exquisite enchantment. It perhaps owed to the present ease which penetrated his proud mind's hard facade that he now saw she was lovelier than the Venus herself. Yet, noting her attention fixed so contentedly upon Jago — in whose carriage, smiles, and keen eyes, he traced several marks of peculiar affection — he soon found cause for criticism. *How easily she accommodates her friend.*

Over to her he stalked and extended his hand, requesting, or rather commanding, she would join him on the tour. Though this gave her some perceivable confusion, she, at length, yielded her hand, and Peter led her away from Jago.

Certain it was, the parents' persistent flattery, claiming to discriminate from the interiors Johannes' "nobly refined mind" — "most undoubtedly edified by a most splendid library" — is what gained them entrance to this very room; the master's room.

With some pique in his voice and looks, Jago noted not even *he* had *ever* breached this sanctum. Johannes sharply replied that not until he would first become the master of himself and his passions would he then understand the prolonged duration of his exclusion.

As patriciate to the Daig, and having allied their affluence, assets, and a seat on the Grand Council of Basel, the von der Mühlls wielded a political puissance in this canton. However, since Jago — the primogeniture destined to inherit the estate and seat — spoke with more ardour of perambulating the canton than one day overseeing its political interests, this might account, among other matters yet to be disclosed, for his exclusion from so sacred a chamber.

Johannes rummaged through his pockets and discovered he had left the key within his escritoire upstairs; he despatched a footman to retrieve the spare from the butler's office. Soon the key was brought, the door was unlocked, and the party entered the inner sanctum, marshalled by the dalmatians, with Johannes proudly officiating as a docent.

That Edmunda commented only on the dusty inconvenience in so many books, Elizabeth did observe Johannes' displeasure; she hushed her mother's remarks and dragged her to the window seat where she could again admire the courtyard fountain.

Seizing the opportunity, Peter stole to the mantel to study the clock, unobserved. So engrossed he soon became, seeking to unravel its familiarity and the strange vision it had produced when he first touched it, that he scarce noted Jago's approach.

Now stood at our hero's side and surveying the clock with an expression of sudden agitation, Jago spun to face his father. "Sir! When did you obtain this?"

Johannes was clearly displeased at the interruption mid-flow in praise of his treasures. He answered his son only with a glare before recommending the exploration of the house to proceed to the first floor. Indeed, this dismissal seemed to add to whatever emotion presently fired Jago's breast as he cast his eyes again upon the timepiece.

Whilst the party quit the library, Peter saw also in his parents some marks of peculiar fascination with the clock; the several glances they directed at the timepiece and each other communicated some hidden meaning.

So much fascination with the same instrument?

After locking the door, Johannes handed the key to the footman and decreed its immediate return to its cabinet. With a condescending stride, he then conducted the gathering up the stairs.

Half-way, however, the mother stopped and begged to visit the wash-room. Further, letting out a feeble whimper and claiming her right knee had locked, she requested the aid of the aforementioned footman, upon whose arm she supported herself.

Jago, too, clearly distempered of mind, stated a sudden recollection of business needing his attention; he quit the party, hurried upstairs and disappeared along the balcony.

The tour did reach its end, and, in point, Johannes, so pleased with it and his guests' encomiums but not yet satisfied with showing off, insisted they sup with him that evening.

Hence, several hours later, an elegant feast was laid out in the main dining hall, whilst a more modest table was arranged in the adjacent garden room.

At the head of the grand table sat Johannes, monopolising the fine silver, crystal, and the company of his wife, Pier, and Peter's parents. Johannes' dalmatians, having a stool of their own on either side of their master, enjoyed each delicacy and morsel tidbit. In the garden room, the rest gathered around the humbler table, where Edmunda did, of course, preside. Midway between the two camps sat Peter, facing fair Elizabeth, flanked by her female companions — those fair nymphs — who did ogle Peter and Jago alike.

From here, wishing to evade their fluttering glances, our hero rather watched the servants, whose evident chagrin had poisoned their physiognomy as they served their guests — particularly himself. Irked by such ill-etiquette, Peter diverted his attention to the hum of divaricated talk:

Ernest and Edmunda perplexed over so much cutlery; Hans and Harris, all scowls and smiles, cursed the whole; Helene compared the occasion to the feast of Thaleia as she exchanged bashful glances with Emil, bringing colour to their cheeks; those fair nymphs merely giggled and blushed all the more with the wine; the surgeon, physician, and apothecary sat further down, disputed the merit of each dish and annotated its texture, taste, and structure; through the open door, the parents' compliments, eulogiums, and almost lyrical paeans heaped on Johannes could not help betray more obsequiousness than sincerity

Strangely, across the expanse of linen, silver, fine plates, and crystal wear, Pier's stare lingered over his wineglass in our hero's direction.

What was it that fascinated that man so much?

Likely perceiving the scrutiny which he was himself now under, Pier looked away.

Jago, for whatever cause, appeared absolutely removed from the occasion; when asked anything, his answers were concise; when the conversation moved away from him, he displayed little interest in re-engaging it.

From the bright chandelier light of the main dining hall, the scent of beeswax flowed through on the elegant, upper echelon air. So, too, did a delectable aroma, which now assailed Peter's nostrils. His head — nay, his nose — besought the direction from which it came. There, upon Johannes' plate, glistened slices of veal, braised in white wine and cream with mushrooms.

This sight and scent struck a chord of familiarity. *Entrée of cutlets in fricandeau!* At last, he recalled the dish!

Saliva did verily pour unbidden as he gaped at so tantalising a sight; till Johannes did rap his plate sharply with his knife, dispelling our poor hero's fancy. Johannes' subsequent glare forced Peter's eyes back to his own modest bowl of chicken soup.

Anew, the parents' voices claimed Peter's attention.

Certain it was, they strove to stamp an indelible impression of their former consequence on the high opinion of their haughty host as the father re-serenaded his heredity of his grandfather, the 1st Baron of Bernberg.

"Ah yes." Johannes wiped the corner of his mouth with his silk napkin. "A great *pity* you are possessed of the heredity, von Graffenried, but not the *wealth* to adorn it."

After our hero learned of his lineage with Worb Castle annexed to it, as pleasing as these prospects were, his joy was speedily eroded. Half of the family estate was apparently lost to colonial pursuits. The other half fell to the mob during the revolutionary on-set. The parents had barely escaped their residence in France with only their souls, their wardrobe, jewellery, and other such valuables that can be easily transported.

As the evening progressed, the cloth was removed, and the party separated; the fairer sexes to the parlour and the men to a game of cards.

The evening being fine, Peter asked Elizabeth to join him in the gardens.

Though neither of them had prior opportunity to discuss their respective interviews with Father Francis, since they were now less averse to each other than at the outset of his holy tyranny, a pleasant atmosphere enveloped their stroll along the gravelled pathways, permeated with the sweet delights of freesia scent and cherry blossom.

Despite Peter's prior objections to the union, in studying Elizabeth at supper, he found an elegance and dignity in her person that would have well become a finer lineage. Certainly, whatever erudition she had enjoyed from Pier's munificence, its effect was more and more apparent. Beyond merely the preservation of his own reputation by not abandoning his future bride to the hazard of her own, in scrutinising his heart, he could not help remark it had, perhaps, permitted her greater longitude over his thoughts than he would have before easily surrendered to.

Elizabeth, too, obliged as she was to choose between two men of diametrically opposite, yet equally unappealing character, she could not help encounter in her breast a peculiar proclivity for Peter. Beyond all filial duty, neither could she help perceive that despite his monumental vanity, stupidity, genius for condescension, and gift for chaos, how much of her sensibility he had gained the ascendancy. Reflection was all it took upon his saving her father and Pier from certain death; she rightly deduced the emergence of her new feelings had to be found there.

Drawn as they were to the grand fountain amidst the grounds, they paused their stroll.

"I am certain," said our hero, suddenly parched, "you will easily ascribe my purpose in requesting this audience." With a tremulous voice, she answered she did. "As to the formalisation of our understanding, I ask your forbearance until the carnival. I would wish the occasion furnished with some ceremony. Also, I must visit Bern immediately after; I mean to return the scroll and would be honoured if you would join me?"

Nodding her ascent, she smiled. Yet from the expression that followed, and that her trembling hand inclined to reach inside her coat pocket, unknown to him, she was now about to approach that delicate subject of the accusatory letter.

But Peter, all merry, moderately intoxicated gaiety, clasped her hand and prevented her from doing so. "Heavens! Why did you not say you are cold? We must return inside."

In haste, he led her back along the gravelled walkways to the schloss.

As they reached the veranda steps, our hero espied a footman concealed in the shadows of a small grove, conferencing with an unfamiliar man.

The footman, having noticed Peter, bowed to the other, at which the men hurriedly parted ways. The one went towards his living; the other mounted a horse and rode into the distance and obscurity of the enveloping night.

Indeed, there was something in their exchange, something almost ominous that raised a degree of uneasiness in our hero's breast. Some ill wind, surely, was to blow across these grounds...

After the guests had departed and disappeared beyond the end of the avenue, Peter re-entered the vestibule en route to the library to bid Johannes goodnight.

Raised voices spilling up from the basement, however, brought him to a halt. Next, hurried steps reverbed up the stairwell, and the butler, with a face of fury, stalked past, commanding Peter to remove himself from his path at once.

Rapping on the library door, the butler requested admittance.

Granted such, he vanished inside and apprised his master in quavering tones that somehow, in the rush of the tour and the unplanned soirée, the key to the garden room and the spare to the library had been misplaced. "I assure you," said he, "I have castigated the servants for their carelessness."

"And *I* assure *you*," replied Johannes, "that not a wink of sleep will pass over your eyes until the keys are found! I expect them to be returned to their place by morning!"

07 – 08 APRIL 1792

While Peter crossed the courtyard to the main building early the next morn, before he reached its entrance, a heated dispute burst from the library. Supposing that the dastardly Johannes was berating the servants, he diverted his steps towards the gardens. Certainly, he had neither proclivity nor patience to suffer such an arrogant, volatile species of man at this hour. However, he went but a few paces before he stopped; the rising voices gave to his understanding that the contention was not between Johannes and the servants, but rather a battle of interests between that villain and his son.

"You *cannot* be ignorant," said Johannes in a tone of haughty severity, "of your *rank* and the *duty* owed by you to your family?"

"My family and rank, sir," replied Jago, irrefutably indignant, "appear by your account to be the same!"

"That is because they are the *sole* deciding value of your birth!"

Jago laughed, but with a scornful tone. "I am your son; not your commodity."

"If you wish to retain such a privilege, you will quicker grasp your negligence of such an entail. Your obduracy in this matter is vain, indeed, boy! Desist from it this instant! And dare not to disavow the filial obligations due the honour of your house!"

Could this have been the same matter Johannes alluded to yesterday outside of the library?

"And what of the paternal honour due to a son's felicity?" rejoined Jago.

"Arrogant, *obstinate* child!" cried Johannes with sterner emphasis. "Are you yet to apprehend it is you who belongs to the name of your house and not the reverse?"

"But what of love?"

"*Love*?" Johannes' tone pervaded with sickly, malignant irony. "Am I to understand your objection to this arrangement is because someone elsewhere has enticed your heart? Surely, you cannot have laid your interest at the feet of that woman?"

Footsteps hurried across the library floor.

"Jago? Return this instant, boy! Unless you wish to be forever disowned as my son, you will dare not to countenance disposing of yourself in any way unworthy! Do not let your vanity indulge such a wild and ungrateful delusion! *Jago*?!"

The library door slammed, and footsteps thundered towards the main entrance.

Swift on his heels, our hero darted to the stables and began readying the horses.

Moments later, Jago burst in, his countenance ablaze.

Seeing Peter, he seemed to check himself and assumed an air of indifference while straightening out his morning coat. The cheerful Znüni was soon at his feet, and Jago bent down to pat the creature. "Intriguing," said he, after a moment, "that I had not before correlated this."

Peter craned his neck from behind the horse. "Correlated what?"

Jago again recounted his sojourn in the hamlet of Gunten, and the commotion up shore at Oberhofen Castle, adding: "At the inn where I stayed, the coachman had a Bernese dog named Znüni."

Of course, the name itself was hardly unique; but the several particulars which Jago continued to narrate were. "That same evening, I saw a Bernese dog limping heavily along a lane. I later learned from the distressed ostler it belonged to him. The next day, the coachman had grown more dejected. All subsequent searches for his companion had profited him with no success. As you may have noticed, this dog happens to limp."

Peter admitted he had failed to observe this distinguishing feature.

With a bemused look, Jago continued, "since its name, its evident past injury and, moreover, its arrival at Bubendorf aligns too convincingly to be happenstance, I shall write the ostler to come here. If it is the same animal, the man must claim his companion."

Though it saddened Peter to consider losing Znüni, he could not refute that restoring the dog to its rightful master was the honourable course.

Johannes' quarrelsome voice bellowed anew from the house.

Horse untied and mounted, Jago drove it into a swift gallop out of the courtyard, all the while pursued by his father's vehement cries and demands.

Had Peter full possession of his faculties, this talk of the Gunten ostler would have disturbed his mind. But bereft of memory, his thoughts dwelt only on the earlier rupture between a father and son. Though having caught but the climax of their tempestuous words, he grasped the dispute pertained to matters of marital alliances.

"Could there be a secret mistress of Jago's affections?" There leapt upon Peter's mind the recent image of Jago's face fixed so fondly on Elizabeth's. The more he examined this circumstance, the more suspicious that peculiar fondness now exhibited itself. "Heavens!"

Jago would not demean himself with an attachment so unequal, would he? Certainly, his family would forbid such a — "Ah! Unless this is what Johannes had vilified him for?" If so, Peter would need to be vigilant for any signs of that man's overtures!

But what of Lizzie? If Jago harboured such intentions, she must have perceived them? There now raced upon his mind the recollection of her smiles and glistening eyes as she conversed with Jago the day before; as well as the many blushes which did overspread her cheeks.

Indeed, the sting of jealousy now drove deep into our hero's breast!

As it was that blessed — nay, pagan — Ostern morn, where all good heathens — I mean Christians — prepared to worship, tantalising smells of festive baking and roasting presently wafted into the stables.

Enticed by these delectable aromas, our hero followed them, soon finding himself in the kitchen just before the appointed breakfast hour.

There he discovered the jovial chef, singing merrily as she laboured over a feast fitting for the Resurrection Day. His hollow footsteps alerting her to his presence, she lifted a finger to her mouth and drew the command of silence. With a knowing wink, she then showed him her illicit horde: a braided Butterzopf bread, golden Fastenwähe dripping with butter (which she sprinkled caraway seeds over), and plain Ankeweggli rolls; though the pious canton had prohibited the baking of all but one kind of bread.

Caring not for such cantonal baking injunctions, Peter only said, "what a prodigious feast!" His eyes devoured where his mouth rather wished to join in gluttony. "A paradise of aromas that entice as much as they punish me with instant, ravenous hunger."

Alas, such feasts were only for such beasts as reigned upstairs!

Soon the whole troupe of house staff, enticed the same, entered from the stairwell, seeking their share of Ostern delights. Turning sharply to them and brandishing a knife, the chef's look was instructive enough to hurry them silently to their seats at the table.

A modest egg and bacon were soon served with a side plate of bread and jam — Peter enjoying an extra portion seasoned with several winks from the chef.

The present conversation about the disaccord between the cantons and surmises and wagers about Father Francis' most likely sermon soon took another turn.

"I don't blame him at all," said one footman to another, taking up an earlier theme. "I doubt I would have ever put up with it for half so long."

The dour butler shushed him with a stern look and a rap of his spoon against his cup.

"You'll be off soon, too," however continued the footman, looking at Peter. "Only a madman would keep serving that tyrant overlord upstairs."

Our hero leaned forward. "You will, I dare say, explain your meaning?"

This time with his knife, the butler rapped his plate. "Propriety!"

Only after the repast was eaten and the irascible butler had quit the kitchen to dress for church, did the conversation return to that earlier indecorous topic which pertained to the former coachman, who had not been fired but had resigned from his post.

"What?" Peter shook in his seat. "Have I been *lied* to?"

Indeed, he had. The footman explained that Johannes' recent "dance with death" was not his second, but at least his fifth. And the former coachman, done with confronting the Grim Reaper, had packed his bag and disappeared one evening without saying a word to anyone.

This revelation was beyond appalling. And what of Peter's own safety? Would he too soon confront a similar danger? Again, he repented of having accepted any employment from such a species of man. "A tyrant overlord, indeed!"

***

Once more, we find our hero seated in the pews amongst the flock under the stern watchfulness of Father Francis. Again, the latter preached on high from his creaking pulpit and delivered an Ostern sermon in agreement with those expectations earlier alluded to at the breakfast table.

But whatever the Father preached passed by without Peter's proper attention. So preoccupied was he by Johannes, that serpent in their midst, he got to wondering what malignant — nay, deserved — force drove these repeated attacks on the wealthy patrician's life. There now came to Peter's thoughts his earlier inkling of how easily such an arrogant man must want not for enemies. Yet, who from his list of haters should want him dead and for what reason both alarmed and intrigued Peter; and how Johannes could appear so flippant to the danger he courted again and again, both perplexed and piqued him.

Since it would distress Edmunda and Elizabeth to learn that Ernest, in his helpfulness, had unwittingly thrown himself in the way of imminent danger, Peter dared not voice his shocking discoveries. And considering that he himself now held the same perilous post, they might fret all the more. Let the women enjoy their holiday cheer untroubled. Besides, with Providence's favour, perhaps no more attempts would be made on the contemptible Johannes' life?

Meanwhile, around Peter, the congregation fidgeted and whispered thoughts on feasting, not sermonising. Beneath the pews, the children traded coloured, sugared, and chocolate eggs; their greedy faces soon smeared with the confections their parents had hidden for them in the gardens. Behind their prayer books, even the grown-ups passed clandestine bottles wrapped in linen cloths, cheeks flushing from stolen sips, giggles preceding the occasional hiccup.

Thus, distracted as they were by gluttonous thoughts, the congregation bolted for the church doors as soon as they were freed, homeward bound to bedeck themselves in their holiday best and join the riotous festivities of the afternoon and evening in Liestal.

***

'Twas nearing seven in the evening when our hero, accompanying Elizabeth and her family, arrived by the pony and wagon at the ancient walls of Liestal. Beneath the turreted clock-tower, they passed and found themselves amid the Chienbäse carnival: a bacchanalian scene of revelry and flame. Despite all worry over the growing ruptures between the cantons, the cobbled main street still thronged with elegant carriages, humble wagons, processions of brightly clad musicians, and spirited dancers garbed in fanciful costumes and masks. Even the stern-faced abbess led her cheerless flock of nuns through the masses, scowling at the inebriated impenitents urinating in the alleyways.

Besom brooms and lanterns, carried by cheerful men, women, and children, lit up the darkening night, whilst man-drawn carts hauled bonfires as tall as houses, saturating the air with heat. From amid the choking soot, smoke, and fire, voices chanted, "winter, melt away." The stout city fortifications reverberated with the deafening cacophonous rattle of wheels, folksong, raucous jokes, and laughter. Merrymakers raised their flasks, played the Eiertütschen — the egg smash — and threw about the broken, brightly painted egg shells.

Because the coaches and carts were so innumerous and tightly packed, it was with some difficulty that Ernest finally found a space to park the wagon on the banks of the Ergolz. Not less irked to be so crammed together, groups of wealthy persons attired in a manner more elegant than carnivalesque also complained about the proximity of peasant masses and the smoke pollution.

After an hour's ramble through the noisy, smoky, crowded streets, a vexed Edmunda demanded an escape from the heat, flames, drunken revellers, and egg yolk. The Inn Zum Engel was the proposed sanctuary according to the arrangement Peter had made with his parents.

This location, they soon found, was, of course, not less packed with drunken bodies and choked with smoke than the streets. Neither was it any cooler, for a prodigious amount of candlelight which lit up the interior of dark panelled walls and low ceilings only added to the unbearable heat. A vacant bay window seat spotted, Edmunda hastily cut — nay, *pushed* and *elbowed* through the crowds to claim it, driving away a young couple who were just about to sit down. Shouting and waving her arms, she signalled her victory. Peter and the others at length found their way to her and squeezed about the table as best as they could.

Shortly after, Hans, Harris, and Helene arrived. About an hour later, Johannes and Jago entered the inn, swathed with patricians and guards — all of them serious and sour-looking.

Try Edmunda did to call out to them over the drunken din, but they heard her not, or appeared so. They moved to another side of the interior and disappeared behind a large tapestry, leaving the guards stood as sentry in front of it.

Seeing so many guards, Peter supposed Johannes must finally have given greater heed to his imperilled person — and, by extension, himself. But what occasion could lead them so solemnly to their secret cavern? He now recalled Johannes' glee in anticipating rich spoils from civil conflict. Doubtless, this convocation aimed to deliberate and determine which rewards each man would claim from the suffering populace once war erupted.

Most truly, the prospects of upheaval spurred the avarice and ambition of they who saw only potential for enriching themselves of the common people facing deprivation and chaos.

The large tavern hall, so cramped with boorish, inebriated townspeople, now saw its rowdy atmosphere displaced by local nobles usurping their seats. The air also grew rife with murmurings from the latest influx of fashionable French émigrés, who descended upon the establishment with equal entitlement. As the profit-hungry innkeeper drove out the lowly folk in favour of the francs soon to line his purse, the strident talk of "*liberté*, *égalité*, *fraternité*!" sooner incited wary looks from Swiss natives and patrolling guards alike.

Since some time passed with no sign of Peter's parents, the party got to wondering where they might be. Another hour gone by, and our hero imagined some dark misfortune might have befallen them. But peering through the thick smoke, he believed he spied his mother near the bar. The churning wall of people, however, quickly enveloped her from view.

Peter cut through the masses in that direction, yet ere he could reach her side, she was gone.

Neither did he find her at the entrance nor outside in the busy street. It was impossible to distinguish anyone among the drunken, noisy crowds. But feeling unseen eyes watching him, he turned to look, yet found not the source.

Dissatisfied with his ill-success and doubting his eyes, he returned to the party and sank back into the brown velvet seating. Seeing him thus out of countenance, Elizabeth kindly sought to assure him his parents were likely delayed and would soon come.

But the evening moved on, and arrive still they did not. Perhaps they remained averse to the proposed engagement? Perhaps forgoing this occasion was their way of showing their disapproval? But if it was his mother he saw, perhaps she was in favour, and it was only his father who still opposed the union?

Then where did my mother go?

Nearby, at the bar, downing one jug after the next, a small group of guards with little else to occupy their soused minds did ogle the fairest maidens gracing the crowded hall. After much discordant debate, all agreed one belle outshone the rest; the delightful Elizabeth.

Though by no means the youngest of that species, nor bedecked with the fineries of many of her female competitors, her handsomeness alone excelled that of her junior's having just come out.

Anyhow, these guards having admired her countenance for some moments, one of them noted her companion.

As if struck sober, his posture stood tall. "Does not he look familiar?" To his comrades, he pointed out Peter. "The man next to that enchanting female."

Let us, however, return our attention to our hero, who, were it not for the frequent jugs of beer forced upon him and guzzled down his own gullet, obliterating his anxious thoughts for his parents, may not have so readily risen to Edmunda's challenge.

"Well, get up!" shrilled she over the loud music and heavy footfall; pulling the lovers off their seats, she pushed them into the crowds. "Just flap your arms and move your feet. But try to look as if you know what you're doing!"

Thus, an abashed Peter led an equally abashed Elizabeth forward to a space at the centre of the hall cleared for such purposes as dancing. Beneath the rays of a large wooden chandelier, they stood, exposed to the clearer scrutiny of their watchers.

"Since they're both so handsome," said Edmunda, "and I must say what a pretty face Peter has without that beard, it won't matter if they stand as still as statues."

Stand like statues they did not! To the surprise and wonderment of all, Peter executed and led with the finesse of a lead ballerino the Schottisch, Walzer, Ländler, Marsch, and Polka. And since Lizzie, not less expert herself from her readings on the art, kept up pace and with an air of accomplishment, they were soon the pride and not a little envy of the hall.

Amidst their exertions, Peter panted in Lizzie's ear, "a great pity the confines of this hall suit not the allemande."

She pulled away a little, studying his expression as if for sincerity. "Allemande?"

"Yes, *enchaînements,* and *passés*."

"I see your memory must be returning?"

Scarce had Lizzie uttered this, when a grand ballroom indeed flashed across Peter's mind.

We resume with the guards for a moment. That most curious soldier had turned his watchful eyes from the lovers to the party at the window, when he spied another young man rise from the table and make his way through the masses towards the bar.

"You there!" said he, tapping the young fellow on the shoulder.

"*Me*?" stuttered Harris as the warmth of intoxication instantly drained from his face. "What can you want with me?"

"That *man* with that elegant female who was at your table — who is he?"

Easily interpreting whom he referred to, Harris grunted, "Peter."

The guard's brow gathered heavily over his deep-set eyes; he asked where Peter was from. Harris replied France, or Germany; he could not remember which. The guard enquired how long he had known him. Again, with a grunt, Harris explained only a few months, for Peter was new to the area. Lips pinched, eyes narrowed in thought, the guard probed Peter's prior whereabouts.

"Volunteering with the Guard," answered Harris, once more with a grunt.

"Ah!" The guard's brow flicked into an arch. "Then he is one of us?"

Doubtless being as much eager to escape this topic, the guard's interrogatories, and to refill his jug, Harris begged the man to speak directly with Peter should he wish to know anything else. At this, the guard waved him away.

This, of course, would not be the end of this matter. For as soon as the guard shifted his focus back to Peter, dubiety claimed the man's features.

Meanwhile, seeking relief from the crowded hall and needing cooler air, our hero and heroine took their temporary leave of the party, at which an impatient Edmunda bade them get to it promptly, embellishing her injunction with a cheeky wink.

Soon strolling together, the lovers reached the gently flowing Ergolz.

Here, upon a lesser occupied bridge, the breeze, the purling of the current, the distant hum of revelries, the nearer murmured endearments of other couples, and the rich reedy diatonic melodies of the schwyzerörgeli played on the banks, all blended to create a scene of tranquillity.

Elizabeth's eyes wandered the environing hills cast in the purple ambience of evening; while the silvery lustre of the full moon ruling the cloudless heavens gazed back upon her, heightening the charm of her countenance and the smiles which overspread it.

Just then, notes of spirited music stole across the water, and the smile lingering on Elizabeth's lips transformed into one of wonder. She leaned forward, with delicate poise, to peer more fully at a flotilla of boat parties below, drifting past; their oars dashing across the river of the trembling moon, stirred the surface into a sparkling welter.

From a torch-lit broad barge, several instruments poured forth their sounds, woven with a female voice singing an aria vivace.

This was one of those moments where the world seemed to have stood still, for all whom had taste, sensibility of heart, and breath within their lungs surrendered all to the sublimest of expression and modulation.

Whilst Elizabeth listened and watched, our hero's gaze rather fixed on the play of flambeau light, which flickered across her serene countenance. Each delicate shift of expression that rippled across her features like the moonlit waters below evinced a depth of sensibility he had, until now, been blind to. Scarce possessed of half the courage to pronounce his declaration, he found his spirit melt with awe, anxiety, and a perplexingly piercing enrapture.

A peculiar buzzing flushed his limbs. *What is this sensation?* His stomach seemed to wrap around his racing heart. *Is this a strange effect of mild intoxication?*

Commanding his shaking legs and wiping his clammy palms on his breaches, he turned fully to her and called her attention. That he now dropped to one knee is what doubtless drew from her a gasp. That he struck that same knee against a sharp cobblestone and consequently jumped back up, hopping about, cursing the bridge, is what indubitably drew from her a light laugh.

"Are you quite well?" said she, with concerned amusement.

"Perfectly well, I thank you," insisted he, still hopping about, rubbing his knee, cursing still the bridge and its architect.

Determined nonetheless to gallantly perform his duty, he squared himself and, again facing her, dropped to the ground, albeit more steadily, feeling for additional abutments.

"Elizabeth." He wobbled momentarily. "Though still bereft of all recollections and having not the testimony of my earlier regard for you, since spending together these past months, I..." he drew courage from the night air, "I..."

Quite possibly intimidated by Elizabeth's gaze, the words he had planned to speak did desert his nervous mind. Little wonder for there was something so bewitching in her countenance, limned in the lunar radiance, that compelled even his heart to kneel.

But grasping at what few words yet lingered peripheral to his thoughts, he resumed, "having had the privilege of reacquainting with you all over again and the opportunity to rediscover my..." Here sensations, oh, such strange — such *delightful* sensations to which Peter had erenow been a complete stranger, did acquaint him with some remarkable secrets. In his mildly besotted state, as when a drunk's tongue loosens to breach discretion, so too his heart felt at liberty to bring forth the shocking truth: "My feelings — my warm feelings?" He leapt up. "Lizzie! Heavens above! Where my mind still does not remember you, I believe my body finally does."

"Your body?" Natch, there was great perturbation in Elizabeth's tone. Had it not been for the night, verily her paleness as the blood forsook her cheeks would have been easily observed.

But back to Peter: as lengthy wars oft wear down and compel staunch defenders to surrender or defect, so too did vanity, that militant, zealous commander-in-chief, outmatched by love's artillery, resolve to abandon her post. Stormed thus by the passion that marched in to claim his beating throne, our ardent hero knelt anew, heedless of Lizzie's disquiet — for she was surely struck by her conscience. Fumbling in his pocket, Peter resumed:

"This band," he held it up, "long-concealed in the inner pocket of my blazer, I no longer doubt for whom it was intended. Indeed, while it serves to humble my obduracy, my arrogance, and to chasten my harsh words spoken to you — my behaviour has been entirely wanting since my return — it also illuminates the quiescent devotion I had undoubtedly always held for you."

It was only natural that upon seeing the ring, hearing these words, and finding her hand again taken by his, Elizabeth would gasp several times and begin a-trembling.

Ensconced as our hero and heroine were in Cupid's thrall, they saw not the two pairs of peepers spying their moonlit tryst; these prying orbs belonging to Edmunda and Ernest. Having snuck off from the inn, they presently crouched on the river bank and peered over the wall. Yet unbeknownst to these snooping snoops, four more sets of mischievous eyes peered from behind a nearby tree trunk, spying upon their spying. These orbs did belong to the roguish Hans and Harris to the right and the sly Helene and Emil to the left.

"Has he popped the question yet?" whispered an impatient Edmunda to her husband, who did instantly shush her.

"Your heart," professed Peter, "I have come to learn merits only the conquest of a noblest of men. If you would bestow on me the unparalleled distinction of becoming its sole guardian and protector, I shall make it my lifelong study to prove deserving."

To be sure, Lizzie's principles engaged in a most violent battle with certain passions. For not only had she deceived the inamorato regarding their relationship, but this ring he presented, she knew, was meant for someone entirely else. Divided indeed were the sentiments vying for her resolution as she deliberated her next words. Had she gone too far to retract? Whatever shame she must bear, her virtue must be retrieved if she were to speak up now. Yes, now she must tell him the truth. Yet her heart yielded to the sovereign of her affections, ruling every objection of her mind and rather inspired her to respond: "Yes."

A smile broke through her mien.

Again, were it not for the night, Peter may have noted where before the blood forsook her cheeks, it now rushed all over her face with such violence as to paint her in scarlet hues.

"But please," said she, "concern yourself no longer with the past. In saving my father and Pier, you had already obliterated from my mind much of your earlier representation."

Instantly, our hero swept her up in his arms and endeavoured to kiss her; but she, though sans that earlier violence of indignation, freed herself from his enclasp and put a finger to his puckered lips, gently easing them away.

"Let us forget not your injunction, that I ought not to lay upon you a finger until your memories are fully returned."

"Ah!" Peter was brought back into himself by these words. "Yes, quite right..."

"There is something I need to ask you," said she, and reaching for her pocket, she was, we doubt not, about to produce that letter; but there came tolling upon the air:

"Praise the Lord!" Edmunda sprang onto the bridge, unable to any longer contain herself. "Praise the Pope! Praise Father Francis!"

To consummate the occasion, the party returned to the inn to enjoy drinks, congratulations, and more dancing. Hans, though defeated at this turn, had already devised his next scheme. After observing his daughter at the Ebenrain gathering and noting the smiles, giggles, and blushes she bartered with Emil, though it at first displeased him immensely, he now sought to encourage and best steer such attentions where they were more warmly reciprocated. Thusly, into Edmunda's ears, he did drop hints — may we call them so — that she needed only to now settle her son's romantic interests.

Johannes and Jago appeared from behind the tapestry with their cohorts. Beckoned forth as Jago was, even though he felicitated the newly affianced, a lack of genuine enthusiasm pervaded his air. While this confounded those of the party who noted this, which they likely contributed to some disagreement with his father, who presently darted several indignant looks at his son before quitting the building, Peter easily divined the secret nature of his displeasure and antipathy.

***

'Twas now past midnight, and a farewell thus bid to Elizabeth and her family, Peter, and Jago returned in the chaise and four to Ebenrain in silence.

Absorbed as Peter was pondering an affection which, whether new or dormant, had stormed the fortress of his heart and seemed to grow with each beat, he did not fail to remark Jago glanced at him now and then with cold eyes; eyes which confessed a distinct aversion.

Still but an initiate in the sphere of amours, Peter's vanity and pride relished in this triumph over his companion. But recalling his parents' absence, all feelings of victory soon bowed to the trial he imagined he would still need to negate.

No sooner had they arrived at Ebenrain courtyard when Jago observed the main house door was wide open; as were several doors to the staff dwellings.

A loud groan burst from the schloss.

The coachman having been ordered to wait, Jago rushed inside.

Following him, Peter beheld a semiconscious footman strewn across the bottom steps of the staircase, bound with rope to the newel post. By the moonlight seeping through the vestibule, Peter noted Jago's eyes were, however, fixed on the ajar library door.

"What happened here?" Jago now sprang to the footman. "Speak man!"

The footman only groaned and sighed.

Collar seized, Jago shook him. "Wake up, man!"

"Jago," tried Peter, staying him with his hand. "The man is *clearly* harmed!"

"I need him to speak!"

Brought to, the footman gasped. "You are returned home." He grabbed onto Jago's sleeve. "I tried to stop them..."

"Stop *who*?" Jago removed the man's grip.

With broken sentences and spluttered pleadings for mercy, the footman confessed that while on duty, he had slipped down to the kitchen to enjoy a tipple — or two. Maybe an hour later, the dogs' barking drew him back upstairs to the garden room to find the exterior door ajar and the dogs outside on the terrace, licking something up off the ground.

Though perplexed as to account for this, he only fetched the key, called the dogs inside and locked the door. After returning the key to the butler's office, he went back to the kitchen to top-up his tipple, for he claimed to be feeling quite alone and sorry for himself; being as all other servants were making merry together at the festival.

Into a shallow stupor, the footman slipped; but Jago again shook him, bringing him back.

Lulled as he then was by drink, he had not heard the intruders until too late. Upstairs he rushed and found the garden room door open again and the dogs asleep beside it! "Noises then came from the library..." The footman grew more confused and slurred of speech. "... Spurred on by foolish courage, I investigated... three plunderers... one lunged at me."

In the ensuing scuffle, which was intense, the dark figures lunged at him, and one assailant's mask was ripped off.

Jago clung to the man. "Then you saw the scoundrel's face?"

The footman again regressed in and out of consciousness; his eyes rolled in his sockets

"His face?" Jago slapped him. "Tell me, man! *His face*?!"

"His face," eventually replied the footman with a gasp. "It was..."

But without finishing, he sank fully into a state of oblivion.

"Wake up, man!" Jago shook him anew. "*Wake up*!"

As appalling this sight was, a whimpering and pattering of paws drew Peter's attention to one of equal aghast. "Znüni!"

Having limped from the garden room, the animal presently collapsed; the white tiles of the chequered flooring revealed in the moonlight bloodied paw prints.

Jago, too, turned to Znüni, and his eyes stretched wide. "Where are the dalmatians?"

09 – 12 APRIL 1792

What a cruel torment our hero now suffered, torn between aiding the footman or the dog. But labouring most assiduously to first revive the former, Peter found his efforts were all in vain. The footman remained as insensible as any politician to human suffering. Thus, Peter recommended the man be removed to his quarters, after which he would see to Znüni.

But imagine Peter's appall when Jago, plainly caring for neither footman nor beast, rather flew into the library.

"Jago?"

A clangour as of books hurled across that sacred chamber soon broke upon the awful silence.

"They have taken it!"

"What is it, Jago?"

Znüni let out another whimper and the servant presently convulsed.

While supporting the unconscious man's head, only now did Peter recognise his face for the very servant he had before espied conversing mysteriously in the garden. "What strange mischief is —"

"Too late, yet again," boomed Jago's voice. "*Another* object stolen away." A tremendous crash erupted from the library. "Would to heaven that I could *rid myself* of every such obstacle!"

Indeed, as Peter listened to this din, he could scarce account for what had provoked such behaviour.

Library door flung wide, Jago reappeared. "The fiends have *taken* it!"

"With respect, what have they likely not taken?"

In that instant, Jago rounded on him with such ferocity that Peter could hardly believe him to be the same person. In fact, even in the shadows, his face, touched by a single shaft of moonlight, so astonishingly resembled every characteristic of his domineering begetter.

"Let us remove him before my father returns," hissed he. "It is probable he will destroy this incompetent fool for permitting such an atrocity."

"The footman? Permitting this atrocity?"

"Quickly, man! Or do you wish to suffer a similar fate?"

Though Peter did wonder at the cruelty of such puffed-up men, he complied and helped carry the man to his quarters, eager to get him safely away from Jago and his inordinate furies.

The poor bludgeoned footman's head had but hit the pillow when Jago, growing more impatient to rouse him from his stupor, flung out into the courtyard and ordered the coachman to search out the surgeon, physician, and the apothecary. Peter too, momentarily breaking from the servant's side, entreated the coachman to return with the veterinary as well.

With a nodding gesture and the utmost expedition, the coachman drove off, cracking his whip with a fervour equal of Helios racing his chariot across the sky.

Peter now hastened inside the vestibule and, with utmost care, collected Znüni — who did whimper — in his arms, and carried him to his quarters.

There, he discovered the door had been forced open.

As gently as Peter could, he laid the dog on his bed before searching about the gloom and disarray for the candelabra to produce light. This was, of course, gone. He further clambered about the disorder, sifting through the chaos of toppled draws and bed sheets scattered over the floor. His liveries were gone. His money-purse too. But his sack and, praise be to the Almighty, the all-important scroll secreted inside its pocket, remained in the room's corner.

Znüni did whimper some more, drawing Peter back to his side. As he endeavoured to comfort the whining creature, he gleaned what injuries he could from the moonlight. But as Peter ventured to pull back the blood-matted fur, Znüni's cries turned to snarls and snaps.

Presently, there came from the courtyard the rumble of carriage wheels and the clattering of hooves. Then Johannes' voice erupted. "*What*?! My dogs, too?! I will tear those thieving fiends, limb from limb!"

An intermission of chaos now burst forth from the schloss. Wishing not to abide Johannes' subsequent eruptions, Peter kept clear of the storm's eye. Though unable to render aid either to Znüni or the footman, he watched over them alternately, repeatedly checking the pulse of one and the breathing of the other.

After what felt an eternity had elapsed, the sound of horses and carriage wheels again reverberated in the courtyard, announcing the arrival of the surgeon, the physician, the apothecary, and the veterinary.

Alas, for all their vaunted titles, these learned men of science could no more revive the footman than raise Lazarus from his tomb. After volleying a variety of disparate opinions, they agreed only that his injuries appeared not mortal, and he remained deep in unconscious arms' embrace. He was to be kept comfortable, undisturbed and, after regaining consciousness, prohibited from movement — and most certainly subjected to no prosecutions.

Such injunctions of leniency could not but vastly displease Johannes and his son — the latter demanding the heavens be pulled down to awaken him while the former thundered: "There is not a moment to be lost! As this fool slumbers, those villainous rogues are making their escape! I will apply to a better qualified physician."

At that, the father and son sprang from the room, shouting at the coachman to fly to Liestal.

During the above-mentioned, the dexterous veterinary set calmly to work, removing the lead ball from Znüni's hind leg. His job done, he swiftly bandaged the creature and prescribed the same conditions as for the footman.

Suffice it to say, with the return of the house-staff, the entire estate was thrown into shock and dismay. Sleep was forbidden to all. The housemaids were driven like slaves to restore order to the rooms. The hired coaches, having just deposited their weary passengers, were commandeered forthwith for the footmen sent to fetch Johannes' closest acquaintances. These fine gentlemen, swift as hounds on a fox's scent, did race to the schloss, more eager to receive recognition and benefaction than to provide sincere consolation; they affected every greatest concern and significant commiseration, uttering unending streams of hollow sympathy.

Perfectly exhibiting their bankrupt humanity, Johannes, his son, and their ensemble of fawning beasts lamented only the loss of the dogs, this Ming vase, that French escritoire, or some Italian painting, while sparing no thought for the bludgeoned footman beyond rage at his failure to safeguard such invaluable possessions. Even the servants verily declared, albeit in hushed tones, their antipathy for their master and indeed all patriciates.

Peter too-well divined the treatment which the prior coachman must have endured. *No wonder he vanished in the night.*

Meantime, Johannes grew frantic for the footman's revival and bade his son take him away to Liestal himself. Immediately, Johannes' companions insisted on the use of their personal carriages for the commission; each promising their conveyance the most commodious means of transport; each one faster than the other. Since there could be only one successor to this office, the unchosen preened and sulked like spurned debutantes.

This spectacle of vanity and avarice filled Peter with a sickening displeasure. Though lavish the scenery, rich the food, elegant the carriages, and opulent the attire, it was anything but a specimen of distinction. All was a gilded existence; a fine costume painted over rotten souls; a tight-fitted corset bursting at its seams with the gluttony of superficial refinement.

There now opened before our hero a chasm. He found himself questioning the very fabric of his high opinions and doubting even the integrity of his own taste.

***

Having snatched barely a few hours' sleep, Peter was abruptly roused by a thunderous rapping at his door. A footman relayed a summons that he should attend the butler's office straightaway.

In the office, sat Johannes at the butler's desk. His countenance bore the clouds of the storm raging within while his eyes were fixed upon the key cabinet, which hung aslant off the wall. "This is a despicable atrocity worthy of death," avowed he. Rising from the desk, he stalked across the office to a rather less than pretty painting. "But my only comfort is that they did not make off with my recent acquisition."

Only comfort? Surely, he meant not this hideous painting? Truly, Medusa's snake-tressed visage could not have been any uglier!

"Despite the present ordeal, there is little point in delaying the journey." Johannes took down the dreadful oil. "I have obtained for you a carriage; you shall hasten to Lucerne."

"Lucerne?" Peter spied a small vault in the wall. "But if you recall, I intend to go to Bern today. For I wish to return the scro —" Peter did stop himself, regretting the slip.

"*Scroll*?" replied Johannes with chilling austerity. The cogs turned behind his cold eyes. "You mean to refer to that scarcely decipherable message, which, even could they understand, will by now have very little authority? No! Indeed, for you shall go to Lucerne. But take the scroll to the garrison there if you are so concerned with what is already past."

From his waistcoat pocket, Johannes produced a key and inserted it into the steel door. With two loud clunks, the vault opened to him; he removed from it a box and, placing it upon butler's desk, removed the lid.

Peter sprang forward. "The clock?"

Johannes' brow did not approve of such familiarity. All the same, he said, "it is rather fortuitous it stopped ticking, for I would not have brought it down here. But had I only been more felicitous in employing a braver, more dutiful footman! Perhaps my satisfaction will have been complete and all my possessions in their rightful place — why do you shake your head?"

Marvelling at so triumphant a pride over a clock while so disparaging a faithful servant, it was impossible not to shake one's head. "Fortuitous, indeed," replied Peter with an affected smile.

"Anyhow, while I consult my grief," resumed that man, "and the loss of my beloved animals, I must concede that the vile brigands are not entirely devoid of my estimation..."

Pausing, he seemed to half-laugh.

Really, with each passing hour, Peter's distaste for the man turned only the sourer. "Sir?"

"For though vast were the items of true value they appropriated, they can at least distinguish the vulgar from the fine." Across the room he advanced, and picking up the grotesque canvas, eyed it with indisputable rapture. "For what else could so cunningly sequester the treasure concealed behind it?"

Now grimacing at the painting, he flung it into a corner, the frame cracking loudly.

The box Johannes pressed into Peter's hands and charged him to guard it with his very life, letting it not leave his sight till it reached the horologist, who would restore the timepiece to its working state. Directions provided, Peter was recommended an inn of repute, where, should he provide Johannes' name to the manager, he would be accommodated in the best quarters.

Peter now requested Johannes' permission for Lizzie to accompany him — at his own expense, of course. Such permission granted, though at the stipulation of taking Emil along as a chaperon, "we cannot have you exposing that woman to infamy," said Johannes, "nor tainting my name by association."

Our hero had already anticipated this etiquette; but since Johannes spoke of it first, rather than defend his scruples, he chose to bow his appreciation. "Ah, there is something else I ought to mention. On the evening of the dinner, I noticed a footman speaking in a, I must say, suspicious manner with someone — I know not who — in the gardens."

Johannes' eyes sparked. "Do you know which footman?"

"The very one struck down by the intruders."

***

All at the chalet were not less astounded to learn of the events at the schloss. Yet, as shocking as it was, Peter begged a deferral of Edmunda's inquisition until after Lucerne. Thus, with hasty packing done, the travellers bid adieu — Edmunda shouting after them how fortunate they were to be travelling to a city where "it had chased out almost every protestant."

Wishing to inform his parents of his journey and discover what had prevented their attendance at the festival, Peter bade the coachman stop at the inn where they were staying.

Alas, his parents were not there. The manager relayed they had quit his property the evening prior; he then handed to him a note, which gave the following explanation:

> *Peter,*
> *Forgive our abrupt departure. Your father has been taken ill again. I have insisted he see his trusted physician in Bern; he will soon put your father to rights! We shall rejoin you*

as soon as his health permits. Until then, your affectionate mother.

Though relieved to read no aversion expressed against Elizabeth, a portent still clawed at his breast. That his father had been taken ill again, perhaps it was a fear of losing him so soon after their reunion? Whatever it was, there presaged an ensuing woe.

***

Now, whilst our travellers jostle along to Lucerne, each occupied by their respective thoughts, let us pause to reflect on the adventures — or rather misadventures — of our hero thus far. Certainly, from the outset, burdened with delivering so future determining a scroll, he did endure much tribulation: grievously wounded, relentlessly pursued, nursed by hob-goblins, seized by the Swiss Guard, then by bandits, and, on the cusp of finally reaching Lucerne, to suffer so monumental a setback in the most inopportune loss of his memory!

Fortune, as we then saw, having chosen him as her most amusing plaything, then rained upon his poor head further indignities: deception, poverty, gruel, toil, scandalous ignominy, hurtling milk-buckets, and near-death beneath a block of ice.

Yet, where Janus wears two faces, Fortune, fickle as she is fiend, did deign to toss Peter the occasional morsel of good luck: the recovery of the scroll, the cryptic correspondent, the reunion with his parents, and the revelation of the elusive personage, G.V.V.

But again, cunning as Fortune is capricious, she watched unsympathetically from her lofty throne as the chaos unfolded between Bern, Zürich, and France, only to divine an opportunity for further sport at Peter's expense. For in despatching our guileless hero straight into a viper's nest — a territory still bestrewn with posters and swarming with the Swiss Guard — she now sets the stage for fresh calamity.

***

Evening had wrapped her starry mantle over the world by the time our travellers gained an eminence which overlooked the ancient Lucerne, nestled below: a jumble of rooftops, turrets, and moats, all hemmed in by the city walls, and touched here and there by the moon's lustre. Beyond, a glimpse of the Rigi, Hochflue, Kulm, and Bürgenstock peaks rose on the far side of Lake Lucerne, claiming the black horizon with their snow-crowned peaks.

After ten long hours and roughly fifty-one miles, all were weary, yet invigorated, to see their destination. The carriage descended a trail into a thick wood. After some distance, the declivity levelled out, and an opening presented the glinting waters of the river Reuss.

Instantly did Lizzie and Emil crowd the window. Though unable to observe the passing scenes for himself, Peter was not deprived of the same spirit of excitement. In studying Elizabeth's countenance through the glances of felicity she paid him, he experienced perhaps an even greater satisfaction than had he personally beheld the Musseg walls, which, across the river, climbed a steep elevation and punctured the sky like a crown. And listening to her relate to her brother the history of the town, he experienced a certain pride in the apparent proficiency of her knowledge. Again, our hero pondered the education Pier must have bestowed on her.

The carriage passed under a clock tower which told it was already past eleven, and they entered a warren of streets, dwellings, and structures forming Lucerne New Town.

Within minutes, they arrived at the Inn Schlüssel.

Emil, all novelty and excitement, sprang out first, hurrying his eyes over the stone-floored square and its sundry buildings, while Elizabeth, stepping out, regarded the square with admiration and intelligent curiosity. Last to alight, Peter removed the luggage.

"As agreed," said the coachman, "I shall return to collect you at eight-sharp, the day after tomorrow." And without indicating his own lodgings, he cracked his whip and drove the horses forward and disappeared behind a church.

Peter now turned to survey the property's exterior. It was neither opulent nor extravagant, but perfectly undistinguished; an odd recommendation for one so perversely wealthy.

"Shall we?" gestured he to Elizabeth to proceed through the door.

While crossing the threshold, Peter noted the date of 1545 carved into the sandstone lintel. Below stretched a shell lunette bearing two crossed keys framed by an engraved arch supporting a grotesque pair of dragons; their clawed feet resting atop a lion and lioness. Something in this imagery arrested Peter's interest, as though struck by a spark of recognition.

Just then, Elizabeth looked back; noting his distraction, she enquired into its cause. As Peter studied the square and the entrance to the inn, he confessed a nagging feeling of some prior acquaintance with this location. Elizabeth asked what it was that he recalled. But Peter, unsure what it was, he replied thus.

"If you've been here before," said Emil, "the innkeeper might recognise you?"

"Yes, perhaps?" Encouraged by this prospect, Peter's stride took on a sudden alacrity.

As they ascended the brightly lit stairwell, their path was obstructed by a retinue of noblemen and guards who descended in a hurry. A distracted Emil, gawking about and paying no consideration to his steps, stumbled into one of the men-at-arms.

"Watch yourself!" voiced the man with inordinate vehemence as he reached for his hilt.

Intervening, Peter steered Emil away. "Please, forgive him. It is his first time in Lucerne."

The glowering guard's eyes did now alight on Peter, at which some apparent confusion seized his expression. The man's strange stare was, however, interrupted by the impatient nobles avowing their aversion to lingering thus on any level with such persons of inferiority and clumsiness. Hence, while clearing their throats and motioning the aforesaid inferior persons to remove themselves from their paths forthwith, the men continued their downward march — the guard, as he quit the property, shooting peculiar glances back at Peter.

Though Peter did grasp not the significance of the guard's odd behaviour, with each step he now took up the stairwell, something boded ill.

***

So, to rightly decode this puzzling encounter, though our sager reader may have already guessed at it, we must revert to the Liestal festival. We will recall that small band of guards who had subdued their indolence with beer and admired the prettiest maidens until one of them had fixed on Peter. Well, it turns out that this man on the stairwell was that very same one.

Despite the account Harris gave of Peter being a volunteer to the Guard, doubt yet plagued this man's thoughts. More so after his inebriation wore off, his mind grew thick with a conviction of having seen Peter elsewhere. But unable as he was to recollect where, and that his comrades uniformly dissuaded him from his opinion, he let the subject drop.

Fortune, however, that meddlesome mistress, verily saw to staging a reunion, bringing guard and hunted together under the same roof and on the same stairwell. From this occurrence, and we shall peer a little into the future here, recognition stirred anew in this guard's mind and 'twould require only a visit the next day to a comrade to reach its culmination.

Thus, the arrival of the next morn would dawn, and during this visit, his fellow man-at-arms — commissioned to join a neighbouring canton — would be busily packing up the last of his impedimenta when, from among a bundle of old papers about to be delivered to flames on his hearth, a WANTED poster would catch the eye of our increasingly preoccupied guard.

"Stop!" would cry he, and snatching it from the bundle, he would compare the symmetry in the printed face with that he recollected of the man on the stairs — the truth seizing him like a thunderclap.

I am sure it will take no great deductive prowess to determine what this guard would instantly wish to expedite that morning. But let us refrain from outrunning our narrative and wait but the passage of one night to observe how it will all go forward.

***

At the front desk, Peter endeavoured to substantiate the possibility of having visited these premises. After scrunching his mouth and bobbing his thick black eyebrows, the manager allowed Peter seemed vaguely familiar but could offer nothing else. Peter thus gave his surname; but the manager again rumpled his mouth and bobbed his brow, only to then reply he had no recollection of it.

To prompt the man's better recollection, Peter proposed he would have possibly been in uniform the last time he visited. The manager only claimed that the endless procession of soldiers made one indistinguishable from another.

How vexing!

To be sure, though our hero did still strive to snatch even the faintest memory from that impervious vault of his mind, he had found some small solace in she who had filled, though but part, of so vast a void. Yet, while such romantic felicity might assuage certain distresses, it cannot forever act as regent to that deeper, more material sentiment termed contentment. For despite instinct's assurance that he was somehow rediscovering his path in delivering the scroll, the shadow of uncertainty still haunted him.

Not less a stranger to perfect serenity was our heroine. For where before she had solely wished for Peter's memory to return and to be rid of him and to reinstate him to his true world, her heart and mind were now so confused by affection that she had begun to dread the severance of their relationship. Her intuition could not help but instruct her that what had brought them together would, once the spell was lifted from Peter's mind, drive them apart.

***

Peter awoke the following morn, beset by new apprehensions of the incident on the stairs. While he readied himself for breakfast, he pondered the general comportment of the guard, which, however abstruse, seemed to betoken some impeding prosecution...

The food bell rang, and he descended the stairs en route to the food hall.

... But having no justifiable grounds on which to expound his presentiment, as much as Peter examined and endeavoured to warrant this, he equally strove to disprove and to chase away the ill-feelings which clung to his breast.

The morning fare of breads, jams, cheese, eggs, and cold and cooked meats — a fine recommendation of the Lucerne cuisine — was eaten with gusto.

From the attire and the hum of conversation drifting in German, French, and Italian, Peter understood the company to be affluent and influential. Though this property lacked ostentation, it was clearly in vogue. Perhaps its clientele is what recommended it to the snobbish Johannes?

One particular group of men sat nearer to the window, gradually inclined Peter's ear more to their subject of discourse: that of the colossal disdain Zürich now held for Bern.

"And to add to it all," exclaimed a fine-dressed gentleman, "the rupture with France! I mean, how could he expect anyone to believe his ludicrous fiction of despatching an impetration of trust and assistance? We are left now with the inevitability of war!"

His equally fine-dressed companions grunted assent between bites.

"Had there been any message," continued the man, "it was but a ruse to wipe out the troops sent to his aid. He would then have marched to Zürich to overthrow it. These revolutionists, they all scheme the same."

In between swilling their beverages, the others accorded how wisely the Bernese Small Council had intervened in ordering the renegade Gustav's present house arrest.

"Have they not yet found that other traitor?" spoke another.

"Vanished off the face of the earth," answered the former. "The villain could be hiding in any canton, gathering forces as we speak. That Bern Canton certainly bears the spawn of rebellion — and it all began with that woman!"

Indeed, hearing mention of a Gustav, revolutionists, and a message, so much roused our hero's curiosity that this advanced his desire to probe it. "Pardon my intrusion," said he, "but do you, perchance, speak of the Schultheiss Gustav von Villeroy?"

After scanning Peter's modest garb with an air of contempt, they asked what of it and, hearing of the scroll's existence, merely mocked him. Peter now explained that he, a former Swiss Guard, had apparently been employed to deliver the very scroll. Yet:

"*Impossible*!" cried they. "This alleged letter?"

Hence, quitting the disbelieving men, Peter then returned and held the scroll before their now huge, widening eyes.

"Good lord!" gasped they, snatching it off him. "So, 'tis *true*!"

Now, more angered than amazed, they berated Peter for having so foolishly and for so long withheld so crucial a piece of evidence, putting the world on the threshold of war. But yielding a very little of their indignation to his account of amnesia, they entered a short, hushed debate on what to do with the scroll. To take it directly to Zürich would occasion only a belief of deception and duplicity. To return it to Bern would avail the schultheiss of only further suspicion. In the end, conceding on its entrustment for now to the neutrality of the Lucerne garrison, the men ordered Peter to take it there forthwith, along with a letter they would draft apprising the garrison of its consequence.

Ready accord nodded, and averring it was already his intention to take the scroll there, Peter asked to whom he had the honour of speaking.

"We are of the Schaffhausen Small Council," replied the stout noble, "myself and him." He indicated the man beside him. "And with us, the Military Commissioner, and Guild Master. We break our journey here for we are just returned from an emergency diet in Bern, which, according to this new discovery, its outcome might now take a very different turn."

***

With ease, our trio procured a carriage coupé outside the inn and were soon whisked through the open air towards the famed horologist's store, Die Goldene Schlüssel.

As the carriage rattled along, the wayfarers discussed the astounding happenchance that occurred at breakfast, of which Peter celebrated the providence of finally confirming the scroll's significance.

Whilst it may appear that Fortune herself did most obligingly stage-manage events to steer our hero within earshot of so decisive — nay, advantageous — a conversation, do not even we lesser mortals find that this is quite plainly how matters sometimes unfold? Yet, alas, more oft than not, the intelligence gained tends rather to our disfavour or disservice...

As they crossed a bridge towards the Old Town, the driver enquired which route they preferred. Peter and Emil deferring to Lizzie, she requested the historical Weinmarkt.

Thither the driver steered the horses.

Our party soon observed clusters of people, all drifting in one direction.

"Is there some event today?" enquired Peter of the driver, who replied there was none that he knew of.

The carriage had just turned onto the bustling street which led to the square when a thickening crowd came into view, all pressing towards some activity ahead.

As the carriage crept along, the press of bodies swelled, further slowing their advance. From his higher vantage, Peter spied a large gathering around a man who gestured emphatically and clung to an ornate fountain column — the man's makeshift stage — which Lizzie identified as a tribute to Lucerne's power and the solidarity of the early Swiss confederacy. This living monument, its patron saint, and ornate sculpturing now formed only an ironic frame for the man's fiery cries against the fracturing alliances.

The zealot presently hurled pamphlets aloft, which came swirling down upon the crowd; several landing inside the carriage.

Inflammatory political language and propaganda were the theme.

"'Tis a shame," said the driver, "to think this sacred spot once hosted the oath uniting our cantons. And this fight between Zürich and Bern, 'tis adding to our problems everywhere."

Several aggressive shouts stole over the swelling agitation as a detachment of guards arrived, warning the crowd to disperse. There came a rock flying over Peter's head, preceding an explosion, frightening Elizabeth as glass from a bright-painted guildhall window rained down sunlit shards. Anxious to flee the rising tension and the crowds pressing harder in on the carriage, Peter bade the driver whisk them away posthaste.

Thus, the sequence of squares hemmed by tall painted houses, gabled facades, guildhalls and boutiques, all linked by cobblestone streets, blurred past in their hasty retreat.

Soon arrived at their destination, the trio alighted the carriage and entered the clock-inundated shop. The door bell's ringing drew the brief glance of a white-haired fellow behind a counter, engaged with a customer. "Be with you momentarily."

As minutes continued to tick loudly by with no further acknowledgement, Peter proposed Elizabeth and Emil to take a stroll along the promenade, but to be careful to avoid all commotion. He would follow shortly after, and together they would walk to the garrison.

A few minutes after Lizzie and her brother quit the premises, the customer also took his leave; Peter approached the counter and presented the box.

"Yes, yes," said the horologist, wiping his monocle. "What can I do for you?"

"I am come on the very particular behest of Johannes von der Mühll."

"Ah!" The man's countenance was of that pinched character, reminiscent of hours spent squinting at the minutiae of clockwork; his eyes, narrow, keen, and sharp, did sparkle with monetary anticipation. "His Lordship sent you?"

Peter removed the lid from the box and drew the man's attention to the sacred apparatus.

"Oh!" said he. "The honeybee?" Timepiece removed from the box, he held it up as one would a newborn. "So, His Lordship is the owner of the sixth clock?"

"Sixth clock?"

While he placed it on the counter, the horologist paid our confused hero a conspiratorial look. "*Vive le futur Empereur!*" He embellished this mantra with a roguish wink.

"*Vive le futur Empereur?*" echoed Peter, struck by some faint chord of memory.

The horologist said he would lock the door. This done, and the curtain drawn across its glass, he returned to his counter. "I had no idea His Lordship was a partisan of our future saviour. Does he have any message for me to convey?"

Indeed, Peter was too confounded to reply; he could only shake his head while "Tick-Tock. Tick-Tock. Tick-Tock" filled his ears, and his eyeballs twitched left to right.

"Never mind," resumed the man. "I shall get to work."

With hands as swift as Hermes, he removed the backplate and, employing several tools quite unfamiliar to Peter, poked and prodded the inner workings of the timepiece. The sound of several cogs turned in succession, resulting in a small drawer springing open from the bottom side of the clock.

"There you are!" cried he, triumphant, handing to Peter a small billet.

More so confounded than at the first, Peter could only stare alternately at the billet and the apparent secret compartment. This was all so very singular. Had not Johannes despatched the clock here solely for its repair? As Peter turned the billet over, he remarked a wax seal stamped with a honeybee emblem.

Indeed, with the next "Tick-Tock's" reverbing around him, his mind buzzed from one bewildered thought onto the next, unable to alight on any understanding.

"You said there are six clocks?" said he to the horologist.

The man drove a final screw into the backplate and placed the clock on the counter. "Precisely six," affirmed he while seemingly admiring his handywork. "Identical, too."

"Six identical clocks?" Our hero now noted the want of a pendulum swing. "Is it still not working?"

With a chuckle, the horologist explained that Johannes would already be aware that all six clocks were pointedly manufactured to stop working at the same time, only to then resume their ticking at a pre-determined date, which would herald a *certain* event.

The door bell ringing violently interrupted them as a red-faced Harris burst in with gasps and coughs, doubling over and rubbing his knees. "Peter!" panted he. "What a..." More coughs seized him before he espied a chair and collapsed into it.

"Harris?" Peter inserted the curious billet into his pocket. "What brings you here?"

Enough air gasped: "Edmunda," said he. "I don't know *where* to begin."

"Edmunda?"

"I've news — *shocking* news!"

"Pray, then tell me this instant!"

"Johannes..." He again gasped and coughed whilst his eyes flashed with some sinister expression. "He's in the greatest rage ... He'll have the Guard arrest you!"

"The Guard? Arrest *me*? On *what* charge?"

"The footman... He's awakened."

"The *footman*? What does this —? Speak to the point, please!"

Harris gulped more air. "The footman... He says it was *your* father he saw at the robbery."

12 – 13 APRIL 1792

As if our poor hero's horror and disbelief were not enough at hearing of his imminent arrest and that it was none other than his own father who attacked the unfortunate footman; but to be then told that his mother was also present at the robbery, why, Peter was nearly bereft of air!

"No!" He gripped the countertop to steady himself. "You must be mistaken! This cannot be! The footman must be confused?"

***

Alas, it indeed proved just as a somewhat triumphant Harris declared. After reaching Liestal, the footman had come to his senses and avowed to Jago the whole sordid account. During the altercation, the very brigand whose mask got ripped away was the father's own! A woman then rushed into the vestibule, and, upon seeing her fellow ruffian — nay, husband unmasked — and the splayed footman with the husband's mask in hand, she screamed and denounced the heavens for so cruelly conspiring against them that her voice did betray her to be the mother.

No sooner had Johannes learned of this perfidy, he flew into the aforementioned rage with violent promises of retribution, even upon the heads of all they connected by blood.

Since tongues were so expedient in spreading this report, it quickly reached Edmunda's ears. To the farm she raced and with very little difficulty obliged Hans — who we know was already eager to attach his daughter to her son — to send a warning to Peter.

Young Harris became the chosen courier and, having taken the night carriage, he first tried the inn, from where he was directed to the horologist and, as we have seen, found Peter there.

***

This disastrous appendix to Harris' tale did indeed overwhelm our hero. But apprehending the urgency, he bade Harris to go find Elizabeth and Emil while he — forgetting the clock — set off for the inn to pack up their belongings.

Is it possible that the very beings who brought me into this world are wretched swindlers? Could it be the memories I seek are but stained with a history of disgrace and depravity?

The magnificent stone fortifications he passed, enveloping him in their cold shadows, served only to symbolise the towering menaces of his present situation and the possibility of, if not his parents' ill-fate, mayhap his own.

What persecution will I endure in the connection? Doubtless, my own character will suffer from the pollution — He stopped. *What if I am cut from the same cloth? Destined to follow their path and meet the same destructive end? Could it be those visions of chains and prison wagons which haunted me indeed alluded to past villainy?*

This consideration so distressed our hero that his legs went from under him, and he fell against an oak.

Several passers-by, seeing him thus, did scowl before hurrying their children away.

Some moments our hero passed in this forlorn posture.

Oh! To have such profligates as parents; such villainous beguilers to have used me so — but wait! Another possibility shot to his brain. *What if they are not my parents at all? This could not be so, could it?*

This was a possibility of far worse villainy than if they *had* been his true parents. His indignation fired by this consideration, he stood tall. *The monsters!*

When our hero arrived back at the inn, the manager made his way over.

"Not now!" Peter put his trembling hand up to him. "Not now, I beg you."

Without speaking a word, the man handed to him a small billet.

More impatient than curious, Peter tore it open and read the following:

> *We know who you are and your attempt to assassinate the Bernese schultheiss. We have taken captive your fiancée and her brother. In exchange for their freedom, you must forfeit your own. Come to the Kapellbrücke, alone, at midnight. Do not, we advise you, mention this to anyone.*

"What is —?" He grabbed the innkeeper's arm. "*Who* sent this?!"

Startled, the man shrank back. "A detachment came —"

"The Swiss Guard? But why?" There rushed upon his mind the incident on the stairwell. Yet, if it were the Guard, would not they have instructed him to go to the garrison? And why take Lizzie and Emil? Confusion, desperation, vengeance, and retribution had perhaps never so pierced the heart of any man. "Are you certain it was they?"

"They waited a good while. But seeing you didn't come, they fell into an angry debate until one of them penned there that note and gave me this." He handed Peter a rolled-up sealed document. "They said if you pretended not to understand the note, this would remind you..."

Seal broken: "Good lord!" Our hero's heart and viscera shuddered.

Beneath the bold-font WANTED, his own face, etched in ink, stared back at him. At this sight, there not only now surged afresh through his remembrance that earlier conversation at the jailhouse, but there stormed across his mind the fullest, prismatic carousel of the explosion at Oberhofen; the subsequent pursuit; the cause of his injuries — which again stung — and that very cabin, where he first laid eyes on these very same posters.

"Good heavens!" He tottered, seeking support against the wall. "Is this *truly* who I am?" So aghast he was at this visitant to his anamnesis, a sudden headache split his skull. He would have instantly abandoned this city; but there were his dear Elizabeth and her brother to consider.

"How she will despise me!" spoke he without even realising it. *How she might rather cling to her captors and recoil from the arms of salvation.*

The manager, watching the procession of emotions which could not but otherwise contort Peter's face, asked what was wrong. Without answering him, Peter searched the hour from the cuckoo clock above the reception desk. It was but approaching eleven. The passage of thirteen hours would drag with the agony of an age. Knowing not where the guards could have taken their captives, he quit the bemused manager and hastened to his chamber.

With long strides, he paced the room, clawing at his forehead and growing breathless as he stared at the note. At length, overpowered by despair, he collapsed into an armchair.

***

Casting our minds back but a chapter to when the guard had snatched from the flames the condemning poster, thus validating his suspicion, we now learn that he had then gathered several others and hastened to the inn to seize the outlaw and claim his bounty.

Peter was, however, already gone to the horologist's store. Hence, after obtaining from the innkeeper the direction in which Peter went, off went the guards in impassioned pursuit.

Doubtless it is that fickle Fortune, ever disposed to confound expectations, did momentarily swap sides and conspire against them most frustratingly, for they rushed in upon the startled horologist but shortly after Peter had (for the reasons we are aware) already quit the premises for the inn.

Thusly apprised as to where their prey had fled, they turned sharply on their heels, growing violent with impatience and restive at the hazard of missing their opportunity.

It was then that the leader of so rapacious a pack spied hapless Elizabeth and Emil strolling along the promenade in his direction. To seize the innocent pair as surety came fast to his corrupt mind. This effected, the villainous gang then split ranks; half, dragging Lizzie and Emil away while the others raced to the inn to lie in wait.

Alas, that Peter did not return directly (for we will recall his forlorn embrace of that oak) and that these guards were due to be on duty from ten forenoon at the garrison, and no one would they allow to steal from them their triumph, they schemed as was written in the note.

***

Poor Elizabeth and Emil, meanwhile, seized upon as they were from behind, their screams silenced by sturdy hands and their pleadings choked by roughly woven gags, they were carried off into a carriage, blind-folded, and conveyed to some location.

Led stumbling up several staircases and across a creaking floor, they were flung into chairs, having their legs tied fast and their arms wrenched behind their backs. As their gags and blindfolds were ripped away, to their astonishment, they discovered a group of guards; two stood in the light shafts and several others lurking in the shadows.

From the various bulky joists and the slanted roof, they understood they were in an attic.

"Where are we?" said Elizabeth, tremulous of voice. "Why have you brought us here?"

The guards only looked at her with cold eyes and unfeeling countenances.

"I demand to speak to your superior," tried she, summoning what courage she could.

"You are in no position to demand," came a deep voice from the shadows. A guard appeared, and, snatching up a paper off a table, he stalked over. "Are you not in league with that traitor?"

"Traitor?" Elizabeth shrank from the teeth-gnashing man. "Of *whom* do you speak?"

The grimacing guard held up the paper to her face. "*This* traitor!"

So great was Elizabeth's shock at beholding the representation so identical to Peter that the power of language cannot describe it. Unable to look away, she studied with horror-filled eyes every detail of the face beneath the words WANTED.

"Put their gags back on!" bellowed the brute.

***

Slumped still in the armchair, environed by shadows which crept about the chamber as the sun crawled along the sky outside, Peter lamented his deplorable situation. Agitation for the safety of Lizzie and Emil swirled about the tempest of his mind. And like lightning flashes, terrifying representations of this Schultheiss Gustav snaked among the despairing blasts of so unendurable an inner storm.

Could I truly have ventured so shocking a machination upon so illustrious a soul?

How could he ever again face his beloved Elizabeth? He rose, uncertain what course to take. *Yet, what of the scroll?* Surely, was Peter this eminent man's adversary, so critical a despatch would hardly have been in his possession? An alarming notion arose against this: *But what if I was not its intended courier? What if, after I attacked the schultheiss, I had merely seized it by equally terrible means? Am I the very instigator of the calamity undoing the confederacy?*

How short a period can entirely overset one's life! Where hope would have before led him to Bern to reclaim so vital an element of his past, horror now utterly restrained him. Hopelessness did attract his every thought to despair's abyss, urging him in the opposite direction to flee to the ends of the world.

Among the shadows still encircling him, now taking on phantom appearances and seeming to whisper taunts in his ears, there slithered through a fresh remembrance of his reprobate parents. Whether they were his parents mattered no more, for his own elusive history was but marred by a far worse degeneracy. How he wished only to destroy and not recall that lost part of his life.

As one struck paralysed by grief, so our poor hero was.

Who really am I?

This was a black moment, indeed.

Unable to moderate the insurgence of devastation which overthrew his dwindling courage, he sank to the floor, where the cruel torture of self-loathing and desolation coiled about his already struggling heart, strangling even his very breath.

A frantic rapping at his door tore him from the deepening abyss.

'Twas Harris, panting and spluttering, declaring he had found neither Elizabeth nor Emil anywhere. He had gone back to the store hoping to discover them, but they were still absent. "And what's this the horologist says about the Swiss Guard?"

Answering him not, nor confessing the additional horrors of his dilemma, Peter begged Harris immediately return to Bubendorf; shoving him out of the chamber, he closed the door.

The mantel clock struck eight, its sound reverbing on Peter's every nerve.

With unceasing agonies, he had passed these several hours. As no mortal threat was made against Elizabeth and Emil, only that their freedom hung on the forfeiture of his own, this fact gradually moderated to some extent his despair.

There was only one thing to be done — he must hand himself over! Yet there now came into his heart a dubiety where earlier he had so freely countenanced the destitution of his character. Certainly, he was vain. Most certainly, haughty. Perhaps a little judgemental. Mayhap even marginally inconsiderate. But he was guarded in his conduct towards the fairer sex. Principled in his beliefs and notions of right and wrong. Despised the wanton corruption he observed in Johannes. He detested all unjust treatment — especially against himself!

I cannot be what I am accused of? There has to be some mistake. There has to be some other explanation — some extenuation — for my memories?

Nightlight and poster seized, he stood before the looking glass. The resemblance was indisputable. But could this poster depict one merely identical to him? Again, he scrutinised the face. If the portrayed outlaw were our hero and he had indeed ventured to assassinate the schultheiss: *why then did I possess the scroll imploring for aid? Surely, I would have simply destroyed it?*

Something was amiss. Something... and *then* it struck him:

***

"Keep this safe," had urged a masked man in the cold, dank tower cell as he pressed the scroll into his hands. "Get it to Zürich!" His voice was deep and austere, issuing from behind the cloth which concealed the lower part of his face.

The man also shoved into his hands a small bag, avowing it was of utmost importance.

"Take this as well. But should your journey face impediment, you must hide it."

***

"Yes! A masked man gave me the scroll! But who *was* he?" Why entrust it to our hero? And who was it to go to? Such fragmented memories! "And the bag!" — he had secreted it inside the tree! Yet what was *this*?

Despite all endeavour, every such detail eluded still his memory. Nonetheless, that he recalled what he had, he now knew: "This *must*, despite all else, *prove* my innocence!"

Where crushing defeat had heretofore obliterated courage and hope, there rose self-assurance and an exigency for vindication, fired by indignation, rage, and zeal.

Midnight fast approached. Growing more suspicious of the guards' motives, Peter pressed the fretful innkeeper as to where a sword could be procured at so late an hour. Despite the man's protestations, Peter prevailed and was directed to the local swordsmith, who, woken up by the loud banging at his shop door, reluctantly came down from his window.

Sufficient indeed was the instrument of our hero's vengeance — flashing with a slickness in the moonlight. With this, the scroll, and the letters from the Schaffhausen Small Council members in his satchel, he hastened to concert with they who dared stir the fervour of a man who, however without memories, grew ever more convinced, with each stride, of his honour.

At a street corner which overlooked the ancient wooden trussed Chapel Bridge, Peter scanned the torch-lit length. No soul stirred — save one! Armour plated and bearing a halberd, a man positioned himself vigilant at the entrance on the near shore.

Lizzie's words of the watchmen patrolling against vandals came fast to his head. Confident the man was no enemy, Peter advanced. "Has anyone passed here?"

"None," came the reply as the watchman raised his lantern. "State your business."

The distant clock tower pealed midnight, each iron knell piercing the frigid air, striking Peter's soul with grave foreboding. "Are you certain?" answered he. "The hour already tolls."

"One minute before," corrected the man; he would have launched into the history of this rarity had not Peter interrupted him, begging he let him pass.

With a displeased brow, the man relented, and Peter hastened onwards.

Midway across the bridge, an imposing octagonal water tower gave him pause. Shadows retreated inside its passerelle. Indeed, the structure exhibited every impression sufficient for such acts of villainy. This had to be the villain's den.

Glancing up, he remarked a pediment painting in the flickering torchlight:

St George on horseback slaying the dragon and rescuing the princess. So too would Peter save Elizabeth.

Hilt grasped in hand, he approached the heavy wooden door stood ajar.

Poised to step through, our hero heard hollow footfalls thudding behind him.

Two guards charged from both ends of the bridge.

In a breath, Peter spun, unsheathing his sword, when darkness smothered him and stole the stunned air from his lungs.

Strong hands wrenched away his weapon and tackled and restrained him. Ropes bit into his wrists. The trap was sprung.

More figures were now upon him, hauling him through a creaking door and inside what he understood to be the tower; his heart pounded in his ears.

Up a musty, cold stone spiral staircase, he faltered, his feet slipping on the steps.

Two iron portals groaned open, and Peter was forced to his knees inside a frigid space.

"Remove the sack," came a guttural voice.

As the blackness ripped away, a vaulted armoury appeared, lit by a hellish glow. Central to the vault stood a Swiss Guard; the very one from the stairwell at the inn.

"It's him," said he; poster in hand. "Take this outlaw and —"

"Wait!" demanded Peter as the men's boots crushed his shoulders. "I know not why my face is on these posters, but my innocence I can prove."

The man's savage expression was exacerbated by the awful shadows. "Innocence?"

While Peter discreetly untethered his hands and glanced about counting five men, he implored, "search my satchel. Inside lies the proof."

"I care only for my reward," spat back the guard. "Destroy his claims of evidence!"

"You cannot do this!" Peter did thrash against the men hauling him off the floor.

Of the belief that he could do whatever he wished, the man stalked forwards as if to lay hold of Peter and strike him. But with lightning speed impulse, Peter pressed his weight against the two men clutching his arms and launched his feet into the approaching man's chest. The blackguard fell backwards, almost keeling over the iron bars of the open dungeon below.

With hands now freed, our hero flung off the men holding onto him, sending them crashing into the stone walls.

Another drew his sword and charged forward. But Peter was ready. Former bonds employed as a lash, he struck the guard's throat. The villain staggered back, breathless, and collapsed over the bars into the dungeon as his blade clattered to the floor.

Already, the next attacker came on; his sword-tip hissed past Peter's chest by inches. Before the next thump of our hero's racing heart, another steel whipped the stale air.

As the blade sliced but a hair's breadth from his face, Peter dropped to the floor and swept his leg under this second assailant. The man crashed down, head smashing against the planks.

Fallen sword snatched up, Peter swung it at the third assailant coming at him with his blade and a face full of vengeful retribution.

With a reverbing clang, the two steels collided. And against each other they pushed, eyes locked, veins bulging.

With a mighty heave, our hero gained the ascendancy and pitched the screaming foe over the railings, joining him to the other in the dungeon below.

In the next blink, the fourth rival advanced.

Seizing a dangling rope pulley overhead, Peter swung its iron hook and snagged the man's habiliments. With a fierce yank, the rogue was ripped off his feet and sent plunging over the barred precipice.

Four had fallen. One remained.

The sharp clatter of a flintlock rang out! Peter spun towards the sound.

By Fortune's favour, the pistol had early misfired.

Weapon tossed aside, the last of the aggressors fled the chamber.

Rather than pursue, Peter raced up the stairwell to the next floors, seeking the captives. Door after door thrown open presented only shadowy spaces lit by pale moon shafts.

"What goes on up there, men?" echoed a voice up the stairwell.

Assailed with fresh consternation, Peter flung back down, colliding with the watchman.

Backwards the man tumbled and smashed into the stone walls, helmet flying off, head spitting out blood.

Seized by sickening dread, our hero stared at him. Was he dead?

Benumbing anxiety forced aside, he flew to him. A pulse... He would live.

Time being against our hero, he quit the injured man, rushed back into the main chamber, and grabbed the leader, demanding the captives' location. Only after forcing a blade to the villain's throat did the man finally reveal this. They had been taken to the garrison.

"The garrison?" Peter sank backwards with despair at so distressing a challenge.

Worse still, the leader had ordered the hostages moved elsewhere if he did not return by the first hour. How was Peter even to infiltrate the garrison, let alone rescue them in so short a time? Opportunely, the answer to half his plight was lying right before him: the man's regimentals.

Once more disguised, Peter quit the suffocating water tower and staggered into the chill night air. Not a soul was on the bridge. While taking but a few moments to regather his strength and arrange his wits, he recalled the other guard who ran off. To the garrison, he must have gone!

Alone and without recourse to friend or ally, Peter drew from within the hero and set off.

The looming five-storied garrison rose ahead; its three-winged stone facade etched against the black night. A stiff breeze snapped the cantonal flags hanging high above; rows of arched windows stared down like hollowed eyes, guarded by patrolling sentries. Guards in vast numbers came and went from the entrance at so late an hour.

Why was there so much movement? And what if he were to be recognised? The whole gave to our hero's understanding of the near-impossibility of his quest.

Head lowered, he held onto his tricorn and braved entering the building.

A deafening, confusing hum assaulted his senses: blazing torches, echoing footfalls, a maze of stone corridors teeming with redcoats and shadows. Passing guards shot suspicious glances, but none challenged his disguise. Knowing not which way to proceed, Peter hesitated.

"You there!" came a sharp voice from behind.

Dread slithered up our hero's spine as he turned around.

"Stop loitering about," ordered a square jawed, white-powdered-wigged colonel glaring in a doorway. "Help carry a chest to the Lieutenant General's office! Have you forgotten we are possibly at war with the French at our borders?"

"War...?" Had it come to this already? "But...?" His eyes shot to his satchel; a violent conflict broke out in his breast. The scroll, he knew, could put an end to the hostilities. But a clock on the wall showed it was already quarter-to-one. To hand over the evidence now would cause a delay. He would return once he had liberated the hostages.

"Will you continue to *stand* there?" The colonel stormed over and, seizing Peter by a tuft of his hair, dragged him inside an office. "Move this *now*!"

The cumbersome leather trunk strained our hero's arms as he and another guard lugged it the entire length of the building.

A clock they passed showed it was now nearing ten-to-one. Every moment lost to delay drove torturous blades of madness into Peter's skull.

Just then, three guards hurried past. Their hushed talk caught Peter's hearing: men had gone back to the water tower, and hostages were kept on the wharf.

Elizabeth and Emil!

His heart pounding against his ribs, his flesh flushing hot and cold, Peter feigned exhaustion as he looked behind, watching the guards exit the stone corridor onto a cobbled forecourt which overlooked the river and, beyond, the wharf.

The guard demanded they keep moving, but our hero, in the grips of gut-wrenching suspense, was deaf to all but the screaming urgency within. Almost at the point of delirium and unable to breathe, he dropped the trunk and raced outside, following the moonlit embankment.

Onto a bedarkened roofed jetty, he soon turned and rushed along the planks above the surging river to the wharf decks.

The endgame was upon him.

The two-floored wharf was a mesh of buildings — several rows of doors concealing the captives. Wind screamed between the structures as Peter tried each door until one opened to him.

Sword thus unsheathed, he slipped inside a narrow, dark hallway.

At the end of the passageway rose a staircase. He ascended it.

Several indistinct voices drifted down and brought him to a halt at a turn on the stairs. Keeping low, he peered through the balustrades. A lantern descended an encased stairwell several meters away. Then, several men gathered in the dark corridor, discussing the hostages.

Something surged through Peter's veins; something like an avenging fire. Something akin to instinct set ablaze his whole; his body seemed to remember the battle, and all fear died to valour. With a loud cry, sword aloft, he raced towards his destiny.

In the shadowy attic, Elizabeth and Emil, alerted to the rattle of a clash somewhere below, could only listen with dreadful anticipation. Four of the ten guards about the attic shifted uneasily. Then, swords drawn, they rushed out.

The shrilling clatter of steel followed with muffled cries and unintelligible invectives; all loudening as the conflict seemed to climb the stairwell.

Unable to distinguish from the vociferous cacophony who contended — whether friend or foe — our captive siblings swung between bursting hope and trembling despair.

The tumult soon reached the other side of the door. Swords clashed; bodies slammed; why, the very flooring in the attic creaked, and the walls shook, dislodging plumes of dust from the joists above.

Over the shouting and cursing, Lizzie believed she caught Peter's voice.

Just then, a frightful cry rang out, preceding a final crash and rumble as of a body tumbling down stairs. Elizabeth could scarcely breathe. Was it Peter?

The door to the attic burst open, and there stood salvation embodied!

From the moon shafts and the orange smoulder of flambeaux, Peter no sooner espied Elizabeth than he turned his gaze on the six men surrounding them. Though disarmed of his sword, our hero was not without courage to defy the glistening blades pointed at him.

Two guards broke rank and raced forwards.

Into a tumble, Peter threw himself and toppled the first.

Feet adroitly gained, Peter then propelled a kick at the second, sending him across the attic with such force that the man smashed into a post — dislodging from it a flaming torch.

The other foe climbed back to his feet and charged anew at our hero; as did another.

With no little awe, did Lizzie and Emil watch the fight unfold as Peter grabbed a rolled arras, unfurling it at his enemies — the dust rendering them blinded.

A sudden burst of light lit up the shadowy space. The fallen flambeau had ignited several rugs and boxes!

Filled now with apprehension at the flames and with increasing awe at the battle, our captives witnessed a guard wielding two swords charge at Peter, who, snatching another torch from the wall, then scaled several crates before leaping onto a thick joist; all the while pursued by his double-sworded adversary.

Beneath the combatants' heavy tread, the beams creaked and groaned; the red glow of the rising flames casting their contending shadows across the sloped ceiling.

As Peter drove back his assailant, images of past combat ignited athwart his memory. His body moved, involuntarily, unparalleled. He sensed — nay, trusted — he was always the victor. It would be no different now!

With a rush of determination, he again lunged forward with his flambeau.

Meanwhile, the crackling flames, fuelled by the howling draughts, whipped through the splintering timbers, hissing and crackling.

A stifled scream pierced the thickening smoke!

Two guards dragged the hostages away.

Distracted, Peter left himself open to attack. His aggressor's sword thrust, barely missing his chest, sliced through the satchel's strap — the bag fell onto the beam's precarious edge.

Again, the assailant's sword came at him.

Jolted back into himself, Peter swung his torch at the opponent's legs, thus unbalancing him and sending the blackguard crashing down into the flames; screams of agony and clouds of noxious smoke now spat out of the violent, hot, and roaring blaze.

Another scream rang out. Elizabeth and Emil, still being dragged to the door.

But the satchel?

The climbing flames clawed at it; our hero moved to grab it; yet Lizzie's next scream stayed him.

Torn between love and duty, he hesitated.

Just then, a groaning tremor shook the attic, and part of the roof collapsed.

Lunging desperately for the satchel as it fell from the beam, Peter's fingers brushed the leather as it slipped past — missed by an agonising hairsbreadth!

Its strap, though, he caught onto, saving it from the flames.

"Thank heavens!" Relief flooded through him.

Yet, as our hero drew it up, its flap fell open; the letters and the scroll slipped out.

"No!"

Time seemed to slow as the parchment floated, unfurling as it fell. Its edges blackened and curled before the flames consumed it — our hero's last hope of salvaging his innocence turned to ash below.

The loss crushed him. His body went numb; he collapsed onto the beam.

Elizabeth's cry, however, cut through his despair, snapping him back.

He had lived his choice!

Jaws clenched against the sudden emotions which combusted within, Peter turned from the cinders and leapt down from the beam.

With blistering determination, anchored now to Elizabeth alone, he grabbed a small wooden table and charged at the last two standing foes.

Elizabeth collapsed, choking on the smoke-drenched air, and the villain, still dragging her, raised his sword to strike our hero.

But swooping beneath the blade, Peter got two steps past the assailant; grip tightened on the table's legs, he turned and crashed it over his head.

The man crumpled to the floor.

With but one table leg remaining in each hand — thus emboldening the courage of the last standing antagonist — Peter, with eyes watering and stinging, fought with every twitching fibre of his power until, at length, he felled this assailant unconscious.

Blindly, Peter now stumbled to Elizabeth and Emil and unbound them.

Together they crawled beneath the noxious clouds towards the outline of the door while gasping at the heat searing their lungs.

A shower of sparks reigned down as another part of the roof collapsed. Peter shielded Lizzie from the flaming debris. Behind, the splintering floor groaned as if it threatened to plunge beneath them.

Barely had they escaped the blazing attic — coughing, heaving, arms outstretched, and feeling their way down the staircase strewn with groaning, half-conscious bodies — when, as they exited into the corridor, a blur of four figures blocked their path.

"You won't get away *again*!"

By the voice alone, Peter recognised the man for the guard from the water tower.

Swords in hand, the men forced them back into the stairwell, now billowing thicker clouds of smoke. "They will give me double the bounty when you're delivered dead!"

Elizabeth and Emil clung to Peter as he shoved them behind him.

The blade was now raised, ready to strike.

Our hero was spent; all hope seemed lost.

Just then, a gunshot rang out; the sword clanged to the floor, and the enemy collapsed to his knees in screaming agony — a smoking hole in his blood-spouting hand.

From behind the remaining foes, another blurry figure raced upon them and a clash ensued.

The vanquisher, attired in a haze of senior regimentals, swiftly prevailed over the antagonists before hurriedly leading our trio down to the stairwell, up which several guards raced.

First, commanding these men to quell the fire, the mystery saviour then continued to hurry the liberated out of the building and led them back to the inn's entrance.

After enquiring into the well-being of the delivered, the liberator — a colonel — instructed them to pack their belongings for he had arranged a coach to convey them back to Bubendorf immediately; he presently pointed it out to them.

Through his still stinging eyes, conjoined with the night's blackness, Peter struggled to identify his deliverer's face. "To whom are we indebted?"

The man answered he must be away at once but promised to communicate with him soon. Peter asked his meaning, at which, with a departing bow, the man explained he would write via the columns.

"The col — the newspaper...?" Peter staggered after him. "But wait! Come back!"

14 APRIL – 01 MAY 1792

The journey back to Bubendorf was as deathly silent, grave, and as filled with the perturbation and anxiety as one might expect following such tumultuous events. Not even the comfort of the remarkably fine, silk-brocade upholstered carriage interior could lift the travellers' spirits.

So consumed by shock, Elizabeth's mind was trapped in a maze of conjecture. Could it truly be that Peter was — is a felon of such notoriety? Certainly, after seeing his likeness affixed to so alarming a poster, she could not dismiss this possibility. Yet as she pondered the brutish guards themselves, who dealt so menacingly and so clandestinely with her, something did not add up. Further, the mode in which Peter resisted their prosecutions and liberated her, chiefly without inflicting mortal harm, served not to guide but only to perplex her all the more!

Thus, her heart, which had at last grew warm towards him, was now torn by the violent and destructive agitation of uncertainty. She dared not to turn her eyes from the landscape which flew past the window for fear of meeting his; but glancing at him now, she noted from a shaft of moonlight how utterly unscathed he appeared.

Awe thrilled her nerves; she could only wonder: *Who is this man?*

As for Emil, whether from amazement or fear, each time his eyes would land on Peter, they quickly darted away again.

As for our hero, indeed the most distressed of the trio, he found the incalculable ramifications of the incident just passed soon eclipsed the triumph of his heroism. Having lost the scroll to the flames, how was he ever to invalidate the crimes of which he was accused?

Cruel misery did rob his mind of all light and hope. And from within the deepening gloom, there bounded ever more dreadful apprehensions of the next set of events which awaited him in Bubendorf: the wrath of Johannes; impending arrest; the sting of ignominy; Elizabeth's decided disfavour and the probable end of their union.

He glanced at her disquieted countenance and easily deduced her thoughts. Yet, how he yearned to embrace her. How he feared he might have lost her. But doubtless, once apprised of every awful circumstance, she would never allow him near her again.

Such a thought was too much to endure. He instantly expelled it from his mind. And what of the colonel who had liberated them — his mystery correspondent? The very person who held the key to his lost history so happened to be the man whom, without his intervention, Peter would now certainly find himself incarcerated; if not dead.

Moreover, what of the war with the French? Peter was too late. If *only* he had earlier handed over the letters and the scroll!

About halfway into their journey, one of the carriage wheels dislodged, causing their conveyance to collapse on the road. As repairs would cause at least a half-day's delay and that the hour was so late, they found the need to secure lodgings.

Fortunately, a suitable establishment was about an hour's walk ahead, which they found had rooms free to provide them with accommodation.

***

They reconvened the following day in the cheerless food hall of dark wainscotting, dark chairs and tables, and dark velvet drapery that smothered what little sunlight braved so unwelcoming an interior — 'twas truly an atmosphere blacker than any pauper's grave!

No sooner had Emil left our hero alone with Elizabeth than she, visibly shaking, turned paler with each tremulous breath that drove her breast up and down.

Peter took her trembling hand in his and enquired if she was unwell.

How good it felt to hold her this close.

But without replying, all the while keeping her eyes fixed downwards, she retracted her hand.

The tension in the air was too palpable to deny. Peter also drew back. His breath forsook him as his chest constricted with that crushing sensation known only to surging anxiety's peak.

"You are understandably perplexed and alarmed by the recent events?"

Eyes still downcast, she let out a sigh and acknowledged his words with a nod. Again, Peter reached across the dark oak table to take her hand. Again, she pulled back.

Though indebted to Peter for his brave rescue, one restless night was sufficient to obliterate such valour. Every uncertainty weighed upon her breast while her mind threaded each unfavourable circumstance of his character into a tapestry no less tangled than the one which was on the far wall, depicting a violent battle scene. Thus, pleasure's warm beam now withdrew from her bosom, doubt's chill occupying its place and altering her every look towards him.

At length, with a disturbed and impatient air, she retrieved a folded paper from her pocket. "As we crawled out of the attic," said she, unsteady of voice, eyes still averted, "my hand landed on this. It is my sole wish that you can disprove such a *horrendous* claim. Yet if not, I ask only that you honour me with an explanation."

After darting a glance about the food hall for any watching eyes, Peter unfolded the paper; from its creases, it had clearly been folded and unfolded many times.

WANTED.

So, she was already aware. How foolish can be a heart which yearned otherwise! His own sleepless night had solely weakened his nerve to reveal this damning truth, for she would have to suffer enough upon their return to Bubendorf.

"Please," said Elizabeth, eyes raised, "tell me this is *not* you?"

"I... I am..." stammered he as he met her distressed gaze. "That is, I mean to say..."

Confusion mingled anew with his distress and so ambushed the workings of his mind that his words fell flat.

"Even were it I," resumed he at length, "I could not..." Again, he faltered. Swelling anxiety compounded the hammering affliction of his heart as he laboured under the oppressive weight of other words now recalled — the note left for him. "There is something I must... show you."

From his pocket, he withdrew the billet. "This came after your abduction. Certainly, those men — those violent beasts — believed it was me. And considering the likeness..."

With a countenance of incontrovertible consternation, Elizabeth read the message. "An assassi —?" She stopped-up her mouth with her hand.

Presently, a dour maid came to refill their coffee.

"Do you think this is possible?" resumed Elizabeth after the damsel waddled off. "You cannot be capable of these crimes, can you?"

"Had I the full ascension of my memories, only then could I answer you with perfect integrity." Anguish of heart concealed, he affected to hope where in truth he despaired. "But in the absence of such, and with what I do recall, which leads to me to believe I am innocent, I have my conviction to trust, which alone leads me to despise the very possibility and veracity of this. For even when my own eyes first saw it, my soul repulsed."

Since matters of such alarming gravity were being thus exposed, Elizabeth now presented the letter from Peter's so-claimed former betrothed, further impugning his character.

Scarce able to credit the lines which accumulated more calumny, he sank back into his chair. Really, this entire set of woeful circumstances worsened by the minute. And still, he needed to apprise her of the additional appalling state of his affairs: the account of his parents.

"There is more that I must tell you."

"There is?"

***

Indeed, this revelation had reigned another night of terror upon Elizabeth's mind and again robbed her entirely of sleep. Having had cause enough since Lucerne to doubt the wisdom of connecting herself to a man so enshrouded in conspiracy, this additional obstacle left her no alternative than to expel him from her life. Yet affection, that injurious and often deceitful allure, having gained too eminent a jurisdiction of her heart, rebelled against reason. Fondness became his advocate. Bravery rushed to his defence. Mercy, too, mitigated his banishment — for 'twould still be uncharitable to penalise any man, guilty or not, for crimes he had no recollection of.

Then, there came the remembrance of her own duplicity and deceit. Whether her betrothed indeed wore any mask, her own conscience castigated her for the same. Had not she used an entire stranger to her own advantage? And at the peril of the confederacy's stability? For had she not acted with such subterfuge and did her all to restore him to his true life, mayhap the cantons would still be at peace.

Hence, tortured by perplexity, conflicting considerations tore her every which way. 'Twas also now that she wondered whether the ring was in fact intended for that mystery correspondent. Had not Peter lost his memory and delivered the scroll, he may very well have been en route to place the band on the former lover's finger. Had she, in her dishonesty, been the cause of the annulment? Also, Peter's timepiece, was that interior watercolour a representation of the same woman?

Oh, how Lizzie detested herself at this moment!

By morning, however, she reached her decision. That she was not inculpable of violations of virtue and propriety, she, before they departed, thanked Peter for his candour and promised to reserve judgement of his character until all facts had been incontestably proved.

***

Mid-afternoon, saw them arrive at the gate to the chalet. Having concerted together to conceal the events of Lucerne, the trio, though tired and troubled, assumed a calmness in their bearing as they alighted the carriage.

Edmunda presently came charging towards them. "What are we going to do about your arrest?" shrilled she. "And what a business about your parents; nothing but dressed-up kobolds!"

A grave-face Ernest followed with Hans and Harris — less grave-faced.

Behind floated Helene, all smiles and blushes, beaming at Emil, who, all smiles and blushes too, easily forgot his own share in the past tribulations.

"Never mind what everybody else says," continued Edmunda. "I'll set'em down! You might be stupid, but methinks that's your greatest crime! And though your parents turned out to be such villains, it doesn't mean you —"

"Yes, thank you, Mother," interjected Elizabeth as she noted Peter sink deeper into despondency with each thoughtless syllable she let drop. "Shall we all go in?"

Not wanting to delay the fate hanging about his neck, our hero said he would make his way directly to Ebenrain. But Edmunda dragged him inside and permitted — nay, forced him into her own chair before she began the operations of preparing and pouring out tea for all her guests, serving Peter his in her best chinaware. "There you go, dearest."

After the shocking events of Bubendorf were lamented, the gathering now enquired of the travellers' trip to Lucerne.

"'Twas certainly eventful," ventured Emil before shutting his mouth and closing his hand over it.

"*Eventful*?" rejoined Edmunda.

"I think he means city life is always so," attempted Elizabeth.

Edmunda laughed. "Though a city, I doubt it was as eventf —" She too stopped herself and turned to Peter. "What'll we do if the Guard hauls you off again to some blackened dungeon?"

"I really must go," cried Peter, rising suddenly.

***

The atmosphere, the accusations, the antagonisms — it was all precisely what Peter had anticipated of Ebenrain on his return; though Johannes appended to him further flagrancy for so freely bringing himself forth as if he feared not to be arrested, and further vilified him for having failed to return to him his precious clock.

"Again, where have they gone?" demanded that man, standing amidst the empty library space where once reigned his high-back chair and ornate French gilded rosewood desk, now vanished with its carved lion paperweight, too. "You cannot pretend to any ignorance of their intentions nor feign to know them not for the rotten scoundrels they are. I would *dissuade* you from *prolonging* this *spectacle* of denial and enjoin your *immediate c*onfession!"

After enduring above an hour's vitriolic verbal assault, vilified as much as the robbers themselves, with great difficulty, Peter, hands bound, flanked by guards, remained calm.

"Must you stand there silent?" Violent contractions did distort Johannes' features; his eyes twitched, and his hands hovered as if seeking some missile to hurl while he stalked the room of plundered bookshelves and vacant pedestals, once exhibiting glorious objects. "Speak, boy! Before I have your head pitched on a stake over my gate." He tore at his hair. "Oh! To be the spawn of such *confrères* of Satan!"

Large drops of perspiration gathered on Peter's brow; lather pooled in his clenched palms. Though possibly guilty of some atrocities, he knew nothing of his parents' schemes.

Jago entered and stationed himself by his father. Though silent and refusing to look at Peter, he communicated in his countenance his own enmity and abhorrence for the accused.

"That *mother* of yours," continued Johannes, "over painted! Over-dressed! Seducing me with her *unctuosity*! And that *heinous man* who I repulse to call a *father*; overstuffed! Over-airing! Filled with covetousness and cacoethes! Abusing my affability, liberality, and hospitality! The both of them the whole time bent on ransacking my effects!"

Fists clenched tight to his chest, Johannes glared at the trompe l'oeil ceiling, looking as if he wished to drag down the pudgy cherubs and pluck their wings for their failure to have protected so sacred a chamber. "Oh! Would to heaven I could get my hands about their necks." Veins engorged his purple face as he darted his blood-shot eyes at Peter. "Where *have* they gone?!"

Our hero only reiterated his ignorance of their schemes and location. "So, please, desist your prosecutions. As grievous as this is, I am certain that my own loss is greater, for —"

"Your loss *greater*?" interrupted Johannes, rending him with his long sword glare. "How *dare* you juxtapose your negligible and immaterial concerns with mine! The perverse lineage you spring from and the destitute family with whom you align yourself have no doubt blunted what few faculties you perhaps ever had! Enough of your prevarications! Guards! Take him away!"

At this moment, a footman entered and informed his lord that a visitor wished to see him. Johannes hurled a book at him. "We are not to be disturbed!"

The servant narrowly sidestepped the missile and explained the man brings news of the theft.

"He does? Well, what are you waiting for? Send him in at once!"

Hence, an elderly, impoverished man hobbled in on a worn stick and bowed. Johannes eyed him with disgust. "What is it that *you* could have to inform us of?"

Clearly unnerved by such looks and tone of question, and only after some hesitation did he reply, "I come, as I overheard some talk yesterday in Liestal. I don't think they suspected my being so close to overhear what they said. But I couldn't sit quiet until I came."

"Are you here only to test my patience?" Johannes picked up another book — which Jago prevented him from hurling. "Speak to the point!"

What followed, punctuated with nervous twitches and complaints about his back, was mostly known to his auditors; but what was not now came to their astonished attention. "Laughing about it, they was. Raising their jugs. Congratulating themselves for duping Bubendorf's finest family — who I knew could only be you, my lord."

The old man bowed again.

Too aggravated for courtesy, Johannes only threatened him anew to get to the point.

"And 'the best part' says one of them," resumed the old man, "was, this was all made possible because their leaders pretended to be someone's parents."

In the ensuing silence, Johannes and Jago's wide eyes did swing on Peter.

"Pretended to —?" stuttered our hero. "Are you absolutely certain this is what you heard?"

Seeing Peter held thus by the guards, and though eyeing him with judging scowls, the old man replied, "as sure as I live and breathe."

The room now spun so violently that Peter rather willingly sought the guard's supporting grip. "Then," said he, "they are most definitely *not* my parents!"

***

So, these adventurers were not only inveterate ransackers by trade of fine households of almost every canton, but being clock-hunters too, a twist of fate brought them to Bubendorf with dual intent: continue their ransacking whilst searching out a certain timepiece — yes, dear reader, the very one which, by another twist of fate, found its way to Johannes's library.

For a moment, we must cast our minds back to when our ailing hero had just fled the hobgoblin's cabin and spied from the mountains what he believed to be the Swiss Guard. 'Twas not they, in fact, but other men connected to these curious clocks. How this sixth timepiece reached that humble cabin is not material enough to here yet relate.

Upon learning the old couple had pawned it, these men hastened after it and, after much ado, traced it not only to Bubendorf but Ebenrain itself — thus setting their sights and schemes on that schloss.

Recall too, the rogues from the jailhouse who recognised Peter from the posters: well, turns out they were the faux parents' corrupt underlings, sent to reconnoitre Ebenrain. There, they did auspiciously confirm the clock's location, and there they were, however, inauspiciously apprehended for their suspicious snoopings and endeavours to bribe a footman.

Though the ringleaders failed in their first exploit to obtain entrance to the schloss and seize the clock, Fortune was about to cast at them another opportunity.

It chanced one afternoon as they dined at a Liestal inn, idle talk spilled off the next table and caught their ears. A party of ten feasted on pheasant while they discussed a certain man without memories — very troublesome to his caretakers and still more so to his ill-fated employers.

At first, listening with disinterest, the tricksters' interest soon escalated as the gossip progressed. The amnesiac was the supposed lover of an Elizabeth; so said the fishmonger. A volunteer to the Swiss Guard; so added the baker. Seemed by his lofty speech to be of family; so continued the ironmonger. Treated by Jago von der Mühll's personal physician; so contributed the physician himself. Had placed a peculiar advert in the press, alluding to a fortune; so the printer himself also added to the tittle-tattle.

Independent of the amnesiac's supposed wealth, it was his connection to the name of the wealthy von der Mühll which crowned our adventurers' interest. It was then that a devilish notion did spark and whisper to their corrupt minds their next contrivance. And being too great a temptation to pass-by without testing it out, all that was needed was to secure an interview with Peter and monopolise on his amnesic state.

The cunning woman conjured the ideal ruse, suggesting they loiter outside and when the gossipers departed, loudly bemoan their missing son Peter, doubting not the ingenuous fools would take pity on them and convey them post-haste to the amnesiac or his lover.

That these knaves found success in the first part of their scheme we have already witnessed. That they found an almost perfect success with the second part we have also observed: for 'twas that certain missing key to the garden room being obtained through bribing a maid that gained them entrance to that fine house; and 'twas also that other key being stolen from the footman's pocket — on whose arm the woman rested en route to the restroom on the day of the banquet — by her nimble fingers, which gained them entrance to the library. Though they failed to seize the clock, they still made off with much spoils.

As to their true names and histories, this, for now, must wait; as must wait addressing the legitimacy of the birth certificate. Since we have not seen the last of these impostors, our patience and, I hope to claim, curiosity, will oblige us to suffer the interim.

***

Johannes fluctuated white to red to purple and back before rounding on Peter. "You are still to blame! Lacking the sense to distinguish complete strangers — vile brigands, at that — and introducing them to my world. You are dismissed from service!"

***

Freed from the guards, Peter collected a mending Znüni and gladly returned to the cottage. The draughty loft, noisy animals, and chores of mundane hell, compared to Johannes' harsh treatment, were a paradise calling. The rusty bedpans glistened. The hay-stuffed bed somehow surpassed cotton. Even the mangle, he had to poke a finger through — yes! It caught! Never were flaws so perfect.

Despite the absence of Johannes' tyrannies, sleep stepped in to torment our hero with bizarre nightmares, stalking him as steel-wielding redcoats and pike-brandishing bandits, portending capture and prophesying unending misery.

More fractured memories conjured ominous characters and events which, though he refused to believe factual, planted seeds of doubt that plagued his waking hours. Furthermore, the disaccord between the cantons and the impending war with the French beset him with grief incalculable. And each time he would attend martial training at the garrison, he found himself overwhelmed with despairing anger — unable to utter a word to anyone of the scroll's former existence, for the tumultuous fears which held him back.

Of a sudden, he gasped aloud. "The members of the Schaffhausen Small Council!"

They themselves had viewed the scroll and recognised its authenticity. If found, might their testimony offer protection? *Moreover, they must surely have notified Bern of the scroll's existence?* Also, could this stay the imminent war?

However long a duration before such matters were to be resolved, for our hero, time alone would heal him from the recent train of events and reveal to him the truth of all matters.

But on the positive, since he was not the spawn of those impostors, he found, if not serenity in his obscurity, resolution. Whoever his true parents, they could still be yet decent, worthy, even honourable citizens; having raised him to be the same. With that in mind, there was redoubled a belief in the error which connected him to the conspiracy against the Bernese schultheiss.

Putting to one side Peter's cogitations, we find Elizabeth, too, despite her own misgivings, took comfort in this re-orphaning of his ancestry. Doubting not Peter's relief to be released by blood-connection to such criminal persons, she drew from it an optimism for his character, and a renewed desire to help him rediscover his history bloomed within her breast. To locate his true parents became her chief objective and, hoped she, to somehow, and safely so, find absolution in the other charges laid against him in the posters.

Ignorant of such unresolved incriminations, Ernest and Edmunda found only joy in our hero's return to the loft. Ernest would teach him the sundry skills of his many professions. Edmunda would teach and busy him with groundskeeping. Fearing, however, the looming strictures of Father Francis, they both would do their all to speed along the wedding preparations.

Hans, having resigned obtaining Elizabeth as bride for his son, now eyed other pretty church maidens while Harris, though not quite ready to relinquish his rejector, had pride enough not to prolong that passion. Helene, freed from one impossible assignment, did most eagerly oblige her father in the next: for independent of his commands, her own fancy for the bashful Emil was sufficient to spur her on in the knowledge of meeting with reciprocation.

Meanwhile, Johannes and Jago, embroiled as they were in disputes and disharmonies pertaining to alliances, associations, and the ill-mixing of class and rank, soon found their attentions stolen away by more pressing matters: the threat of the French at the Swiss Genevan borders and the profits to be found in this.

Forgetting not the thwarted Lucerne Swiss Guard — several permanently scarred from the fire and filled with rage and retribution — they reconvened during their recovery to discuss their next offensive. They would bolster their numbers for the apprehension of so formidable a man and would soon march to Liestal, where they had first spotted Peter.

***

Now, there is still that other matter yet unresolved: our hero's true identity. Whether Fortune, who now and then does show us her better side, had taken pity on Peter, I cannot tell, but another turn of event was about to unfold which would finally bring this back to his mind.

Two weeks had gone by before Pier learned of the harsh treatment with which Johannes used Peter. Thus, his own compassion moving him to the offices of friend and succourer and, being a bit of an archery enthusiast, he visited mid-morning to invite Peter out on a noonday hunt. Readily accepting his offer, our hero penned a note for Lizzie and left it with a mightily distracted Emil and Helene as they mended one of her boots. But too diverted by Helene's blushes to heed his words, Emil simply placed the note on the kitchen table and forgot all about it.

About an hour later, when Edmunda returned, prattling away about the village gossip, she unknowingly put a water-jug atop the note. Later still, when Elizabeth then came in commenting on the promising weather and that she would go to her favourite woods to sketch the environs of the awakening spring, no one apprised her of the hunt or the note.

Around another hour had passed before Edmunda finally noticed the damp message stuck to the bottom of the jug. Seeing this, only now did the smitten Emil, still mending Helene's boot, finally relay that Peter and Pier were gone hunting. Edmunda seized him by his shoulder and shook him. "They've gone to the woods?"

Startled, Emil nodded, confusedly.

"Why didn't you say so earlier?" Edmunda whacked him. "You know that Lizzie's favourite spot in the woods is close to where Pier goes hunting!"

At once grasping the peril, boot and blushes were instantly forgotten, and Emil, pursued by Helene, sprang out of the cottage, pursuing the likely path that Elizabeth could have taken.

***

"Very well done," cheered Pier. "Though you claimed you had not practised archery?"

"I believe I said I had not any recollection of practice," replied he, hanging a pheasant over his shoulder besides the two hares he had already scored. "Not until I pulled back the string and aimed — there! Look!" He pointed ahead. "Do you see it?"

At a distance, among the tall trees which surrounded them, was an unsuspecting fawn; its red coat shimmered in the light shaft as it stepped clumsily across it.

"I see it," replied Pier.

Arrow readied, Peter stalked slowly forward.

Just then, flickering images flashed before his mind's eye: a forest of old stretching high above; colourful, regal tents pitched all about; guards and noblemen atop horses; a man of imperious, yet strangely familiar countenance. These brief, fractured glimpses clawed at the edges of his consciousness.

Beneath his tread, a branch snapped; the fawn glanced in their direction and took off.

"Stay here," said Peter as he hastened after it.

Before long, the creature vanished, leaving Peter lost among the bowls, roving through the moist, garlic drenched woods of trees beyond differentiation.

He called out Pier's name; but only echoes of his own voice came back.

Just then, a rustling snared his attention. In a small break in the distant boscage, the fawn reappeared.

Bow drawn and arrow nocked, he aimed and released it.

What alarm he met with, however, when the arrow just missed the darting fawn and whistled past it, preceding the shriek of a female voice.

What subsequent horror Peter then encountered when he rushed through the snagging growth and arrived at a small, grassy clearing with Elizabeth, curled sideways on a blanket, grasping her calf as blood trickled from beneath her hand.

The arrow protruded from the ground mere inches away from her.

"Lizzie!" He sprang to her side. "Let me help you —"

"Why are *you* here?" She waved him off and sat up. Thankfully, the arrow had seemingly only torn the top layers of her skin as it slashed by. Yet, as she tore a strip from her skirt to stuff and bind the wound, she noted the bow in Peter's hand. All remaining colour vanished from her cheeks. "You shot at me?"

Too aghast to answer, Peter gathered up her items and promised an explanation at the chalet.

An air of unease enveloped them as they quit the vicinity; it was only that Elizabeth found it necessary to bear her weight on Peter's arm that she accepted his repeated offers.

The trail they followed at length connected to a long stone bridge.

Seeing Lizzie's struggle increase, Peter suggested they rest awhile.

Hence, on the wall, she sat and eyed him with indubitable distrust. "Why ever did you shoot at me?" Most likely, in that moment, she verily believed him to be the outlaw, wishing to remove all obstacles to his safety.

That Peter explained so passionately and regretfully the cause of the accident; her looks went from aggrieved to sceptical to placated, and she permitted his words to be the truth.

"This misadventure would convince me I am accursed!" said she. "For I now realise that, on the same date three-and-twenty years ago, I was injured in the same manner."

"You *were*?" Peter was stung with guilt at the blood trickling from under her bandage.

Something of sadness filled her eyes. "But other events of that day..." She fell quiet.

"What is it, Lizzie?"

"Too many things I would rather wish to forget." Some ill-ease arrested her countenance. "But it was also the day that my older brother was taken from us."

"Your older...?" Now Peter understood that extra place-setting at the table. Observing the grief which now filled Lizzie's eyes, Peter's heart could not help entering into the sorrow it spoke of. "Your mother still awaits his return?"

Elizabeth nodded. "Even until now, she wishes fire-and-brimstone upon that family. Though I believe they have already suffered enough for..." Again, her expression betrayed some anxious working of her mind. "For on that same day..." she seemed to labour under some heavy burden, "the Frau Schultheissin Vivienne von Villeroy passed away."

A strange buzzing beset Peter's brain. "Vivienne von Villeroy?"

"I know not if I can ever forgive mys..." she sighed. "Many acknowledged her as the only kind soul of that family. I was fortunate to have met her several times; although I knew not who she was until the day of her death... But her warmth and charity I shall never forget... If only I had known it was she, that night, then..."

Her words faded away.

Something of a poignant eloquence penetrated the pounding of Peter's breast. The account of this Frau schultheissin rang with haunting familiarity.

Disjointed images now exploded across his mind: a sullied hemp cloth thrown over a body; deep red pooling down a lifeless arm; a hand lacerated and dripping blood.

Grown breathless, sweating, and dizzy, our hero slammed his fist against his now struggling lungs as an unaccountable anguish stole the air.

"Peter? What *is* it?"

"I do not know. A *sudden...*"

Amidst the storm unleashed upon his mind, depictions of a childhood thundered forth — seeming fragments from his own: of hunting, of horses, of an arrow in flight, of the screams of a red-headed girl.

Struck with stupefaction, he lifted his gaze to meet Elizabeth's.

Staring back at him, however, was not she, but rather the face of that same little girl whose hair was as red as that fox he had hunted.

"Is it *really* you?" murmured our hero as he reached out to touch her face.

She drew back. "What do you mean?".

He went to answer, but the next violent surge of phantasms stifled his words; a dark stairwell of ill-boding, a mournful courtyard, a horse-drawn cart bearing the dead thrashed his recollection.

On Peter's memory, the image of a deceased woman grew like a terrible apparition, conjoined with the excruciating stabbings of sorrow and despair.

Overwhelmed, trembling, and nauseous, he fell against the bridge, nearly toppling over its wall into the rolling waters below.

"*Peter*?" Elizabeth grabbed his arm. "What is it?"

But her voice again faded, drowned by the river's rush and recollection's clamorous agony, erupting upon his faculties with profound, aching loss.

More visions flooded without cessation. A man's cries. Weeping servants' shrieks. Guards crowded about that blood-soaked, shrouded body.

This woman — a gruesome memory so seared into his psyche — her visage took form; he knew who she was!

In that moment, the bitter truth broke through at last. Our hero remembered who he himself was.

I am Valentin von Villeroy.

The Bernese schultheiss' first-born.

To be continued...

ABOUT THE AUTHOR

Justan Autor is a newcomer author to the world of novels, bringing a passion for the arts to historical fiction.

Throughout his youth and adulthood, Justan has been painting, landscape gardening, tailoring, playing the pianoforte, and composing classical music. It was only 5 years ago that he discovered his true calling in narrative and novel writing.

Inspired by a love of 18th and 19th century literature, Justan aims to bring seldom-told tales of the past to life. His first novel will immerse readers in the sights, sounds, and struggles of 18th century Switzerland, employing evocative settings, multilayered characters, and dramatic storytelling — all with an element of the burlesque — that should, he hopes, resonate with readers, transporting them into a living past.

Justan's diverse artistic talents and passions come together to shape his unique voice and perspective in the realm of historical fiction.

Visit Justan's website at

Visit Justan's Facebook page at
www.facebook.com/JustanAutor

20
S
23
Staten House

Printed in Dunstable, United Kingdom